PENGUIN CANADA

THE KING'S MAN

PAULINE GEDGE is the award-winning and bestselling author of thirteen previous novels, ten of which are inspired by Egyptian history. Her first, *Child of the Morning*, won the Alberta Search-for-a-New-Novelist Competition. In France, her second novel, *The Eagle and the Raven*, received the Jean Boujassy award from the Société des Gens de Lettres, and *The Twelfth Transforming*, the second of her Egyptian novels, won the Writers Guild of Alberta Best Novel of the Year Award. Her books have sold more than 250,000 copies in Canada alone; worldwide, they have sold more than six million copies and have been translated into eighteen languages. Pauline Gedge lives in Alberta.

Also by Pauline Gedge

Child of the Morning

The Eagle and the Raven

Stargate

The Twelfth Transforming

Scroll of Saqqara

The Covenant

House of Dreams

House of Illusions

LORDS OF THE TWO LANDS

Volume One: The Hippopotamus Marsh

Volume Two: The Oasis

Volume Three: The Horus Road

THE KING'S MAN

Volume One: The Twice Born

Volume Two: Seer of Egypt

THE KING'S MAN

PAULINE GEDGE

PENGUIN
CANADA

PENGUIN CANADA

Published by the Penguin Group

Penguin Group (Canada), 90 Eglinton Avenue East, Suite 700,
Toronto, Ontario, Canada M4P 2Y3 (a division of Pearson Canada Inc.)

Penguin Group (USA) Inc., 375 Hudson Street, New York, New York 10014, U.S.A.
Penguin Books Ltd, 80 Strand, London WC2R 0RL, England
Penguin Ireland, 25 St Stephen's Green, Dublin 2, Ireland
(a division of Penguin Books Ltd)
Penguin Group (Australia), 250 Camberwell Road, Camberwell, Victoria 3124, Australia
(a division of Pearson Australia Group Pty Ltd)
Penguin Books India Pvt Ltd, 11 Community Centre, Panchsheel Park,
New Delhi – 110 017, India
Penguin Group (NZ), 67 Apollo Drive, Rosedale, North Shore 0632, New Zealand
(a division of Pearson New Zealand Ltd)
Penguin Books (South Africa) (Pty) Ltd, 24 Sturdee Avenue, Rosebank,
Johannesburg 2196, South Africa
Penguin Books Ltd, Registered Offices: 80 Strand, London WC2R 0RL, England

First published 2011

1 2 3 4 5 6 7 8 9 10   (WEB)

Copyright © Pauline Gedge, 2011
Original map copyright © Bernard Ramanauskas, 2011
Revised map copyright © Crowle Art Group, 2011

Quotations from *Egyptian Mysteries: New Light on Ancient Spiritual Knowledge* by Lucie
Lamy. Reprinted by kind permission of Thames & Hudson Ltd., London.

Manufactured in Canada.

LIBRARY AND ARCHIVES CANADA CATALOGUING IN PUBLICATION

Gedge, Pauline, 1945–
The king's man / Pauline Gedge.

(The King's man trilogy ; v. 3)
ISBN 978-0-14-317077-8

I. Title. II. Series: Gedge, Pauline, 1945– . King's man trilogy ; v. 3.

PS8563.E33K56 2011   C813'.54   C2010-907621-4

Visit the Penguin Group (Canada) website at **www.penguin.ca**

Special and corporate bulk purchase rates available; please see
www.penguin.ca/corporatesales or call 1-800-810-3104, ext. 2477 or 2474

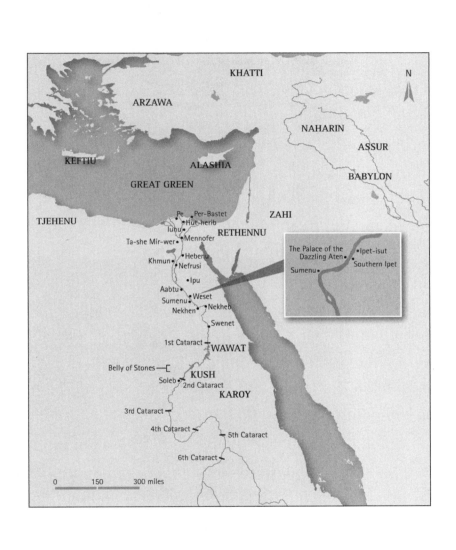

KHATTI

ARZAWA

KEFTIU

NAHARIN

ASSUR

ALASHIA

BABYLON

GREAT GREEN

TJEHENU

ZAHI

Pe   Per-Bastet
     Hut-herib
Iunu
     Mennofer   RETHENNU
Ta-she Mir-wer

     Hebenu
Khmun   Nefrusi

     Ipu

Aabtu
     Weset
Sumenu
Nekhen   Nekheb

     Swenet

1st Cataract
                  WAWAT

Belly of Stones
Soleb   KUSH
     2nd Cataract
                  KAROY

3rd Cataract

4th Cataract   5th Cataract

6th Cataract

The Palace of the
Dazzling Aten   Ipet-isut

                  Southern Ipet
Sumenu

N

0   150   300 miles

PART ONE

I

ON THE TWENTY-FIRST DAY OF MEKHIR, Huy's barge, together with one he had borrowed from the Mayor, pulled away from his watersteps and turned south. The morning was sparkling, the breeze warm, the air full of the optimism of spring. Huy, with Amunmose beside him, stood at the deck rail and watched the small group of servants recede. He did not wave and neither did they. He did not know when he might return, and had told them so as he bade them take care of his home. There was no need to instruct Merenra; the staff would be disciplined and nurtured as always under his control.

The barges tied up for the night just north of Iunu. Huy had decided to take an escort of guards and visit Thothmes and Ishat before he realized that his plan was nothing more than a delaying tactic. Angry with himself, knowing that his reluctance to reach Mennofer was deeply anchored in the resentment towards his god that still sometimes came and went, he took a reed mat and a blanket and slept on the riverbank, close to the fire his servants had kindled. At dawn the next morning they set off again, passing Iunu's gleaming watersteps and the forest of palm trees all but hiding the ancient White Walls, and by late that afternoon the barges were tacking towards the left bank and nosing into the canal that would take them to the palace. Uncomfortably, Huy, leaning on the deck rail, remembered the last time he had seen the encircling wall. He had been answering another King's summons, had failed to defend Ma'at, and had slunk away in distress. Grimly, he turned his mind from that memory. The barge was slowing as a group of liveried soldiers approached, led by a figure Huy recognized. He waved. "Supreme Commander Wesersatet! It's good to see you again! You look well!"

The soldiers halted on the stone edge of the canal and Wesersatet smiled. "It's good to see you also, Great Seer. Thank the gods, I remain healthy. You are expected. The palace is full of the tension of waiting. The second barge is yours also?"

"Yes."

"Then continue to the apron. Chief Herald Maani-nekhtef will direct you from there." Bowing, he spoke a quick order and his men wheeled about, retreating to stand in the shade cast by the trees ranked against the high wall running from the palace to the river, east to west. It joined the one abutting the edge of the wide stone concourse leading to the great double doors of beaten copper, and hiding the whole of the Fine District of Pharaoh from the gaze of commoners.

Huy caught his captain's eye, an order was shouted, and the sailors submerged the oars. Soon, too soon for Huy, his barge bumped gently against the wide stone concourse and his ramp was being run out. Huy crossed it alone, feeling naked without his scribe walking just behind him. An aging but still capable Tetiankh had dressed him in gold-bordered linen of the twelfth grade, combed perfumed oil through his long black hair, and braided it so that it brushed gently against his spine as he walked. His blue faience earrings in the likeness of Ra-Harakhti with the yellow chalcedony sun-disc on the god's head swung from his lobes. Tiny pieces of jasper attached to his sandals glowed dully red. The Rekhet's sa amulet hung on his chest together with the young Prince's Naming Day gift to him, the heavy collar with its golden frogs and lizards. His face paint had been flawlessly applied. The amulet rings of protection graced his hands. No one watching him pass by, tall, handsome, his expression closed, could have imagined the turmoil within. As he neared the massive copper doors, the metal tinged faintly pink in the first intimation of dusk, another man he remembered stepped forward from his stool beside one of the colossal seated figures with their blue and white flags flanking the palace entrance, and bowed. Then he waited. So did Huy. It was some moments before Huy realized why.

"I am not a noble, Maani-nekhtef," he said. "Don't wait for me to speak."

The man bowed again. "Your pardon, Great Seer. I am flattered that you have remembered my name. The King and the Regent are in the King's quarters. My orders are to take no errands but keep watch for you here until your arrival and then to personally escort you to the royal apartments. Do you wish the company of your scribe?"

How tactful you are, Huy thought as he shook his head. *You hide your surprise at my lack and make no verbal blunder. I had forgotten the extreme politeness of the courtier.*

"Then be pleased to follow me," the herald invited. One of the tall doors stood open. Huy followed his guide into the echoing vastness of the reception hall. A wave of longing for the poppy swept over him as he surveyed the deep blue of the lapis-tiled floor, the flecks of pyrite glinting like sparks as the lights from the many tall lamps reached them, the pillars marching into the distance where an empty dais and a golden baldachin spoke to Huy of audiences and formal banquets. He had not taken his midday dose for fear that Mutemwia would read his drugged state in the size of his pupils, but now, with a spasm of nausea, he regretted his decision. He had been using the poppy for so many years that only a very large quantity affected his thought or his speech. He was grateful that it still had the power to kill his pain and lull him to sleep.

They crossed the hall and entered the first of the wide corridors criss-crossing the complex, which were lined with ebony statues of the gods and symbols of every sepat. Huy remembered trying to find the totem of his district, the Am-khent. As before, he was soon lost in the maze of this city within a city. The passages were busy with hurrying servants all wearing the white and blue, and Huy and Maani-nekhtef often encountered groups of courtiers ambling along. At a sharp word from the herald they melted back against the walls to allow Huy to walk by. Once he heard a swift exchange of loud whispers as he slowed to negotiate a particularly crowded corner. "It is he! I know it is! Look at that hair! They say he's still a virgin. I wonder how old he really is."

"Hush. He'll hear you. If he glances at you, don't respond. They say he can put a spell on you just by looking into your eyes."

Maani-nekhtef swung round. "I cannot put a spell on you, my Lady, but I can certainly recommend to the Queen that you be reprimanded for your rudeness. Get about your business!" Calmly he resumed his place in front of Huy and walked on. *So the authority of a Chief Herald extends further than the safe delivering of documents and the calling of titles,* Huy mused as he followed Maani-nekhtef. *Is he a noble himself?*

Huy had expected to be led out into the central garden space with its pools and many flower beds and shady trees, but the herald turned right into an area of the building Huy did not recognize. Guards stood along the walls of the quiet corridors. Great royal likenesses frozen in mid-stride or seated peacefully with hands on their kilted thighs punctuated the few closed doors Huy noticed. *I will never learn to negotiate this maze,* he thought. *I'll need a servant just to lead me about.* At that moment the herald slowed. Directly ahead were double doors of what Huy knew was electrum, the beautiful blend of gold and silver favoured by every King and every noble who could afford to have it made into jewellery. Four soldiers were ranged across them. As Maani-nekhtef halted, they moved apart, saluted him, gave Huy a cursory assessment, and one of them pulled open one of the doors. *It must be heavy,* Huy thought again as his heart began to race. *He's leaning back and the muscles of his arm are taut.*

The herald stepped beyond, murmured something, and returned. He bowed. "It has been an honour to serve you, Great Seer. I leave you in the care of Chief Royal Steward Nubti. Should you need the services of a herald, feel free to send for me. If you wish, I can appoint one for your use alone."

"Thank you, Maani-nekhtef," Huy replied. "I shall do so." The man smiled and strode away, and Huy turned to see Nubti in the doorway.

At once the steward bowed. "Great Seer, you are very welcome," he said in the deep voice Huy remembered so well. "Their Majesties are eager to see you."

"Nubti." Huy, following his hunched back, found himself in a wide hallway that opened out almost at once into a large, brightly lit room whose walls were covered in paintings of giant, anonymous kings wearing the Double Crown and sitting on the Horus Throne or aiming an arrow at a confusing mass of enemies or standing in a skiff surrounded by reeds, throwing stick in hand. He had no time to do more than briefly notice the pretty ebony-and-ivory-inlaid tables, the gilt chairs with their inviting cushions, the gleaming lampstands bearing alabaster lotuses and furled lily petals in whose depths the oil wicks glowed and flickered. At the far end, a shrine stood open. From its interior Amun's benign face and tall double plumes seemed to exude an air of peace. Someone had laid a small bouquet of tiny white narcissus blooms across the god's feet. Huy could smell them together with the heavier scents of lotus and henna flowers and the almost undetectable tang of spiced satke oil. Mutemwia's perfume. Huy inhaled and closed his eyes for a moment. When he opened them again, he saw Nubti's oddly misshapen form gliding towards one of the wide doorways in the walls, but he had hardly reached it when he was forced to move aside. Amunhotep hurried past him towards Huy.

"You came!" he exclaimed. At once Huy went to his knees and then put his forehead on the floor. He could hear the patter of the King's sandals slow and then stop. "You may rise," the familiar voice commanded, and Huy scrambled up. Amunhotep was smiling at him. "Oh, Uncle Huy, it's so very wonderful to have you here," he said. "I wasn't sure you'd come."

Huy's eyebrows shot up. "You sent me a direct command, Majesty. Of course I obeyed as quickly as I was able. You've grown a great deal since I saw you last." Indeed, the creature standing before him was almost unrecognizable. In the months since Huy had seen him, Amunhotep had become taller and more slender, as though the remains of childhood fat had been used to impel his growth. His face was thinner also, although his cheeks remained pleasantly rounded. He was at the awkward stage when girls as well as boys suddenly become all arms and gangly legs, chests slightly concave, heads too large. *Why, he's twelve,* Huy thought with shock. *He's the same age I was when I came back to life in Hutherib's House of the Dead after being attacked at school in Iunu.*

The boy's large brown eyes rimmed in black kohl were watching him with humour. "You are assessing the changes in my body and adjusting to them. Before you ask, I am exceedingly healthy. Is Anhur with you? I long to see him." He indicated one of the two chairs drawn up to one of the opulent tables. "Let us sit." He flung himself down. "You are more than my Personal Scribe," he went on as Nubti and a white-kilted servant with a blue ribbon tied around his shaved skull appeared out of nowhere and silently placed wine, cups, and a dish of almonds by the royal hand. The slim fingers waved once. Nubti poured the wine. "I will not forget that you are Egypt's Great Seer. I will always invite you to sit in my presence, an honour no one else but my Majesty Mother has, because I love you and because I must never insult Atum by showing you the slightest indignity. You may also touch me sometimes."

Huy took the other chair at once. Amunhotep pushed a cup towards him. Huy lifted it and drank. The King laughed at his expression as he swallowed. "Year two of my Osiris grandfather Amunhotep, high quality, three times good, from the Food of Egypt. Our best. Now, is Anhur hovering beyond the doors?"

"No, Majesty. I wish he was." Briefly, Huy described Anhur's illness and the steps he himself had taken on his soldier's behalf.

Amunhotep grimaced. "I shall dictate a letter to him at once. It will be your first task as my scribe. So you are now without a captain of your guard or a scribe. I'm sorry." Huy expected the boy to continue, to say that he knew exactly the replacements Huy needed, but he did not. "Have an almond," he said after a short pause. "I wanted to command a great feast in your honour the day you arrived, but my Majesty Mother advised me to wait until you had been here for some weeks. She said you would be utterly lost for a while. So the three of us will eat together here in my private quarters tonight."

Nubti appeared again and bowed. "Majesty, the Seer's servants and goods have all been unloaded and taken to his apartments. If you wish, I can guide him there."

"No." The King took a last hurried gulp of wine and rose. "I'll take him myself, but you must come so that you can meet his steward Merenra." Huy would have liked to sit over the

excellent vintage for much longer, but Amunhotep was frowning impatiently.

"Merenra has remained behind to administer my estate," Huy
told him as they approached the double doors. "I have promoted
Amunmose instead."

"I remember him." Another servant was suddenly and silently
present, pushing open one of the doors, and a soldier on the
other side at once held it open. "He used to prattle on at greater
length than I did in those days. Have the passages cleared!" he
barked at the guards. As he and Huy fell in behind the soldiers,
Amunhotep slid his arm through Huy's. His perfume, rosemary,
wafted into Huy's nostrils. "My uncle Amunhotep is on his way
back from Mitanni," the King continued as the five of them set
off. "I have sent a contingent of soldiers from the Division of Ra
to meet him at the border. To escort him safely home." Huy
repressed an urge to glance at the smoothly painted face. Out of
the corner of his eye he saw that the hennaed mouth was faintly
smiling. "I don't remember him really. It will be good to
welcome him back. Pa-shed is looking forward to serving him
again."

Huy filed both snippets of information away. The guards were
already slowing after no more than two turns of the corridor.
Ahead, a pair of tall cedar doors stood open. Two of Huy's own
soldiers were already standing guard outside. He greeted them
and they returned his words with obvious relief at seeing him. As
he stepped over the threshold, Amunmose came hurrying. At the
sight of Huy's companion, he fell to his knees and his forehead
audibly bumped the tiles. Amunhotep told him to get up, which
he did with alacrity, only then rubbing his forehead. Huy prayed
that he would not speak first. The steward waited.

"I remember you very well, Amunmose," the King told him.
"You often brought me forbidden sweatmeats when I stayed in

Huy's guest room. Are you happy with the domain you will oversee?"

"Oh, Majesty, it's wonderful. Wonderful! Master, there are more and bigger rooms than your house has at home, and several of them give out onto a huge lawn with trees and flowers and two ponds! On this side"—he pointed—"the apartment joins by a door to your servants' quarters. There's a door on the opposite wall beyond, but it won't open."

"It will open from the other side." Amunhotep pulled his arm from Huy's. "My Majesty Mother's apartments are between yours and mine, Uncle Huy. If she wishes to speak with you, she will send a servant through. It is the same for me. I don't spend much time in my quarters, though. I must continue my studies until my sixteenth Naming Day like every other Egyptian pupil, and as well as my lessons, I must give audience to any minister who needs to consult Mother and me. There are a lot of them, not to mention the ambassadors who come and go from barbaric foreign countries." He turned to face Huy directly. "I must leave you here, but tonight you will be summoned to my rooms. I'll send you an escort. After the three of us have eaten, I'll dicate the letter to Anhur. Nubti, explain to Amunmose exactly where your quarters are, and how the stewards in the palace go about their duties. Stay here."

Everyone bowed and Amunhotep left. Huy felt that the boy had taken his energy with him. He was all at once tired. A wave of homesickness for his house and Thothhotep's light voice and Anhur's lined face washed through him.

"Master, would you like to see the layout of this place, or would you rather sit quietly while the rest of your belongings are unpacked? Your sleeping room is ready for you now, and Tetiankh is there."

Huy fought off his exhaustion. Nubti was waiting in the

motionless patience of the good servant. "If Tetiankh is there, I'll find it myself," Huy replied. "Nubti, tell him everything he has to know."

He wandered farther into the airy room with its white and blue tiles, its pretty red or yellow reed mats, its chairs and tables and lampstands, its cushions stuffed with goose down. The surface of one of the tables formed a sennet board, the figures inside the squares exquisitely painted on bone or ivory, the squares them- selves formed of thin, criss-crossing strips of gold. Under the table was a drawer where, Huy surmised, the rods, spools, and sticks for the game were kept. The walls around him did not have much decoration on them. They were broken by rectangled doorways leading into other rooms and perhaps even to rooms beyond them, until there was a solid wall against which some noble lived. The layout was simple, pleasing, and easy to grasp.

Huy found his body servant folding linen in a large, dim room dominated by a capacious couch with its head pushed against the far wall. Over it on the ceiling the body of the goddess of the sky, Nut, was arched, surrounded by stars, the sun just about to disap- pear into her mouth. Pink light, the early light of sunset, dribbled down from the three clerestory windows cut high in the only wall clearly fronting the garden Amunmose had mentioned, and pooled weakly on the blue and white tiling of the floor. The table by the couch was gilded, and already held Huy's night lamp. So was the chair resting against the right-hand wall, with two of his chests beside it. Tetiankh had already dressed the couch and placed Huy's shrine with its likeness of Khenti-kheti against the last piece of free wall.

The air smelled faintly of vinegar and jasmine. *The jasmine must be flowering outside*, Huy thought. It had been years since he had worn that particular perfume, not since the disastrous evening at Nakht's house when Nakht had refused him a position in his Governor's office and Anuket had kissed him so deliberately and so coldly in the dark of her father's garden. Huy hated this room at once, then silently reprimanded himself. *You are tired and a stranger here. Besides, you know there won't be much time for sleeping, don't you?*

"I need a small dose of poppy and an hour on the couch, Tetiankh," he said, stepping reluctantly forward. "Go and find out from Royal Steward Nubti where the palace physicians keep their mortars and pestles and whatever else you'll need. Later, you and I and Amunmose must discuss the safety of our belongings, how to keep everything secure, but for now just let me rest." He stripped off his kilt, sandals, and jewellery, placed his headrest on the couch, and lay down, watching the glow from the two standing lamps in the room gradually seem to brighten as the daylight waned.

When Tetiankh returned, Huy drank then dozed, listening as the man set up Huy's cosmetics table, opened a chest to retrieve a clean kilt, brought out a piece of jewellery with a soft clink. There was sanity in the gentle sounds, and relief from heartache in the drug. He came to himself with a start when a hand descended on his naked shoulder.

"Master, I let you sleep for two hours, but I dare not make you late for the King," Tetiankh said. "A servant from the nearest bathhouse is here with hot water. I will refresh you."

Later, in white kilt and shirt, a plain gold chain hanging with the sa around his neck and golden ankhs in his earlobes, his eyes kohled and his hair newly braided, he sat in his new reception room, now full of shadows, glad to be away from the aroma of jasmine and feeling wholly unreal.

A herald came for him not long afterwards, and by the time he had followed the man the short distance to the King's dully gleaming electrum doors, he was familiar with the way. He entered the royal apartments to a blaze of cheerful lamplight and the pleasant trills of a plucked harp. Nubti flowed towards him, reverenced him, and led him to where Amunhotep and Mutemwia were waiting, three little dining tables laden with fresh flowers behind them.

Huy made his obeisance to them, and Mutemwia held out both silver-hung arms. Astounded, Huy found himself loosely embraced, enveloped in her perfume, the blue enamel flowers surrounding her coronet brushing the middle of his chest. His own arms went around her automatically. It was like holding a child. She stepped back, but only a little. "I have missed you a great deal, Seer Huy." She smiled. "Many times during the worries of the past months I have needed your counsel and gone without. I hope you will be happy here. I will do everything I can to make it so." The tiny hands laden with rings flew apart in an expansive gesture. The beautiful black eyes were full of warmth.

Huy bowed profoundly. "Majesty, you are generous and kind," he replied. "Know that I will serve my King and you for as long as my love and devotion are needed."

"Let us eat together, then." Still smiling, she indicated the floor, and once she and Amunhotep had settled themselves behind their tables, he joined them.

At once the room sprang to life with a file of servants carrying trays that filled Huy's nostrils with appetizing aromas. He suddenly realized that he was hungry. He was offered date, palm, grape, shedeh, or fig wine. The choice of delicious salads at that time of the year was large. Ox liver with parsley and onions, roast duck in a cumin and marjoram sauce, grilled fresh inet fish, its skin crisp with thyme and coriander, were all paraded before him. The meal ended with a small bowl of dried figs and currants in a date syrup. Huy, leaning back replete, realized that nothing he had eaten had been tasted, and then decided that it did not matter. Their Majesties would have their own tasters, and any meal shared with them was safe—unless one or both of them might want to poison him in the days ahead. He stirred uneasily, dismissing the ridiculous thought.

Amunhotep was talking about his chariot horses. Mutemwia was watching him, her rings glinting as she moved her wine cup slowly to and fro. Huy, glancing from one to the other, saw more than the physical likeness between them. Both carried their noble blood with a grace Amunhotep was just beginning to display, but now a subtle aura of easy confidence surrounded them, the mutual satisfaction of a task accomplished. Huy did not feel left out; indeed he had understood Mutemwia's goal and the caution with which she had proceeded to accomplish it, and had complied without words. He came to himself with both pairs of large black eyes fixed on him inquiringly.

Amunhotep laughed. "Have you eaten too well, Uncle? What were you thinking?"

"I was remarking to myself on the many similarities between you and your Majesty Mother, and yes, I have eaten far too well. My physician will compel me to fast all day tomorrow." The comment was a small test. Huy had not known that until the words left his mouth. Would Mutemwia tell him that the royal physicians would be caring for his health from now on? Or would she not care, seeing that her network of spies was incredibly efficient? Mutemwia said nothing.

The King rose and Huy followed. "I keep forgetting that I must not call you Uncle anymore now that my blood relative is returning," Amunhotep said ruefully. "I'll miss that freedom, but I'll enjoy calling you Amunhotep. Now I want to dictate to Anhur, and afterwards my Mother wants to speak with you in her quarters."

Mutemwia bowed to him then kissed his cheek. "Sleep well,

my son." Acknowledging Huy's obeisance with the slight tilting of her head, she walked towards the door. At once a bevy of servants followed behind her. Huy recognized Nefer-ka-Ra, her scribe, in the group. The door was closed.

Amunhotep beckoned Nubti. "Go and find the Seer a palette and bring papyrus and ink as well." He turned back to Huy as the steward floated away. "After you've taken down my letter, we'll play a game or two of sennet. I still can't go to my couch until the middle of the night. Neither can my Mother, and it's always a struggle to leave my sheets in the morning. I do like those rare days when my presence isn't needed to give audience or bless some god's festival and I can go on snoring! Mother deals with the administrators and then tells me what she's done. If I disapprove, I must tell her why and give her strong arguments or she overrides me. She's making sure that when I reach my majority and have full control over Egypt, every official, both governmental and religious, owes me something and is utterly loyal to me. So many of them!" He cocked an eye at Huy. "You are exempt," he added. "You are my scribe because I love you and you are Egypt's Great Seer and I don't like being here without you."

"But my brother Heby and my nephews are not exempt."

"Well, partially." The King's glance became shrewd. "They are your close kin, therefore I feel warmly towards them, and Heby has made an honest and competent Mayor for Mennofer. Ramose is still only eleven and cannot yet perform any duties as a steward in the Mansion of the Aten at Iunu, but his appointment lets everyone know that I intend to personally supervise the worship of that god."

Huy looked at him curiously. *Was Ramose's elevation Mutemwia's idea or Amunhotep's?* he wondered. *Would I have been as astute at twelve years old? Or is Amunhotep so anxious to show me how capable to rule he's becoming that he is taking his mother's farsightedness for his own?*

"I think the choice of your other nephew for Superior King's Scribe of Recruits is very good, don't you?" the King went on. "He's a competent-enough scribe at twenty, but added to that is his reputation among the officers and men. He's comfortable with them. He shares the soldiers' rough jokes and speaks to the officers in the language of the barracks and the training ground. Ah! Here's a palette for you."

Huy was about to say that his nephew Amunhotep-Huy was a harsh, quick-tempered man, but Nubti was handing him a scribe's tools and withdrawing.

"Tomorrow you can use your own palette. I'm ready to begin."

Hastily, Huy went to the floor, murmured the usual prayer to Thoth, and picked up a brush. *So it begins,* he thought as the King began to pace. *Am I still within your will, mighty Atum?*

When the letter was finished, Amunhotep took it, beckoned to Nubti, and handed it over. "Take it to Nebmerut for sealing and then to Maani-nekhtef before you retire," he ordered Nubti. "Now, Uncle, we will play sennet."

No we won't, Huy thought. *If I don't lay down the white cord delineating my boundaries now, this wonderful boy will take over my life completely.* Placing the palette on one of the tables, he faced Amunhotep. "Majesty, I am fifty years old," he said steadily. "If I am to serve you as I would like, I must keep my hours of rest intact as often as possible. This is my first evening here. I'm tired and just a little homesick, and I must speak with the Queen before I retire. Please dismiss me."

An expression of sullenness flitted across the intelligent features. King and scribe stared at one another in a pregnant silence. Then Amunhotep dropped his gaze. "You're right," he admitted. "You reprimand my selfishness as gently as you used to do when I misbehaved in your house. I am corrected. Make your reverence, go to my Mother, then sleep without danger. The servants fall over one another, so be sure to ask for whatever you need. Until the morning, Amunhotep."

Huy bowed, straightened, and smiled. The relief he felt did not show on his face. "Majesty, I will gladly be called by your powerful name when dealing with everyone but you and the Queen your Mother. I've been Uncle Huy to you for years, but now you are almost a man I would like you to call me just Huy."

Amunhotep returned Huy's smile. "I'd like that too. Your name holds many good memories for me." He turned away.

Huy backed down the room then strode to the door. *He is still irritated at my presumption to gainsay him,* he thought as the soldier pushed it open and Huy walked through. *Nevertheless, I cannot allow him to control me or he will begin to believe that if the Great Seer is biddable under his hand, then bending everyone else to his desires is permissible. I hope Menkhoper and his other tutors are still able to hold on to the invisible leash. Besides, if I always give in to him, I'll be no use to him as an adviser. His respect for me will erode.* In the passage he paused and one of the guards approached him.

"I am to escort you to Her Majesty's apartments," he said with a bow. "Her walls abut yours, Great Seer, so if I take you there today, you will need no help in the future." Huy followed the wide, muscled back as the man took him not far past his own quarters and halted before another pair of electrum doors. Huy was too tired to scan the figures beaten into the metal except to notice that they wore feminine dress. Again there were guards and again a consultation with someone beyond. A young man in an ankle-length white sheath bordered in blue emerged, bowing several times.

"I am Ameni, Chief Steward of Her Majesty, Great Seer," he said. "You are expected. Please enter." Huy did so, wondering if

Pa-shed, the steward who had served Mutemwia in his master's absence, was even now preparing the Prince's old quarters for his return.

Finding himself alone, he paused in the middle of the room and looked about. The Queen's apartments were little different from those of her son. The evidence of opulence was everywhere, but softened by the influence of a woman. Or women, Huy mused, his gaze travelling his surroundings. Mut, Hathor, Sekhmet, Isis, Neith, all goddesses, graced the white-painted walls, making them bright with the vivid colours of jewelled belts and coronets. The lampstands flowed, the fine alabaster lamps themselves curved into flower buds, fruit, and bulbous seed pods. A shrine at the far end was closed, but the air held a faint whiff of incense smoke. Yellow reed mats covered the tiled floor. Several cushions were thrown about between the tables and intricately inlaid chairs.

All the apertures leading to other rooms showed darkness but one. A shaft of light came from it, mingling with the many lamps burning around Huy. As he stepped towards it, Mutemwia appeared, her diaphanous sleeping robe momentarily blurring its radiance. Her tiny feet were bare. She wore no adornment, and her hair fell in a gleaming shower to her shoulders. Watching her, Huy realized that she reminded him of someone, but he could not remember who that might be. He felt immediately at ease with her, this most powerful woman, even though she looked to be no more than a vulnerable girl. He bowed, smiling, and she waved him forward.

"This is like old times, isn't it, Huy, when I used to wander about your house and garden at night, and we would often meet because you could not sleep and I was not tired." She raised her chin at the nearest wall. "These are the rooms reserved for the Chief Royal Wife of the King. Neferatiri used them last, and as

my son is still only twelve and will not be taking any wives for a
while, I have sent Neferatiri back to the women's quarters. As a
dowager Queen she is entitled to wear the royal vulture on her
head. I am perfectly happy to keep the gazelles' heads. Sit down,
my friend. It's late and I will not hold you with silly chit-chat.
Thank you, Ameni." With a start Huy saw the steward at his
elbow, placing beer and water on the table. "Are you hungry,
Huy? Would you rather drink wine? No? Then you may go,
Ameni. When the Seer leaves, summon Tekait."

The man made no sound as he crossed the long floor and went
out. Mutemwia poured water for them both. Huy drank thirstily,
but the Queen's cup remained full.

"The King and I have tasks for you," she began, pulling a footstool towards herself with her naked toes and settling her feet on
the cushion. "Firstly, I have prepared for you a list of High Priests
and ministers in positions of responsibility at court. The King
inherited some of them from his father. Some of them I myself
have appointed. We want you to give audience to each of them.
We need to know who will remain loyal to my son, who will work
honestly and diligently, whom to trust. I have determined these
qualities as best I can. You may See for them if requested, but if
there is anything detrimental towards the Horus Throne in the
visions, you must bring a record of them to me. You need not
bother with my list tonight. Bring it to the Hall of Audience
when the King sits. Maani-nekhtef will call out the names of
those in attendance as they approach the Horus Throne.
Nebmerut will note down their needs, and if necessary the King
will see them in their several offices. Nebmerut, Beloved of the
King, Royal Scribe and Seal Bearer," she explained in answer to
Huy's raised eyebrows. "He will work under you or take your
place if you are ill or absent. You will have much to do with him,
so learn his character well."

She paused to lean forward and lift her cup, and as she did so Huy was suddenly enveloped in a miasma of jasmine perfume. At once he was overcome by a confusion of emotions. Despair, desperation, rage, desire, deluged him as they had on the night when Anuket accosted him in her father's garden. The aroma had seeped into his earlier sleep, and his rest, though deep, had been full of unwanted dreams.

"You don't wear jasmine!" he blurted, half rising from his chair.

Mutemwia glanced at him sharply. "I have it sprinkled on my night robe occasionally. For some reason it helps me to sleep. What's the matter?"

Huy sat down slowly. *I'm so tired tonight*, he thought resignedly. *That's unusual for me unless I've been Seeing. I want to be dismissed and drink my poppy in silence.* The Queen was sipping her water, her eyes on him in speculation. Huy grimaced. "The smell of jasmine returns me to a time of great misery," he replied. "Forgive me for startling you."

"You didn't startle me." She put her cup back on the table. "But I must say that I have never seen the marks of exhaustion on your face before. I'll be brief."

She didn't ask me what that time was, Huy's thoughts ran on as she began to speak again. *She probably doesn't need to ask. She knows already.*

"The King's uncle will arrive in a few days," she was saying. "He will be treated with every honour to which he is entitled as a Prince. The King is most eager to get to know him. I remember him well and of course you do also. You made a Seeing for him. He will doubtless send for you before long." She met Huy's eye. "If he asks for another Seeing, I must know. If he sends such a request, it may mean that he has secretly decided to make a bid for the throne, in which case I must have him very closely watched, and Neferatiri also. The Prince will need her blood and position. She seems content, but I leave nothing to chance." She ran both hands through her hair, lifted it, and, letting it fall back into place, folded her arms. "Apart from the hour of audience, the King won't require your presence tomorrow. It might be wise to go to the administrative offices and let the ministers begin to get to know you. You remember the wording of your summons?"

"Of course, Majesty."

"Good. You must restrict the use of your gift to those I send to you. The common people have had you long enough!" Her smile was infectious. In spite of his fatigue he found himself smiling back. "Amunhotep loves you very much," she went on. It was the first time Huy had heard her use her son's name. "Before he gives audience tomorrow he wishes to confer two titles on you: smer and erpa-ha. He intends to elevate you to the ranks of the nobles. It's something his father should have done, but of course Thothmes would have reduced your power if he could, not added to it. What do you think?"

Huy did not answer her at once, although he knew exactly what he would say. He tried to read the thoughts behind the black eyes, which often seemed full of an innocence that was, in fact, utterly misleading. Was this a challenge? A test? *I deserve this*, he told himself. *I have served Egypt well and will serve her even better in the years to come. But I don't want it. Have never wanted it.*

Leaving his chair, he knelt before her, and taking her little foot in both his hands, he kissed it and set it gently down. "I am more than grateful for this honour, but I must refuse it. I can't serve the King and you if I hold a title."

"Why not?" There was no edge to the words, but Huy sensed the wariness beneath them.

"Because you have brought me here to be an adviser to His Majesty. You know that I love him and hold the greatest respect for you. You stand behind the throne as Regent. When the King reaches his majority, you will no longer have that power, although you will of course always have influence with him. My position as his adviser will not change. I must be seen to be above the politics of both the nobility and the priesthoods, to favour neither the servants of the King nor the servants of the gods. Only then can I be seen as incorruptible. The priests will not be able to accuse me of a bias towards my fellow nobles. The nobles will not see me as a contender against them for the positions and preferments available through His Majesty's generosity. As Huy the peasant, I am completely impartial. As Huy the Seer, I am seen to serve only the King."

She had been motionless while he was speaking, the gossamer linen that fell to her ankles stirring only with the rise and fall of her breast. Now she reached out her hands, lightly stroking down his hair and then taking both of his long braids and tugging them gently. "Get up. You are very wise, aren't you, my Seer? I had not considered your argument, but it has validity. Very well. I shall explain it to the King." She rose, went to another table, and returned holding a thick roll of papyrus, which she passed to him. Now standing, he took it reluctantly. "Not for tonight," she said. "You are dismissed. And before I forget, you have our permission to hire anyone you like to be your new scribe and the captain of your guards. Choose well. The palace is not always a safe place."

Bowing, Huy made his way to the door. Beyond it, Ameni acknowledged him and entered, closing it behind him. The passage was full of moving shadows between the torches on the walls, but Huy had no reason to share his fellow Egyptians' fear of the night. Not anymore. He came to his own door without difficulty, bade the two guards a good night, and made his way to his bedchamber. Tetiankh was asleep across its entrance. Stepping over him, Huy had just enough energy to rid himself of kilt, loincloth, and jewellery before crawling onto his couch with a gusty sigh. On the table beside him was a stoppered vial. After picking it up and shaking it, Huy pulled out the stopper and drank his poppy. Almost at once his fatigue became a pleasant lassitude and he drifted easily into unconsciousness.

He dreamed that he was sitting in his garden at Hut-herib drinking wine with Ishat. Even in his sleep he knew that drinking wine was a good omen. It meant that he would open his mouth and speak important words. He turned his head to tell Ishat so, but the woman beside him was not Ishat. It was the Queen. Mutemwia was wearing the crown with the gazelles' heads. There was no wine cup in her graceful hands. Instead, she was lifting a wreath of jasmine and ivy over his head. "I love you also, Huy," she said. "I have loved you almost as long as you have loved me. But what can I do?" The garden suddenly darkened and the hennaed lips so close to his own became ebony in the uncertain light. "Kiss me, Huy," she whispered, and it was Anuket wearing the crown, Anuket whose fingers pressed the wreath against his skin. Huy cried out softly, but he did not wake.

2

HUY HAD EXPECTED THAT AMUNHOTEP would hold audience in the Throne Room he remembered so uncomfortably from the time when he had lost his nerve to expose the sphinx dream as a sham. But the servant who arrived the following morning did not lead him through the palace and out into one of the gardens; he stayed within the main complex, and once again Huy was lost.

He had spent a restless night but could not recall his dreams, waking with the first grey light of dawn filtering weakly down from the high clerestory window. He had lain quietly for a moment, sure that he had not woken of his own accord. His sleep had not refreshed him. He felt tired in body and stale in mind, with the need for poppy already beginning to agitate within him. He was about to shout for Tetiankh when he heard music coming from somewhere fairly close by. One lone voice was raised in song. Huy could just make out the words and decided that they were drifting in through the clerestory above him. "Hail Mighty Incarnation, rising as Ra in the East! Hail Emanation of the Holy One!" A chorus at once answered, "Thou art risen, thou art in peace. Rise thou beautifully in peace, wake thou to life!" There was more, but Tetiankh appeared with his first dose of poppy and the simple meal Huy preferred in the mornings. Huy, rightly assuming that his body servant would have wasted no time in becoming acquainted with the routines and rumours of the court, asked him who had been singing. Tetiankh paused, Huy's tray in both hands.

"The chanter is Ptahhotep, the High Priest of Ptah here in Mennofer. At least, he was Ptah's High Priest. Apparently the One has made him High Priest of Amun and Fanbearer on the Left Hand. The responders are priests from Amun's shrine." He set the bread and fruit down by Huy's hip and poured his milk. "The King is supposed to go to the shrine at dawn to break the sanctuary seal and be present when the Hymn of Praise is sung just as Ra emerges from the vagina of Nut, and then to perform the necessary tasks in the Holiest of Holiest. But our King finds it difficult to leave his couch, being something of an owl as we know, so unless it's a god's feast day, Amun's High Priest and his acolytes come to sing the hymn to him outside his bedchamber every morning after they've sung for the god himself."

Huy, a wrinkled fig halfway to his mouth, suddenly looked at it, frowning. "Thank you, Tetiankh. Now tell me if you saw Amunmose taste this food and milk."

The man nodded, lifted a starched white kilt from one of Huy's tiring chests, and laid it carefully over the chair. "I did. Amunmose knows what you like to eat. He chose and sampled everything himself. He did the same last night with the water beside your couch. I'll go to the nearest bathhouse now and make sure everything's ready for you."

Huy ate and drank slowly. He did not relish having to be washed and oiled in the company of others every day, but he supposed that given the hundreds of people inhabiting this warren it was unavoidable. He wondered how long it would be before he could have a home built for himself, just out of the city perhaps, by the river.

Now, dressed simply as a scribe but ornamented as a favourite of the King, he strode after the servant, his palette and the scroll the Queen had given him under his arm. At last the man halted at a tall doorway. "This is where His Majesty discusses matters with his ministers," he told Huy, bowing and waving him through. "I will return later and take you wherever you wish to go."

Huy thanked him and plunged into the throng of men milling about and talking loudly. As he moved, he caught a glimpse beyond them, into a vast room he recognized as the main reception hall. He was behind its rear wall, looking through an open door and across its dusky expanse to the wide, pillared entrance of the palace. Feeling a little less bewildered, he studied the officials around him. Amunhotep had complained in a letter that he was surrounded by old men, Huy remembered, but the faces he saw were mostly young. For a while no one noticed him, but at last he saw someone he knew. Heqarneheh approached him, beaming and bowing.

"Great Seer, you are here! It's been a long time since I chased a Prince around your garden."

"It's good to see you," Huy replied, pleased. "I presume your days of nurse to Amunhotep are over. Are you still a Royal Tutor?"

"I am, but I spend most of my time at the harem in Mi-wer, seeing to the care of our late King's lesser children. Menkhoper still teaches Amunhotep, of course, along with an army of experts in every field His Majesty must conquer. Oh, here comes Maani-nekhtef! I hope we may speak again and at length."

The Chief Herald had mounted a dais on which two thrones and a rather large cushioned stool were placed. His Staff of Office hit the wood three times and a hush began to settle over the crowd.

"His Majesty Amunhotep, King of Upper and Lower Egypt, neb-maat-ra, Ka-nakht kha-em-maat ..." He went on calling

Amunhotep's titles while every back was bowed. When he was at last bidden to stand, Huy saw that the chairs were occupied. Amunhotep, in a plain white kilt and a blue and white striped linen helmet, had crossed his legs and placed both arms along the golden lions' spines making up the arms of the throne. Mutemwia, in a long yellow sheath belted in gold and with a coronet of red faience flowers on her head, was surveying the company. Catching Huy's eye, she beckoned him. At once the assembly drew aside and Huy went forward. At the same time a man of about Huy's own age came hurrying through the door behind the dais, bowed peremptorily, and settled himself cross-legged on the cushioned stool beside the King, setting a large box on the floor beside him and a palette across his thighs. *That must be Seal Bearer and Royal Scribe Nebmerut,* Huy thought as he halted at Amunhotep's feet.

"Come up and stand behind me, Huy," the King said. "You slept badly, I see." Then in a louder voice he addressed those present. "I have been pleased to appoint the Great Seer Huy Son of Hapu to the position of King's Personal Scribe. I desire his wisdom and value the gift the gods have bestowed upon him. In token of his love for me he is now known as Amunhotep. Reverence him and then let us get on with the matters of the day."

Every head went down then lifted. Every eye was fixed on Huy. No response was necessary. Huy unrolled the scroll Mutemwia had given him and prepared to put faces to the daunting list of names and then try to remember them all.

Afterwards, Amunhotep disappeared to his lessons and Mutemwia, her entourage behind, walked Huy and his escort out into a garden Huy recognized though he had once entered it from a different door. Mutemwia indicated one of the many buildings enclosing it. "The lesser audience hall," she said. "Reserved for occasions less formal than those that take place in the reception hall but more official than the meeting of the King with his ministers. You have been inside it, I think."

Huy did not answer. He was revelling in the blue sky and bright sunlight of a spring day. A warm breeze pressed the Queen's yellow linen against her legs and freed wisps of black hair from Huy's one thick braid. The grass, watered earlier and now quickly drying, sparkled with moist droplets. Petals from the trees growing everywhere showered the ground with every gust of air and Huy, passing the spiny arms of a plum tree, caught the spicy scent of its little greenish-yellow flowers.

Mutemwia pointed, ignoring the trio of gardeners now flat on their faces as she walked by. "That whole building continues into the next area of garden. You can see the path that cuts off the end of the wall. All the ministers have their offices there. No, Tekait, don't bother with the sunshade—the wind is too strong. Huy, I am taking you to meet a few of them, and that will be enough for today. We eat the evening meal in private again tonight, the King, you, and I. Greetings, Ptahmose!"

They had halted at the doorway of the first cell. At the sound of his name a man came out swiftly, bowing as he did so. "Majesty."

"I have brought Amunhotep Son of Hapu to meet you. Huy, this is the Vizier of Upper and Lower Egypt, the noble Ptahmose."

They exchanged a few light pleasantries. Huy endured the other's polite scrutiny. These men knew nothing of him but rumour. The Osiris-King Amunhotep the Second, who had generously rescued Huy and Ishat from poverty, had sometimes sent court officials to Huy for Seeings, but his son Thothmes had not dared to do so. Thus a generation of nobles had never seen him.

"As His Majesty's Personal Scribe, you and I will be sharing many private matters," Ptahmose told Huy. "I hope we may become friends in our service to the Horus Throne."

"So do I," Huy agreed. He was sure he would enjoy this noble's company. The eyes met his with quiet confidence. Although Ptahmose was obviously not a young man, his lean body and well-muscled arms spoke of a balanced life. Huy was surprised by how much the Vizier knew about Hut-herib and its environs.

"Part of my work for the King lies in examining all land transactions from the Great Green in the north to our border with Wawat, where Nehemawi serves His Majesty as Viceroy of Wawat and Kush," Ptahmose explained. "I have representatives with every Governor and I tour the sepats twice a year, once to assess the health of the fields and once to settle any major disputes between the noble landowners after the Inundation has destroyed the canals. I have met your uncle Ker."

Mutemwia held up a hand and immediately Ptahmose stopped speaking. "We must continue on our way," she said. "Is there anything I need to hear, Vizier?"

"No, Majesty. I shall not need to trouble you with any governmental matters until I return from Weset."

"Very well." She turned towards the next cell and Ptahmose bowed and withdrew. "The Vizier is a very powerful man," she remarked to Huy. "He reports only to the King and to me. His most difficult task lies in making sure that Thothmes' lesser sons receive estates or trade revenues commensurate with their station. They can be a quarrelsome horde, always demanding more because their blood holds the tincture of royalty. Ptahmose handles them firmly and with tact. He refuses to give any of them government posts. He prefers to promote the young men under him who have worked hard to improve their station. This cell houses the Overseer of the Treasury, Nakht-sobek. The Sobek family comes from Sumenu, south of Weset. They are lovers of the desert, but live here because they are entirely trustworthy. Nakht-sobek reports to me on the state of the Treasury every day. Of course, I have a spy in the Treasury as well."

Of course, Huy thought with a flash of humour that rapidly became gratitude. *She has obviously decided to confide in me completely. She must know the power over both herself and her son she's giving me. Eventually I would be able to destroy them both.* He was exchanging greetings with Nakht-sobek while these thoughts flitted through his mind.

He and Mutemwia moved on, and soon Huy gave up any effort to remember the many faces that smiled at him. *I simply must hire a scribe who will walk with me and remind me what titles each person holds and what positions they fill,* he thought a trifle anxiously, *and I urgently need a captain who will organize the few guards I brought with me, someone who will have my welfare and the care of my staff at heart. Who can I go to for advice? Heby? My nephew Amunhotep-Huy?*

"You look worried, Huy," Mutemwia said, and Huy came to himself.

"Not worried, Majesty," he responded, "but I've already forgotten the names of half the men I've seen."

"That will change." She had halted and turned to him, and with a curiously possessive gesture she lifted the golden sa amulet he always wore and, setting it against his naked chest, once more patted it lightly. "I must leave you here," she went on. "I have my own office adjoining the hall you were in earlier, and ministers waiting for decisions. You will be summoned this evening." Huy watched her walk away in the direction of the main building, her steps smooth and graceful, her escort hurrying to catch up to her. He could still feel the mild touch of her hennaed fingers on his skin.

The day was becoming warmer. The sun was almost overhead.

Huy re-entered the palace, and by asking directions from the many soldiers and servants filling the corridors, he made his way back to his quarters. Amunmose met him just inside the doors. "If you want a meal, I'll have to take Tetiankh to the nearest kitchens so I can watch him fill your platters," the steward grumbled. "Honestly, Huy, we might as well be back in the temple of Ra at Iunu with me still an apprentice cook and you a schoolboy! At the very least you need more staff to fetch and carry. The soldiers are complaining that they can't organize themselves. Anhur must be replaced, and soon."

"I know. Send Tetiankh to the kitchens for food. You can taste it here. Talk to Chief Steward Nubti about having sealed flagons of beer sent in regularly for all of us, and see to the procuring of water yourself. I miss the estate also," he finished as Amunmose was nodding unhappily. "In the future I'll use the income from the poppy fields and caravans to build us all a new home. Until then, do the work I promoted you for."

Amunmose wheeled away, calling for Tetiankh, and Huy walked through his reception room to stand at the small open door giving out onto a garden. Several nurses and attendants were sitting in the shade of the sycamores and watching a gaggle of children playing on the grass. *I'd completely forgotten about my litter-bearers*, Huy thought suddenly. *I suppose Amunmose sent them to the nearest servants' cells. I'll need them this afternoon to take me to the barracks. I must find Amunhotep-Huy.* The need for his drug had begun to nag at him. Abruptly he retraced his steps and flung himself into one of the ornate chairs scattered over the floor.

After his meal, he did not sleep. Sending Amunmose for his litter and bearers, he made his way to the main entrance of the palace with two of his guards, and this time he became lost only once. The bearers greeted him effusively. He questioned them briefly about their welfare. They had no complaints. Privately

Huy wondered how he might gather every member of his house-hold into one large apartment close to his own; their scattering was a cause for concern. The Queen had not told him anything about the living arrangements the dozens of officials had. Were they and their families all quartered in the palace, or did they have homes somewhere within the Fine District of Pharaoh, itself inside the enormous walled Ankh-tawy area comprising the temples of Neith and Ptah, the ancient citadel girded by the equally ancient White Walls, the barracks and arsenal, and the Peru-nefer docks?

He gave the men his order. They lifted him and set off towards the canal up which he had been rowed, across the vast sweep of concourse in front of the palace entrance. Several small skiffs were moored close by. He and his men settled themselves in the boat, together with the litter. Huy told the man whose job it was to pole courtiers and visitors wherever they wanted to go that he needed the barracks. It was good to be on the water, to look ahead to the line of palms on the river's bank and above to a cloudless blue sky, to see the rivulets of the canal sparkle under a bright sun. At the canal's mouth the skiff turned south against the current, but it was still spring, Peret, and only the one man was needed to pole Huy slowly past the noise and dust of the portion of the city lying between the Fine District of Pharaoh and the busy river. They passed the waterway leading straight to the temple of Ptah, and were jockeyed into the last mooring space available at the watersteps leading up to Peru-nefer and the barracks beyond. To Huy's left another canal vanished past Amun's shrine towards the temple of Hathor, and ended at the drainage canal far behind the western edge of Mennofer. A large body of water opened out between the river and the shrine, and here many of the King's ships were docked. The verges of the lake were choked with sailors, heralds in royal livery, and naval soldiers hurrying to and fro or loitering in raucous groups or fingering the merchandise offered on the stalls of the tradesmen loudly calling their wares.

Leaving the skiff, Huy waited impatiently for his litter to be unloaded. The din around him, though cheerful, was trying. With a vision of the often-deserted and quiet river path between his estate and the town of Hut-herib itself, he climbed into the litter. His bearers moved cautiously through the throng, none confident enough to demand a passage for him, but once past Peru-nefer itself the crowd thinned. The guarded arsenal loomed on Huy's right, and once past it the bearers swung that way, pacing by its wall until suddenly the huge parade ground opened out in a dazzling expanse. Across it Huy could see a row of cells and behind them, he knew, there would be many more where the King's military and naval officers lived while on duty. He heard the whinny of a horse coming faintly from his left and presumed that the stables lay beyond yet another line of similar structures.

Once across the hard-packed earth of the parade ground, Huy ordered a halt. "Go into any cell and find out where the Scribe of Recruits works," he said to his nearest guard. In spite of the gentle season the sun was reflecting harshly off the dusty area around him, making him sweat. He felt exposed and vulnerable without Anhur's solid figure standing beside him to block out not only the sunlight but also any threat. He and the other bearers waited.

Presently the man came back and pointed. "The scribe's cell is the one right on the nearest end."

Huy got off the cushions. "You two, come with me," he ordered the guards. "The rest of you, find some shade until I need you."

It was a matter of a few steps to arrive at the open door. As Huy and his men approached it, a servant rose and bowed. "Is the Scribe of Recruits within?" Huy asked.

The man bowed again. "He is. I will announce you, Great Seer. Yes, I know who you are." He smiled. Vanishing for a moment, he quickly reappeared and ushered Huy inside.

The cell was bigger than it had seemed from outside, the ceiling higher, the rear farther away from the entrance than Huy had supposed. One square archway led off to what must be his nephew's sleeping room. The floor was beaten dirt. One brown reed mat covered most of it. The interior was pleasantly cool. Three spears were propped in one corner with a gazelle's hide shield at their foot. Niches pocked the walls. In the centre stood a desk half buried in scrolls, and Amunhotep-Huy himself was rising from behind it, a startled expression on his face.

"Uncle!" he exclaimed. "I'm surprised to see you here! I knew that you'd been summoned but didn't expect a visit from you. Get the Seer a stool," he barked at the servant. "Pour beer!" The man scurried to obey. Huy sank onto the stool, waved Amunhotep-Huy back into his chair, and gratefully took a mouthful of beer. "This is not an idle call, is it, Uncle?" the young man continued. "You and I never did enjoy one another's company, but I suppose I have you to thank for my elevation from one of the anonymous scribes waiting on His Majesty to the Scribe of Recruits. His Majesty gave me the appointment in his own person."

"Actually, you owe your promotion to the Regent," Huy remarked. He pushed a few of the scrolls aside and set his cup on the table. "Our whole family is enjoying her favour. We are blessed indeed. Are you happy here?"

"Yes." Amunhotep-Huy folded his arms. "I already knew almost every officer of every division before I took this position, and many of the common soldiers too. Being out under the sky is a great deal better than hurrying about the palace maze with a palette clutched to my chest."

"You look very well." The man did indeed look healthy. His skin glowed a deep brown. Any courtier would regard the colour as proof of a loss of status, but plainly Amunhotep-Huy did not care for such niceties. His body was tight, his eyes, so like his father Heby's in shape, were clear, the whites contrasting startlingly with the dark features in which they were set.

"I am." A smile came and went on the generous mouth. *Generous in shape*, Huy thought, *like his mother's, the placid Sapet, but not at all generous in the speech that issues from it.*

"I exercise every evening, I eat much the same food the soldiers eat, and I am moderate in my enjoyment of wines. I take no poppy even when I am in pain. I rely on more mundane remedies."

Unlike me, Huy finished the unspoken criticism. *You arrogant man. What do you know of my pain?*

"Your rigorous way of life agrees with you, then." Huy managed to swallow his annoyance. "I need your advice, Amunhotep-Huy."

The attractive sweep of the dark brows drew together in a frown. The muscular arms were unfolded and placed on the desk. "From me, Uncle? What can I possibly do for Egypt's Great Seer?"

Huy ignored the faint mockery in the words. "First of all, you can remember that you and I, your father and Ramose, are tied by blood and as such owe one another respect and loyalty," he replied. "Next to the King, of course. Do you agree?"

Amunhotep-Huy grimaced but inclined his head. "I agree. Even if we do not particularly like our kin. Respect, perhaps. Loyalty, definitely."

"Good. The captain of my household guard has retired and I need to replace him with someone who will answer to no one but me, someone who cannot be bribed or coerced."

"So you came to me rather than Wesersatet because his loyalty goes first to the King. You need an ambitious soldier who is prepared to gamble that you will continue to rise in the King's favour and will therefore remain trustworthy to you. I applaud your reasoning." The young man began to drum his fingers on the surface of the table. "You have also concluded that in this matter my allegiance goes to my family first. You are correct. Let me see." He was staring unseeingly at the far wall. Huy waited. "Someone young enough to see an appointment with you as an opportunity to rise," Amunhotep-Huy muttered. "Older officers only imagine promotion as rising within the ranks. Someone with the authority to command. You have set me a difficult task, Uncle." He fell silent and his hands relaxed. Huy sipped his beer and waited.

Presently Amunhotep-Huy sighed and sat back. "You'll have to request him from Wesersatet, but I think I know who you need. He's a Captain of Ten in the Division of Ra. A fine soldier, popular with the troops, and not too rough to rub shoulders with his betters." Rising abruptly, he went to the doorway. "You!" he shouted. "Fetch Captain Perti and be quick about it!" Returning to his seat, he smiled at Huy. "If you don't like my choice I'll find someone else, but it'll take time and you'll have to wait. Speaking of choice, I've decided to sign a marriage contract with Henut-nofret. She's the daughter of one of the King's Naval Troop Commanders, Nebenkempt, but he's a noble, so it's an advantageous match for me. Father's pleased. He'll be giving me a wedding feast and of course you'll be invited."

Do you like her? Huy wanted to ask. *Is she more to you than a rung on the treacherous ladder of court preferments? Does Heby worry about her welfare under your thumb?*

"There's no point in asking you to See for either of us," Amunhotep-Huy went on. "I know you would, but I'm confident about my future as your nephew, and Henut-nofret is as healthy as one of old Yey's horses."

"I wish you both long life and prosperity," Huy said politely. "Will you be building a house for her?"

"Well, I certainly won't expect her to live in this cell!" Amunhotep-Huy got up again and moved restlessly to the doorway. "I've already commissioned an architect to oversee the work. The Regent has given me a piece of land at Ta-she. Henut-nofret loves the lake. She'll be happy there while I pursue my duties here."

You remind me a little of Sennefer, Huy thought sadly, *although you are more handsome than my unhappy attacker. Already at twenty you have a furrow of discontent between your eyebrows. Dissatisfaction has driven you from the time you were born.*

There was nothing else to say. They waited, Huy with his hands in his lap and Amunhotep-Huy pacing from wall to wall. But at last a shadow fell across the floor and a young man entered. His blue-edged kilt was grey with dust. So was his crumpled linen helmet. In one grubby hand he clutched a bow and two arrows. He was panting lightly. As he executed a short bow to Amunhotep-Huy, a few specks of dirt sifted slowly to his equally grimy feet. A pair of bright brown eyes slid to Huy, then widened. The obeisance that followed was deep and reverential.

"Yes, you are in the presence of the Great Seer Huy, my uncle," Amunhotep-Huy said crisply. "He wishes to speak to you. Are you thirsty? Help yourself to beer."

The young man nodded his thanks, showering yet more dust onto the floor, went to a shelf, took down a cup, and poured, first laying his weapon carefully by the lintel. But he did not drink. He stood still, his gaze going from Huy to Amunhotep-Huy and back again without anxiety. Huy looked him over. He was undeniably striking, with a bronzed, lithe body and even features holding an open expression of calm anticipation.

"You are Captain Perti?" Huy said at length. *He's little more than a boy*, he thought. *The last thing I want to do is waste my time worrying about whether or not he's keeping order with my guards. What is Amunhotep-Huy thinking?*

"Yes, Master." There was confidence in the voice. "It is my privilege to command ten of His Majesty's soldiers in the Division of Ra."

"Indeed. And where are you from?"

"I was born at Het-nefer-Apu in the Anpur sepat."

"Do drink your beer, Perti. If there's as much grit in your throat as you're leaving on my nephew's floor, you must be extremely thirsty."

The boy flashed a smile that lit up his face. Quickly he emptied the cup. Amunhotep-Huy indicated that he might fill it again. Perti shook his head with a word of thanks. His attention returned to Huy.

"What military action have you seen?" Huy pressed him.

Pride infused the answer. "When the Osiris-one King Thothmes went south to subdue the troglodytes of Kush, I marched with the division. I took five hands. His Majesty praised me and promoted me to Captain of Ten, and so I remain."

"How old are you?"

A moment of hesitancy darkened the pleasant face. "I am sixteen, Master. I joined the army when I was twelve and fought the men of Kush at fourteen. My father is very poor." He offered no other explanation for his early entry into Pharaoh's fighting ranks. None was needed. A silence fell, broken only by Amunhotep-Huy's loud breathing and a shouted order echoing across the empty parade ground from somewhere far beyond it. *Do I offer a post to this stripling?* Huy wondered. *Would my nephew recommend him to me for a personal reason having nothing to do with my need? Can Amunhotep-Huy be trusted in this matter?*

"Perti, I need a captain for my household guard," he said at length. "The King has given me permission to appoint whom I will, and my nephew the Scribe of Recruits has recommended you. Would you be willing to take up this post, and also allow me a window into your future?"

Now Perti looked startled. "I'm not sure, Master. Your request comes to me as a blow from the heavens. I will need time to consider it. As for examining my future, I live by every precept of Ma'at and consider myself blameless under her scrutiny. I would not fear your eyes."

"Your speech is educated for a soldier," Huy commented. "How so?"

Once more that appealing smile beamed out. "It's no secret that I am ambitious, Master. Many superior officers in the divisions are noblemen. I am well aware that I can go no higher than my speech and manners dictate, therefore I listen to my betters and learn from them so that I may rise in the service of the King. I am a good soldier and my men love me because I am always concerned for their welfare. They expect rewards as I earn one promotion after another."

"You are unusually frank!" Huy was intrigued.

Perti shrugged. "Ma'at is generous towards the man who tells the truth. Besides, I do not have a nature devious enough to remember many lies. I am young, but I have learned the value of a good night's sleep."

Huy understood at once. "Will you think about my offer?" he said.

Perti bowed and set his cup back on the table. "Certainly, Great Seer. You honour me. How many guards have you?"

"I have ten. Anhur was like you, a Captain of Ten. My

guards fall over each other without direction now that he has gone."

Perti's eyes narrowed. "Forgive me for saying so, Master, but you need double that number in order to assure your safety within the palace. His Majesty allows a private guard of no more than twenty anyway. Every powerful official employs the full complement. It would be good for you to accept my ten soldiers along with me, if I choose to protect you and the commander of my division agrees to release them. I know them well, and they obey me willingly."

I am beginning to see why, Huy thought. *You know yourself and your men, and there seems to be no tentativeness or diffidence in you. What you say makes sense. If you bring men to me who already trust you, my worries will be fewer. Providing you yourself serve me with loyalty, of course.*

"I agree. Go away and make your choice, then I will See what's in store for you," he said. "Bring me word by sunset tomorrow. I need someone urgently and will not give you more time. You are dismissed." The boy bowed himself to the doorway, retrieved his bow and arrows, and was gone. "You've made a curious selection for me, Amunhotep-Huy." Huy rose and faced his nephew. "I hope Perti lives up to his name of 'Mighty One.'"

"I'm the Scribe of Recruits, Uncle," Amunhotep-Huy replied irritably. "I meet regularly with the Supreme Commander. Wesersatet has his eye on Perti and is only waiting for a few more years to go by before making him a Captain of Fifty. Snatch him and his men while you can. You won't regret it. Is there anything else I can help you with?"

"No. And I thank you. Be sure and invite me to your wedding feast." Amunhotep-Huy also stood. His attitude did not encourage an embrace. He bowed stiffly and Huy left him, stepping onto the unforgiving surface of the training ground with relief. Behind him he heard Amunhotep-Huy berating his servant. The litter-bearers were coming out of the shade, stretching and yawning, and Huy's guards quietly took up their stations to either side as Huy climbed onto the litter's cushions with relief. The prospect of a dose of poppy seemed more welcoming than usual.

The time of the afternoon sleep was almost over, but Huy retreated to his bedchamber, sent Tetiankh for the drug, and lay on his couch staring up at the busy ceiling with its dozens of stars surrounding Nut's arching, elongated body. The faint scent of jasmine added to the depression that seized him. In spite of the thousands of people inhabiting the palace, he was alone. He needed to discuss his invitation to the young Perti with Anhur and Thothhotep. If he had been at home he would have aired the prospect with them, put his thoughts in order by expressing them aloud, listened to their opinions. Now there was no one. Impatiently he pushed the self-pity aside, together with a sudden inner picture of his green and quiet garden lying deserted under a bright noon sun. *This is my home now,* he told himself sternly. *Why do I bleat after Hut-herib like a hungry calf? I have known for years that my destiny lies with the Horus Throne, but now its fulfillment is beginning I can only look back over my shoulder. I hate this place,* he knew suddenly. *I hate its noise, its crowded corridors, its servants painted like aristocrats, and its nobles with their backs bent like servants. I will soon be familiar with its design and may perhaps find empty corners where I can enjoy a temporary peace, but I do not believe that my distaste for this god's house will change.*

When Tetiankh returned, Huy drank his poppy, retrieved his palette from one of his chests, and tried to compose a letter to Anhur and Thothhotep, but his words were both stilted and hesitant. He could not speak to them as though they were present, both because he knew that his letters would be opened and resealed before being carried south and because he could imagine their concern for him if he wrote the truth. *I must have a scribe and a herald who will have no conscience about circumventing Mutemwia's spies,* he thought gloomily as he replaced the palette in the chest and sat on the edge of his couch. *Where may I find such servants? It's not that I have anything to hide from the King and the Regent. My loyalty to them is without blemish. But I must not express a dissatisfaction that would worry them or cause them to see my mild unhappiness as the prelude to a more serious discontent.*

The drug had not made him sleepy. The dose he had requested was large, but no more than the amount to which he had become inured. It had gradually begun to rob him of a healthy appetite for food, this he knew, and on the rare occasions when he was unable to get to his supply he would slowly begin to sweat and tremble as though he had a fever. He contemplated his addiction calmly, not only regarding the poppy as a gift from the gods for easing pain, as every Egyptian believed, but also convinced that for him it was a strange compensation for his inability to become drunk, a pastime every citizen enjoyed, or to gratify the sexual desires he had ruthlessly repressed a long time ago. For obscure reasons of his own, Atum had forbidden these pleasures to Huy, and in their place had set the poppy, a drug that aided the Seeings and enhanced Huy's visions as well as easing the terrible headaches that assailed him after each encounter with the future.

Now he reached to his table and, pouring water, drank absently, his mind on his problem. *I could go into one of Mennofer's many markets and hire another scribe as I did Thothhotep, but would I be fortunate enough to find someone not only highly literate but also unaffected by the power and riches abundant in the palace? Someone incorruptible? And am I myself powerful enough to demand absolute fealty from a herald who will refuse to allow anyone access to my letters and will carry them directly to the recipients? Shall I talk to Heby about all this? Ask his advice?* He felt cold with defencelessness.

Later, bathed and dressed in fresh linen, he made his way alone to the King's quarters for the evening meal. For the first time he was not comfortable in Amunhotep's presence. It seemed to him that the young Pharaoh was pouting over some event or word that had upset him during the day, and Mutemwia's glances Huy's way seemed fraught with hidden meaning.

As the empty dishes were deftly removed and honeyed dates and the last of the wine were set out, Amunhotep sighed deeply and leaned towards Huy. "I have endured a day of annoyance and frustration, Uncle Huy. First of all, God's Father Yey is ill. Again. And Yuya's gone south to the Akhmin sepat to see to his duties as Overseer of Min's Cattle at Ipu. He'll be back tomorrow morning. Therefore I spent an afternoon trying to improve my chariot skills under the fumbling and inept instruction of Yuya's assistant." He grabbed up his goblet, drained its contents, and held it out to be refilled. "This morning I acquainted Nakht-sobek with my plans for a few building projects. He behaved as though he has no idea how full my Treasury is, although he's supposed to be its Overseer. He dared to tell me that to begin construction now was precipitate and I should wait until this year's taxes come in. If I'd had Kha with me, I'd have been able to argue with him." He stuck one ringed finger in his wine and twirled it impatiently. "Well, am I sole ruler here or am I not?" He withdrew his finger and licked it, giving his mother a sidelong look.

"Not until your majority," Mutemwia retorted crisply, "and Egypt deserves better than a sulky child guiding her. This is ridiculous, Amunhotep! What do you have advisers for if you fume at their advice?" She turned to Huy. "You have met Treasurer Nakht-sobek. Yey has been God's Father, a valued adviser to the Horus Throne on both secular and religious matters, for many years. He has been Master of the King's Horse and Chief Instructor of the King in the Martial Arts to both Amunhotep's father and his grandfather. Unfortunately, he's old and prone to the usual infirmities of approaching Beautification. Yuya is his son and will inherit his responsibilities when he dies, as well as his position as Chief of the Rekhit. You were not at Amunhotep's coronation, so perhaps you are unaware that as such, Yey is accorded the privilege of being the first noble to pay homage to the new King." She swung back to her son. "Instead of resenting Yey's infirmity, you should be visiting him with gifts and words of appreciation. As for your building plans, put them away for a while. To do so will reassure your Treasurer that he is heard."

"Why should I have to reassure anyone about anything?" Amunhotep muttered, but in telling Huy of his day, his gloom had gradually dispersed. He smiled, his whole face lifting. "Uncle Huy, if I give my plans to you, will you consult Chief Architect Kha regarding their cost and validity? I won't pursue my Treasurer this year, but I intend to have my monuments begun when the flood recedes next Tybi! And will you come with me to Yey's house? I want you to ask Atum to heal him."

"You should meet him in any case, Huy," Mutemwia put in. "But Yey is very old, Amunhotep. No god is able to prevent us from aging and dying, not even Atum." She gave Huy a wry smile. "Although when I look at you, Seer, I wonder."

For a while there was silence. A servant entered, bowed, and lit the brazier standing in the corner, for the spring night had become chilly. Huy's gaze was immediately drawn to the swiftly growing flames beginning to heat the charcoal. Shadows gyrated on the walls close by. The air began to warm, and with its softening, Mutemwia's perfume drifted into Huy's nostrils. *Lotus, henna, narcissus,* he thought idly. *I must tell Tetiankh to sprinkle something calming around my bedchamber, essence of lilies in ben oil perhaps, to mask the scent of that accursed jasmine.* His glance strayed to Mutemwia. She had removed one heavy golden earring cast in the likeness of the goddess Nephthys and had laid it on the table in front of her. She was staring into the dimness, obviously lost in thought, absently stroking the piece of jewellery with one slow hand. The other rested against her cheek. Suddenly Huy wanted to leave his chair, cover the small distance between them, take both her tiny hands in his, and press them to his forehead. In a rush of sensory images he felt their warmth and the coolness of her many rings against his flesh, inhaled the increased intensity of her perfume as her arms rose, looked down at the outline of her slim thighs under the pleats of her diaphanous linen sheath. The impressions were so strong that he must have inadvertently made a sound, for she laid both palms flat on the table and faced him. Amunhotep appeared mesmerized by the fire as Huy himself had been, his face tinged a dull orange, his black eyes glittering in the leap and fall of the blaze.

"I hear that you have already chosen a captain for your household guards," she said. "Your nephew may be a harsh man, but he is an excellent Scribe of Recruits and has chosen well for you. Wesersatet will be disappointed. Perti shows much promise as an officer. Don't be deceived by his youth—he is fully capable of protecting you."

Huy gathered his scattered thoughts with an effort. *She has used red antimony for her lips instead of henna,* the voice in his head said clearly. *It makes her little teeth look very white. Everything about her is little, and delicate, and graceful, except for the eyes that dominate her perfect face. I want to pick her up and hold her close to me, feel her hair against my naked skin. She would be as light as an armful of feathers.*

"I have given him until tomorrow night to make his decision," Huy replied, pushing the image away. "Then of course I must seek a glimpse into his future." He turned to Amunhotep with relief. "If Your Majesty will give me a list of the building projects you wish to begin, I'll consult with your Treasurer and Chief Architect."

Amunhotep's grin lit up his face. "Threaten them with a disastrous spell if they won't give me what I want!" he joked. "Go to them in the morning, Uncle. Kha already has my list. In the afternoon we'll visit Yey."

"He doesn't live in the palace?" Something in Huy's voice must have given him away. Mutemwia's glance at him was keen.

"He and his family have a house by the river in the northern suburbs," she answered. "Are you homesick, Huy?"

You are the one who can cast a spell, not me, Huy thought in the moment before he answered her. *I must force myself to maintain a distance between us so that I do not lose the ability to do the work you and your son require. That small detachment has been present ever since you first brought Amunhotep to my house, even though we became friends and allies. What is happening to me now? And why?*

"I miss the peace of my estate and my servants miss its convenience," he replied with complete honesty. "But Majesty, we will adapt."

"So you will." She studied him, her head on one side. "For some time to come His Majesty and I will need you close by. Be patient. Many changes are in our thoughts." She rose. It was a dismissal. Standing and bowing, Huy left them.

The corridors were quiet, and empty of all save the motionless palace guards. Quickly Huy approached his own apartment, but before he reached it he could see the two young men sitting huddled uncomfortably on the tiled floor to one side of the double doors and one of his soldiers watchfully blocking the entrance. Seeing him come, the pair scrambled up and reverenced him several times before he came to a halt.

"Who are you and what do you want?" he demanded irritably. "Whatever it is, my chief steward Amunmose deals with domestic matters, and not this late at night. Come back tomorrow."

One of them stepped forward. "Our apologies, Great Seer. Your chief steward quite rightly would not let us through your doors, but it's difficult to encounter you. You are so busy on His Majesty's business. We have both left scrolls of reference with Amunmose. He told us that we could wait for you here. I am Paneb, underscribe to Vizier Ptahmose."

"And I am Ba-en-Ra," the other put in. "Chief Herald Maani-nekhtef sent me to you. I had not met Paneb before this evening. We have been getting to know each other."

They waited, eyes on Huy. In the new silence, he studied them. Neither was as young as the dim light of the passage had led him to believe. He judged them to be in their twenties. Paneb, the shorter and stouter of the two, had an air of steadiness about him. The gaze that met Huy's own was calm and direct. Ba-en-Ra seemed entirely relaxed and confident, hands loose by his sides, his shoulders back. Huy noted that both of them had the remains of orange henna on their palms, and although the hour was late the linen of their expensive kilts was unstained. Both wore amulets. A red carnelian sweret bead rested on Paneb's naked chest. Huy could just make out Thoth's hieroglyph etched into the elongated curve of the object. Paneb's name would be incised on it also. It was a logical protection for a scribe. Ba-en-Ra's sinewy wrist was encircled by a series of golden hares chasing each other. The hare was a desert animal and as such was a symbol of regeneration, but everyone knew that it also slept vigilantly with its eyes open and was venerated for its speed. In spite of his weariness, Huy began to smile.

"Now, why should I hire either of you?" he said. "Give me good reasons before I look at your references." They exchanged glances.

"To our great astonishment we discovered as we talked that we had each dreamed the same thing on different nights last week," Ba-en-Ra began. "We were sitting in the reed marshes of the south, eating crocodile flesh. The meaning of such a dream is clear: we are destined to become important officials."

"This was before our masters commanded us to seek your employment, Great Seer," Paneb said quietly. "If you doubt us, then take our hands. The gods will show you the truth of Ba-en-Ra's words."

"Serving me will not always be easy," Huy told them. "I require complete loyalty in my staff, even if a disagreement between myself and the King should arise. Are you here simply because the Vizier and the Chief Herald ordered it?"

"Yes," Paneb answered at once, passing the small test Huy had set. "But the opportunity to join your household exceeds my wildest hopes and I believe I speak for this herald also." He waved at Ba-en-Ra, who nodded briefly.

"Have you wives? Children?"

Paneb shook his head.

"I have recently signed a contract with my brother's wife," Ba-en-Ra said. "My brother died of a snakebite, and it is my duty to care for his family. They understand that a herald's work often keeps him away from home for long periods. I have a reliable steward in charge of their welfare." Huy found himself warming to this man, who understood and acted upon his responsibilities so selflessly.

"You are both nobles," he commented. "I am not, nor ever will be."

Paneb shrugged eloquently. "Nobility does not guarantee a life lived in the favour of Ma'at," he retorted. "Noble or commoner, it does not matter as long as there is honesty and right-thinking."

"A splendid sentiment," Huy said drily. "Very well. Present yourselves here tomorrow evening for a Seeing. Now go." At once they bowed and left him, walking together down the shadowed passage. Huy watched them disappear before turning to the door his soldier now held open. *I need both scribe and personal herald,* he thought as Amunmose greeted him and the door thudded closed behind him. *It seems that I must trust Ptahmose and Maani-nekhtef, two men I do not yet know, or struggle on without scribe or herald until I can make knowledgeable choices.* "I should read the scrolls before I sleep," he said in answer to his steward's question. "I won't have time in the morning. What's the matter with you, Amunmose?" He took the papyrus held out to him, his eyes on the other's haggard face.

"I'm sorry, Huy. I'm exhausted," Amunmose admitted. "I have control of a household in near chaos because my supervision doesn't extend to the palace kitchens or the laundry or anything else involving the general running of this anthill. The soldiers come to me for their instructions. I need an under steward I can delegate to, more servants, a food taster … I need your authority to sort it all out before I collapse. And what about a permanent physician for us all? I don't trust any judgment but your own."

"Have you read these references?"

"No. And that's another thing. Petitioners line up outside the doors, wanting to see you. Scrolls pile up from the gods know who and I've no permission to open them. We've been here no more than a few days and already it seems like hentis."

"I'm the one who must apologize, Amunmose." Weariness and a claustrophobic panic had seized Huy. "Early tomorrow afternoon I must visit a friend of the King's, but afterwards we'll try to establish some order out of all this confusion. Go to bed."

In Huy's own bedchamber, Tetiankh had turned down his

sheets and was trimming the lamps. Huy flung himself into a chair. "Find me a lily perfume and anoint my couch and the walls with it," he said as the body servant knelt to remove his sandals. "Do it every day until the jasmine has stopped flowering. We need a physician of our own, old friend. You already know your way about the palace. Recommend someone. And give me my poppy! My head is full of troubling images tonight."

He was undressed, washed, drugged, and on his couch by the time Tetiankh found a quantity of lily perfume and began to distribute it carefully about the room. Gratefully Huy inhaled the aroma that reminded him of his mother Itu and the little house where he had spent his childhood. Deliberately he called the sunlit garden to mind, and Ishat slipping through the acacia hedge to play with him, and his father Hapu plunging his tousled head into the deep clay basin outside the rear door at the end of a day spent working in his uncle's perfume fields. Yet the heavy blanket of opium stupor he relied upon to wrap itself around his mind seemed unusually thin this night. Itu's perfume filled his nostrils, but it was Anuket's innocent young face that blossomed suddenly, filling his inner vision, waking the ancient passion for her that had destroyed his peace for so many years. Long before her death he had been cured of it, but here it was again in all its distressing impotence. Even as he sank beneath the soporific influence of his drug and unconsciousness waited to claim him, he somehow knew that an old love was not the cause of the mental picture being presented to him. Nor was it a grasping for the familiar in the bewildering ocean of new circumstances. It was something else, something simpler and yet more threatening, but his tired consciousness refused to examine it. That night he neither stirred nor dreamed.

3

IN THE MORNING, HUY ATTENDED the daily audience, once again standing behind Amunhotep's throne with Mutemwia, doing his best to take careful note of each administrator and the matter of business he brought. This time he was able to recognize and name many of them. Ptahmose, Vizier and Fanbearer on the King's Left Hand, he had already met and liked. Amunmosi, Fanbearer on the King's Right Hand, little more than a boy, seemed something of a dandy, with his expertly made-up face and faultlessly pleated linen, the golden threads woven into the many braids of his gleaming wig, the gems adorning his chest, hands, and feet. Amunhotep greeted him affably, sharing with him some private joke that indicated a close and easy relationship between them. Huy made a mental note to acquaint himself with the Fanbearer. As Amunmosi turned back into the crowd, he flashed Huy a spontaneous smile of such sweetness that Huy found himself grinning in answer. Treasurer Nakht-sobek gave a short report on the amount of gold recently arrived from the mines in Kush. The King listened to him in a stony silence and Nakht-sobek's obeisance when he had finished was mildly defiant. There was little more.

Amunhotep dismissed them all with obvious impatience, got up, and took Huy's arm. "Nakht-sobek will be working in his office until the noon meal. I have already sent Maani-nekhtef to find Chief Architect Kha and have him waiting for you with the Treasurer. Make them bend to my will, Uncle Huy! Am I not supreme in Egypt? Nakht-sobek's refusal to open the Treasury to my demands borders on blasphemy! I am eager to begin beautifying the houses of the gods. What's wrong with that?"

Huy glanced about. No one but the Queen was within earshot. "Amunhotep, you know exactly what's wrong," he said, deliberately using the boy's name rather than one of his titles. "You are behaving like a spoiled child who kicks and screams because he cannot get his own way. I will ascertain whether or not your demands are reasonable, but I suspect that if they had been so, Nakht-sobek would have been pleased to accommodate you. Do you think that your uniqueness gives you the right to bully your administrators, the men chosen to serve Egypt for their wit and knowledge? Do you think that Ma'at approves of your high-handed behaviour? Menkhoper your tutor and Heqarneneh your nurse taught you better. So did I."

Amunhotep had gone white under his face paint. Holding his furious gaze, Huy was still able to glimpse the rigid tendons in the royal wrist as the King gripped the back of the gilded throne. Mutemwia said nothing, yet Huy knew that her hidden tension matched his own.

"Majesty, do you know how many uten and deben's weight in gold dust and nuggets rest in the Royal Treasury under Nakht-sobek's excellent protection? Lapis, jasper, ivory, turquoise, ebony, silver?"

Amunhotep's eyes became angry slits. "No."

"But your Treasurer does. Could it be that he is doing his duty in the caution with which he guards it?"

"But it's mine. All of it. Everything in the Treasury. Everything in Egypt. Every cow, every sheaf of corn, every ell of linen, every man, woman, and child—mine. Even you, Great Seer, belong to me." He folded his arms. "My power is supreme. And all I have to do is summon Wesi, the Head Bowman of the Lord of the Two Lands, to have you shot full of arrows."

Huy stared at him in shock. Now the boy was trying to grip his upper arms, but his hands were shaking. So was his outward breath. *This is not about me or the Treasurer,* Huy realized suddenly. *Something else is wrong.* He met Mutemwia's gaze. The Queen raised her eyebrows.

"You are King under the laws of Ma'at, like every one of us, Amunhotep," Huy said, doing his best to keep his voice even. "Egypt is not a private playground where you may indulge every whim. You know this. I have loved you since you first came to visit me on my estate in Hut-herib. Your aides and ministers do your bidding because you are Horus, and their respect will be slowly coupled with love if you show them that you intend to rule with wisdom and compassion. I believe that this is indeed your wish. What is distressing you so greatly? Your Mother and I can help you."

Amunhotep's head went down. With an uncharacteristic clumsiness he fumbled for the arm of the throne, stepped in front of Huy, and lowered himself onto the seat, gripping his naked thighs. At once Mutemwia moved to kneel in front of him. Huy bent beside her.

"Forgive me, Majesty Mother, Uncle Huy," he said unsteadily. "I'm not really angry. I'm afraid, and my fear has found a ready target in Nakht-sobek. Maani-nekhtef brought me a scroll early this morning. My blood-uncle Amunhotep arrives in Mennofer tomorrow." His hands rose in a gesture of uncertainty. "I was a baby when he went into exile because my father and grandfather plotted to disenfranchise him, perhaps even murder him if he had remained in Egypt, so that my father could take his place as the Horus-in-the-Nest. Now he returns. His claim to the Horus

Throne is indisputable and I am still only twelve, a fledgling with my Mother as my Regent for the next four years. I am very vulnerable." The face he turned to Huy was still pale, but the frenzy had left his eyes. "What must I do? Have him murdered and incur the wrath of Ma'at, not to mention every other god? Send him back into exile? Relinquish the Horus Throne to him and become Prince Amunhotep again? Such a move would surely reverse our positions. He would fear a bid to regain power on my part, plot to exile me, even kill me ..."

"You have reasoned well, but your conclusions inhabit the realm of fantasy, Majesty," Huy said. "This matter should have been discussed, at least with your Mother, as soon as I was permitted to invite the Prince's return. She would have reassured you."

Mutemwia settled herself on the step beside the throne. "Your blood-uncle was my best friend and confidant when you were still a baby, Amunhotep. He was, I believe he still is, a devout servant of Ma'at. Tomorrow we will welcome him home with a great feast, and see him settled in his old apartments with his steward Pa-shed. After a few days we will discuss his future with him." She tapped her son's sandalled foot. "I have already prepared to place spies among his new servants and among Dowager Chief Wife Neferatiri's entourage. Huy is ready to See for him if you order it. But wait, Amunhotep. You may yet discover an affection for him."

Amunhotep sighed. "I don't think I'll feel entirely secure until my position as the One is sanctioned on my majority," he said gloomily. "Meanwhile I dare say that both of you will tell me to concentrate on my education. Still"—he looked up at Huy—"I do want you to speak with Nakht-sobek and Kha, and find out when I may begin building in Egypt. Having taken note of your criticism, I shall humbly order a meeting with the Treasurer myself and explore the extent of my wealth."

Huy smiled. "A wise decision, Majesty. In the meantime I see Minhotep and Ptahemhet loitering by the doors. Go and enjoy your friends."

Amunhotep slid off the throne. "I must have my clothes changed first." With a kiss for his mother and a nod to Huy, he strode away.

"His confidence is renewed," Mutemwia observed. "As for our own, only time will tell." She turned a resolute face to Huy. "Nothing must endanger his destiny. I shall want you to See for him again soon, Huy. It has been years since you held him in your arms amid a magical storm of gold dust."

Huy watched her glide to where her attendants waited for her. *I suppose I must make my way to the Treasurer's office. He and Kha will be waiting, and later I am to meet the noble Yey. I wish a scribe was trotting behind me.* Calling for a servant to show him the way, he left the lesser audience chamber and plunged into the maze of corridors leading to the offices of the King's hard-working ministers. He was hungry for more poppy already.

Both men rose as Huy entered, but only Kha bowed. Huy noted quickly that the Chief Architect's palms were not hennaed. He was an older man, the muscles of his arms ropy, the loose skin of his belly folding over his belt. His head was shaved, but the faint shadow of stubble on his scalp was grey. Deep wrinkles scored a weatherbeaten face dominated by two startlingly blue, clear eyes that squinted sharply at Huy as he returned the gesture. Kha's kilt was white and plain. He was bare of jewellery but for a simple gold protecting Eye of Horus resting on his chest. Three clay cups stood beside a flagon of beer on a small folding table to one side. The surface of the Treasurer's desk was invisible under piles of scrolls, each neatly tied together with flax twine. A scribe was already sitting cross-legged on the yellow floor matting, his palette ready.

"Great Seer, this is Egypt's Chief Architect Kha," Nakht-sobek began. "We are here to meet with you at the King's request." His brief smile was polite and noncommittal. "I believe that His Majesty has already acquainted you with his desire in the matter of building projects. Would you like beer?"

Huy nodded. While Nakht-sobek poured for the three of them, Huy greeted Kha. "Do you have family here in Mennofer?" he inquired.

Kha shook his head. "My wife and two daughters remain on my estate outside Weset. That's where I was raised, and where I was educated in the temple of Khons at Ipet-isut."

Nakht-sobek was waving them onto two chairs that had obviously been temporarily provided, making the quarters seem uncomfortably cramped. He himself settled behind the desk. Kha regained his seat with a sigh of obvious relief and reached for his beer. Huy sat close to the end of the desk. Beside him the scribe had finished burnishing his roll of papyrus and was whispering and sprinkling a little water on the floor by his knee.

"That was not the customary prayer to Thoth," Huy said to the man. "What were you doing?"

The scribe glanced up, startled. "Before I beseech Thoth for his aid in transcribing what passes, I cast forth a smattering of water in memory of the mighty Imhotep, god and magician and the greatest scribe of us all," he answered. "It is a common custom here in Mennofer, Great Seer."

Imhotep. The name echoed in Huy's mind with an unwelcome familiarity. "Why here in Mennofer?" he asked.

The scribe had opened his mouth to answer when Nakht-sobek loudly cleared his throat. "Your pardon, Seer Amunhotep, but we must proceed to the business in hand," he said firmly.

Huy experienced a moment of confusion as he picked up his beer. Then he remembered the King's decree that he must be addressed as Amunhotep. He returned his attention to the Treasurer. "Very well," he agreed, aware of Nakht-sobek's continued wariness. "I might as well be honest with you, Nakht-sobek. His Majesty expects me to try and sway your judgment in the matter of his demand that the Treasury provide gold for his building projects. However, he has not shared his plans with me. You have his list of needs."

"So have I." Kha opened the drawstring pouch anchored to his belt and withdrew a scroll. "His projects are ambitious and will add to the glory of Egypt."

Unerringly, Nakht-sobek lifted another from the wealth of papyrus on his desk. "I agree. However, they will be expensive," he said tartly. "The Treasury is healthy. The King's father, the Osiris-one Thothmes the Fourth of that illustrious name, did not live long enough to do much beautifying. But our present Incarnation is still young. If he intends to embark upon a lifetime of building, he will have to find ways of replenishing the Treasury. As for this year, we are nearing the end of the month of Mekhir. The crops everywhere are in full growth. My assessors report the prospect of a good harvest and there is no major disease among the domestic animals. The taxes will be high." He glanced coolly at Huy. "Therefore I wish to reserve my decision on His Majesty's request until the next Inundation."

You want to keep an upper hand, Huy thought, meeting the man's gaze. *You resent the fact that I stand between you and the Horus Throne. How many other administrators are similarly offended? Will my time be wasted in running about and smoothing down ruffled feathers?*

"I want to see the list." He held out a hand across the desk. "I can advise neither the King nor you if I am in ignorance." Nakht-sobek's hesitation bordered on rudeness before he passed the scroll over. Huy unrolled it. "His Majesty is well informed," he said presently with an inward glow of pride. Many of Amunhotep's lessons in architecture and masonry had been taught by Huy himself in his own pleasant office at Hut-herib, while his royal charge squirmed on his stool and appeared to listen with only half an ear. "He wants to hire workmen and overseers to open a new quarry at Berseh for calcite, and repair and reopen those at Tura, just south of Iunu, for white lime-stone. He needs the stone for additions to Amun's temple at Ipet-isut. He wants to make a new barque for the god, raise and finish an obelisk that his grandfather the Osiris-one Amunhotep the Second apparently left lying in the granite quarries at Assuan—"

"He speaks of gold, lapis, malachite," Nakht-sobek broke in. "He does not understand the extent of the Treasury's holdings. They are vast, but …"

Huy tossed the scroll back on the desk. "His Majesty has agreed to meet with you so that he may learn exactly how rich he is," he said crisply. "I have asked him to do this before there is any more talk of opening the Treasury. I'm neither stupid nor craven, Nakht-sobek. Both the King and his mother know that I have not been summoned to court to place a seal of compliance on every royal desire. No decision is required until you and he have spoken." He turned to Kha. "Are these ventures laudable and feasible?"

"Yes, indeed." Kha tapped his scroll against his thigh. "Depending on the details of the designs, of course."

Huy got up. He had not drunk his beer. "Then we may delay any further discussion for the present." He bowed to the Treasurer. "Are you reassured, noble one?"

He received the ghost of a smile in return. Nakht-sobek also rose. "Completely, Great Seer. I look forward to consulting with you again in the future."

It was a capitulation that Huy accepted with good grace. Taking his leave, he went out into the passage that ran the length of the administrative offices and began the long walk to his own quarters. Before long Kha caught up with him.

"His Majesty has already warned me that he intends to arrive at my office one day soon to lay out the details and dimensions of his plans," he told Huy, coming abreast and falling into step with him. "From what he has already said, he understands the rudiments of an architect's task and can speak quite knowledgeably regarding the qualities and weaknesses of various kinds of building materials. He has you to thank for such knowledge, does he not?"

"In some part, yes."

"Then I trust you will be included in the work. I find it very exciting. His father cared little for any such major endeavours."

"How is it that you came to study architecture?" Huy wanted to know.

Kha laughed. "I appreciate your tact, Great Seer. You have already noted my common status. My ancestors belonged to a desert tribe inhabiting the wastes of Tjehenu to the west of the Delta. That's where my blue eyes come from. My grandfather began a trade in desert glass with the Governor of Weset's sepat during the reign of Osiris Thothmes the Third of that name. He was ambitious and enterprising. He earned enough to build a small house within the city of Weset itself, and opened a beer house in the room fronting our street. My father sent me to school. I have prospered, for a peasant. My daughters have made good marriages in Weset and my two younger sons have followed me into architecture. They are both with me here, where we live in a palace apartment. Would you be willing to come and share a meal with us sometime?" Huy found his liking growing for this unpretentious man.

"I'd be honoured, Kha. Thank you." They had come to a halt where the passage branched. "In the meantime, we must be about our duties." They took an easy farewell of one another, Kha to disappear to somewhere in the bowels of the labyrinthine complex and Huy to return to his own quarters.

Amunmose met him as he walked in. "I've hired an under steward named Paroi, Master," he announced, "and I've been talking to Nubti about more staff. Now that you're back, I'll go and fetch your noon meal. The King has sent a message for you. You are to have your litter-bearers ready to take you to the house of God's Father Yey after the sleep. His Majesty will meet you on the main concourse of the palace."

He left. Tetiankh appeared with hot scented water to remove Huy's sandals and wash his hands and feet. The apartment was unusually quiet. Someone had left the door to the gardens open and unguarded, but for once Huy did not care. He sat still while his body servant tended him, his eyes on the shaft of white sunlight pouring onto the tiled floor of the reception room, aware that its brilliance made him feel all at once thin and insubstantial.

When Amunmose returned, Huy ate the food quickly, dismissing the thought that if he took his midday dose of poppy on an empty stomach its effect would be greater than if the drug were mingled with grilled fish and broad beans with garlic. He would need to be alert when meeting Yey, Master of the King's Horse, Prophet and Overseer of the god Min of Ipu, and—as if those responsibilities were not enough—also Chief Rekhit. Stripping to his loincloth, Huy lay on his couch, lulled by the scent of the lily perfume Tetiankh had continued to spread about the room, but in spite of the usual vial of opium he could not sleep.

Each day brings a test. The Treasurer and Kha this morning, the most powerful noble in Egypt this afternoon, and tomorrow an encounter with an exiled prince. Tonight I must not forget to See for the two men eager to join my household, and surely young Perti will have reached a decision by then and will send me word. There has been no letter from Anhur and Thothhotep, far away in Nekheb, nor a report from Merenra on the state of my holdings at Hut-herib. The poppy fields south of Weset will have been sown anew three months ago. Amunnefer has sent me no word on the health of our latest crop. I desperately need a scribe! His belly churned, and although he was able to drowse intermittently, he still felt tired and jaded when Tetiankh came to rouse and dress him.

He chose to be adorned sumptuously for this important encounter, standing with arms outstretched as Tetiankh wrapped a yellow, gold-shot kilt around his waist and secured it with his belt of gold links. His face was painted, his eyes blackly kohled and sprinkled with gold dust. A droplet of gold sat in one earlobe. His glorious earring of Ra-Harakhti swung heavily from the other, the god's golden hawk feathers inlaid with blue faience, the sun-disc on his head a mounded circle of yellow chalcedony. Gold talons brushed Huy's oiled shoulder. A single golden band encircled his head. Tetiankh had braided his hair in one long plait that rested against his spine. His naked chest was bare of any ornament save the protecting sa amulet his friend and mentor, the exorcist Henenu, had made for him herself.

Huy thought of her as Tetiankh slipped onto his fingers the two rings he always wore. Henenu had made them also, the Soul Protector with its hawk's body and man's head, and the golden Frog of Resurrection with its deep blue lapis eyes. Huy could see her quite clearly in his mind's eye as he sat so that Tetiankh could slip on his jewelled sandals. Her name, Henenu, was a secret shared with very few. If the demons she had controlled and exorcised had learned it, they could have used it against her. Huy had never divulged it to anyone. In public she was the Rekhet, a woman of power and magic. With a spurt of nostalgia for a time long gone, Huy imagined her walking towards him, a smile lighting her seamed face, the cowrie shells sewn into her sheath and woven into her grey hair clicking, her magic wand held firmly in one capable hand. She had understood him, his uniqueness, his resentful struggles against the tasks the creator-god Atum required, his anguished love for Anuket, now dead. Comforting and reproving him, advising and disciplining, she had loved and guided him. He missed her a great deal. Every year in the summer month of Payni, when the full moon heralded the Beautiful Feast of the Valley, he joined the crowds flooding Mennofer's cemeteries with offerings of food, oil, wine, flowers, and prayers for their ancestors, and begged Henenu for her continued blessing. He made the short journey to his parents' tomb at Hut-herib also. At such times he thought of the noble Amunnefer, far to the south at Weset, his partner in the poppy trade, crossing the river with his offerings to the place of the dead where his wife Anuket lay coffined in the dark.

"Huy? Master?"

Huy sighed and looked up. "I'm all right, Tetiankh. Call a palace servant to escort me to the main concourse."

His litter-bearers were waiting as he emerged between the soaring pillars of the palace entrance flanked by two of his soldiers. The sunlight was dazzling and momentarily blinding on the pale stone that ran away from his feet to the glittering canal on his left and the great wall, beyond which the central city lay. Two other litters and a gaggle of servants and guards were milling about. Huy glimpsed the King in one of the litters. Mutemwia was about to lower herself into the other one. Huy was suddenly glad that she would be making the visit with him. *Nevertheless, I must make a conscious effort not to rely on her too much,* he told himself as he found his own cushions and heard the captain of the King's escort give the order to move. *Her influence is subtle, gentle, but it is also remorseless and difficult to resist.*

Her litter had drawn abreast of his and her curtains were open. She smiled across at him. "A fine day for a small outing, Huy, don't you think? It's a pity that our reason is so sad. I have the greatest esteem for the noble Yey. He's dying, and I hope that your presence may bring him a measure of consolation. He was born in Mennofer, but his father was a Maryannu warrior of Mitanni, brought back to Egypt by His Majesty Osiris Thothmes the Third as booty. He very quickly proved himself proficient enough with arms to become a royal instructor. We leave Mitanni alone now, of course, in exchange for a yearly tribute, and the members of Yey's family are proudly Egyptian."

Huy filed away the useful information, searching his memory for anyone from the time of Osiris Thothmes who might have been Yey's father. But he himself had been a young student at the temple school in Iunu. He reminded himself to ask Thothmes. Might it have been the haughty Kenamun, Foster Brother and favourite of Osiris Amunhotep the Second? Huy tutted in annoyance at himself. The matter was not at all important. Glancing to Mutemwia's litter, he saw that her curtains were now closed.

The small cavalcade had turned directly north, crossing the concourse in the narrow gap between the end of the canal and the palace's front wall, and then continuing on past the precinct of the temple of the goddess Neith on their left and the noisy northern district of the central city on their right. They entered the northern suburbs, moving along wide tree-lined streets where high walls to either side were regularly interspersed with narrow guarded entrances through which Huy glimpsed lawns and shaded gardens. Soon they swung east and reached the river road, where the guards called a warning to clear a way through the busy crowd, and before long they were veering in under a small pylon to be greeted by a wide expanse of grass and flower beds riotous with vivid blooms. The surface of a large pool bearing open waxen white lilies and the closed spears of the morning's blue lilies rocked gently. Another, smaller pond held nothing but the tall, white, pink-tinged blooms of many lotuses. Huy caught their rich, heady scent as his litter went by. Sycamores shadowed both bodies of water invitingly. Acacias clustered by the path. Tall tamarisks flanked the estate's protecting walls to north and south, their tiny leaves shuddering in the afternoon breeze.

The litters came to a halt. Huy alighted to face a short portico of six white pillars and open double doors in the white wall beyond. A steward stood bowing on the threshold as Amunhotep and Mutemwia walked up to him. Huy followed. Another servant had risen from his perch in the shade of the pillars. He was holding two leather leashes. One was attached to the jewel-studded collar of a tiny grey monkey squatting on the ground and watching the small procession with wary interest. It bared its sharp white teeth to Huy in the parody of a smile as he passed. Involuntarily he shuddered, remembering the ivory monkey his uncle and aunt had given him for a childish Naming Day long gone. It could clap its paws together when a cord in its back was pulled. Huy had hated and feared it from the start, and in the end he had taken it out into his garden one night and smashed it against a stone. Ishat, dear Ishat, had picked up all the tiny pieces that had lain like shards of bone under the moonlight and disposed of them. Huy had never asked where. The other leash was attached to a goose that hissed at him and tried to nip his ankle before the servant pulled it back. Thankfully, Huy stepped into the reception hall.

It was large and airy. Squares of brilliant white light falling from the clerestory windows high above lay at regular intervals across the black and yellow tiled floor, but between them the expanse was pleasantly dim. At the far end, past a wide staircase on Huy's left and a procession of closed doors on his right, the wall disappeared and a large portion of the rear garden could be seen. Drafts of warm air eddied through the pillared space. *This house is almost as sumptuous as the palace,* Huy thought, wending his way between isolated clusters of chairs and small tables that were lost in the vastness around them. The steward was mounting the stairs, the royal pair behind him. Huy followed.

The house's second storey was as harmonious in its layout as the first. The hallway was broad. The aperture leading onto the roof beyond was wide and inviting. To Huy, irritated by the constant noise surrounding his apartment in the palace, the quiet here was glorious.

Turning in through open double doors, the steward halted. "Master, the King and his illustrious Mother are here," he announced to someone Huy, still outside in the hall, could not see. "The Great Seer Amunhotep is with them." He stood aside and Huy entered the bedchamber.

A large couch stood on a dais to one side, its draperies of fine linen dwarfing the frail old man enveloped in them. The odour of expensive frankincense lingered in the air, although the censer itself was scoured and lay on a narrow table beside an ornate golden shrine whose doors were closed. The window hangings were also closed. A bevy of servants had gone to the floor at the steward's words, together with a couple who, judging by their dress and jewellery, were obviously not members of the household's staff. Absently Amunhotep told them to rise, and he and Mutemwia approached the couch. At once a pair of stools were produced, but before he sat, the King reached for one of the thin, mottled hands lying on the sheet and stroked it before gently letting it go. "Please tell me that you feel stronger today," he said. "I need you, Yey."

The man smiled faintly. In spite of the inevitable destruction aging had caused, Huy could see the shadow of a former strength beneath the seamed and sagging face. Yey's waving white hair was spread across the pillow. The pouched eyes regarding Amunhotep were a startling pale blue. *Warrior stock from Mitanni,* Huy reminded himself. *If it's true that Yey's father entered Egypt as a prisoner, what a driving ambition he must have had! In two generations the family has gone from captivity to great wealth and a powerful influence on our three ruling gods in succession. How did they gain such trust? I must ask the Queen for her assessment and form my own.*

"Majesty, I am dying," Yey was saying hoarsely. "Much as I would like to remain in Egypt, I feel the breath of Anubis on my back. He is coming to usher me into the Judgment Hall, but I am not afraid. I have served my country with honesty and I shall be justified before Ma'at. What else can I say? I am old, used up, and Yuya is ready to put on the yoke I have carried for so long." His voice had become more thready as he spoke and the last words were a whisper.

Mutemwia gestured to Huy. "This is the Seer Amunhotep son of Hapu." She had risen and was bending to Yey's ear. "I wish him to minister to you, but most of all I wish him to acquaint himself with your family."

The response to her words was an amused smile that came and went across the sunken features. "You mean you wish his reassurance that our Maryannu blood will continue to support the Horus Throne, not try to usurp it," Yey whispered as Huy stepped up onto the dais. "Have no fear, Mutemwia. We owe the throne more than we could ever repay and our service is given gladly."

Mutemwia kissed his cheek, and Huy saw with surprise that her own painted cheeks were wet as she withdrew. At her silent invitation Huy took her place. Those blue eyes, still clear, met Huy's shrewdly.

"I have heard much about you, Seer Amunhotep," Yey murmured, his voice now little more than a sigh. "There is no need to See for me and you can do nothing to cure what ails me. Be a friend to my family." His fingers shook as they brushed Huy's own and Huy grasped them carefully, feeling the pathetic reality of the barely covered bones. "They only wish to be obedient to the laws of Ma'at and the godhead of the King." He had begun to gasp for breath.

Huy hushed him. "So do I," he said. "I'm honoured to meet you, Noble Yey. May your journey to the Beautiful West be safe and swift."

The man had closed his eyes. Huy stood and at once a physician came bowing and waited for him to move. Huy left the dais. The King waved forward the pair Huy had noted before. Both of them performed a deep obeisance to Huy as they neared him.

"Huy, this is Yuya, Yey's son and heir, and his wife Thuyu," Amunhotep said. "They are dear to me and to my Mother. Well, let's go home now. We've disturbed this house long enough."

Huy answered their bows with one of his own. Politely he expressed his sympathy while privately he made a cursory assessment of them. Yuya was tall and muscular, his skin darker than was considered acceptable for an aristocrat. He too had very blue eyes. His hair, streaked through with slashes of white, was fair and lay below his shoulders in soft waves. His nose was an uncompromising hook over prominent, generous lips. The whole impression he gave Huy was one of physical prowess and a confident control over himself. Thuyu was also fair-haired and blue-eyed. Huy wondered fleetingly whether perhaps Yuya had sent to Mitanni for a wife. He made a mental note to ask the Queen if that had been so, and if it was, whether such a decision would have been seen as insulting to Egypt's native aristocrats. The woman, though obviously in middle age, was undeniably still beautiful. They murmured a greeting, to which Huy responded.

"I can do little but offer incense and prayers for Yey's passage," Mutemwia told them as Amunhotep went out. "Send me word at once when he dies. I love him dearly, as you know." She fell into step with Huy as they started back towards the entrance. Tears still glistened on her cheeks and Huy had to suppress an urge to wipe them away with his fingers. "I've known them all my life," she went on. "Time and again they have proved their loyalty both on and off the battlefield. In spite of their foreign blood, the ministers trust them."

"And you, Majesty?" Huy dared to ask. "It's possible to love without trusting. Am I to be wary of the noble Yuya and his wife?" They had reached the foot of the stairs and were crossing the reception hall behind Amunhotep. He stopped and turned.

"The chariot horses all love Yey and Yuya," he said. "They whinny and nudge at them when they come close, and obey every command eagerly. I think that animals, being innocent, are able to sense any hidden malice or deception in people." He shrugged. "Be wary of everyone, Uncle Huy, but Mother and I rely a great deal on Yey's family. See for them only if you feel you must. We do not want to insult them."

He walked on. Mutemwia remained silent. Privately Huy decided that he must definitely find an opportunity to glimpse into their future. Their influence on both the King and his mother seemed absolute.

Outside, the light was momentarily dazzling. Huy saw with relief that the servant in charge of the monkey and the goose had gone. *Animals may sense evil in human beings*, he thought, *but birds will be faithful to the first face they see as they emerge from the egg.* The litters sat close by and the bearers were bowing.

As Huy bent between his curtains, a movement caught his eye and he straightened. Halfway between himself and the far wall of the estate, a young girl was coming to her feet in the shade of a sycamore. A grey cat was tucked carelessly under one of her arms, its flaccid body hanging against her side. Both the monkey and the goose were tethered to the tree. At Huy's glance she stood perfectly still and gazed at him fearlessly, eyes narrowed. Huy stared back. In spite of her gangly limbs and skinny torso, she had an air of impudent confidence about her that immediately commanded his attention. She neither bowed to him nor looked away. She went on staring at him, the breeze ruffling her reddish-black hair and stirring the hem of her short white kilt, until Amunhotep leaned out of his litter and addressed Huy impatiently. "That's Yuya's daughter Tiye. Take no notice of her. She's rude and pushy and she thinks she's clever. Hurry up, Uncle! Thanks to you I have to listen to Nakht-sobek drone on about the contents of the Treasury before I can take my bow out to the practice ground."

Huy got onto his litter, and all the way back to the palace the girl's unmoving yet alert regard stayed with him.

He was not summoned to dine with the King. Amunmose had prepared a table for him in his reception room, and Huy sat waiting there for the steward to bring him his food. He had briefly met Paroi, his new under steward, on his way to the visit of the afternoon. Paroi was a young man with a permanent expression of sober purpose on his face. His voice was soft, his words delivered slowly. Huy could not imagine a servant less like the restless and voluble Amunmose, Paroi's immediate superior. Huy watched his calm approach. He bowed.

"Master, there are three men waiting outside the door to see you," he said. "Apparently two of them are expected. The third is a young soldier."

"Bring them in." Paroi bowed again and glided away.

In the short hiatus before the three made their obeisances to him, Huy realized first that he had intended to pass the bar of his gift over each of them, and second that he had in fact never deliberately Seen for any of his servants apart from Ishat, whom he had never thought of as a member of his staff. *I will wait and see what my own ka senses about them as time goes by,* he decided. *I have been free of pain for a few precious weeks. I won't risk an unnecessary attack.* Three backs were bent before him. Three heads of black hair were lowered together. Huy told them to rise. At once two sets of dark eyes were fixed on him expectantly. Captain Perti's brown eyes met Huy's calmly. Huy spoke to him first.

"Your decision, Captain? Will you work for me?"

Perti nodded. "Supreme Commander Wesersatet and my division commander have both agreed to release me into your service, Great Seer. I have been allowed to bring my men with me. All of them chose to leave the division."

"Good." Huy's gaze moved to the others. "You two have already made up your minds. I have decided to hire you but not See for any of you just yet. The Seeing is not a small matter either for the subject or for me."

Perti's eyebrows rose. "Your trust is welcome, Master."

"Very well. Paroi will see to your evening meal, and after we have all eaten we will sit down with Amunmose and Paroi and establish a proper routine for the running of this place. Ba-en-Ra, you may go home to your wife. Return tomorrow morning." The herald bowed his thanks and moved to the doors. Huy waved the other two towards a waiting Paroi and turned to Amunmose and the kitchen servants behind him. The food smelled very good and Huy found that he was actually hungry. His appetite was an unforeseen blessing.

He spent several hours afterwards with the senior members of his household, thrashing out a workable arrangement of responsibilities for his two stewards and his soldiers. The small sounds his scribe Paneb made from the floor beside Huy, as he recorded every decision on his palette, were reassuring. At last the wine jugs were empty and Amunmose was making no effort to hide his yawns.

"This is all very good," he said, gesturing behind him to the servants waiting to clear away the cups. "Thank you, Huy. If you will dismiss me, I'll retire to the bathhouse and then to my cot. Tomorrow I'll see Nubti about having Paneb and Perti moved closer to these apartments."

Huy dismissed him and rose, Perti with him. "I want to meet my new guards," Huy said. "Then I'll leave it to you to introduce them to my old ones."

"They are outside on the grass," Perti replied. "With your permission I shall pair them with those who are used to seeing to your safety and begin their rotation at once. For myself, I shall take the first watch on your garden door and be available to the men throughout the night. I pray that this change goes smoothly."

They crossed the room together. Perti opened the door and the guard stationed outside saluted Huy as he walked out into the cool air. The gardens were shrouded in darkness, but there was a small pool of lamplight not far from where Huy paused, and the sound of low voices.

"You do not need my permission to order the twenty in any way you see fit," he told Perti as they crossed the springing lawn, and there was a rustle of movement ahead as the men rose. "All I ask is that the soldiers who accompany me each day be seasoned."

"One of them will always be me," Perti answered promptly, and Huy smiled to himself at the note of pride in the young man's words.

Later, after greeting Perti's contingent, Huy was at last able to enter his bedchamber and close the door behind him. He had digested his meal without difficulty, but the parade of the day's new faces and decisions had left him eager for the dose of opium Tetiankh was holding out to him as he came up to his couch. "I need a massage tonight," he said, grimacing from the drug's bitterness as it slid down his throat. "My neck and shoulders are stiff, Tetiankh. Use plain sarson oil. I don't want to inhale any perfume apart from the lily."

"You need to be bathed, Master," Tetiankh offered as he undid Huy's kilt and removed it. "You are covered in sweat."

"So I am, but I have no desire to stand on the slab tonight. Wash me here. Tomorrow the Prince Amunhotep returns to Mennofer. It will be another taxing day."

As the poppy began to blunt his anxiety and Tetiankh's expert fingers coaxed the tension from his shoulders, Huy became aware that beyond the quiet of his room the palace still whispered and murmured. *How many people serve me now?* he wondered. *Fifty? More? All with their several tasks, all weaving around one another in this apartment that now seems much smaller than my estate at Hutherib. Shall I ever know such freedom again? I remember thinking that the Osiris-King Amunhotep the Second had cornered me, put me in a pleasant prison with his gift of a house and land and gold. But compared to my situation now, I was a bird. Here I must be guarded against the jealous, the envious. My food must be tasted, my doors protected. How soon may I beg the King for a house of my own, big enough for everyone surrounding me? Something the size of Heby's home would suit me well but would not be practical. How soon will my days be filled with the familiar instead of the new, against which I must brace myself?* Tetiankh's touch was withdrawn, and Huy began to doze.

He was almost asleep when he heard the door open and whispers beyond. Drowsily annoyed, he turned over, away from the irritation and the last of the light on his bedside table, but a polite hand descended on his shoulder.

"Master, your pardon, but Captain Perti has sent one of his guards to tell you that he is remaining by the garden door in order to watch a young girl who is demanding to see you and will not go away. He wants to know what your wishes are regarding her."

"My wishes?" Huy sat up. "He is to send her away at once, and if she won't go, he is to have her forcibly escorted back to wherever she came from. This is a ridiculous hour to be disturbing the household."

Tetiankh bowed himself away and Huy lay down again and closed his eyes, but within a few moments he had returned.

"Master, I'm sorry, but Captain Perti asks that you come to him. Two of his men have restrained the girl, but not before her goose inflicted several sharp bites on them. The bird has been tied to a tree and the girl is threatening to scream if you won't see her. If she does, she will attract the attention of the palace soldiers, not to mention waking up half the residents."

"A goose?" Huy swung his legs over the edge of his couch. "Give me a kilt, Tetiankh, and then tell Perti's man that I am coming at once." The body servant nodded, handed Huy the limp kilt he had removed a short time before, and went out. *It must be the girl I saw under the sycamore tree in Yey's garden, the one who stared at me so rudely,* Huy thought as he tied the garment on and followed Tetiankh. *Yey has just died and she's been unable to reach the Queen. But no—that's silly. Such a message would be carried by Yey's chief steward. Tiye. That's her name.* He had crossed his dim reception hall and was coming up to the open garden door. Beyond it the light from a lamp Tetiankh was holding showed him two burly men glowering as they managed to control the struggling form between them. The goose was a bundle of grey against the darkness, and honking loudly. Perti swung to Huy, his face set in what Huy rightly took to be anger.

"This being my first watch in your employ, I have probably erred in not dealing with the situation myself," he said shortly. "I'm sorry, Master. But I don't yet know how you would want such circumstances handled. The girl looks familiar to me, and judging by the quality of her sheath linen and sandals, she's from some noble's house."

"Don't call me 'the girl,' you ignorant peasant!" the girl shouted. "Of course I look familiar to you, or I would if you ever did anything but polish your weapons and idle about on this doorstep! My father is the noble Yuya! I am Tiye!" Perti did not even glance at her.

"Someone go and silence that bird," Huy ordered. "And as for you, Tiye, you are rude and thoughtless. This man is Perti, the captain of my soldiers. He is neither ignorant nor an idler. Surely you've heard the words from the Wisdom of Amenemopet, 'Say nothing that gives injury. Do not you yourself cause pain,' even if you don't know how to read them. You're lucky his men did not drag you back to your father at once. Please apologize to him for your insult."

"Apologize to a servant? I will not! And you're wrong, Great Seer. I can read the Wisdom of Amenemopet for myself, and quote from it too!" At Huy's gesture the men began to drag her away. "Oh, all right! All right! Please don't let that guard hurt Nib-Nib! I apologize for my rudeness, Captain Perti."

"That's better. Release her and let her untie that infernal creature!"

At once he was obeyed. Tiye ran to the goose. It stopped squawking and appeared to be nuzzling her bare legs as she freed its leash and led it back to the group of men by the door.

"I really am sorry, Captain," she said while the goose glared balefully around. "I have a dreadful temper. Father can't seem to beat it out of me." She turned to Huy. "'Be serious of heart, steady your thoughts, and do not use your tongue to steer by.'" She smiled at Huy. "But Amenemopet can be very boring and sanctimonious as well as offering good advice, can't he, Great Seer? My father has me schooled with my older brother Ay and my younger brother Anen. Anen is friends with your nephew Ramose, you know."

"No, I didn't know. What are you doing here without a guard, in the middle of the night?"

"Nib-Nib is a much better protector for me than any guard," she replied promptly, "and of course I'm here because I want you to Scry for me."

Huy stared at her. She went on smiling, standing loosely and easily with the goose squatting by her feet, the cool wind stirring her linen against a body still largely bony and unformed yet held with confidence. Only her eyes were truly beautiful, large and perfectly shaped, the brows pleasingly feathered above eyelids that were already full. Her mouth in repose turned down, giving her an expression of dissatisfaction. Her nose was too wide. Yet she exuded the force of a powerful though still embryonic personality that suffused an otherwise ugly little face and made it strangely compelling. Her dark red hair fell to her shoulders and gleamed with health in the guttering lamplight. Her fingers held the leash with confident grace. *Mitanni blood*, Huy thought. *Warrior blood.*

"I will Scry for you with your father's permission, but certainly not tonight," he said. "Do your parents even know that you're not on your couch? No, I didn't think so. Captain Perti and these two men will rouse my litter-bearers and take you home immediately. I hope that Yuya disciplines you severely."

"So I have walked all this way for nothing?"

"Yes. Don't do it again." His glance at Perti was a permission to move. "Your selfishness has robbed me of sleep and given these good men an extra duty to perform. Captain Perti will give you into the care of your father's chief steward with a full account of your behaviour. Then, if your father agrees, you may send to my chief steward for a suitable time to come to my apartments through the front door. Give no more trouble."

Her eyes blazed at him and that sullen mouth opened, but the moment of rebellion passed. She bowed. "I have deserved your tongue-lashing, Great Seer. I will behave."

Perti left Huy's side and, sending one of his men for a replacement, stepped to Tiye. "By the time your new guard arrives, I will have the bearers up and ready, Master," he said. Gently he took the girl's arm. The goose, after giving him one sharp and beady glance, ignored him. The small cavalcade began to leave, but Huy stopped them.

"Tiye, how is your grandfather?" he asked on impulse.

The girl did not turn. "Yey is beyond healing now," she said sadly. "All that's left to us will be the Prayers for the Dead in a very short time. Thank you for your concern."

Huy did not wait to see her swallowed up by the darkness. Bidding Tetiankh close the door, he swiftly crossed his reception hall, entered his bedchamber, pulled off the kilt, and regained the couch. He was already hungry for more poppy. The encounter with Tiye had agitated him, why he did not know. It was something more than having to deal with the spoilt child of an aristocrat. The incident seemed to have a curious aura around it in his mind, as though every word, every action, even the scents carried on the wind and the flicker of the lamp's flame in a soldier's hand, were imbued with hidden meaning. Though he was very tired, Huy knew that without his drug he would be unable to sleep. Sending Tetiankh away to get it, sitting under his sheet and waiting, he clearly saw those strong little fingers controlling the recalcitrant bird, the downturned mouth widen in a smile of great sweetness, the big eyes light up in a flash of anger at once subdued.

Tetiankh returned promptly, and as Huy downed the opium, he found himself hoping that Yuya would allow her to come to him for a Seeing. He wanted a glimpse into her future.

4

BEFORE HUY HAD EVEN OPENED HIS EYES the following morning, he could sense a change beyond the walls of his apartment. An air of muted excitement drifted into his bedchamber. When Tetiankh placed the tray of water, fruit, and bread on the table beside the couch and went to raise the hanging on the window, Huy saw that it was still early. The sky was only just beginning to flush pink with the dawn.

"I apologize for rousing you at this time, Master," Tetiankh said, "but you are required to present yourself at His Majesty's apartments as soon as you are ready. Chief Steward Nubti respectfully asks that you take no more than two hours for your feeding and ablutions."

Huy sat up, reaching for the vial of poppy beside the food and welcoming the familiar taste of its bitterness. "I suppose the King will be greeting his uncle informally before the public celebration of the Prince's return. What are the servants saying about it, Tetiankh?" He drank the water and began to pull the warm bread apart without much appetite. The poppy had set up a dull ache in his stomach, but he forced himself to eat, knowing that he needed sustenance against the demands of what would surely be an exhausting day. *Like all the others since I left Hut-herib*, he reflected, and pushed the invitation to self-pity away.

Tetiankh was opening Huy's tiring chests, methodically setting out linen and jewels. "They are curious, of course. Some of them remember the Prince before his exile. Many are behaving like good servants, refusing to gossip, but others whisper that the King has put himself in danger by allowing a contender for the Horus Throne to return to Egypt." He straightened, frowning down at the pair of ornately decorated sandals in his grasp. "I spoke briefly with Pa-shed yesterday. He's looking forward to taking up his old position as chief steward to the Prince, who had already sent a formal request on the matter to His Majesty. It seemed to Pa-shed and also to me that all speculation is vain at present anyway. Master, if you wear these sandals you'll need the moonstone earrings and plenty of gold on your wrists to offset their simplicity."

Huy told him to choose whatever he felt would be appropriate, and forced himself to swallow a fresh date. Its sweetness revolted him.

By the time he returned to his bedchamber from the crowded bathhouse with Tetiankh, his stomach had ceased to burn and his head was clear. Absently he gazed at his reflection in the small copper mirror propped behind the litter on his cosmetics table while the body servant kohled his eyes and combed and braided his oiled hair. His last encounter with Prince Amunhotep had been rife with his, Huy's, misery and guilt over failing to expose the younger Prince Thothmes' sphinx dream as a blatant fabrication designed to advance his wholly spurious claim to the throne. Prince Amunhotep had been far more gentle with Huy than he deserved. Those negative emotions came back to Huy as Tetiankh fastened his thick rope of hair with a narrow strip of leather and a golden frog ornament.

"The gold-bordered kilt, I think, Master, and the green turquoise circlet for your head." Huy, fighting the vision of his cowardly self, bit back an impatient retort. Tetiankh's deft hands

THE KING'S MAN   81

dressed him, put on him his jewellery and his sandals, pressed perfumed oil onto his neck, arms, and chest, and Huy was assailed by a sudden and infantile desire to get back onto his couch and bury himself in his sheet.

"Tell Paneb to pick up his palette and meet me in the passage," he said curtly. Inhaling the comforting scent of the lotus now rising from his body, he followed Tetiankh out of the room that was fast becoming his sanctuary.

He greeted his new scribe, who bowed in response. Paneb was wearing a simple but obviously costly linen kilt. A red ribbon matching the sweret bead hanging on his breast went around his forehead. His only nod to his aristocratic roots was the freshly dried orange henna on his palms and simple silver likenesses of Thoth hanging from each earlobe. Silver was worth a great deal more than gold. Huy approved of his new scribe's restraint, and his mood lightened. Perti and two soldiers waited to form an escort. Gesturing at them, Huy set off to walk to the King's apartments.

Nubti admitted Huy and Paneb into a quiet room. Huy had expected to face the Prince amid a crowd of courtiers, but only the King, Mutemwia, and a strange man sat around a table laden with sweetmeats and goblets. A few white and blue–liveried servants stood apart but watchful, Pa-shed among them. He was joined by Nubti. Huy extended his arms in an obeisance to the King while behind him Paneb knelt to perform a full prostration. Amunhotep waved Huy forward.

"Get up, Paneb!" he ordered. "I heard that Uncle Huy had hired you. A good choice, the Queen my Mother says. Uncle Huy, you must remember Uncle Amunhotep." He laughed, a short spurt of boyish hilarity that nevertheless held a note of strain to Huy's ears as he approached the stranger.

The man rose and turned, and suddenly Huy found himself staring into a face he recognized, older, seamed and darkened, framed by a fall of sleek black hair. It was indeed the Prince. Huy bowed profoundly.

"It's very good to see you again, Great Seer," the Prince said, his voice sending waves of both unease and gladness through Huy—unease at the memory of their last confrontation and gladness because his prediction regarding the lifespan of the Prince's usurping brother had been proved true. "The letter you sent recalling me home was worded in exactly the same way as it appeared in the vision you gave me all those years ago. You are indeed blessed by the gods!"

"Uncle Huy can easily predict anyone's future," the King put in. "Sit here beside me," he ordered Huy. "Nubti, have wine poured for Uncle Huy, and I should like some more."

As Huy took the chair Amunhotep indicated, his eyes briefly met Mutemwia's. She appeared to be at ease. Her small hands rested in her lap, the beringed fingers loosely interlaced. Her gold-shod feet peeped out from under a filmy, pure white sheath. She had crossed them at the ankles. Yet Huy, in the moment before he sank onto the chair, sensed her tension. She moved her head once, a swift admission to him that all was not well. Behind him Huy heard his scribe sink unobtrusively to the matting on the floor. Huy had received permission to speak now that the Prince had addressed him directly. He smiled across at the man's clear gaze as a servant soundlessly placed a cup brimming with wine into his hand and moved on to refill the King's.

"I'm very happy to see you safely returned to this blessed country, Prince," he said. "Your enforced stay in Mitanni was long."

"It was, and much of the time I was homesick in spite of Artatama's generosity to me. I've done my best to ensure excellent relations between Mitanni and Egypt that I hope will continue into the future."

"If our vassal King is as loyal to Egypt as Yey's family has been, we'll have nothing to worry about," the King broke in. "Vizier Ptahmose oversees the Office of Foreign Affairs. He tells me that communications from Mitanni are regular and respectful and the annual tribute is always paid promptly."

The Prince could have told his royal nephew that, given where he had just arrived from, he was perfectly aware of the state of Mitanni's relations with Egypt. Huy saw the short reminder in the man's eyes and quick intake of breath before he chose not to give it voice.

"That's very good, Majesty," he replied instead. "The purple gold the Mitanni smiths forge is alone worth Egypt's effort to keep Artatama and his family contented."

"I don't suppose you managed to discover the secret of its making. It would have been a triumph for Egypt, not to mention the rest of the world, if you'd brought it home with you." Amunhotep had swallowed a large gulp of wine. He set his cup back on the table with an unsteady hand and Huy realized that he was quite drunk. The Prince obviously knew it too.

"Artatama gave me complete freedom in everything but the smithies, Majesty," he answered gently. "I did not betray his trust in me, although of course it occurred to me that the secret of purple gold would be a mighty gift to bring home to you. It would have been foolish to endanger the peace our ancestors created between our two countries. I have prepared a full report on all aspects of Mitanni society and government for you. My scribe Ka-set has already placed it in Ptahmose's office."

"And your gifts of purple gold to both of us are truly appreciated," Mutemwia said. "Oh, my dear old friend! It's wonderful to see you and hear you and know that I may visit you in your old apartments whenever I wish, as I used to do when the King was a baby! Do you remember how he would chuckle and smile up at you as you cradled him in your arms?" *Very good, Mutemwia,* Huy thought. *Very good indeed.*

The Prince also recognized the ploy. Leaning towards the King, he spoke with reverence. "I loved you as a baby and I love you as my King, Nephew Amunhotep," he said gently. "I will never do anything to harm you. I know what it's like to live in the shadow of death at the hands of those one loved and trusted. Something inside me was destroyed when my father and brother turned against me. You must trust me when I tell you that I have no wish to put on the shackles of kingship, imprisoned by protocol and carrying the weight of Egypt's health, both secular and religious, on my shoulders. I have lived in freedom for the last twelve years. I only want to stay in the palace until you and I become friends. Then, with your blessing, I'll retire to my estates at Ta-she, find a capable Egyptian wife, and spend the remainder of my days boating on the lake and watching my grapevines flourish."

Huy, watching the King, whose attention had become riveted on his uncle's face, saw the wine-flushed young features gradually loosen.

"I didn't intend to hear my fear expressed aloud by you, Uncle," he rasped. Then, coughing, he went on more clearly. "Still, the Queen my Mother warns me that kings should not place their trust blindly. I want to trust you. I want to be your friend. But for now you will be guarded by my soldiers, not yours. And I may ask the Seer to hold your hand as he did once before."

"Wise decisions," the Prince responded. "I would make them myself if our positions were reversed. Now please dismiss me, Majesty. I want to be bathed and shaved before the feast you are so kindly giving me tonight, and I'm eager to re-enter my old apartments."

Amunhotep nodded, his cheeks now pale. Huy wondered if he was about to vomit out the wine he had consumed so rapidly.

The Prince rose and Huy did also, bowing to him as he backed to the double doors with Pa-shed already holding them open for him. When he had gone, the King looked up at Huy.

"I really want to be happy to see him," he said. "I did not behave towards him as a King should, or even an ordinary member of his family. I'm very sorry."

"I know. Dismiss me also, Majesty. You need to sleep again."

But Amunhotep gripped his kilt. "You love me, don't you, Uncle Huy? You would never hurt me, would you?"

Huy knelt beside the King's chair and put his arm around shoulders that felt suddenly frail and vulnerable to his touch. "You became the child I was never privileged to father," he murmured so that the motionless servants could not hear. "I have loved you ever since you began to spend the months of the Inundation with me on my estate. I vow that I will never harm you or knowingly allow anyone else to harm you. Be happy to see the Prince. Treat him tonight with the esteem he deserves."

Amunhotep let go of the linen and Huy rose, bowed deeply, and walked away, Paneb at his heels. By the time he entered his own domain, his body was tense with the need for poppy. He ignored the throb. "Paneb, find Amunmose and collect any letters that have come for me," he said. "I might as well deal with them before the noon meal."

To his delight, there were scrolls from both Thothhotep and the steward Merenra, now caring for his estate outside Hut-herib. Merenra had little to say beyond assuring Huy that all was safe and peaceful in his house and garden and he was making sure that the domestic servants kept everything in order in case their master should decide to visit his home. Asking Paneb to make sure that Merenra was receiving enough gold to maintain his arouras and feed his staff, he broke the unadorned wax seal on Thothhotep's letter. "To the Great Seer Huy, my Master, greetings," it began, and Huy, seeing the woman's neat, familiar script fill the roll of papyrus, felt a stab of homesickness. He read quickly. Anhur, dear Anhur, who had guarded Huy as a boy on one of his journeys to Thoth's temple at Iunu and had later come to the estate to captain Huy's soldiers, was becoming increasingly debilitated, his breathing more laboured in spite of the medicines Thothhotep purchased for him. She thanked Huy for providing the gold that allowed them to live in relative luxury and spoke briefly of the pleasure of living beside the river in Nekheb, the town of her birth, but at the end anxiety for her husband and her longing for Huy and the satisfaction of her life as his scribe broke through. "Anhur must now sleep sitting upright and I rest on a pallet beside our couch," she said, her voice rising clearly to Huy from the black hieroglyphs. "I give him the poppy your generosity has provided so that he can forget his lungs for a few precious hours. When he is able to talk, his words are all of his life with you, our life with you, and a powerful nostalgia for the past. He often begins his statements with the old oath 'As I love life and hate death.' He will not enter the Judgment Hall easily. We miss you very much, and I envy the person who now walks behind you in my place. Written by my own hand, Thothhotep, scribe. Dated this fourth day of the month of Phamenoth, Year One of the King."

I miss you also, my little waif plucked from poverty, Huy thought. Aloud he said to Paneb, "I don't recognize the imprint on the seal of this last scroll. Whose is it?"

"The chariot depicted is the mark of Yey's family," Paneb told him.

"Then break it and read the contents to me." He placed Thothhotep's scroll lovingly on the table before him, beside the one from Merenra.

"'To the Great Seer Amunhotep, son of Hapu of Hut-herib,

greetings,'" Paneb began in the even tones adopted by most scribes so that their opinions of what they were reading did not influence those of their masters. Huy, who was used to Ishat's very definite inflections and Thothhotep's lilt, found it irritating. "'Please accept my heartfelt apology for the recent behaviour of my daughter Tiye. She has been severely disciplined, but continues to plead for a chance to have you touch her and thus See her future. Knowing that once such an idea comes to her she will importune me until I capitulate, I humbly request that you Scry for her and thus bring peace to this unhappy household. However, I understand that your duties are many. If you wish to refuse her, dictate to her directly or she will not believe me when I tell her that you have no time to indulge such an ill-mannered chit. By the hand of my Chief Scribe Bakenkhons this sixteenth day of Phamenoth, Year One of the King, Yuya, Prophet and Overseer of the Cattle of Min, Lord of Ipu.'"

Huy smiled. "It sounds as though the noble Yuya would like me to refuse the Lady Tiye in order to teach her a lesson she obviously finds difficult to learn. Write to her. I shall See for her tomorrow, the eighteenth of this month, in the evening. She may not bring any of her pets, including that damnable goose that guards her, and she must show the letter to her father and arrive at my doors properly escorted. That's all, Paneb." The man bowed and glided away.

I haven't Scryed for anyone since I left the estate, Huy thought. *Taking her hand in the evening will ensure that any demands on me that the King might make will have been accomplished. My head can then ache all it wants. I confess that I'm rather looking forward to divining for this girl.*

He was not summoned to wait on the King. Calling for Paneb, he lay on his couch while the scribe took him yet again through the list of Egypt's many ministers and officials. Huy had already begun to put names to all the faces he saw coming and going, but when Paneb began a description of the gods' High Priests, Huy sent him away, drank the poppy Tetiankh had already prepared, and fell asleep. He did not wake until his body servant came to light the lamp beside him and usher him towards the bathhouse.

The feast that night to celebrate Prince Amunhotep's return was held in the reception hall of the palace. The vast space was thick with invited guests from the throne dais, where the royal family sat, to the march of lofty pillars through which the night breeze flowed to battle a hundred different perfumes and the smoke from a hundred huge alabaster lamps on their tall stands. Beyond the pillars was the great stone apron that ran to a canal filled by the river. Here the light was a dim orange from torches whose flames trembled in the soft, moving airs. Beneath them lounged the guests' litters and bearers, watched by the palace guards. They too were fed, and passed the time in gambling or dozing, while in the hall their employers sat amid thousands of fragrant blooms as the King's liveried servants in their gold-bordered blue and white kilts wove carefully through the throng bearing trays laden with steaming dishes and jugs full of wine.

Although Huy had not been invited to take a seat with the King, Mutemwia, and Prince Amunhotep, he was accorded his own table close to the foot of the dais and his own trio of servants for his needs alone. Captain Perti and four soldiers stood between Huy and the noisy crowd as he ate and drank, his attention fixed unobtrusively on the gods at the high table. The King seemed happy. Gorgeously arrayed in cloth of gold from head to knee, the jewelled uraeus, the vulture goddess Nekhbet of the South and the cobra goddess Wazt of the north, rising in protection and warning from his glimmering helmet, he was not only a hand-some youth but the embodiment of sacred power.

On his right sat his blood-uncle. Prince Amunhotep's head had been shaved, his eyes kohled, his body obviously massaged with the oil that glistened on his skin. His adornment was simple, a set of plain gold bracelets on his left forearm, a chain of delicate filigreed gold around his neck, and a pair of golden feathers trembling from each lobe. Paired feathers were symbols of the god Amun. Huy knew that the Prince's devotion to Amun, and his refusal to help his father and younger brother raise the sun-disc Aten to prominence over Egypt's mightiest deity, had resulted in the man's exile and the loss of his right to the Horus Throne.

Mutemwia, lovely and gracefully fragile in white and silver, was leaning across in front of her son and smiling up into the Prince's face while she spoke to him. His expression was one of gentle affection. *They make a striking pair, the mother of the King and the King's uncle. Together their authority would be well-nigh invincible.* Shocked at the unbidden words, Huy drew back just as someone touched his shoulder and a soft mouth moved against his ear.

"See that bevy of painted girls clustered at the foot of the dais, just beyond your extremely rude captain? They're the King's sisters. Have you been allowed to meet them yet? The oldest one, Iaret, is a dowager Queen like Mutemwia. Her father married her before he died. Mutemwia keeps her firmly in hand."

Huy swung round and found himself enveloped in the familiar aroma of mingled myrrh, cassia, and henna flowers as two arms went around his neck. "Ishat! What are you doing here? Gods, it's good to see you! Is Thothmes here as well?"

She kissed him on the cheek and settled back, sitting easily on a cushion she dragged towards her. "Of course. So are all the children, and Nasha. Didn't anyone tell you that every Governor and his family was invited to welcome the Prince home from

Mitanni? Mutemwia has been planning this ever since her husband the Osiris-one Thothmes died. Huy, you look positively haggard. Aren't you being treated well in the palace?"

"And you look radiant as always. I see that you've given in to vanity and begun to henna your hair. The rusty red suits your personality. Captain Perti was rude to you?" As he spoke, his eyes meeting her own, he could feel every tension within himself melting away.

She grimaced, a twist of the mouth Huy remembered so well. "Not rude exactly, but he was determined to keep me away from you. At the King's command, he said. So I pushed my way back to Thothmes and made him come and argue with the captain. He's awfully young, isn't he? But full of self-confidence. Thothmes is taking this opportunity to talk Governor talk with his equals. He's anxious to see you, but later, when the two of you can talk in peace. Have you seen your brother Heby? He's here with Iupia. I waved at him. He was talking to your nephew Amunhotep-Huy. Now there's a truly rude young man! None of us can leave until the King does, so I might as well have something to drink." She beckoned to one of the servants standing against the wall. "Bring me beer." Her gaze returned to Huy. "Why don't you visit us more often? Why do you look so strained? Are you Seeing for too many people? Who's your scribe now? Did you hire yet another woman? Have you heard any word from Thothhotep and Anhur?"

Taking her hand, Huy began to answer her questions, aware of her eyes fixed on his mouth as he formed the words, knowing, with an intuition honed by the long years they had spent together, when she was about to interrupt him, and falling silent before she spoke. Her beer arrived. She drank with relish, then the two of them began to reminisce, falling easily into the comfort of their past.

The meal ended, the guests moved back, and the entertainments began. Dancers, fire-eaters, magicians, animal tamers, came and went to roars of appreciation. Huy and Ishat retired to a shadowed corner of the hall, where they talked on, oblivious to the noise, Thothmes' steward Ptahhotep and Huy's Amunmose hovering patiently nearby. At last Ishat yawned. "I wish the King would go to his couch. How can such a young man need so little sleep? It's too late for any visiting tonight, Huy. May we all come to your apartments tomorrow morning? Thothmes has carob pods from Rethennu for your cook, and a bag of almonds, although I expect you eat anything you want here in the palace." She struggled to her feet just as the King rose, nodded at Chief Herald Maani-nekhtef, and left the dais through a door at the rear, followed by the King's mother and uncle. Two men Huy did not recognize began to shepherd the King's sisters away. Harem attendants, Huy surmised. He beckoned Perti.

"Captain, please escort the Lady Ishat wherever she needs to go." He hugged her briefly. "Until tomorrow, Ishat. Come early. Afterwards we can eat the noon meal together in the gardens." Together he and Amunmose watched her walk through the slowly emptying hall, Perti and his men surrounding her, Ptahhotep behind.

"I don't miss her until I see her, Huy," Amunmose remarked. "Then I remember those perfect days on your estate when you and she worked together for the people who lined up at your gate, and I was newly arrived and awed by Merenra and your good fortune. Then my thoughts stray even further back, to the time I was asked by High Priest Ramose of Iunu to accompany a young boy to Thoth's temple at Khmun, the city where I was raised. I was still very young myself. Then I start thinking about how much time has gone by, and how fast. Then I become depressed. Seeing Ishat is not good for me."

Huy laughed. "You'll never change, will you, Amunmose? The Governor and his whole family will appear tomorrow. Find Rakhaka. I want him to cook for us all."

"He won't be happy. He hangs about the royal kitchens and tries to tell everyone what they're doing wrong. We all need to get out of here."

Huy did not reply. Anhur and Amunmose had always been allowed the privilege of addressing him by name and speaking to him in equality. *Amunmose is right,* he thought as they moved between the pillars and out under the starry night sky as though they had agreed to seek fresh air before taking the longer way back into the palace. *I must put the matter before the Queen, but not yet. I must earn the right to a house of my own.* Having walked leisurely around the building, they were almost at Huy's garden door when Heby's steward Prahotep caught up to them. He bowed.

"Great Seer, I have been looking for you everywhere! Your brother and the Lady Iupia wish to greet you tomorrow morning. Will their presence then be acceptable to you? Mayor Heby apologizes for neglecting to approach you at the feast, but he did not want to interrupt your conversation with the Lady Ishat."

Huy answered him with a spurt of pleasure. His family and his dearest friends would be with him together. "Of course. Tell Heby I'll be delighted to see him."

"We might as well be back on the estate, considering the small amount of time you have for visiting your own kin," Amunmose grumbled as he held the door open.

Huy bade the two soldiers on the door a good night and entered the apartment. "Before you sleep, make sure that Paroi goes to Rakhaka with the number of people we'll be entertaining in the morning, please, Amunmose." Huy turned towards his bedchamber with relief.

They poured into Huy's reception room not long after the sun had risen—Heby, Iupia, and Ramose, who had celebrated his eleventh birthday three months earlier, Thothmes, Ishat, and their three children—hugging each other, filling the space with chatter and laughter, and spreading themselves on the floor and the chairs. Ishat's eldest son, named after Huy himself, lowered his tall frame on a mat beside Huy, and Huy, smiling down into the thoughtful dark eyes, was assailed by a momentary sense of unreality. This boy had somehow become a man of twenty-one, and was accompanying his father Thothmes, learning the craft of governorship against the day when Thothmes would die. Glancing around at the cheerful faces, Huy noted Nakht, Thothmes' second son, named after his grandfather, talking rapidly and with many gestures to Heby, who was nodding sagely. Beside him Sahura, Thothmes' daughter, had found a place on the floor and was talking to her mother, sitting with her knees bunched up under her yellow kilt. She resembled Ishat so closely that Huy became even more bemused. *How old is she now? Eighteen, I think. When Ishat became eighteen, we were already living on the estate Pharaoh Amunhotep the Second had given to me. The years between have flowed swiftly. I myself am fifty. How did that happen?*

"Huy, have you received any news from Methen lately?" Heby wanted to know. Huy plunged into the happy babble around him and forgot his brief sadness.

At noon they trickled out into the garden, where mats and sunshades had been set out for them. The growing season, Peret, was well under way, and all around them the flower beds were a riot of brilliant colours, the blooms filling the air with an intoxicating blend of scents. Contentedly Huy watched as Amunmose, Paroi, and Rakhaka served them. His appetite was good. *Probably because I'm free of any anxiety today,* he thought as he ate under the gently billowing white awning. *If the Queen and her son were here, then all those I love would be gathered together in safety.* Presently he saw Ramose get up and run towards another young boy who had just emerged from the shadow of the wall and was crossing the lawn. They embraced quickly and began to saunter back to the small crowd, arms linked. As they drew closer, Huy studied the stranger's features with a faint feeling of recognition that was resolved when both boys came up to him and bowed.

"Uncle Huy, this is my friend Anen," Ramose explained. "We both attend the school attached to Ptah's temple here in Mennofer. He is the son of the noble Yuya. He'll be the Prince of Ipu very soon because his grandfather is nearly dead and the King will promote his father after that."

"Indeed," Huy responded with a gravity he did not feel. "Anen, you resemble your sister Tiye. How old are you?"

"I'm nine, Great Seer," the child replied, "and begging your forgiveness for my boldness in wishing to correct you, but I do not look at all like my sister. Tiye is ugly."

"I forgive you! I merely remarked on the colour of your eyes and the curve of your chin. Now go and play, both of you. Anen, you are welcome to my food and drink."

"Thank you, Great Seer." Ramose slung a nonchalant arm around his younger friend's shoulders and the two of them wandered away. *He does resemble Tiye,* Huy thought, looking after them, *but it's true that his features are more gentle than hers. What aristocratic company we peasants now keep, don't we, Ishat?* She was listening politely to Iupia, but Huy knew by the silent tapping of one foot that she was bored. With a sigh he got up to rescue her.

As the afternoon wore on, Huy's guests took their leave. Huy arranged to visit Heby as soon as possible and promised Thothmes that he would come to Iunu when he could. He was unable to make definite plans; he was never sure when the King might summon him. So far, although he was Amunhotep's Personal Scribe, he had only been called upon to take dictation once and he wondered whether perhaps the title was supposed to be more important than the work itself. He saw everyone go with regret, went to his couch, and slept.

He was not summoned to dine with the King that evening. He assumed that the three members of the royal family were eating together in Amunhotep's apartments. Returning from the bath-house in the late afternoon, he told Tetiankh to put his jewellery away and find the simplest kilt he had. He was not sure why he had decided to See for Yuya's daughter dressed very plainly. It had not occurred to him to try to impress her with his wealth or posi-tion; she had more of both than he. Nor was it an opposite attempt to show her that he was not intimidated by the child of Egypt's most powerful official. He waited for her unpainted, his hair combed and braided but not oiled, reed sandals on his feet. His only adornments were the sa on his breast and the rings of protection on his fingers. These he never removed.

Full night had fallen by the time Amunmose ushered her into his office, a room now used mostly by his chief and under stew-ards and his scribe. "The Lady Tiye," Amunmose said. "I have already explained to Paneb the task required of him during a Seeing. He's on his way. Do you need anything, Master? Wine? Water?"

Huy had risen from the chair behind the desk and had bowed to the girl. She also was dressed simply in an unadorned white sheath that fell to her ankles, sturdy leather sandals, and no jewellery other than a small golden hoop circling one lobe. She looked demure and modest. Huy was sure that she was neither. Nevertheless, she had reverenced him with proper decorum and now stood just inside the door with her head bent and her hands clasped around a small pot in front of her.

"Bring a jug of water and two cups. Has Tetiankh prepared my poppy? Bring that as well." The steward nodded and withdrew. Huy pulled his chair around to the front of the desk and placed a stool before it. "Please take the chair, Lady Tiye. The stool is for me." The lamplight made gleaming bands across her cap of dark red hair as she came forward.

"Thank you, Great Seer," she said easily, "and thank you for agreeing to See for me after my behaviour the other night. My father slapped me and made sure that I had no food on the following day. His punishment was just." She held out the pot. "I know that it is customary for a petitioner to offer a gift on occasions such as these. Please accept this little cruse. It comes from the island of Keftiu and has strange fish called dolphins on it. I've been using it to hold my anointing perfume. I had it filled with ben oil for you so that you may add any perfume you choose. I hope no aroma of cardamom lingers. It's the last scent I used."

Huy took it reverently, running his thumb admiringly over the delicate tracery of blue lines obviously representing the Great Green, and the odd fish with their fat bodies and long snouts gambolling in the waves. It was a delicate, beautiful thing. Even firmly stoppered, the pot exuded the pungent yet pleasantly light tang of ground cardamom seeds. Huy bowed his thanks and set the gift on his desk. The girl settled herself in the chair, and after smoothing the folds of her sheath over her thighs she wound her fingers tightly together in her lap. *So she is not wholly an arrogant brat*, Huy thought, noting the tension. *She is able to feel insecurity, to be sensitive to her surroundings and those in it.*

"Do you often misbehave?" he wanted to know as he positioned himself on the stool so that he would be able to take her hand without strain.

She grinned suddenly and her fingers relaxed. "Quite often, Great Seer, but not always on purpose. Sometimes my brothers lure me into trouble. Anen is younger than I, but Ay is one year older. He leaves me to take the blame for our adventures because he knows how exasperated Father can become with me. It's important for girls to refrain from competing with boys and to cultivate the modest habits of a good wife." She sighed. "I'm nearly eleven, but Father already worries that I will grow up with behaviour unattractive to any suitor."

"I met Anen in the garden today. It's to your father's credit that in spite of his concern he still insists on a good education for you." Huy was surprised that she was so young. She had appeared to him to be twelve or even thirteen.

"I suppose so. I'm just as bored with my studies as my brothers are. Except for the history of Egypt—I like that."

"And does your father tell you about the kingdom of Mitanni?"

Her startled blue eyes met his. "Mitanni? No. Why should he? We are Egyptians. My father says that everyone in the world wants to hold Egyptian citizenship and that we're the most privileged people ever born. This"—she tugged at her hair—"the reddish lights in it, and the colour of my eyes are my only legacy from Mitanni."

They were interrupted by a discreet knock on the door. Paneb entered, bowed to Tiye, and sank to the floor at Huy's elbow. Crossing his legs and placing his palette across his thighs, he murmured the prayer to Thoth and began to burnish his piece of papyrus.

Tiye leaned forward. "Where is the divining bowl and the oil, Great Seer? The statue of mighty Anubis, Lord of the Bau and leader of the Sheseru of Horus? How can you work heka without those things?"

"I am not a hekau, Lady Tiye. I do not practise magic. Heka is one of the forces used by Atum to make the world, but when I See for someone I am not continuing that making as a hekau would do, nor am I using magic to fight magic, like to like. I need nothing to compel the gods to hear me. Atum shows me what I must see, and Anubis speaks to me."

"Then you are indeed a hekau, higher than the King, who receives the power of heka when he is crowned?"

Huy was saved from answering by Amunmose, who glided in, placed a ewer of water and two clay cups on the desk together with a small vial, bowed, and withdrew.

Huy glanced down at Paneb. "Do you want to sprinkle water on the floor for Imhotep, Paneb? Are you ready?"

"I'm ready now, Master."

Huy took one of Tiye's hands in both his own. "I cannot predict any outcome," he told her. "If I see your death, do you want me to tell you about it?"

Once again those cornflower-coloured eyes met his. "No, I don't think so. Perhaps when I am much older. If you see it and tell me now, I will become fixed on it."

Such wisdom in a little girl, Huy thought. Reaching past her, he drank his drug in one swallow. The time was long gone when he reacted to its bitterness.

"You may close your eyes or not, as you choose," he said, "but remain as still as you can. Let us begin." On impulse he closed his own eyes. It had been many months since he had given a Seeing and he thought belatedly that he ought to have asked the King's permission to do so, but it was too late now. The opium was spreading its own enchantment through his stomach, its warmth reaching for his chest and head. It felt good, but his attention did not stay on its progress through his body. Slowly he became aware of Tiye's breathing, a trifle fast, a betrayal of nervousness, but regular. As he listened to its rhythm, a sound beneath it began to grow until it became the measured beat of drums. Had they been there all the time? Now there was the swift trilling of harp music and the wail of pipes. Huy felt himself lifted into it. A voice began to sing, impassioned, fervent, the melody a burst of worship, and suddenly Huy found himself in a temple he did not recognize, hemmed in by a crush of listening people. He was hot and uncomfortable. The air was hazed with incense. He could smell its sweet sharpness, the odour of sanctity, of praise rising with it to please the god. But which god? Huy, trapped as he was, could not glance around. All he was able to do was peer forward between rows of bowed heads to the area before the double doors of the sanctuary.

He recognized the King at once. Amunhotep was no longer a child. He had grown, filled out, his chest broad and glittering with necklets, his arms brawny as he held the crook and the flail out over the crowd, his jawline softened by cheeks that were still full. *Obviously he has reached his majority,* Huy thought. *Is this his final crowning?*

"Why yes, it is, Great Seer." The grating tones, instantly recognizable, came from the left. A pang of terror went through Huy, then faded. All the same, he was glad that the press around him made turning to the side difficult. The god's breath was warm and moist on Huy's left cheek. Its faint animal smell seemed blended with another odour, so foreign that Huy could not name it. "Perhaps it is the scent of the lotus petals drowned in wine and mingled with the taste of human adoration I've been drinking," the husky voice went on. "In the midst of their fear they reverence me, proud Huy. They know that one day I will grasp their hand and lead them into the Judgment Hall."

"Anubis." Huy's mouth had gone dry. He swallowed. "Whose temple is this? I have an impression of immense size although I can see little." A hand fell on Huy's shoulder. Out of the corner of his eye Huy saw a black forearm heavy with gold bracelets. The odour of wild pelt and myrrh now filled his nostrils.

"You are always surrounded by immense size and can see little," Anubis said caustically. "But because I have better things to do than stand here all day, I will tell you. This is mighty Ipet-isut, Amun's glorious home, and you are in the city of Weset, far—oh, very far—from the palace in Mennofer."

"So Amunhotep chose to be crowned here so that all could see his alliegance to Amun. That's very good."

"Is it? Then why does he intend to name his new home on the west bank of the river the Palace of the Dazzling Aten?"

"The west bank? Close to the dead?" Shocked, Huy's head jerked around. The god's mouth was still open, the pink tongue quivering between white fangs, the black lips raised in a sneer. Yellow eyes, bright and feral, narrowed to slits as they met Huy's own. The grip on his shoulder tightened.

"Perhaps if you had bothered to look further than the thrill of pride you felt under the admiring gaze of the royal child and his mother all those years ago, Amunhotep might have given glory where it is due when he named his bold new house." This was blatantly unfair, but Huy let it pass. One did not contradict a god. "I am harsh but not unreasonable," Anubis growled. "Why Atum chose you to steer the fate of this, his favourite land, is beyond me. You knew how threatening the improper worship of the Aten could become, how its elevation to a growing prominence over Amun resulted in an injured Ma'at. Did her wound not bleed in your presence? All you had to do, after you slunk out of Amunhotep the Second's audience chamber like the coward that you are, was to pay attention to the fact that young Prince Amunhotep was spending too much time in the harem at Mi-wer, where he imbibed the Aten with his milk."

"Mutemwia always sent him there to escape the illnesses of the children in the palace," Huy broke in. "I was not prepared to endanger his life."

"Oh. So it was a tussle between his health and Egypt's, was it? No resolution came to you?"

This time Huy could not respond. He had known of Aten worship as a pursuit of royalty and nobles. Egypt's ordinary inhabitants found the Disc too esoteric for their taste. The women of the harems, particularly the foreign wives, found the Aten a comfort. The Disc seemed to speak to a basic but crude religious commonality in every culture.

"Mutemwia," Anubis mused. "Now where is that slender reed with the metal spine? Not standing behind the King anymore. Can you see her, Huy?"

All at once Huy's range of vision became wider. The King's mother was seated to her son's right, but a young woman divided them. The young woman's knees were together and her back was very straight under the sheath of cloth of gold covering her from neck to braceleted ankles. A wig of long black hair was mostly hidden by the golden vulture's feathers cradling her face. Its head jutted imperiously above her forehead and its claws to either side behind each ear grasped the shen sign, symbol of eternity. Gold and lapis likenesses of the goddess Mut, Amun's consort, swung from her lobes. Gold bracelets covered her forearms. A wide collar made up of layers of blue lapis and red jasper squares linked with gold hid her sheath from her neck to her tiny breasts. Huy drew in his breath. There was no mistaking the lustrous, heavily kohled eyes or the downturned mouth. She was gazing imperiously ahead, confidence displayed in every line of her, while the music seemed to surround the royal pair with an aura of sacred invincibility.

"Tiye!" Huy whispered. "I sensed that there was something

about her. So she signs a marriage contract with Amunhotep and becomes Queen. This is Atum's will for her? For them?"

The god's hand was removed from Huy's shoulder. "Patience, Seer. Let us move forward, shall we? Pay attention, for this is the gravest vision you will ever have."

All at once the crowd around Huy began to melt away. He felt himself lifted and stifled a cry of fear as he found himself looking down on a vast sprawl of stone buildings, stelae, wide avenues lined with the likenesses of gods and kings, along which a colourful procession of white-robed priests and gaily dressed citizens came and went. He had no time to glance around at the city of Weset itself. He was being propelled forward at great speed, following the winding glint of the river, going north or south, he did not know which. The banks seemed to flow past and to either side of him in a blur of palms and green fields. Closing his eyes against a fit of nausea, he gritted his teeth, suddenly aware of arms around him and the odour of Anubis's jackal skin in his nostrils. "The years move on beneath us, but we fly more swiftly than they," the god said. His moist nose touched Huy's ear. "Now what would the Lady Tiye like to see, do you think? Any rivals who might arise in the women's quarters? How well she will age? What illnesses she will suffer before her death? But no. She does not want to know the day or the manner in which she will die, and you do not need to know. You yourself will have entered the Hall of Judgment by then. You created a dark path when you chose safety over truth and allowed Amunhotep's father to mount the Horus Throne in his brother's place. Egypt has been stumbling along it ever since. Now open your eyes and see where that path has led."

Huy was unaware of any slackening, nor could he feel his feet touch the ground, but when he obeyed, he was standing on solid ground again, or rather on huge stone flags making up the floor of an enormous temple unlike any he had seen before. He was in the centre of what should have been the inner court, but the customary roof was missing. Instead, a sickening heat beat down upon him and the light was dazzling. Blinking, he surveyed his surroundings. He was alone with Anubis in a place full of offering tables heaped with wilted flowers and mouldering food. There was no closed sanctuary ahead, only a larger table. On the wall behind it Huy made out the colossal carving of a crowned disc with many hands, each grasping an ankh, the symbol of life, and presenting them to a king who knelt adoringly and raised his face to receive the gifts. There was something wrong with the man's figure, something peculiar, but Huy's attention was diverted by an awareness of the music. It had not stopped. It was enveloping him, echoing off the high walls of this sun-baked, shadeless place where he and the god waited. He knew instinctively that they were indeed waiting, but he wanted to flee from this temple, if temple it was, with its blinding heat, its atmosphere of desolation and loneliness.

"Be still," the god growled. "You must remember what you see. You must dream of it, drink in its mute terror with your opium, taste its bleak emptiness with your food. For empty it is, Son of Hapu. Ma'at is not here. Indeed, in all Egypt she is not to be found. This is the ponderous inevitability of consequence."

Huy's heart gave a painful lurch and began to race. He had first heard those words from Ramose, High Priest of Ra, in the temple where he had attended school as a child. They had stayed with him, accusing him of his failures, reminding him of his duty to Atum on the many occasions when he would have given away his ka itself rather than live one more day in the creator-god's invisible chains. Here, sweating and trembling in this dreadful place, Anubis's animal, inhuman tones in his ears, those words seemed to hold the sum of every nightmare Huy had suffered.

"What lives here?" he whispered.

"You know," Anubis replied. "The Aten and its monstrous son live here. Oh, cry for Egypt, all you gods! Weep for the destiny that has overcome her!" His baying subsided into a series of shrill barks.

Huy would have turned and run from him, but all at once the music started to change, and at the same time two shadowy forms began to appear before the large offering table. They gained solidity quickly, a man and a woman standing together facing Huy, and immediately he recognized Tiye. She was dressed in an ankle-length sheath of many starched pleats. Her shoulders were covered by a short cape, also pleated. She was smothered in jewels, but Huy noticed them only briefly. His gaze was drawn first to her crown, a tall, ornate thing with the horns of Hathor rising to encompass a great golden disc set over a Queen's vulture headdress. Not one but two royal uraei curved upward from her forehead, each creature also crowned with a row of small discs. His eyes travelled to her face, and as he stared at it the glorious music changed. The drums fell silent. The voice began a lament, a dirge that filled the temple with harsh sorrow. Tiye stared straight ahead. Those beautiful eyes had become wrinkled and hooded with age. Deep grooves to either side of the painted mouth pulled it down harshly, giving her an air of permanent dissatisfaction. Her expression was imperious, almost cruel, and bore the stamp of some dark knowledge.

Distressed, Huy looked away, only to find his eyes lighting on her companion. He appeared to be younger than she, but his deformities made a conclusion difficult. His chin and jawline seemed malformed. His lips, hennaed a bright orange, were too large, his shoulders too rounded over a shallow chest. His soft belly hung over the belt of his white kilt, which was of such a fine quality that through it Huy could see the outline of wide, almost feminine thighs. A blue and white striped bag wig covered his head, and from its rim rose one uraeus, the vulture Lady of Dread and the cobra Lady of Flame.

"Behold the King of Egypt and his spouse, the Empress Tiye," Anubis said loudly. "Behold the inevitability of consequence. Do they not make a handsome couple?" Huy could not look at them anymore. Heartsick, he turned his back on the apparitions, if apparitions they were. The alien yellow eyes of the jackal god met his, and for the first time Huy read sympathy in them.

"Where are we, Anubis?" he asked. "Who is that … that misshapen creature, and why is Tiye his wife, his Queen? You say Empress. What does that mean? Must I tell the child whose hand I know I'm holding that one day she will be in subjection to …" He could not finish. The music rose to a discordant clash of noise and ended. The air was uncomfortably dry and hot in Huy's nostrils, and the top of his head was burning. It seemed to him that for a henti he watched the god breathing slowly, the black male chest hung with gold rising and falling, before the long jackal snout opened and Anubis sighed.

"We are in the temple of the great city that will be built by that King," he answered. "It will be the most glorious city ever seen in Egypt, and the most cursed. Famine and ruination will follow its construction, until this country shrinks from a great empire to the prey of greedy foreigners."

"Empire?" Huy croaked out the word. Already he felt the weight of the responsibility he knew the god would lay across his shoulders.

Anubis bared his pointed teeth, a feral grin devoid of humour. "Amunhotep, the son you love but did not father, will pile land and riches at Amun's feet in token of Egypt's prosperity," he answered. "Already he plans great things. Atum loves him and will bless him, Huy. Tiye will make him a good wife and a very capable Queen. As for you, take care. Two tasks are left to you. One is to finally solve the meaning of the Book of Thoth. The other is to make what you have seen here a lie, a tenuous mirage dissolving away as those in your care are guided along a different route. The abomination must not be allowed to live. Do you understand?"

"Unless you tell me who he is, I will not know what to do!"

"The only significant choices made in Egypt from now on are yours, and you will indeed know what to do. Use your gift. Stop running away from the Book of Thoth. In time you will know whom you have witnessed today. Meanwhile, go home."

He raised one black palm in front of Huy's face, and Huy had time to see that relentless sunlight sparking on the god's rings before he found himself hunched on a stool in his office and soaked in sweat, his fingers twined around those of the girl in the chair and the lamp guttering on the desk behind her. At once pain seized him. He doubled over with a groan, feeling Tiye's hand leave his.

"Paneb, I need more poppy at once," he managed. "Find Tetiankh." He heard the scribe leave his place and walk across to the door, closing it quietly behind him. Even so, the sound sent waves of agony pulsing through Huy's head. Slowly he forced himself to straighten and meet Tiye's worried eyes.

"Everyone knows that the Seeing makes you ill," she said, "but like this? What can I do?"

"Pass me the water on the desk." Swiftly she did so, rising and pouring from the pitcher then resuming her seat and watching him carefully as he drained the cup. Huy could smell the odour from his damp body hanging in the room, foul and acrid. It must be offensive to inhale, but the girl gave no sign that it was repulsing her. Taking the cup from him, she refilled it. Once more he drank, then crouched over it, holding it against his chest, feeling each rapid thud of his heartbeat echo in his head. "The vision was long," he said to reassure her. "Thus the pain is severe. But it will abate, Lady Tiye. Poppy and sleep will drive it away. Let me take the drug and then I will tell you what I can."

They waited in silence, Huy with his eyes closed. Presently the door opened and Tetiankh's light step came close. Gently the cup was removed and replaced by a vial. Huy emptied it, handed it back to his body servant, and forced his eyes to open. "Thank you, Tetiankh. I don't want to, but I'd better go to the bathhouse before I lie down. Wait for me outside in the passage."

The concern had left the girl's face. She sat with hands loosely folded in her white lap, her expression politely noncommittal, but beneath her good manners Huy sensed a wary eagerness. Paneb had returned and was quietly settling himself once more by Huy's knee. The opium had already begun to dull the worst of Huy's misery and he was able to smile across at Tiye. "You need not be disappointed by what I shall tell you," he began. "Anubis showed me something wonderful in your future, Lady Tiye. Unfortunately, I feel that I must speak of it to your father before I give it to you."

At once the dark brows came together over those blue eyes. "You saw my death? But no. You said 'something wonderful,' but something that Father needs to hear before me." She leaned forward, peering sharply into his face. "The god showed you the man I'm to marry, didn't he, Great Seer? Nothing else would be important enough to take to Father first. I'm right, aren't I?"

"My apologies, Lady. I can tell you nothing at this time." Huy turned to Paneb. "Write a request to the noble Yuya for an audience on my behalf," he ordered. "Do it at once and Tiye can carry it home with her." The scribe reached for his papyrus scraper and Huy eased carefully back to the girl. Any movement meant pain. "Be patient," he said to her, "and you will be glad you waited. Ask my steward to summon your escort, and forgive me, Lady Tiye, both for withholding my vision from you and for neglecting to reverence you. I am not well enough." It was a dismissal.

Tiye sighed, nodded, and came to her feet. "Patience is very difficult for me to learn, Great Seer. Nevertheless, out of respect for you, I shall wait without pouting." Putting out her arms, she bowed from the waist, an obeisance usually accorded all royalty but the King himself. Huy was surprised and touched. Paneb was already standing at the desk holding a candle flame to the base of a stick of red wax. Expertly he sealed the thin scroll, waited a moment for the wax to solidify, then handed it to Tiye with a bow. She snatched it and went out.

Huy waved his scribe back down. "Take a dictation, and keep this and all future records of my visions safely away from the usual business of each day, Paneb. What passes on these occasions must be entirely private." He wanted nothing more than to curl up on the floor and close his eyes, but Paneb's brush was busy for a very long time.

5

THREE DAYS LATER, word came to the palace that Yey was dead. The King and Mutemwia ordered a full seventy days of mourning for the man who had been revered as God's Father, an honorific held by many trusted ministers, Master of the Horse, His Majesty's Lieutenant-Commander of Chariotry, Chief Instructor of the King in Martial Arts, and, last but definitely not least, Chief of the Rekhit, the highest nobles of the realm. Only the most urgent matters were dealt with in the palace, and the King's officials and foreign ambassadors spent the time visiting one another, catching up with unimportant and therefore neglected correspondence, and being leisurely carried through Mennofer's crowded streets.

Huy had received no reply from Yuya regarding his request for a meeting, and did not expect one until Yey's Beautification in the House of the Dead was completed and his funeral was over. It had taken Huy two days to recover from the long and detailed Seeing he had given Tiye. During that time he rested in Tetiankh's care, sleeping and eating, expecting the summons from either Amunhotep or his royal Mother that in fact did not come until the second week of the mourning period. By then the month of Pharmuthi was well advanced, the days were pleasantly warm, the nights cool, and Egypt was bursting forth in renewed life everywhere. Huy had dictated a detailed letter to his old friend Methen, priest to Khenti-kheti, totem of his natal town. It contained everything Huy had seen relating to Tiye's future and begged Methen to make the short journey south to see him. Huy had given the scroll to his new herald Ba-en-Ra with strict instructions to place it in no other hands but the priest's. No one must catch a hint of what it contained until Huy had had an opportunity to discuss the vision with the Queen and Yuya. He divided the things Anubis had shown him into two distinct parts, the first of which was full of promise. Examining everything he knew and had experienced of Tiye, Huy grew convinced that she could very well make an excellent Queen for Amunhotep and for the country. She was as yet too young for anything more than a legal agreement between her family and the Horus Throne, and it would be necessary to supervise her education closely, not to mention sequester her in the harem, but Huy sensed very strongly that beneath the girl's capricious self-will there lay a raw intellect and an early ability for discernment that, if properly nurtured and disciplined, would result in a woman worthy to walk beside a King.

He did his best to shy away from the second vision. The memory of it filled him with foreboding. The malformed King beside the figure of a Tiye whose face held only a harsh ruthlessness, the sense of dereliction emanating from the Disc with hands and imbuing the vast building from whence Ma'at had fled with the aura of hopelessness, the merciless onslaught of the sun, stirred a grief in Huy that was greater than his horror. Why grief he did not know, unless it was to see the bright child whose hand he had been holding become something coldly implacable. He had Seen for Amunhotep when the King was a baby. The vision had been a happy one, promising him great wealth and power in a storm of sun-fired gold dust that made him chuckle with delight, but Huy did not remember any assurance of long life for the little Prince. Was Tiye to outlive him, then, and remain a Queen beside this monstrous stranger who would bring a curse upon Egypt? Were there to be no royal sons for Amunhotep? The riddle would be meaningless until the future solved it, and Huy left it aside.

The god's rebuke regarding Huy's neglect of his work on the Book of Thoth struck home, but with mild despair Huy acknowledged that without further direction he was at a standstill. He knew the Book by heart, every word, every profound concept. He had spent years puzzling over it. He had become convinced that it was not complete, that somewhere lay the ending that would reveal its ultimate meaning, but he had no idea where to look for it. Atum had breathed life into his lifeless corpse and had given him the gift of Scrying in exchange for his agreement to read and understand the Book Atum had dictated to his scribe, the mighty ibis god Thoth, at the dawn of creation. The Book was contained on forty-two scrolls, half of which lay in Ra's temple at Iunu and half in Thoth's temple at Khmun. Huy had read them all. So had Imhotep, architect, Seer, healer, still worshipped as a god himself although he had been beautified uncounted hentis ago. Huy had begun to believe that Imhotep had deciphered the Book, had written the commentary with each scroll that Huy had found so useful, and had hidden the very last of the Book for some reason, doubtless wise, of his own. So much had happened that had driven Huy's duty to the Book into the far corners of his mind. Anubis had warned him to bring it forward, *but how*, Huy thought in despair, *am I supposed to take up my search again when the King may quite rightly command every moment of my time?*

A reply to his letter arrived from Methen. Huy, inspecting the seal into which Khenti-kheti's benign likeness had been pressed, saw with relief that it had not been broken. Cracking it, he unrolled the papyrus and recognized the priest's own writing. Methen had answered the account of Huy's visions in his own hand. "Atum has shown you a terrible thing," Methen wrote.

Anubis warns you that you must on no account allow what you Saw to come to pass. At present it makes no sense. It's a mirage that appears to have no foundation, but we both remember the Osiris-King Amunhotep the Second and his son Thothmes, our last Pharaoh, and how they fabricated Thothmes' dream of the great sphinx he had dug out of the sand before Osiris Khufu's resting place in order to disinherit the rightful heir, our own King's blood-uncle newly returned from exile. Both of them gave Amun no respect. Their adoration went to the heat of Ra and more specifically to the light of the Aten-disc. May Amun grant you wisdom in the coming years, dear friend! Our young King loves you. So does his illustrious Mother. Keep a reverence for Egypt's mightiest deity alive in them. I miss you and pray daily for your health and safety. By my own hand, Methen, Priest to Khenti-kheti of Hut-herib, this twenty-first day of Pharmuthi, Year One of the King.

Huy handed the scroll to Amunmose. "Burn it," he ordered, "and have my litter-bearers rounded up. It's time I spent a day with Heby and Iupia."

Amunmose scuttled away and Huy went to his bedchamber for clean linen. The room no longer smelled of jasmine. Other blooms filled the gardens with their scents and the surface of the pools rocked gently under a weight of fragrant water lilies and delicate pink lotuses. As Huy opened his door, a tiny green lizard darted across the ceiling where Nut stretched out her star-spangled body, and disappeared through one of the clerestory windows high up in the wall. Huy had seen it before, diligently eating flies above his couch. "We should name that creature," he said to Tetiankh, who was opening one of Huy's tiring chests. "He does good work and I rather like him." Tetiankh raised his eyebrows. He made no reply.

Huy was summoned to the King's private quarters before the end of Pharmuthi. Escorted as usual by Perti and a couple of soldiers, he presented himself before the massive cedar doors to be warmly greeted by Chief Steward Nubti and ushered inside. Amunhotep was pacing to and fro before his closed Amun shrine, his arms folded across the gold lying on his chest, his feet bare. When he saw Huy, he hurried to embrace him. "Uncle Huy! It's been weeks since we met! I thought that since we are all in mourning for Yey I might as well fill the time with some dictation. You brought your palette?"

Huy had in fact snatched it up as an afterthought on his way out; it was as well to be prepared. Enveloped in the aroma of rosemary, Amunhotep's favourite perfume, he felt a rush of renewed affection for this young man who had been a part of his life for so long.

"I have, Majesty." He smiled, stepping away and bowing. "I've missed you also. Are you well?"

Amunhotep made a face. "My health is excellent as always, and although I loved Yey very much, I'm getting bored. I can't take my chariot out or even feast with my friends. I've done my duty and visited Yuya and Thuyu. I even miss my studies!" He grinned and waved at the table laden with sweetmeats and wine. "Let's nibble on shat cakes and share the news. Have you any?"

Yes I do, and I wish I could tell you about it, Huy thought as he took the chair Amunhotep had indicated. He shook his head. "I have enlarged my staff, and before the Master of Chariotry died I entertained my family. Nothing more."

Amunhotep flung himself into the chair opposite Huy. At once Nubti clicked his fingers and a servant glided up to fill the waiting goblets. The King drank with relish, dabbing his hennaed mouth on the piece of spotless linen offered to him.

"You seem carefree in spite of your enforced aimlessness, Majesty," Huy ventured. "It does me good to see you this way. It reminds me of so many happy days spent with you and Anhur on my estate, when you were a little boy."

"I miss that time, Uncle." Amunhotep leaned forward, pushing the pastries to and fro. "Being the King sometimes makes me lonely, in spite of the Queen my Mother's companionship. Here." He handed Huy a tart. "This one has almonds on it. A rare treat."

Obediently, Huy took it. The taste of the precious nuts reminded him of his first meal at the school in Ra's temple at Iunu. Those days came flooding back, together with a sudden and brilliant vision of the sacred Ished Tree beneath whose ancient branches he had sat to read the Book of Thoth. Of course the King had no inkling of the unwanted direction Huy's mind was leading him, but it was as though Atum himself was putting the words in Amunhotep's mouth when the King said, "Ra's High Priest still cultivates the almond tree one of his predecessors planted in the temple garden. Apparently it's very temperamental and hard to coax into producing these delectable things, but I receive a small sackful every Mesore, at the end of the harvest season." He was busy picking the nuts from every pastry and audibly crunching them. "There are more if you want them, Uncle," he added apologetically. "Would you like beer?"

Huy declined, and went on watching the boy. "I've seen nothing of the Prince since he returned," he said. "How is he?"

"We are becoming friends, but the Queen my Mother's spies still bring her regular reports." Amunhotep swallowed a mouthful of wine and sat back. At his gesture a servant refilled his cup. "She doesn't think that you'll have to See for him. His actions are open and his conversation is inoffensive. It seems as though he spoke the truth when he told us that all he wanted to do was retire to his estates and live in peace. However, the Queen my Mother will keep him in the palace for a while longer. Now," he said cheerfully, "I am actually going to dictate, Uncle Huy. I did what you told me to do. I listened to Treasurer Nakht-sobek. I now know how rich I am. So take your place and write my plans for the gods and my country."

Hiding his astonishment, Huy left his chair, sank cross-legged onto the floor beside the King's calf, and opened his palette. It was the same one that his uncle Ker and aunt Heruben had given him for his fifth birthday, a cedar rectangle with his name etched in silver on a lid that slid open to reveal grooves for his brushes, compartments for black and red ink powders, two pots to mix them in, and a simple burnisher. Huy and his uncle had parted company a long time ago, but for a moment he was back in his father Hapu's garden, in the sunshine, his admiring family around him as he examined the gift with awe. *Leave me alone, Great Atum*, he prayed silently, bitterly. *Why do you suffocate me with the past? Did I not take those last visions enough to heart?* A servant's hand appeared, holding a dish of water. He took it with thanks, poured a little in the pots, and began to mix his inks. He had replaced his brushes many times, and the scrolls of papyrus hung in a leather pouch from his belt. Taking one and unrolling it, he burnished it, murmuring the scribes' prayer to their patron, Thoth, as he did so. On impulse he shook the remaining water onto the mat beside him in honour of Imhotep.

The King was tapping his bare foot by Huy's knee. "Are you ready?" he asked crisply.

Huy looked up and nodded.

"Then begin. 'These are the tasks that I Amunhotep, Mighty Bull, the One Who Causes All to Be, have set myself for the beautifying of Egypt and the gods. My monuments shall be more splendid than those of any King before me, and my works shall amaze and confound those who will come after. First it is necessary to open the calcite mine at Berseh on the east bank of the river opposite the city of Khmun, and to repair the ruined mine at Tura south of Iunu so that limestone may again be quarried to complete the work my father began and to provide material for my own building projects.'" He paused. Huy dipped his brush in the ink and waited. "Nakht-sobek was my father's Master of Works as well as being responsible for the Treasury," Amunhotep mused.

Huy, as a good scribe, realized that the young man was simply thinking aloud.

"I need someone new, someone whose attention will not be divided. My father did not have much time for beautifying in Egypt before he died." Was that a hint of scorn underlying the words? Huy wondered. Had Mutemwia, who disliked and distrusted her husband, sown a seed of disdain in her son for his royal father Osiris Thothmes the Fourth? "Continue," Amunhotep ordered, and Huy bent over his labour. "'The noble Men, our Chief Sculptor, will make a capable Master of Works. He can see to the mines at once.' I'll consult the Queen my Mother, but I believe that Men will be happy working under Chief Architect Kha and perhaps his sons Hori and Suti. You know them, Uncle Huy?"

"I have met the noble Kha and liked him, Majesty. I have yet to become acquainted with his sons."

Amunhotep laughed. "You will certainly be amused by them. The whole family is expert at designing. You must meet them as soon as possible. They're most interesting as well as talented. In fact I think I'll put them to work at Weset. They've been idle since they finished the small project at Aabtu." He flung out his arms. "I shall show my love and devotion for Amun to the whole world! Ipet-isut will become the greatest testament to a King's worship the world has ever seen! Uncle, I am on fire with plans, with visions of what I want to see rise on that holy site! I am indebted to you and to my tutors, who deluged me with boring lectures on masonry and architectural design and forced me to learn! Without you I would have no dreams of proper homage to offer to my Divine Father." He rose to his feet and began to pace once more, and Huy realized that he had been bursting with this enthusiasm the whole time. *Men—new Master of Works. Kha—Chief Architect, Weset,* he wrote. *Sons Hori and Suti—Ipet-isut?*

"New gardens for the temple filled with flowers, servants— monuments of gold, lapis, malachite—Amun shall have every- thing his heart may desire. There is one more thing to be noted down." Amunhotep resumed his seat. "Uncle Huy, did you know that a very ancient Osiris-one, Senwosret Glorified, caused to be built a palace-temple at Weset named Senwosret Is Observing the Primeval Hill? And even before that, a small temple already existed at Ipet-isut? But of course you did. The whole of Weset, city, temple, and surrounding land, has been holy since the beginning, when Atum became 'Hill' and birthed the world. I intend to move us all to Weset, and the Queen my Mother agrees that it is our joyful duty. What do you think?"

Shocked and yet filled with an enormous relief, Huy glanced up at the boy's eager face. *All those months under my care. All Mutemwia's anxious determination to counteract any influence his father's heresy might have on his childish mind. It has come to this magnificent fruition: a King who will wield supreme authority in Egypt in a very few years and who already chooses to follow the way of*

Ma'at and the elevation of the god who has always been Egypt's champion and protector.

"I think that your love for Amun will make you the greatest Pharaoh this blessed country has ever seen," he said. Quickly, he wrote *Move to Weset and new palace. Renovation of existing building?* "Have you decided on an architect for its design?"

"So far I only trust Kha and his family, but I'll hire anyone he recommends to work under him. No more dictation, Uncle Huy. I can tell that you're very pleased with my surprises. I like to please you, you know," he added earnestly. "I love you. I can dismiss you now. Acquaint those I have chosen with my decision. Oh, and please find Nehemawi and send him to me. The Queen my Mother and I want to grant his request and let him retire. Send me Merimose as well. He'll take Nehemawi's position as Viceroy of Kush and Wawat and Overseer of the Gold Lands of Amun."

He was still smiling a trifle smugly, a boy pleased with his surprises, as Huy bowed himself out, palette under his arm, and Nubti closed the doors. Perti and the soldiers came to attention.

"Captain, do you know where I might find the Viceroy Nehemawi and the noble Merimose?" Huy asked as they began to walk. "I haven't yet met these men."

"Of course, Master, and while you were busy with His Majesty a message came for you from his Mother the Queen. She requests your company this evening in her quarters. Shall I send Sarenput with your reply?"

"Sarenput? Who's he?"

"Your new herald under Chief Herald Ba-en-Ra, who hired him yesterday. Ba-en-Ra will doubtless approach you regarding the matter as soon as possible."

"Doubtless." Huy sighed, absently noting the waves of bowed heads in the passages as he went by. He had no appetite for the impending noon meal. He knew that he would need a dose of opium and an hour on his couch once he had met these two strangers and delivered the King's demands.

Ra had entered the mouth of Nut and the light of the stars was strengthening when Huy sought admittance to the Queen's apartments. In spite of the fact that he had not eaten during the day, he had done no more than pick at the broiled goose, broad beans, and garlicked cabbage Paroi had set before him. He had woken with an intense craving for yet more poppy and an ache in the pit of his stomach that had nothing to do with a hunger for food. Resignedly he fought the urge to call for Tetiankh. He had been bathed and dressed in fresh linen, but when his body servant began to braid his hair, Huy had pulled away. "Leave it loose," he said. "My scalp hurts." Tetiankh had reminded him that he would be meeting the Queen. Huy snapped back some brusque response that he instantly regretted, and Tetiankh had bowed.

"At least let me gather it into a ribbon," he said. "Master, do you need to consult a physician? You eat less than you should, and your belly is not happy."

"A physician would only tell me what we both know already," Huy replied. "I take too much opium. Have Amunmose mix me garlic and juniper, and brew me an infusion of thyme for the pain." He had allowed Tetiankh to tie his hair with a white ribbon, and later he downed the remedy his chief steward had prepared. The ache became a tenderness, but still he could not eat. He was glad to leave his quarters.

The Queen's steward Ameni admitted him to her rooms. She had been wearing jasmine perfume the last time he had entered, but to his relief the mingled scents of lotus, narcissus, and henna flowers wafted towards him as he went forward and bowed. As before, she was casually dressed in a voluminous linen sheath and a filmy coat with soft wide sleeves from which her tiny hands extended like the centres of white lilies. She was unpainted and unshod, her feet planted together on a low stool. The bud-shaped honey alabaster lamps on their tall stands filled the warm space with a golden glow that barely reached the depiction of flowers, birds, and fruits covering the walls in glorious profusion. *There is no woman sharing my quarters anymore,* Huy thought as he straightened, *and I do not realize how much I miss the aura of a feminine presence until I come here. I am sexless. I forget that I am a eunuch by the will of Atum, but in Mutemwia's presence I become a man again for a while. It is not a comfortable awareness.*

She beckoned him. "Come and sit down, Huy. You look unwell. Take a little date wine. It's fortifying."

Obediently Huy took the empty chair beside her and at once Ameni was at his elbow, pouring the dark liquid into a silver goblet. Although he had no desire to do so, Huy drank, and felt the dull ache in his belly subside.

Mutemwia smiled. "That heavy brow of yours has begun to clear, but you are gaunt, dear friend. Do you not eat enough?"

"You have no need to spy on me, Majesty," Huy said. "In all the years we have known one another, I have given you no cause to distrust me."

"I know." Her hands left the arms of her chair and were folded in her lap. "I have no active spy in your entourage, Huy, but servants talk, and I have always had an ear for the conversations of those closest to their employers. One would think that family members are closest, but it's not so." She nodded once. "Good servants do not gossip, but of course neither are they dumb. For example, your chief steward Amunmose enters the kitchens with mortar and pestle where many cooks work at all hours. He requests a clove of garlic and a juniper berry to grind up, and a handful of thyme leaves in order to brew an infusion. He says no more. One cook comments to another that the Great Seer must be suffering from an upset stomach. He too says no more. Much food is being returned to the kitchens from your quarters each day and distributed among the servants. Again, a brief word to me in passing is all that is needed for me to draw certain conclusions. Your appetite is lacking, your stomach is giving you trouble: you are of course addicted to opium." She leaned towards him and, taking his hands in hers, shook them kindly. "I have learned to make correct deductions over many years when the knowledge of what is passing behind palace doors is vitally important for me and for my son. I trust you utterly, my Huy. Do you understand now?"

Her fingers were warmly alive. He wanted to lift them to his face and set her palms against his cheeks. He met her eye. "Yes. And therefore I suppose that I need not tell you that I Scryed for Yuya's daughter."

She burst out laughing. "That's certainly one reason why I asked you to come to my quarters. Are you willing to tell me whether or not you Saw something that I or the King should know?" She released him and sat back.

He glanced around at Ameni and two other servants, alert and motionless in the shadows. "If you had not called for me, I would have petitioned Ameni for an audience with you before long. But what I have to tell you is most definitely for you alone to hear. Please dismiss your men."

At once she gestured, a flick of the wrist, and Ameni ushered them out, closing the door behind himself. Her attention returned to Huy. She became very still as she waited for him to speak, her body relaxed, her attitude one of complete patience.

Huy's thoughts flowed quickly as he considered how much of the two visions he ought to relate. The first had been one of triumph, the temple full of incense smoke and joyful music that soared in praise to Amun and spoke of the eternal power of Ma'at. But the second ... Mentally, Huy shook himself. This was Mutemwia, the woman with whom he had shared the dangerous years of her husband's reign, who had spent many nights with him in the office on his estate, talking easily and intimately as the night deepened and the house fell silent. But here, in this noisy conglomeration of hundreds of living quarters, the clusters of building after huge building, a small city within the larger maelstrom of Mennofer where she ruled as Regent to her son and could wield absolute power if she so chose, had she changed? Become altogether a goddess? What was he to her now? A friend and adviser, or a gaming piece to be used? On the wave of a familiar doubt the yearning for poppy suddenly returned, smothering his mind, seeping into his limbs, and he fought it with a desperate spasm of his will.

When he spoke, the words were forced out through stiff lips, but he recounted everything. It took a long time, and only when the lamps stopped crackling did Huy realize that the Queen had left her seat, replenished the oil in them herself, and regained her chair. Picking up his goblet, Huy drained the last of the date wine. Her gaze followed his movements. Huy could tell that she was thinking deeply. Her fingers had begun to tap out an absent rhythm on her linen-clad thighs, and she was frowning.

"This is the last message from the gods that I expected," she began at last. "I had been waiting until Yey's funeral was over to request your advice regarding Iaret."

"Iaret? One of Amunhotep's sisters, the eldest one who became Osiris Thothmes' wife?" Huy vaguely remembered a letter from little Amunhotep years ago when his father King Thothmes had taken him on a punitive expedition into Wawat. Iaret had accompanied them. Amunhotep had told Huy how the Queen, his sister, had complained ceaselessly about the heat and discomfort of their surroundings, and about how much he disliked her.

"Yes. I had expected Neferatiri as Thothmes' Great Queen to attempt a union with our returning Prince in order to supplant my son as King. But the Prince simply wants to go away from court and live as a provincial noble. I believe he is sincere in this. Neferatiri will remain in the harem indefinitely." Mutemwia slid to her feet. "Iaret's petition caught me by surprise. She is a fully royal sister. She has a right to occupy the Queen's throne beside my son." She spread her arms, a gesture of frustration. "So do Amunhotep's other sisters, although Iaret's claim is the strongest. But you tell me that Atum has chosen Tiye. Only two generations separate her from her Mitanni grandfather, a commoner, and moreover a prisoner brought into Egypt by Osiris Thothmes the Third." She squatted in front of Huy, placing her hands on his knees, anxiously scanning his face. "She's still a child, Huy, soon to be eleven years old. Amunhotep doesn't like her very much, although a King's personal preferences when it comes to marriage are not important—an eligible girl's lineage and character matter far more. Remember how precarious my son's claim to the Horus Throne is! His first wife should be of royal blood, his own and his father's. She should be his sister. Since ancient times it's been the royal women who carry the power of divine succession in their blood! Tiye's blood is neither royal nor even Egyptian! Gods, Huy, what are you doing to me?" Rising abruptly, she swung away from him. Huy expected her to begin to pace, but she stood immobile, chewing her lip and still frowning. "Who else knows about the visions? Your scribe? Tiye herself?"

"Paneb definitely. I was not stupid enough to tell Tiye what I Saw, but eventually I must. The first vision anyway."

"The first vision." Mutemwia exhaled and her body lost its rigidity. Bending over the table, she poured herself wine. Again she did not do what Huy expected. Instead of gulping it, she took two sips and set it down. "The second vision is dire, Huy. Anubis gave you no instruction regarding the first, but he was adamant that what he showed you in the second must not come to pass."

"Yes."

"Tiye is linked to some grotesquely malformed man? A King?"

"Egypt's King. Yes."

"So Tiye will outlive my son and still be young enough to marry his successor? Then where are my royal grandsons? If Tiye signs no marriage contract with the Horus Throne, if she is denied the Queen's crown and I command her to wed with some eligible nobleman, both visions will dissolve into nothing."

"Would you defy the Great He-She?" Huy rose and faced her. She was sweating lightly, the heat of her body releasing gusts of perfume that clung to him, making him giddy with the flare of an emotion so old and yet so familiar to him that in her anxiety and his urgency he did not pause to name it. "Mutemwia, my gift, my curse, this door Atum opens for me—I ignore what it shows me at my peril, and I beg you not to put yourself in danger from the hosts of Khatyu Anubis, which may unleash on both of us if you flout the King's immediate destiny. The god uses me. Believe me, it's often more of a punishment than something others envy. Consider Egypt's destiny also. Who knows what disasters may come upon the country without Tiye at the King's side?"

Her eyes narrowed. "We believe in fate. We believe that from the time we are born our lives are ruled by whatever decisions the gods have made regarding our every move. I think about this often." She grasped his arm. "But what if the resolutions the gods have made for us can be altered by our own choices? What if Atum can only show you what might be, because what might be depends on the large and small choices of your petitioners each day? Do your predictions always come true?"

Huy stared down at those deceptively delicate features without really seeing them. "They always come true," he answered finally, "but not always in the way I was shown them. I too have pondered this question. Whether illness or death or a contented life, the end is as I have Seen it, but the path leading to that end sometimes differs from the vision." *Yet the first Seeing Atum forced upon me was for Nasha,* he remembered with a jolt. *I had no control over the visions then. I Saw Nasha knocked down and killed in the Street of the Basket Sellers at Iunu. I warned her to stay away from that place and she did, and it was her mother who died under the wheels of a donkey cart. Is a certain destiny set, then, and must be fulfilled at any cost? What am I really Seeing when I take a supplicant's hand into my own?*

"So no matter what I decide, Tiye will become Queen of Egypt." Mutemwia sat down. "Is that what you are saying, Huy? And what of the second vision? Is there any use in trying to obey the god's injunction if what you saw is inevitable?"

I was punished once, Huy thought. *The fate Atum had decreed for Anuket became Ishat's for one terrible day before I humbled myself and bitterly repented my cowardice.* "Our daily choices only lead to the fate already chosen for us," he said at last. "Atum reveals that fate to those brave enough or foolish enough to come to me. But he has also made the future of Egypt my responsibility. That is why you chose to send your son to my estate. That is why he grew to love me, and you and he summoned me to court, where I may guide and advise you both." The turn in the conversation had woken a kind of desperation in him. He felt tense and suddenly ill. "You make many decisions on his behalf, Majesty, and they are good and necessary if he is to become Pharaoh. But the decisions arising from my visions you must leave to me. You must trust that Atum desires only prosperity and peace for his favourite country." His knees had begun to tremble and he eased himself into a chair.

She was staring at him speculatively, her lips pursed, her expression cool. "My last question has not been answered," she said stiffly. "Moreover, one does not say 'must' to a Queen. Even if Atum owns this ship and tells you in which direction it should sail, yet my son and I remain at the helm and may steer towards its destination as we see fit." Huy had not seen her angry before. She had not raised her voice or made any gesture, nor had her cheeks flushed, but he sensed an icy rage beneath her calm exterior.

"I apologize for being so blunt," he said. "You have showered me and the members of my family with favours and preferments because you know that we, all of us, are utterly loyal to you and to Egypt. You brought me to the palace to be close to the King, to continue to guide and advise him just as you yourself do, out of love for him. Are you angry with me, Mutemwia, or with the god?"

Her narrow shoulders slumped. Pushing back her hair with both hands, she sighed. "I don't know. Everything you say is true. Everything. Perhaps I resent having the decision of a suitable wife for Amunhotep taken away from me. It is one of the few occasions when I may be a mother as well as a Regent. My mind fills with acrimony when I imagine him coupled with a commoner chosen by a commoner." She pointed ruefully at Huy. "You. Nor do I like humbling myself before the gods. If you see a fragile, dainty aristocrat in me, my friend, you are deceived. I admit that Amunhotep needs you, but I need you also, to remind me that even a Queen must face the judgment of Ma'at's feather. I have grown arrogant since my son mounted the Horus Throne." She grimaced. "Very well. Why did I bother to bring you here if I refuse to listen to you? Or to Atum? But promise me, Huy, promise me that you also will obey the god and do your utmost to make the second part of the vision a lie. We will say nothing of it to the King. It has nothing to do with him. As for Tiye, why should she imagine her husband dead before she's even been betrothed? You may approach Yuya when his father has been entombed, and then the King, who will protest the god's imperative very loudly, and then Tiye. She will have to be moved into the harem with her mother, and her education must change. Iaret will be furious."

A silence fell. Mutemwia drew up her knees, hooked her heels over the edge of the chair, and folded her arms around her linen-clad calves. Huy had seen her perform the same informal movements countless times in the office of his house outside Hut-herib during the long nights when the two of them talked closely and effortlessly together. Mutemwia, like her son, found sleep difficult and early morning risings even more onerous. The memory was sweet and Huy began to relax, expecting her to look up at any moment and dismiss him. Instead she said, "Vizier Ptahmose will be making his regular tour of all the sepats at the beginning of the month of Mesore. The harvest will be in by then and we will be waiting for the Inundation. He visits every Governor in order to assess the general well-being of the country. I want you to go north with him. Pay special attention to the state of the Delta and our borders with Rethennu and the tribes to the east that pay us tribute. There have been reports of pirates landing on our coast and complaints from the King of the island of Alashia that they have begun to plunder the towns on Alashia's coast. We import almost all of our copper from Alashia, and we have a very friendly relationship with the ruling family. Your nephew Amunhotep-Huy can go with you in his capacity as King's Scribe of Recruits. His mind has been overfull of his impending marriage. I suggest that you spend time in the Office of Foreign Correspondence. You need a better sense of Egypt's influence." She smiled. "The King and I agree that as his Personal Scribe you have had little to do. He wants you to continue taking down his future plans in private, as you have already done, but we are wasting your talents, Huy, especially as you will no longer See for anyone we do not send to you. Is that acceptable?"

It was a warning, and the new task she had set him was a confirmation of her trust. Huy nodded. "The King has told me that he intends to move the court to Weset," he ventured. "Am I to keep an occasional eye on the progress of the new palace's design?"

"Talk to Kha." She uncurled and stretched. "If he has any problems, he'll probably bring them to you anyway. Amunhotep has already scandalized him."

"How so?"

"By deciding to build on the west bank instead of the east." She shot Huy a keen look. "Yes, I know that the City of the Dead lies on the west bank, but our reasons are sound. We are ushering in a new age for Egypt, an age of wealth. Amunhotep intends to strengthen our hold over our vassals, make the gold routes coming up from Wawat finally secure, extend our reach into the east and north, to the Bend of Naharin, Assur, Babylon, Arzawa, invite an ambassador to Egypt from the Khatti, the new power rising in the northeast. In short, we will create an empire. The old palace on the east bank is large, but the city itself has grown around it and hems it in. Over the years we will need room to expand as more and more foreign delegations arrive. Besides"—she linked her hands and bent over them towards him—"we want our citizens to see that Weset is supreme, the home not only of Amun but of his divine son also, that Mennofer belongs to the past."

"You say 'we,' Majesty, but I am perfectly aware that the future you describe was born in your own mind. You are an admirable visionary and a shrewd Regent." She grinned at him. To Huy she looked to be no more than a young girl. *That's an advantage when dealing with men in authority: they will bow to a woman while grossly misjudging both the level of her acumen and the sophistication of her mind.*

"Are you with me in this, Great Seer?" she demanded. "Shall you and I together make my son the richest and most powerful King Egypt has ever seen?"

A tide of elation swept over Huy, swamping all fatigue and strain. *I am guilty of underestimating her also,* he thought as he held out his hand. *She is entirely capable of ruling Egypt on her own.*

"Yes," he said. "Yes!"

She clasped his fingers briefly. "Go and sleep." She was dismissing him. He rose and bowed. "Drink date wine before you eat and it will rekindle your appetite. I warned you about the poppy a long time ago, if you remember. Now, is there anything you need, apart from a way to escape from your apartment? I know how much you hate the palace after your quiet little estate, but be patient. Amunhotep has set aside for you a portion of land by the river opposite Weset, and if you offer one of Kha's sons enough gold he will design for you. You will need a place of escape, for I intend to work you very hard. Do you love me as well as my son, Huy?"

The question had come out of nowhere, but oddly Huy was not surprised. It was as though the words had been drifting fully formed about the pleasant room and had found expression through her mouth instead of his.

"You are my friend, Majesty. I have always had a deep affection for you." But that was not what he meant, nor what she wanted to hear. A sadness passed over her dainty features and was gone.

"I must tell you something you will not like before you go," she said as he turned to leave. "The King is determined to call our new home the Palace of the Dazzling Aten."

Huy froze. "What? Why? That's totally unacceptable, insulting to Amun who inhabits Weset, and dangerous, Mutemwia! Does he harbour a secret devotion to the Disc? I—"

"I agree," she broke in, "but believe me, he cannot be swayed. He argues that the foreigners will not be insulted by this god who in fact means nothing to him, and that Egypt will seem less insular, have more in common with other countries."

"Egypt is insular," Huy said hotly. "She is unique. What other country is privileged to live by the laws of Ma'at, which even a divine King must obey? Why should Amunhotep care for the opinions of our inferiors?"

"Attempt to change his mind if you can," Mutemwia said, "but he'll simply quote one of the hymns to Amun at you: 'Aten of the day, creator of mortals and maker of life.' Oh, Huy, does it matter that much? After all, the Disc is merely light not heat, and its rays become lions when they strike the earth. Shrines to the Aten are so very few, and the Disc is boring to our commoners. I'm inclined to let the matter rest. Sleep in safety."

Huy arrived at his quarters with his mind full of everything Mutemwia had told him. In spite of his nightly infusion of poppy, he could not rest. His room was dim, his couch comfortable, his sheets smelled faintly of the vinegar in which they had been rinsed, but no matter how he positioned his body, unconsciousness would not come. In the end he got up and, tying on the limp kilt Tetiankh had recently removed, made his way quietly to the garden door. The guards outside straightened, saluted, and prepared to accompany him, but he waved them back. The grass was soft and cool under his bare feet, the air redolent with the scents of the night-blooming flowers. Starlight shivered on the surface of the pool as he walked past it. He went on until he entered the deep shadows of the sycamores. Here he turned. A few high clerestory windows in the wall of the palace showed a dull orange where a small number of residents remained wakeful.

Otherwise he was surrounded by darkness. Lowering himself to the ground, he leaned back against a wide tree bole and felt every tension begin to leave his body.

I should do this more often, he thought. *Nowhere else is there silence and privacy, and I miss both so very much.* For a while he allowed his mind to lie fallow, but then the day's events began to demand attention and reluctantly he considered them, knowing that he would get no sleep until he did so. *I'm not concerned about a journey through Egypt. Vizier Ptahmose and I need to get to know one another better, and I am easily able to fulfill the task I have been set. Hut-herib is on the way to the northern coast; I may be able to spend a little time on my estate, even visit Methen. I don't look forward to travelling with Amunhotep-Huy, though. My nephew has always been a bad-tempered, sulky young man who tried my patience every time I visited Heby. No, it's the speed with which changes are coming that distresses me. The pace of my life is increasing, and in spite of the way Atum has preserved my body, my ka tells me that I am growing old. I passed the age of fifty some time ago. Tomorrow I must spend the morning with the Minister for Foreign Correspondence. Who is he? I don't know, and Mutemwia did not tell me.*

An image of the Queen sprang vividly into his thoughts, her lithe little body swathed in filmy white linen, her huge eyes fixed on him as she leaned forward on the gilded chair. He stirred, folding his arms against the sudden flutter in his chest. *Every time I am in her presence she reminds me of Anuket, the Anuket of my early days at school, when Thothmes' family welcomed me into their home during the weeks the school was closed*, he mused. *My mind refuses to remember the Anuket of the later years, lined and raddled, drunk every day. The likeness I see with such painful clarity is a slim and lovely girl sitting cross-legged on the floor of the herb room surrounded by fragrant blooms, a festive garland in her lap, her long fingers stilled over it as she lifts her face towards me with a smile. I will* carry that vision with me into my tomb. Yet sometimes the features raised to me belong to the Queen, a flash of mental confusion soon righted. It's no wonder that in her company my senses occasionally lie to me and I become uneasy.

But they did not lie to you during the years when she and her son spent much time on your estate, another voice whispered in his head. You formed a bond of friendship with her, you enjoyed her conversation, but not once did you see Anuket in her place.

Huy frowned into the dimness. She gives me dreams, he thought all at once. I go from her quarters to my couch and I dream of Anuket. Somehow I must substitute those perilous images waiting to fill my sleeping mind with something safer before they lead me to my own destruction. I could so easily come to desire her, that's the problem. That's the truth I've been trying to avoid. Oh, Atum, why do you allow me to teeter on the edge of this pit? Do you intend it to strengthen the channel between the Queen and me, or is it a malicious caprice? Both loving you as my creator and hating you as my torturer is exhausting.

He came to his feet slowly, wanting to shake himself free of his thoughts like a dog coming out of a river. Very well, he told himself with savage force. Very well. I shall make sure that each of my days is full of duties and my nights dulled with poppy. If by chance I cannot sleep, I shall watch the contents of the Book of Thoth scroll past my inner vision, a futile exercise that may prove useful in my need to evade reality. Tomorrow Ba-en-Ra or this Sarenput he's hired will invite Chief Architect Kha and his sons to dine with me. After that I'll make my plans with the Vizier, talk to the King and Yuya about Tiye, dictate a letter to Thothhotep and Anhur, so far away in the south. Yet under the rebellious determination that was quickening his steps as he made his way back to his door was a lake of grief and despair in which he feared he would drown.

In the morning, Ba-en-Ra and a younger man with short, curling hair and a large, upturned nose were waiting for him as he emerged from his bedchamber. Ba-en-Ra bowed profoundly and apologetically. "I beg your forgiveness for not consulting you before I hired this person, Great Seer," he said. "It was becoming obvious to me that one herald to deliver your letters and messages would not be enough. Sarenput comes from the noble May's employ, with May's permission."

"You are my Chief Herald and I have already spoken to you regarding my expectations of all those in my service," Huy replied, looking Sarenput up and down. "You may hire as you see fit. So. Sarenput. You are as thin as a twig, and a herald's life is a strenuous one. How have you fared under the noble May?"

Sarenput bowed. Huy could see the bones of his spine as he bent. "I eat prodigiously but become no fatter, Master," Sarenput answered. "I am skinny but very strong. I had to be. I have spent more time out of Egypt than within it since the noble May became the Minister for Foreign Correspondence. Before then he was one of His Majesty's palace stewards."

Huy's interest was kindled. "So you grew tired of travelling in alien lands?"

"I grew tired of delivering Egypt's greetings and instructions to the petty kings of our vassal states and standing before them while they pretended that they were conferring some mighty favour on Egypt by having the scrolls read to them. In my opinion the Regent should instruct His Majesty to occupy these little kingdoms and declare them Egyptian territory. Half a division would provide enough soldiers." His speech had become progressively hotter, his gestures more pronounced. Those stick-like arms opened wide. Huy noted with amusement that the silver arm band denoting Sarenput's profession had slid from his upper arm to dangle from his wrist.

"I hope that you will serve me with the same fervour you invest in the future of Egypt's holdings," he said. He nodded at

Ba-en-Ra. "We will put him on sufferance for three months. Now find Chief Architect Kha and invite him and his sons to a meal with me at sundown. And you, Sarenput, go to your previous superior and request an audience for me within the hour." They bowed and left, and Huy turned to Amunmose. "As soon as Ba-en-Ra returns, you may begin to organize a feast. Make very sure that every dish will be tasted."

"Under Steward Paroi will be delighted," Amunmose muttered half under his breath. "Gods, Huy, will there ever be a break in this frenetic pace?"

"Soon, I think. Write to Merenra on my estate at Hut-herib and warn him to expect us sometime during the first week of Payni, after Yey's funeral. Paroi will stay here."

Amunmose's eyebrows rose. "A reprieve?"

"For you, not for me. I'm to tour the sepats with Vizier Ptahmose. If the gods smile on me, I'll manage a day or two at home." The word felt strange on Huy's tongue as he dismissed Amunmose. *Could it be that in spite of my dislike of the palace, it's truly becoming my home?* he wondered. He heard Paneb's polite but authoritative voice as the scribe was admitted, and presently the man approached. Huy bade him a good morning, outlined the tasks of the day, and they both settled down to wait for Sarenput's return.

Minister May's office adjoined those of His Majesty's other administrators, but it was larger than any Huy had seen, and at first glance the space appeared utterly disorganized. Scrolls and clay tablets lay piled everywhere, and in order to greet him, May wove a course between them.

"Great Seer!" he said cheerfully with a bow. "It's my pleasure to welcome you to my domain. Pay no attention to your surroundings. My scribes will arrive soon to take everything to the palace archives, and then we start again. Correspondence

between His Majesty and Egypt's vassals is regular and copious—
I mean, between the Regent and the vassals in the King's name,
of course. His Majesty signs the letters. He comes here and listens
to them and to the replies every morning. He is most anxious to
open trading negotiations with the foreigners who are not yet
under Egypt's sway. Not yet." He smiled widely. "I do have a stool
by my desk somewhere, and my servant hurried to bring cheese,
bread, and beer once Sarenput acquainted me with your desire.
Incidentally, Sarenput is more intelligent than he seems on a first
meeting. He has been all over the empire on His Majesty's business and can answer many of your questions." He had been lifting
an armful of scrolls to reveal a chair. He indicated it to Huy with
another bow and edged his way around the desk to pull a stool
close to Huy as the latter lowered himself gingerly and Paneb
carefully made himself a place on the floor for the mat he had
brought. "Neither His Majesty nor the Regent will be joining us
today." May sat down on the stool. "Queen Mutemwia sent me a
message telling me to expect you instead."

At the sound of her name, Huy felt his heart give one large
thump before resuming its usual rythmn. *Stop this*, he said
silently. *I will not allow it.*

May waved at the food and drink on the edge of the laden
desk. "Please help yourself, Great Seer. Now, where shall we
begin?"

"I think with the vassal states and the strength of their attach-
ment to the Horus Throne." Huy poured beer, passed a cup down
to Paneb, who had already prepared his palette, and then poured
for himself. The brew was very dark and tasted sweet. Date wine.
She forgets nothing, controls everything, he thought both admiringly and grimly. *I have no hope of an independent life—not yet.
Neither does Amunhotep. We are both her willing tools in her plans
for Egypt's future.*

May was nodding, his fingers linked under his ample stomach. "Good. First we will consider our relationships to the east. You know of course that the Horus Road runs directly through Rethennu, our nearest eastern neighbour. Rethennu was conquered hentis ago, and our hold on it renewed most notably by the Osiris-King Thothmes, the Third of that name. The princes of Rethennu's cities have been paying us a handsome tribute year after year. Beyond Rethennu we exact tribute from Canaan, Apra, and Amurru, mostly precious woods, metal, live-stock, and workers of various kinds. The natives are expected to provide soldiers for our garrisons. I would rather see them manned by loyal Egyptian men. Egypt has governors in these areas who make regular reports to me and thus to the Regent. Incidentally, Huy, the Horus Road is garrisoned along its length in order to monitor the traffic of foreigners in and out of Ta-Mehu, but the Queen has become concerned that the commanders of each of the strongholds are less vigilant than they should be. After all, we have been at peace with the east for some time now."

So that is at least one reason why Mutemwia wants me in the Delta, in Ta-Mehu, Huy thought fleetingly.

May helped himself to a piece of brown goat cheese and put it in his mouth. "Further east we enter Zahi and Shinar," he said once he had swallowed, "and then we come to two mighty rivers within whose arms we deal with several provinces lumped together under the name Naharin. They are Mitanni, a power that we treat at present as an equal, and Katna, Niy, Kinanat, Senzar, and Nukhashshi, tribes of no consequence, although we watch them in case Mitanni attempts to enlarge its holdings by appropriating them. I forgot to mention that Amurru and Byblos are often at each other's throats, and each writes to the King demanding troops to aid in their quarrels with one another. The Regent has been providing soldiers to both Amurru and Byblos.

In her letters to the chiefs she stresses her concern that there be peace between them, but of course she instructs her commanders to maintain a balance between the two tribes."

He took a hearty swig of beer, and at that moment five or six men darkened the door, bowed to both Huy and May, and began to place the scrolls and clay tablets in reed baskets with a care that told Huy how well they knew where each would be stored.

"Far to the northeast we find the Khatti," May continued. "So far all we know about them is that for hentis past they have been nothing more than warlike barbarians, but our spies tell us that a chief calling himself their King is trying to organize both a viable army and a feasible government. They care for no one but themselves, and must be watched. Do you read and write Akkadian, Huy?" Huy shook his head. "It would be as well to learn it if you are to keep your finger on the pulse of Egypt's foreign dealings," May pointed out. "Akkadian is the accepted language of diplomacy, trade agreements, any business conducted between the nations. Besides, the Regent wishes you to do so."

"She does? So it's not enough for me to receive regular reports from you?"

May shrugged. "Apparently you are to appear here every morning at the same time as His Majesty and the Regent, and listen while the information flowing in and out of this office is dealt with, until you are fluent in Akkadian and have a firm grasp of the strengths and weaknesses of every country in the empire and outside it. Then you are to take the Queen's place in guiding my work and you will report to her instead of me."

"But why? She has not spoken to me about this!"

May gave him a level look. "She trusts you above all of us— your loyalty, your judgment, your ability to see every difficulty Egypt faces in terms of her future growth and security. Of all her ministers, I am the most important to her. She is determined to increase Egypt's influence in the world, and thus her wealth also. She consults the Scribe of Recruits almost as often as me."

"He is responsible for the safety of our borders." Huy's mind was racing. "You said 'empire,' May. Is His Majesty lord over an empire?" He knew that the question betrayed his ignorance, but May smiled.

"Not quite yet, but by the time he reaches his majority his Mother believes that he will be eligible for the title of emperor."

For the first time since coming to court, Huy saw Mutemwia's plan in its entirety, her stratagem a series of fragile filaments snaking towards a unity where there were no longer any areas of uncertainty, where every design had come to fruition and Egypt was truly the centre of the world. *She's been working towards this for years,* he thought feverishly, *ever since I held the baby Amunhotep in my arms and we were engulfed in a storm of gold dust. She saw me then as a potential ally, and she began the long years of testing my intellect, my loyalty, my dealings with both servants and those of purer blood who came to me for Scrying—in short, my whole being, all my behaviour. Everything within me and without was carefully scrutinized. Such ambition! And all for her son.*

"She trusts her ministers to be faithful and honest in their work for Egypt," May was saying, "but she only gives her full confidence to you. Your destiny is as vital to her as that of the King." The laden scribes had gone. Once more a shaft of undisturbed sunlight lay across the dusty floor.

"She has discussed these things with you?"

"Not directly, but everyone labouring in these offices knows that you have her ear. Some have begun to fear you. Some do their best to hide their jealousy. Most of us respect the man who will soon become the King's principal adviser." He stretched and lifted his wine from the cleared surface of the desk, holding up the cup in a salute to Huy. "As for myself, my load is heavy. I shall be glad to do nothing more than what I am told. But first, Akkadian." He drank, then pursed his lips thoughtfully. "If you agree, I'll send one of my scribes to teach you every evening. I don't suppose your own scribe is familiar with the language?" Paneb glanced up, pen in hand, inclined his head in a bow to May, then shook it. "A pity." May eased himself off the stool and surreptitiously rubbed the small of his back. "Is such an arrangement agreeable to you, Great Seer? I'm required to report on your progress to the Queen. I realize that you and Vizier Ptahmose will be absent from court for a couple of months. My scribe will go with you." He bowed. "May the soles of your feet be firm as you travel. We shall meet again upon your return."

Huy left the chair, bowed shortly, and walked out into the heat of mid-morning, Paneb at his heels. He felt as though May's words had been imbued with some unseen force that had pummelled both his mind and his spirit. *I understand everything that was obscure to me before,* he thought as he made his way through the crowded corridors. *After summoning me to Mennofer, she made sure that I would stay by giving every member of my remaining family, even my younger nephew Ramose, an exalted position. She showered Heby with titles and the corresponding responsibilities. He was already Mayor of Mennofer when she made him Overseer of the Cattle of Amun and Overseer of the Two Granaries of Amun in the Sepats of Ta-Mehu. All this, to hold me tightly to her side.*

By the time he entered his own apartments, it was noon and the air was full of the pleasant aroma of leek soup and hot herbed ox tongue. He had given his senior servants permission to eat their meals in his reception room. They were spread around the furniture or sitting on the floor, eating and chattering—all but Amunmose, who was hovering by the door, obviously waiting for him. At his side was an elderly man with a shaved skull and seamed face. As far as Huy could see, the only paint he sported was a thick layer of black kohl protecting two bright brown eyes, but his long white linen skirt was bordered in blue, and as he turned to Huy's approach, the kohl glinted with tiny gold specks. His fingers were free of rings, the nails filed very short. One golden band of office grasped the loose flesh of his left upper arm. He greeted Huy with a low obeisance.

"Master, this is Physician Seneb," Amunmose said. "With your permission I shall return to my meal. By the way, Ba-en-Ra brought a message from the Chief Architect. He and his sons will be here at the appointed time."

Huy waved him away and gave his attention to the man already straightening. "How may I serve you, Physician Seneb?" he asked politely.

"No, no, Great Seer, I am here to serve you," Seneb replied. "Her Majesty the Queen has appointed me as your personal physician. I come to you from the household of Chief Herald Maani-nekhtef, where my erstwhile assistant has been elevated to Chief Physician. I was born in the Am-khent sepat and know the town of Hut-herib well. I am also acquainted with the facts of your death and miraculous resurrection. Khenti-kheti's priest Methen is distantly related to my mother, who passed into the Beautiful West some time ago."

"Why are you telling me all this?" Huy said abruptly. He was angry and did not understand why.

Seneb spread out his hands, palms up, in a gesture of submission and apology. "Queen Mutemwia wanted you to be at ease with me, to know that I will require no information regarding your childhood and upbringing. A physician must be aware of such details. Her Majesty wishes to spare you the need to revive painful memories."

"What else does she want?" Huy's tone was sharp. In spite of the craving for his midday dose of opium, his appetite for leeks and ox tongue was blessedly growing also.

"She wants me to keep you healthy." Seneb smiled. "Neither of us may disobey her, Great Seer. I am to examine you every week, take charge of your meals, prescribe fasts and exercise when necessary, and supervise your intake of the poppy."

"No. My body servant Tetiankh has sole custody of the opium." He felt hot with an anger that he now knew was directed at Mutemwia, a confusing compound of desire, extreme irritation, and now fear that the substance on which he relied for his sanity would be taken away from him at the will of a ruthless goddess.

Seneb bowed again. "I do not intend to control your intake, merely supervise it. The form in which your body servant prepares it makes it weak. You need too much of it for a comfortable effect. I have already inspected the yield that comes to you from your fields by Weset. The noble Amunnefer, your partner, sent me a sample. The quality is good, almost as good as the crops imported from Keftiu. Believe me, Great Seer, the Queen is passionate regarding your care, and I share her zeal. I have an apartment not far from yours. I have already given your chief steward instructions on how to summon me if I am needed. Otherwise I shall present myself with the tools of my profession tomorrow, and every week thereafter. Are we agreed?"

"I can hardly disagree," Huy said tartly. "Now may I eat?"

Seneb smiled again, an expression that already seemed habitual with him. "As much as you like, noble one. Please dismiss me."

Huy was about to protest that he owned no such title, but Seneb was already halfway to the door, his linen flowing majestically with him.

6

CHIEF ARCHITECT KHA AND HIS SONS were admitted to Huy's suite shortly after sunset, and looking at the two younger men as they bowed to him Huy understood why the King had laughed when speaking of Kha's family. Kha's sons were identical twins, gazing solemnly at Huy out of almond-shaped grey eyes, each wide jaw cleft with the sign of a stubborn nature, each generous mouth with the same slightly upward quirk to the left side that would make them appear scornful to anyone who did not know them. But there was no hint of mockery in their expressions as they waited for their father to introduce them. Kha's own blue eyes were merry.

"Great Seer Amunhotep, these are my children Hori and Suti. They have been anxious to meet you." Both shaven heads were lowered again. They had both been painted with the same light grey tinge of colour on their eyelids, above heavy kohl.

"You are most welcome," Huy said, making no attempt to hide his amusement. "Now, which of you is Hori and which Suti?"

"We are asked the same question almost every day, Seer Amunhotep," one of them replied promptly. "I am Hori. He's Suti. I am the more intelligent, of course. I draft the most original designs." They looked at one another and laughed.

"So original that no one wants to see them actually built," Suti retorted gaily. Huy noted that the modulation of his voice was very slightly higher than that of his brother. Suti raised his braceleted right arm and pointed at himself. "I have a small mole halfway down the side of my chest. Sometimes even our mother can't tell us apart until I show it to her."

"You mentioned two daughters on your estate outside Weset," Huy said to Kha as Amunmose ushered them farther into the room. "Are they also twins?"

Kha shook his head. "Thank all the gods, no! These two provide problems enough!"

Paroi was waiting with wine jugs in both hands as Huy and his guests took their places and lifted the garlands before them on the low tables.

"This is not, strictly speaking, a feast," Huy told them. "The noble Yey has not yet been buried. There are no perfumed cones and no entertainment. However, we may enjoy the fresh flowers."

Both Hori and Suti were holding the garlands to their faces. "One of the advantages to living close to the perfume fields ..." one began.

"... is the variety of lovely blooms in the Delta," the other finished, quite naturally and without even glancing at his brother. "White lilies, creamy henna, pink tamarisk, even the yellow bak flowers that smell so sweet." He set the wreath around his neck and looked across at Amunmose, who was setting out cups and finger bowls. "I don't suppose ..."

"... you have any bak pods hidden away?" Both sets of dark eyebrows were raised in anticipation.

"I'm sorry, honoured guests, but the season is still too early for them. My master enjoys them also." The conversation became general as the wine filled the goblets and the food was served. Huy, having drunk a mouthful or two of date wine earlier, was surprised that he was mildly hungry for the lettuce and cucumber salad drenched in garlic and sesame oil and the ox liver with chickpeas that sent the aroma of majoram and coriander drifting through the air. He ate carefully, however, aware of the delicate state of his stomach, while Hori and Suti consumed everything offered to them politely but steadily.

"Your cook is excellent, Huy," Kha remarked as Paroi began to clear away the debris and Amunmose stood by with a platter of honeyed figs.

Huy nodded. "He has certainly done well. Please tell him so, Amunmose."

The steward rolled his eyes. "He'll only look conceited and then begin to grumble about the restrictions of trying to work in a common kitchen, but I'll give him the compliment anyway. I keep searching for someone cheerful to replace him." He set down the figs and bustled away.

"Your chief steward has an unusual temperament," Kha commented as the twins descended on the figs. "He is not at all in awe of you."

"He's an old friend. I've known him for many years." *He and Anhur,* Huy thought fleetingly, *in the days when I was still engaged in a fruitless struggle to understand the Book of Thoth and my own astonishing regeneration.*

He and Kha watched the figs disappear, and two pairs of beringed hands dabble in the warm water of the finger bowls and reach for the squares of crisp white linen set ready for them. At once Paroi signalled and the tables were removed. "Let's go out into the garden," Huy said, getting up. "Amunmose has set a mat and cushions on the grass and lamps under the trees. Paroi will bring more wine." Together they left the room and, accompanied by Perti and three other guards, walked the short distance to the welcoming lamplight.

"So this is where Perti ended up," one of the twins observed, flinging himself down beside his brother. Huy tried to decide which one had spoken, but failed until the other chimed in.

"We thought he'd been disgraced." This comment belonged to Suti. "One day he was drilling his favourite ten men on the practice ground and the next he and they were gone." He turned to Huy. "We regularly liked to watch the various army divisions go through their paces when our own work was done. The Scribe of Recruits allowed us to stand with him on the dais. We competed with Perti at archery, too."

"And he always beat us." Hori held out his cup to Paroi, who had emerged from the darkness. "He recognizes us but won't acknowledge us without your permission, Seer Amunhotep."

"Then be good-mannered enough to stop talking about him as though he can't hear you," Kha put in testily. He had placed his cushion between the small of his back and the trunk of a tree. "Why must you both behave as though you are still children?"

"Because their work is difficult and requires their utmost concentration," Huy said. All evening he had been quietly watching the silent, almost unconscious interplay between them. Their words were light, frivolous, but their thoughtful glances had missed no detail regarding the people around them, including himself. "They find relief in meaningless talk. Don't be concerned on my account or Captain Perti's, Kha. I have already taken their measure, as I'm sure Perti has. I'm ready to discuss the tasks the King has set us all."

There was a moment of silence. The twins stared into their wine cups. Their father folded his long legs one over the other and smoothed his kilt across his thighs.

"All three of us will be returning to Weset," he said. "It will be good to see my wife and daughters, but the duties assigned to us are heavy. The King intends to make the most ambitious changes to Amun's temple at Ipet-isut that Egypt has ever seen."

"I have already given orders that limestone from the mines at Tura must be routed south once the mines are repaired." The voice was Suti's. "I'll be demolishing the late King's sandstone court within the sacred precinct. It is not worthy of either Amun or our Pharaoh, who wants something there in white alabaster from Hatnub. I dislike designing for alabaster—it's so friable. And the obelisk that's been lying on its side unfinished for the last thirty-five years is a disgrace to the temple. It must be finished and erected."

"We're going to need Master of Works and Chief Sculptor Men, and his son Bek." Hori drained his wine in one gulp and nonchalantly held his cup out to be refilled. "I've sent to Iunu, and both of them should be on their way to Weset by now. His Majesty has ordered me to draft a plan for a new Barque Shrine in Ipet-isut, and he has his royal eye on the southern Apt a mile or two south of Ipet-isut. I've seen the ruins of a small, unfinished limestone chapel there."

"As your superior, I anticipate your designs, both of you. I assume that Men appointed his junior Masters of Works to see to the repairing and opening of the various mines." Kha turned to Huy. "You are completely in the King's confidence, therefore you are aware of his wish to build a new palace on the west bank directly opposite the temple of Ipet-isut."

"I am aware of it, and I am horrified. The Regent has stated the reasons His Majesty gave, but they seem spurious to me. The dead will not be pleased."

"Nevertheless, he has made up his mind. All three of us, Hori, Suti, and myself, will be designing it. It's true that the existing palace will eventually become too cramped." He sighed. "The design itself will take many months. In the meantime His Majesty will occupy the old palace. But before we begin our work at Weset we've been commanded to plan and erect a shrine to

Nekhbet the vulture goddess at Nekheb, at the mouth of the desert valley where the eastern gold route begins. We must depict our King's father Osiris Thothmes sitting with his son, and elsewhere the goddess herself with her protecting wings over Pharaoh."

Why? Huy wondered immediately. *Does Amunhotep feel that he needs the shield of the Lady of Flame because of his uncle? Has he always held Nekhbet in especial esteem? Did his father, and so by honouring the goddess with a new shrine, he is keeping his father's spirit peaceful? In all the time I've known him, he's never preferred one god over another, and indeed when he was a little boy he confessed to me that he found matters of religion boring. Well, I suppose that as long as he is keeping the Aten in its proper place I need not fret.*

"I didn't know that," he said aloud.

The evening was over. Full night now permeated the garden, and lamps had begun to wink off within the palace. Kha rose to his feet and his sons scrambled up at once.

Suti yawned. "I was dozing. Thank you, Great Seer, for your hospitality. We shall be seeing much more of you as the King's projects progress. We wish you safety on your journey."

I suppose that every inhabitant of the palace knows that I am travelling with the Vizier, Huy thought, returning their bows and leading them back inside, where Amunmose waited to alert their escort. *At least I don't leave tomorrow. I need poppy, and a sound sleep.*

Yey was entombed on the last day of Payni. The weather was slowly warming towards the stultifying heat of the harvest season, but the day of the funeral was mild, with a pleasant breeze. Huy, far back in the procession snaking slowly westward through the palm groves to the desert beyond, gave himself over to the delicate scents intermittently wafted to him. He had decided to attend the first day of the three-day rite out of respect for the man who had commanded such affection from the King and his mother, but he himself had not known Yey. The customary wails of the dozens of mourners in their blue sheaths trailing behind the coffin reminded him only that Yey's family was wealthy enough to hire a small army of them. He reflected briefly on the power Yey and his survivors wielded. However, the sunlight was dazzling on the churned sand ahead, the white linen held over his head billowed gently in the moving airs, and with a mild pang of guilt that was immediately dissipated he gave himself over to the pleasure of the morning.

He and his entourage returned to the palace after sunset. The halls were unusually quiet. Every minister and nobleman had gone to accompany Yey on his last journey. Huy took the opportunity to dictate a letter to Thothhotep and Anhur, telling them that Nekheb would soon be full of workmen and introducing Kha and his sons, who had already left for Weset. Nekheb was not far south of Weset, on the east side of the river. Its twin town Nekhen sat on the western bank. He was tempted to dictate a formal request for a meeting with Yuya, but before he lay his vision of Tiye's future before her father, there loomed the necessity of presenting it to the King. *Better to wait,* Huy thought as he stretched out on his mat under the shade in the deserted garden and gazed sleepily up through the thick leaves of the sycamore. *Amunhotep will doubtless pout and protest. He will capitulate in the end, of course, but there's no need to antagonize him by anticipating his surrender. I wonder if the Queen has already prepared him for the news?*

ON THE FOURTH DAY, the palace began to fill again as the inhabitants came straggling back. Their mood was light, and Huy, listening to the loud chatter and frequent bursts of laughter, knew that their cheerfulness sprang from relief. Yey was dead, left behind in the darkness, but they had survived to pick up the commonplace threads of their everyday lives. No need to fret about Ma'at's feather weighed against their hearts in the gloom of the Judgment Hall. Not yet.

As Huy emerged from his bedchamber on the fifth day, a message came from Vizier Ptahmose requesting that Huy be ready to leave Mennofer in two days, on the seventh of Epophi. Huy passed it on to Amunmose with instructions to pack his belongings. "You'll accompany me, of course," he told the steward, "along with Paneb, Ba-en-Ra, Tetiankh, and Perti and half my soldiers. I suppose Seneb will come also."

"I heard him arguing with Tetiankh. Something about your opium." Amunmose was frowning. "Seneb was trying to insist on taking charge of the portion of the shipment Tetiankh sets aside for your use during the year. The physician doesn't want Tetiankh to dry it and grind it up. Tetiankh's getting old, Huy, too old for the labour of a body servant. He needs nights of uninterrupted rest and less bending and lifting. Not to mention the effort of your daily massage."

"Why do you tell me this now?" Huy retorted more sharply than he had intended. Indeed he had always taken Tetiankh's quiet service for granted. "Is there some reason why Tetiankh can't approach me himself?"

"He's too proud. He'd rather work until he drops than admit that he needs help."

"Well, speak to him. Find him an assistant. Gods, Amunmose, it's your job to see to the welfare of my staff! Use the authority I've given you!"

Amunmose looked at him keenly. "I'm glad we're going away. You need plenty of time sitting on the deck of your barge doing absolutely nothing. Except learning Akkadian, unfortunately. The scribe Minister May has assigned to you is waiting outside in the corridor with a bag full of bits of broken pots for you to prac- tise on as though you are back at school." His tone was scornful. "Also, Physician Seneb wants to know whether morning or evening will be a more convenient time for him to examine you. Also, the Queen demands your presence in His Majesty's private apartments as soon as possible. She sent Maani-nekhtef here with the message. Huy, I need a scribe of my own!"

"Then hire one and deal with Seneb and May's servant. Both of them will travel with me. We'll need at least one other vessel besides mine. Get Paroi to see to it."

Amunmose nodded curtly. He was already barking orders as he walked away.

With his guards before and behind Paneb and himself, Huy made his way to Amunhotep's now familiar double doors, waiting while Captain Perti knocked and Chief Steward Nubti appeared and bowed, greeting him politely and ushering him inside. Before he bent in reverence, Huy noted that the room was unnaturally empty. He extended his arms, bowed from the waist, and moved towards the two at the far end. Mutemwia was sitting with her feet on a low stool, her yellow sheath falling softly across her legs and brushing the floor. A coronet of thin, twisted gold wires studded with artificial lotus buds sat on her brow above a care- fully painted face, the lustrous eyelids glinting with specks of gold dust mixed into the kohl, the perfect little mouth gleaming with red antimony rather than the more common orange henna. Rings weighed down her thin fingers. A tiny silver likeness of the vulture goddess Mut, consort of Amun and Mutemwia's totem, hung from one lobe. Huy, going to his knees, thought with a throb of distress that she had never looked more regal.

Amunhotep was standing beside her chair, feet apart and sturdy arms folded. A starched linen helmet of white and blue stripes brushed his shoulders. Its rim, surmounted by a small rearing cobra with its hood flared, cut across his forehead. *The Lady of Dread, ready to spit venom at any who might wish him harm*, Huy told himself as the King gave him permission to straighten. *Why are they both arrayed with such powerful symbols of divine defence? Are they protecting themselves against me?* Amunhotep strode towards Huy with a broad smile, however, and Huy's nostrils filled with the scent of rosemary as he was embraced.

"I'm almost as tall as you are, Uncle Huy!" Amunhotep exclaimed. "And did you remember that my Anniversary of Appearing is almost upon us? You'll have left with Ptahmose by then, but I expect you to open the shrine in your cabin and offer incense to Amun on my behalf. My father died on the fifteenth of Mesore. Thus I ascended to godhead. Leave us, Nubti."

The steward bowed and went out, closing the door behind him. For the first time Huy noticed Mutemwia's personal scribe Nefer-ka-Ra, sitting cross-legged on the floor a little apart from her. His ink pot was open, papyrus unrolled across the surface of his palette, and a brush was in his hand. At Huy's motion Paneb sank down beside his fellow and began his own preparations. Amunhotep swung back to Mutemwia's chair. She had not stirred, merely acknowledging Huy's veneration with a brief nod, but their eyes had met. Huy looked quickly away.

"So, Uncle," the King continued. "My Mother tells me that you have had a vision concerning me. She has refused to say anything about it, although I've begged and threatened her, but it seems that she relents today. Yey has gone to the Beautiful West and we mourn for him no longer. Speak!" His words were light, joking, but beneath them Huy sensed the young man's apprehension. He was tense himself.

"Sit if you wish, Huy." The voice was the Queen's. She was watching Huy with composure, her hands clasped loosely in her lap.

Huy declined. "The vision concerns you," he said to Amunhotep directly, "but the Seeing was for Yey's granddaughter Tiye, at her request and with the permission of her father the noble Yuya."

Amunhotep grimaced. "Poor Uncle Huy! What a burdensome task for you! I hope your vision showed you that evil goose of hers taking after her for a change. It slips its leash far too often and attacks anyone it pleases, including me, but my Mother won't allow me to order it beheaded and stuffed for one of my feasts. I swear Tiye sets it against me on purpose. Now." His expression became solemn. "Tell me how a Seeing for Yuya's daughter can have anything to do with me."

"I didn't expect it to, Majesty. Indeed I anticipated a very simple, perhaps even frivolous glance into the girl's future for which I needed no permission from you. However, the god showed me something momentous."

The boy had begun to drum his fingers impatiently against the back of his mother's chair. Mutemwia herself had not stirred. Her gaze remained fixed on Huy. He could not read the thoughts behind it. With an inward sigh, he went on.

"Atum desires that Tiye should become your wife," he said deliberately. "I Saw her beside you at Ipet-isut, crowned and clad in gold, on the day your Mother relinquishes her authority as Regent and you become a divine Incarnation. She was wearing the vulture headdress of female royalty, and gold and lapis hung from her earlobes. Mut's claws held shen signs. You yourself were holding the crook and the flail in protection and blessing over the crowd. No matter how strange this seems," he pressed on as the King's fingers were stilled and his spine stiffened, "the will of the god is clear. For your own sake and for the health of Egypt, you must sign a marriage contract with Yuya's daughter."

He had imagined a violent outburst from Amunhotep and had

steeled himself for whatever reaction his words would cause, but he was unprepared for the silence that fell, in which his voice seemed loud and domineering before it died away. Mutemwia remained still. So did the King. Huy, watching him carefully, saw his eyes gradually narrow. Presently he folded his arms, but the silence continued. Huy saw that he was thinking furiously, his hennaed lips pursing and relaxing, looking at Huy with a slitted gaze but not seeing him. At last he exhaled noisily, stepped from behind his mother, and sat, waving Huy down at the same time. Huy obeyed, bemused. Obviously there would be no display of royal bluster. Amunhotep crossed one leg over the other and leaned towards Huy.

"My trust in you has never been tested before," he said, "but now I am forced to examine all the years behind us to assure myself that your own honesty has always been genuinely selfless. Year after year my Mother the Queen placed me in your care. She trusted you enough to guide my education during the months I spent on your estate, plant in me a reverence for the laws of Ma'at, rebuke my arrogance, and correct my childish restlessness. I came to love you, but was that because you set out to conquer the affections of a boy who would one day be a King? Bind me in affection to serve your own ambition for the future?"

Huy listened to him appalled, wanting to refute such insanity at once, but out of the corner of his eye he saw Mutemwia raise one hand, a quick gesture Amunhotep did not see, and he kept quiet.

"My Mother the Queen warns me often that a pharaoh may trust no one, that in the end the Incarnation of the god can rely on no advice but that of the god," Amunhotep continued huskily. His hennaed palms drew apart, an evidence of doubt. "This instruction from Atum, this glimpse of what must come, it could be a plot hatched out between you and Yuya to place both of you in positions of immense power." Suddenly he buried his face in his hands. "How may I know the truth?" he groaned. "Today I realize that in fact I do trust no one, not even you, my Mother."

Mutemwia made no move to touch him. However, she laid her arms along the arms of her chair and turned to look at him. "You need to trust no one and nothing but the accumulation of evidence, Amunhotep," she said crisply. "Firstly, my spies confirm that Huy has visited Yuya's house only once, and that was with us, to greet Yey before he died. Secondly, they confirm that Tiye caused a nuisance at Huy's door in the night, that Huy had her escorted home immediately, that Yuya punished her but gave her permission to request a Seeing, and that Huy Scryed for her only once. His recovery took two days. If you paid more attention to the daily reports of both your ministers and our spies, you would know these things yourself instead of being content to hear them from me. You may thank the gods that I am to be trusted. As for Egypt's Great Seer, why would he attempt to ingratiate himself with the Lady Tiye and her family when he already enjoys the esteem of a King?"

Amunhotep had lifted his head and was staring at her. She rapped him smartly but gently on the cheek with the back of her hand. "You are almost thirteen years old," she chided him. "In three years' time the Horus Throne and absolute power in Egypt will be entirely yours. Wake up! Listen to me, to Huy, to your ministers, with more than one ear tuned to the urgings of your friends who want you to spend your time careening in your chariot out on the desert. I think that I have been too lenient with you. Today the Seer has woken me. Do you intend to trust him or not?"

Huy saw no sign of resentment on the King's face in spite of Mutemwia's tongue-lashing. Instead he recognized an expression of serious consideration that returned him briefly and vividly to the halcyon years when he oversaw the tutoring of his royal charge during the months of the Inundation.

"I hear you, my Mother," Amunhotep said.

He reached across and touched Huy's wrist, a charmingly tentative action that filled Huy with warmth. *This is the child I know, the kind-hearted boy I remember.*

"Uncle Huy, I truly dislike Tiye. Are you sure it was her that you Saw? Why her, a commoner, and not my sister Iaret, who is fully royal and quite legitimately claims pre-eminence? Not that I like her either—she whines a great deal—but marriage to her would reinforce my seat on the Horus Throne."

So Amunhotep still doubts his blood-uncle's desire to relinquish any right to govern Egypt, Huy thought. *Does Mutemwia?* "It was definitely the Lady Tiye," he replied, "and Majesty, the Atum did not see fit to acquaint me with the reasons for his choice. All I know is that, commoner or not, you are to make her Chief Wife."

"You do realize that if I marry Tiye I'll be giving her family precedence over every other noble in Egypt," Amunhotep commented. "The title Yuya has inherited, Chief Rekhit, will be more than just an acknowledgement of gratitude to Yey and now to Yuya. Must I truly do this thing?" He rose and stood irresolute. "I suppose that Atum's reasons will eventually become clear, and if I disobey the god I will certainly incur a punishment. May I consider the matter for a while, become used to it, before the Minister for Protocol draws up a contract?" His grin was rueful. "At least I won't be expected to do my duty and consummate the union at once, and by then there will be concubines to compensate me. Are you sure of what you Saw, Uncle Huy? I am shocked by this astonishing turn my life must take."

Huy also left his chair, and bowed. "Majesty, if you wish, I will See for you," he offered. "You must have no qualms regarding such an important matter."

The young man's eyes were clouded as they met Huy's. "If you have lied to me about Tiye's Seeing, then you can just as easily fabricate a vision for me. Perhaps I should consult one of my astrologers. All they do so far is tell me which third of each day is lucky and which unlucky. They all promised me a very lucky beginning to this morning, but they did not say why."

"It's your privilege to command an answer from the oil in the Anubis bowl," Huy replied. "In any event, make a sacrifice for clarity of mind to Atum, and to Amun also. I leave very soon for a tour of the Delta with Ptahmose, so your decision is required by the time I return. Forgive me for distressing you, Majesty, but believe that I have spoken the truth. Egypt will need you and Tiye together. Please dismiss me now."

Amunhotep nodded. Thankfully, Huy backed out of the room, Nubti entered, and the doors were closed.

THE VIZIER'S FLOTILLA left Mennofer at dawn two days later. Five barges were strung out in the centre of a river whose level was slowly dropping towards the sullen current that would hopefully presage the annual Inundation. Huy's two barges followed those of Ptahmose. To Huy's relief, his nephew had decided to bring up the rear in his own vessel. "I can't cram my staff in with yours, Uncle," he had told Huy the day before, "and there'll be no room on your barge for me, my scribe, or my guards. I refuse to share the common servants' space. I usually make this annual inspection aboard the Vizier's barge, but the Regent has requested that you sail with him instead." His tone had made it clear that he resented giving place to Huy, who responded with a polite apology and a sense of liberation.

So Huy sat and talked with Ptahmose under the large awning set up on the deck of the Vizier's boat while their scribes and body servants drank beer in the shade of the cabin and the rowers moved them slowly past the dusty, drooping palms lining the banks. Beyond the trees, the air was often thick with chaff from the scythes and billhooks of the reapers who moved across the golden fields, the crops falling before them. But soon the Delta harvest of blooms took the place of barley and wheat, wafting the mingled scents of narcissus, lilies, jasmine, the aromatic tang of heliotrope, and a dozen others, forcibly returning Huy to the days of his childhood when his father had toiled for his uncle in fields like these.

Vizier Ptahmose was a charming, approachable man and Huy was soon entirely at ease in his presence. He could speak as knowledgeably about Egypt's attempts to grow and harvest frankincense as about the strengths and weaknesses of the governors who answered to him. "Her Majesty the Regent has asked me to acquaint you fully with the responsibilities of my position," he told Huy. "Your nephew knows them well. In the past he has accompanied me on my tours of duty while he saw to his own task of military inspection. However, Her Majesty wishes you to form your own opinion regarding the forces patrolling Ta-Mehu before you hear any report from the Scribe of Recruits." He had cast a humorous sidelong glance at Huy. "Her Majesty says that she commanded your nephew to take you into every fort, garrison, and encampment over which he has jurisdiction, but to make no comment to you whatsoever regarding the officers and men you meet, or their deployment. I believe that your nephew has not yet spoken of this to you?" The tactful words were partly a question.

"Amunhotep-Huy and I have little but our blood in common," Huy replied heavily. "I love him as my brother Heby's son and I remember the difficulties of his childhood. I wish him only good. Although we are not close, I do know that where his loyalty to Egypt and to the King is concerned, he is an honest man. He will tell me of the Regent's injunction when he is ready to do so."

"Her Majesty spends much time pondering the future of this country," the Vizier responded with seeming irrelevance. "We will see many changes in the months to come."

The city of Iunu, where Thothmes was Governor of the Heq-at sepat, was their first stop. Huy, Ptahmose, and Amunhotep-Huy disembarked in the brilliant red of a late sunset to be greeted respectfully by Thothmes' elder son. Bowing first to the Vizier, the young man indicated the litters resting on the broad watersteps. "You are expected, noble ones," he said. "A meal has been prepared for you."

"Assistant Governor Huy," Ptahmose responded with a smile. "Of course you know the Great Seer and his nephew, the Scribe of Recruits."

Huy embraced his namesake with delight. "You look more like your father every day! I trust he is in good health? And Ishat?"

They chatted as they moved towards the litters resting above the wide public watersteps. The Vizier had a litter to himself, but Huy was forced to share one with Amunhotep-Huy, who refused to answer Huy's attempts at light conversation as they set off, and looked so miserable that Huy reluctantly asked him if he was well.

"There is nothing wrong with my body, Uncle," Amunhotep-Huy blurted as though he had been waiting for an opportunity to unburden himself. "But I am troubled in my mind."

Startled, Huy looked across at him. In all the years Huy had known him, he had never once confided anything of importance. The litter's curtains had remained tied back. The evening was still and hot. Red dust from the sandy street rose in thin clouds from the feet of the accompanying soldiers, and Huy could hear Paneb's deep, measured tones and Perti's lighter answers as they strode behind the bearers. Amunhotep-Huy leaned closer. Huy could smell his sweat mingled with the faint scent of sam flowers.

He had time to wonder at his nephew's choice of wild wormwood blooms for perfume before Amunhotep-Huy passed a tentative hand over his shaven skull. His brown shoulders were hunched.

"Yours are not the ears I would choose, but there's no one else I can ask about this," he went on huskily. "At least you have a reputation for keeping your counsel. I am the Scribe of Recruits. I am known for my forceful speech and strong decisions. By my own diligence and with help from my military tutor, Officer Irem, I won a position as a scribe in the palace, and then as an under steward. You didn't know that, did you?" For a moment the usual caustic quality sharpened his speech, but Huy had merely begun to shake his head when Amunhotep-Huy plunged on. "Then Her Majesty the Regent became aware of the time I spent enjoying the company of the soldiers and was pleased to promote me yet again, to my present position as Scribe of Recruits. I am responsible for administering the army and navy and regulating the defence of the Delta. I enjoy my work. I do it well."

He bit his lip and fell briefly silent, obviously struggling for words of anxiety that must surely, Huy thought, be foreign to him. Huy was entirely bemused by this uncharacteristic outburst. *I could point out that every member of our family received a preferment when I was summoned to court,* he thought. *Your father became Mayor of Mennofer and Overseer of the Cattle of Amun, not to mention the added prestige of being appointed Overseer of the Two Granaries of Amun in the Sepats of Ta-Mehu. Your half-brother Ramose was made steward in the Mansion of the Aten at Iunu although he was only eleven at the time, a wise and crafty way for Mutemwia to ensure the loyalty of a future spy among the devotees of that god. Certainly Her Majesty fixed upon your talent, my cantankerous young relative, but her true incentive was to lure me into her service.* Huy said none of these things. He waited for Amunhotep-Huy to compose himself. At last the handsome features so like those of his father were turned down to the fingers clasped tightly across the burly thighs.

"But now Her Majesty summons me and tells me that I am to accompany you—not that you are to accompany me—with Vizier Ptahmose as he holds his annual consultations," Amunhotep-Huy continued, his voice uneven. "Everyone at court knows that you have her ear and that your influence over the King is absolute. I decided that perhaps you had petitioned His Majesty for the position of Vizier instead of Ptahmose. I thought nothing of it."

No, of course you didn't, Huy wanted to snap at him, his temper rising. "You do not know me at all if you think—" Huy began, but Amunhotep-Huy cut him short. Hot fingers closed over Huy's wrist.

"That wasn't it at all!" he said urgently. "I am to take you into every fort, every garrison, I am to make every officer in the Delta aware of you, I am even to travel with you east along the Horus Road, and I am not to say one single word regarding the deployments I have effected or the reasons why I have chosen to distribute the troops in the manner you will see! The gods know that I do not yet hate you, Uncle, in spite of our differences, but if my position as Scribe of Recruits is taken away from me and given to you, the Queen's willing lapdog, I shall beg Set for vengeance!" His voice had risen and he had begun to shake.

Huy hushed him savagely, aware that the men surrounding them were now quiet. He pulled himself loose from his nephew's clutch. "I have always known of your antipathy towards me," he said, fighting the surge of anger that threatened to spill over into words that could never be withdrawn. "I have never understood it, unless its roots lie somewhere in your discontented childhood. You do me a terrible disservice if you truly believe that I would deliberately seek to undermine you. I have no desire whatsoever to take your title away. Think, Amunhotep-Huy! You have already been promoted three times. Have you no confidence in your ability? In the Regent's wisdom? Your assumption is nothing but a fantasy."

"I do not trust you!"

"You should. I came to you, seeking your advice regarding my need for a suitable captain. You agreed that no matter what hostility lay between us, a loyalty to the family came first. You remember?"

"Yes."

"Her Majesty understands that allegiance. She will not force a choice on me between my duty to my family and my duty to Egypt, because she acknowledges my honesty. Where's your courage and the faith you have in your own talents, nephew? Do you want me to See for you after all?"

"That is not necessary," the other said stiffly. "I apologize for my loss of self-control."

The bearers were slowing. Amunhotep-Huy was struggling to recover his composure as quickly as possible, and dismally Huy realized that in confessing his inmost fear to him and thus his vulnerability, his nephew would now hate him all the more.

His reunion with his two oldest friends and their remaining children was joyful, and Huy filed away the painful exchange with Amunhotep-Huy to the back of his consciousness as he embraced each one and allowed himself to be led into Thothmes' reception hall. To his great pleasure another familiar figure rose from among the scattering of little gilded dining tables, goblet in hand, a cluster of blue faience cornflowers pinned behind one ear. "Nasha!" he called, and hurrying towards one another, they hugged fiercely. Thothmes' older sister smelled of wine and Susinum, a blend of lilies, myrrh, and cinnamon in balanos oil, which Huy seldom encountered.

"You never write to me," Nasha complained as they drew apart. "Here I am, bored and lonely, rattling around in the house next door, reduced to playing with my jewellery and dyeing my hair, while you share the exalted confidences of our young King and think yourself too good for us ordinary folk!" She raised herself on her toes and kissed his cheek. "You must eat beside the Vizier and then talk of serious things with him and Thothmes in the office, but afterwards we have planned to drink the rest of the night away on Thothmes' raft. You remember the last time we did that, Huy? It was after the celebration of Thothmes' marriage to Ishat. Father was dying. Those few days were a strange mixture of sadness and pleasure."

A lump formed in Huy's throat as he looked down into her painted face. The eyes were as sparkling and alive as ever, speaking to him of Nasha's indomitable and optimistic nature, but her age had become increasingly evident in the sagging of her cheeks and the lines around her hennaed mouth.

"You should have married, dear one," he said. "The gods know, you had suitors enough!"

She wrinkled her nose. "They all had something wrong with them. Besides, I have father's house and estate. Why should I share the riches? We can talk later."

Thothmes' steward had approached and was waiting politely to show Huy to his table, and as Huy followed him one of Thothmes' servant girls reached up and laid a wreath of quivering blooms around his neck.

The feast was a happy one, full of banter and good conversation. Even Amunhotep-Huy, sitting on Ishat's left, became flushed with Thothmes' wine and hummed to the music of the harp and drum as the sweet nehet figs in date syrup were offered and the warm night air made the lamp flames tremble in their alabaster cups.

Afterwards, Thothmes, Huy, Ptahmose, and Amunhotep-Huy, together with their scribes, gathered in the office, and Thothmes in his capacity as Governor gave the Vizier an overview of the business of the sepat: the quantity and estimated value of the various harvests still in progress, the legal disputes adjudicated, the advancement of building projects, any problems concerning the administration of both secular and religious institutions, and the overall mood of the populace in general. There were few areas of concern. Iunu was an ancient and wealthy city, its priests and nobles content, its commoners well fed, and the peasant farmers and retired soldiers coaxed abundant fruits and vegetables out of the fertile soil. Huy, watching his friend's sensitive and intelligent face, found himself giving thanks to Atum for the warmth and intimacy that had been his since his childhood days at school here in the temple of Ra, when he and Thothmes had been drawn together, the peasant and the noble's son, and Thothmes' family had made him one of their own.

When Ptahmose and his attendants had returned to the barge, Huy dismissed Paneb, and arm in arm with Thothmes he walked to the watersteps, where torches blazed, illuminating a raft piled with cushions and rocking gently. Amunhotep-Huy had refused Thothmes' invitation to join them. "You and the rest of my uncle's friends will doubtless while away the hours in reminiscences, Governor Thothmes," he had pointed out. "I thank you for your hospitality, but I think I'll retire to my cot."

"He is not a happy man, is he, Huy?" Thothmes had remarked as they watched the darkness gradually swallow up Amunhotep-Huy's rigid spine. "How's the rest of your family, by the way? Heby and Iupia? What's your other nephew, Ramose, doing?"

A peace stole over Huy as he lowered himself onto the raft between Ishat and Nasha. Much as he loved Thothmes' children, he was glad that none of them had joined the group. True to

Amunhotep-Huy's prediction, there were memories to share, but much of the talk centred around Huy's daily life in the palace.

"Who would have thought that the awkward boy with the inarticulate passion for our sister Anuket was destined to advise the King himself," Nasha commented at one point. "You must be incurring a flood of jealousy among His Majesty's other counsellors." Huy answered her lightly, examining himself as he spoke for any remaining vestige of the obsession for Thothmes' manipulative younger sister that had almost destroyed him. He found nothing but a faint echo from the past, and gave himself up to the familiar pleasures of the present company.

Ptahmose's advance through the sepats of the Delta followed much the same pattern as his visit to Iunu. In the centre of each district, whether city or town, he, Huy, and Amunhotep-Huy were feasted, the business of local government was discussed, and the following morning the barges would set off to negotiate whatever tributary of the river they must follow. During the idle hours Ptahmose gave Huy his personal assessment of the loyalty and efficiency of the various governors, his thoughts on the resolution of their difficulties, and a brief sketch of their family histories. Huy listened, noted, and formed his own opinions. He was aware of the Delta as never before—a vast, lush garden where fat livestock grazed, where the air, heavy with the humidity of the many rivulets and canals in spite of the time of year, carried the odours of a riotous fecundity to his delighted nostrils. Both Amun's overseers and those of the King pastured their herds here, but Huy began to notice many small flocks of sheep and groups of fat swine occupying the grassy fields. Their guardians, wearing rough skirts and thick cloaks, stared at them impassively as the barges slipped by.

"Tribesmen from Rethennu," Ptahmose told him. "I don't suppose you would have encountered them at Hut-herib when your father worked in the perfume fields. They like to keep their animals grazing fairly close to the Horus Road. The governors of our northeastern sepats are endlessly settling quarrels that arise between our farmers and the slaves over the use of the land." Any non-citizen or seasonal labourer from beyond Egypt's borders was called a slave. It was a light, rather scornful word, and Ptahmose's tone was condescending.

"I know it's been the custom for hentis to let them in," Huy said. "How many drive their herds into the Delta along the Horus Road?"

Ptahmose shrugged. "You must ask your nephew. My only concern is whether or not my governors are handling the situation."

Huy was about to remind the Vizier that during a dark time in Egypt's history those same tribesmen had managed to take control of the country without a drop of blood being shed and had ruled for more than two hundred years, but he closed his mouth again. *Better to see for myself, to talk to the garrison commanders. The Queen will expect the information I glean to be in my report.* Reluctantly he turned from the pleasant scenery slipping slowly by to May's scribe, waiting patiently by his elbow. Huy's lessons in Akkadian, the language of diplomacy, were progressing well. The meaning of the stark, thin symbols was much easier to learn than the tangle of hieroglyphs he had struggled with in school.

Once the Delta sepats were behind them, the barges were left in the care of Ptahmose's captain and the litters were readied. The way led northeast along the Horus Road that began in the Khent-abt district and ran through the marshy Sea of Reeds, well-nigh impassable during the Inundation, towards the coast. It then curved east to disappear into Rethennu and the foreign terrain beyond. The garrisons set every few miles along it began at once. Huy expected to see a military presence between them, but there was none. The Road was choked with the flow of animals and their keepers leaving Egypt to return home before the Inundation drowned the rich fields they had enjoyed, and the Vizier's entourage moved slowly in spite of the guards who walked ahead, calling a warning. Huy did not mind. There was time for a leisurely look at a swiftly changing topography, and the bearded herdsmen in their garish colours fascinated him. At each garrison, after the obeisances and a hospitable meal, he listened to the report given to Amunhotep-Huy. Paneb quietly noted it down. Huy had questions of his own regarding the policing of the Road. How were the foreigners controlled? Were daily records kept of their numbers coming and going? How often were the soldiers manning the garrisons rotated? The answers to the last question began to bother him. Many of the men were mercenaries, returning regularly to their native territories. These were places that paid tribute to Egypt or, more rarely, were governed directly by one of Pharaoh's resident ministers.

"Every garrison is commanded by an Egyptian officer," Amunhotep-Huy had responded testily to Huy's query. "The men under them are entitled to a piece of Egyptian soil when they're too old to fight. What better incentive is there to keep them loyal to us?"

Huy thought his attitude naive but consistent with his character. Harsh discipline and the promise of reward would be sufficient to maintain order in the garrisons. A more subtle lure leading to treason or revolt would not occur to him. *Is our army full of mercenaries also?* Huy wondered. *And what of the navy?* Ptahmose had struck out east before any inspection of the coastal forts had been made. He considered the state of Egypt's eastern dependencies more important, probably quite rightly. Huy decided to travel the northernmost shore roads of the Delta by himself if necessary.

Ptahmose held meetings in Rethennu not only with the Governor and his assistant stationed there but also with the chieftains of the tribes whose members were permitted temporary entrance into the Delta. Collectively the Vizier called them the Habiri, but Huy heard how politely he gave each his title. He knew all their names and the names of their elder sons, those who would inherit both the control of the tribes and the yoke of Egyptian domination. Without exception they grumbled at the amount of cedar wood Egypt demanded, and to a lesser extent at the number of cattle included in the annual tax. Ptahmose dealt with them tactfully but firmly. There were no forts within Rethennu's borders, but the Governor maintained a large contingent of Egyptian infantry. Huy approved. "What lies beyond this land?" he asked the Vizier as the three of them, Ptahmose, Amunhotep-Huy, and himself, walked towards the tents that had been set up for them.

"Zahi and Shinar," he was told, "Apra, Amurru, and a few small collections of unimportant clans between the Amurru and the kingdom of Mitanni. We deal with the Amurru diplomatically. Her Majesty periodically sends soldiers to both the Amurru and the city state of Byblos to help discourage any plans of southward expansion that Mitanni might concoct. They provide a buffer between Mitanni and Rethennu. Are you confused yet, Great Seer?"

No, Huy was not confused. A rapidly growing map of Egypt's strengths and weaknesses was being etched in his mind. It seemed to him that although Ptahmose was an excellent Vizier, his interest did not extend into conjecture beyond the limits of his responsibility.

Huy did not like Rethennu. Its mountains were clothed in the precious woods Egypt needed, but it was on the whole a bare, unlovely place, the ground sharp underfoot with gravel, the growth of fodder sparse on the foothills. He understood why so many slaves, non-citizens, chose to drive their livestock into the verdant little hayfields of Ta-Mehu. He was relieved when Ptahmose gave the order to retrace their journey along the Horus Road.

At the city of Per-Bastet, sited on the main eastern tributary of the Delta and home to the cat goddess Bast, they amicably parted company. It was necessary for Amunhotep-Huy to inspect the forts and army training centres as far as Swenet, far to the south, and the Vizier had to continue his own assessment of the middle and southern governorships. "I usually make my head-quarters at Pe when I evaluate the annual state of the navy," Amunhotep-Huy told Huy, "and I do it well before the Inundation. This year you'll have to take my place. The noble Nebenkempt is our Naval Troop Commander. A good man and an able sailor. He captains the royal barge *Kha-em-Ma'at* when it's needed. You also need to speak with Standard Bearer Hatmesha. He commands two hundred and fifty marines, but there's no one who knows more about the history of the navy and its current state. Good luck, Uncle."

His manner had been offhand and he would not meet Huy's eye. Paneb was rapidly taking down the information in his neat hieratic script. Huy had wanted to ask his nephew to carry his greetings to the noble Amunnefer, his partner in the cultivation and harvest of the opium crops, and to visit Thothhotep and Anhur at their home in Nekheb, but thought better of it. He bade both men farewell, climbed aboard his barge with an inward sigh of relief, and began to read over the information Paneb had accumulated. May's scribe had accompanied him in order to continue his lessons, but Huy hardly needed him anymore. Akkadian was a very logical language.

7

HUY RETURNED TO A PALACE agog with the news that on the first day of the month of Thoth the King had signed a marriage contract with the daughter of his most senior nobleman. Tiye and her mother Thuyu had been moved to the harem. With a shock Huy realized that he had been away from Mennofer for almost two months. Every harvest was in. The land lay parched and bare, waiting for the benison of the Inundation. Mutemwia had chosen a most auspicious day for such a momentous occasion, Huy reflected. The first of Thoth was New Year's Day. It was also the day when worship for the god Thoth began with universal rejoicing, and continued more quietly until the next month, Paophi, began. *In spite of her objections to the match, she has obviously trusted my vision,* Huy's thoughts ran on as he sat in his reception room with the chaos of unpacking going on around him. *She put the matter before Yuya without waiting for my return. This is good.*

Under Steward Paroi was hovering close by. Amunmose was trying to bring order to the laden servants milling about. Huy had given Paneb, as a scribe, permission to take his annual gift to Thoth's shrine, and so it was Paroi who patiently clutched a sheaf of scrolls. Huy wanted to be bathed, but Tetiankh was busy putting Huy's clothing and jewellery away. Resignedly Huy beckoned Paroi close. "It's good to see your sober face again, Paroi. Please tell me that those letters are utterly unimportant."

Paroi bowed and, taking the chair opposite Huy, tipped the scrolls onto the table between them. "I thank the gods that you have returned to us in good health, Master," the man replied. "We have no heart when you are away. Indeed, Amunmose has dealt with most of these scrolls." He poked through them. "There is a report from the noble Amunnefer in Weset regarding your poppy investment. The quality of the opium is slowly improving and the harvest has been copious. He has hired another expert in the cultivation of the plant from Keftiu. This man advocates leaving the juice on the pods for a few more days to increase its potency, and the transplanting done so far is not rigorous enough. The noble Amunnefer has petitioned the King for additional land to enlarge the venture. He asks for more gold in the event that he is allowed to do so."

"I can read all that for myself. What else? Is there any news from my caravan?"

"Not yet. The myrrh must come from a long way away, Master. The Prince of Ipu has sent you a formal expression of gratitude for advancing his daughter's prospects. There is no need for an acknowledgement." It took Huy a moment to remember that Tiye's father Yuya held the honorary and hereditary title of Prince, and his fiefdom was far to the south in the Akhmin sepat. "The Lady Tiye herself has asked for an audience with you at your earliest convenience."

"Has she indeed? Put that scroll aside and when Paneb comes back from his devotions I'll deal with it. Anything more? If not, tell Tetiankh I need a wash and my drug."

"There is this. I offer my condolences, Master. I did not know this man, but Amunmose did. He is grieving." Paroi rose and bowed again. "I will send Tetiankh to you."

A shadow seemed to pass through the room. Huy glanced up sharply, but nothing had changed. *Anhur*, he thought as he fingered the papyrus Paroi had handed him. *Anhur my friend, my protector. I had hoped to put my arms around you yet again, but you have gone to be with Osiris, and left me.* Unrolling the scroll, he recognized Thothhotep's confident hand. His own hands were cold. The noise in the room ceased, all but for his former scribe's voice, as he read. "My dear Master," she had written.

I am sorry to give you this sad news. Anhur is dead. He was taken to the House of the Dead for Beautification here in Nekheb yesterday. I was unable to write until today. I mourn him and miss him as I know you will, but at the end he was gasping for every breath and my only consolation is that he has passed through the Judgment Hall with his full health restored. I beg you to send me a letter. Thothhotep, by my own hand, this thirtieth day of Epophi, Year One of the King.

Huy let the scroll roll up and closed his eyes. Gradually he became aware of the cheerful din around him, but under it he was an anxious child again, standing at the massive entrance to Thoth's temple in Khmun with Anhur's comforting presence beside him. He could smell the leather of Anhur's jerkin, and if he turned his head he knew he would see that weatherbeaten face with its bright brown eyes looking down at him. *Anhur never minced his words*, Huy remembered, a lump in his throat. *He spoke his mind, a soldier's mind, practical and yet with a wisdom on which I came to rely. The King loved him too. Anhur taught him to fish and wrestle, and let him ride about the garden of my estate on his shoulders. He will be as sad as I.* Sensing someone close by, he opened his eyes. Amunmose was bending over him.

"I want him back the way he was, Huy," the steward said. "I want to be home in your house and hearing his footsteps walking the hallway in the middle of the night. I want to sit with him and drink beer on hot afternoons. I want to see him watching over you in that unobtrusive way he had when we ventured out. Will you at least invite his wife back into your employ? Can we have Thothhotep here after we've mourned for Anhur?"

Huy came to his feet. Amunmose was doing his best to control his expression, and at the sight of his struggle Huy felt his own tears begin. He threw his arms around Amunmose, holding him tightly, and with a sob Amunmose responded. Gradually the clamour in the room died away. Huy's servants stood nonplussed, watching their master and the man who gave them their orders every morning weep on each other's shoulders.

By the time Paneb returned from Thoth's shrine, Huy had been bathed and had drunk his poppy. The scribe glanced swiftly at Huy's swollen eyes before politely lowering his gaze and folding onto his mat at Huy's feet. Huy waited while Paneb prepared his palette for the dictation. *I was leaving the Delta for Rethennu on the day Anhur died. The twenty-ninth of Epophi, and the harvest in full swing. Osiris's harvest also, although I did not know it. Today is the fourth of Thoth. The astrologers wait to see the rising of the Sopdet star, and with it the first eddies of the coming Inundation. Thothhotep has been observing the customs of mourning for thirty-five days. She will see Anhur entombed in another thirty-five. If I set off at once, do I have enough time to reach Nekheb by then? How far from Mennofer? Four hundred, five hundred miles? My sailors would be pulling against the current of the Inundation, but I must try.*

He began to dictate a reply to Thothhotep, not trusting himself to put brush to paper. His hands were still cold and shaking. Pouring out his love for Anhur, he told her that he was sending gold for the sem priests who were even now attending to

Anhur's preservation, and begged her to return to his employ. "Seal it and give it to Ba-en-Ra with instructions to leave for Nekheb immediately," he said as Paneb passed the papyrus up to him to sign. "Go to Amunmose and ask him for a pouch of gold to include with it. If no request for my presence comes from the Regent this evening, send a formal appeal for an audience with her on my behalf. I can't deal with anything else today, Paneb. I'm going to my couch. Tell Captain Perti to keep everyone away from me."

Walking into his bedchamber, he closed the door and opened his little shrine to Khenti-kheti, the totem of Hut-herib. In spite of the debt he owed to the creator-god Atum, who had raised him from death when he was twelve, he seldom prayed to him. With returning life had come the gift of Seeing and the curse of a eunuch's existence, an inability to engage in the act of sex. As a young man Huy had tried to rid himself of this blight, to no avail; Atum's proscription had remained firm. So had Huy's grudge against the god, an emotion that had moderated considerably over the years but had not entirely dissipated. The sight of Khenti-kheti's long crocodile snout emerging from the shrine always reminded Huy of his childhood, of long, carefree days as the spoilt only child of adoring parents, of playing with Ishat in the orchard amongst the sweet aroma of spring blossoms, of Khenti-kheti's priest Methen, who had found him naked and terrified outside Hut-herib's House of the Dead and had carried him to his father's house.

Huy put a sliver of charcoal in the cup of the long incense holder and lit it. While waiting for it to turn to hot ash, he allowed his memory to wander back to the time when Anhur had come to the estate with his ten soldiers, and the friendship between the apprehensive boy and the battle-hardened man, begun years before, became firm. Huy sprinkled a few grains of frankincense onto the

ash and at once the room began to fill with a haze of fragrant yet
unsweetened smoke. Reverently he censed Khenti-kheti's likeness,
laid down the holder, and, prostrating himself, prayed for Anhur's
ka, his khu-spirit, and his heart. Knowing that a man only came
into being when his name was pronounced for the first time, and if
his name was not carved or written so that the gods could find and
recognize him, he then ceased to exist, Huy repeated Anhur's name
many times to his totem.

When he had finished his prayers, he closed the shrine and lay
on his couch with his hands behind his head. He was tired but
did not want to sleep. The memories of his life with Anhur filled
him, vivid and satisfying, slowly blunting his grief and bringing
him a morsel of peace. He was still awake when Tetiankh
knocked on the door and entered with a tray of fresh fruits and
goat cheese, which he set beside Huy's hip. "The Regent has
summoned you, Master," he said. "There is time for you to eat
and for me to braid your hair and apply your face paint. Their
Majesties will be dining with the ambassador from Mitanni for
some hours yet. It is a meal they share with him regularly." Huy
sat up and, finding himself hungry, began to eat.

He and Paneb were admitted to the King's quarters several
hours after sunset. The corridors were choked with revellers and
their servants coming and going, their jewels glinting in the
torchlight, their carefully kohled eyes flicking to Huy and away
again before they accorded him a bow that released clouds of
perfume from their filmy linens and starched white kilts. Huy
acknowledged their reverences while Perti called his advance
and the stream of humanity parted. "They are celebrating a small
rise in the level of the river," Paneb explained in answer to Huy's
query. "Isis has begun to cry, and the priests have proclaimed the
rising of the Sopdet star at last."

So Ma'at is content with her realm, Huy said to himself as Perti slowed before the King's huge double doors. *The equilibrium between cosmic and earthly principles is being maintained.*

Nubti ushered the two men inside with a smile and a swift obeisance, his misshapen left shoulder blade no more than a hint of distortion until he turned to precede Huy into the long, lamplit room. The King was sitting sprawled in a chair, one braceleted arm slunk over its back and his legs crossed. Beneath the paint on his face Huy thought he looked tired. *He has a great deal to contend with and he's only just turned thirteen,* Huy told himself as he walked forward and knelt to prostrate himself. Mutemwia, looking as ethereal as a cloud in floating white linen, rose from her own chair. Tiny silver vultures hung from the circlet around her brow and from her earlobes. A wide plate of silver studded with deep blue lapis flowers covered her breasts, and pellets of lapis dotted her sandals. A large ankh hung from the centre of her thin, silver-linked belt.

"Rise, Uncle Huy," Amunhotep said. "I've missed you and worried about you and prayed to Amun for your safety among the barbarians in Rethennu and beyond."

"Your Majesty is kind." Huy rose to his feet. "I missed you also. You would have found much to intrigue you in the wilds beyond your eastern border."

"No doubt." Huy, invited by the Regent's gesture to step closer, now saw that the young man looked distressed rather than tired. Amunhotep straightened and uncrossed his legs. His kohled eyes under the rim of the blue and white striped linen helmet were puffy. "You know about Anhur?"

"Yes. There was a message from Thothhotep waiting for me when I returned." He turned to Mutemwia. "Majesty, there is just enough time for me to travel to Nekheb and attend Anhur's funeral. He was so much more than my friend. Please give me permission to go."

"I'll come with you," Amunhotep said loudly. "I have wept for him a great deal since the news came to me. The Mitanni ambassador dared to ask me if I was ill." He flung a challenging glare at his mother. "There's no use asking the Queen if we may make the journey. She has already refused my request to do so."

"Sit down, Huy." The voice belonged to Mutemwia. Her doll-like face was set, the hennaed lips pursed, the vulture-spangled forehead furrowed. Huy did as he was told, taking the proffered seat opposite Amunhotep. "I need not explain myself to you," she continued. "Nor to you, my son. Not for another three years. If you cannot see the wisdom in my decisions, you obviously still need the guidance of your teachers." Stepping quickly to Huy, she placed her hands on either side of his neck. Her palms were hot. It was a shockingly intimate action that took Huy by surprise so that his own hands came up to grasp her wrists. Her delicately chiselled features were so close to his that he could smell spiced wine on her breath. "You are indispensible to me," she said quietly. "Allowing you to travel with Ptahmose was necessary, but while you were gone my mind was filled with every disaster that might have befallen you. I cannot permit another long voyage unless it is in the urgent service of this country. You surely know that I was fond of Anhur also." She moved back, and Huy repressed the urge to touch his neck where he could still feel the pressure of her rings.

"She told me much the same thing," Amunhotep said irritably. "Here, have some nedjem wine and we can at least drink to Anhur's Beautification." Nubti came forward swiftly at his words, but Amunhotep was already filling a silver cup. He pushed it across the table at Huy, who raised it, mirroring the King's action, and took a mouthful. It was indeed nedjem, sweetened, a fig wine far too honeyed for Huy's taste, although the blend of spices in it was welcome. He replaced it carefully on the slippery surface of the ivory-inlaid table.

"Majesty, such vain imaginings are unlike you," he said to Mutemwia. "I am under the sunshade of Atum; and Anubis, though he often chastises me during the Seeings, makes sure that I come to no harm. Atum has imbued me with heka to ward off the blows of fate." *It's true, isn't it? My destiny to advise these royal beings has been clear to me since Mutemwia put little Amunhotep into my care every year, and as I age I am able to look back and see the god's gift of magic that has averted every danger in my life. I have not said any of this aloud before.* "The Kings of Egypt are also blessed with Atum's heka. Weret Hekau Great of Magic does not leave their side unless they commit some terrible blasphemy against Ma'at. Where are your fears coming from? Your dreams?"

He was desperate to change her mind. He wanted to be with Thothhotep in her little house beside the river, to walk behind Anhur's coffin as he was carried to the hollowed-out cave Huy's gold had prepared for his beloved captain's resting place, to make the offerings of food, wine, and oil. He wanted to hold Thothhotep's skinny, wiry body against his own, to see her reach up to tuck the one unruly strand of her short hair behind her ear in the unconscious gesture he had loved. *I'm homesick for the past,* he realized suddenly. *Not just missing the peace and orderliness of the estate, but genuinely ill with desire for it. Such disorder in my ka is an invitation to attacks from the demon Khatyu in spite of Atum's protection.*

Mutemwia was shaking her head. The silver vulture likenesses of Mut tinkled dully against one another. "No. But surely you see that the King must stay here and he must be seen to have the god's protection your presence provides. Besides, I have work for you. Have you become proficient in Akkadian yet? Did your scribe bring me a copy of your report?"

The subject of a journey to Nekheb was closed. The King audibly blew out his lips and sank his nose into his wine. Huy grimly forced down a spurt of pure anger. Was she exercising her power frivolously or was there a legitimate reason for keeping both the King and him under her scrutiny? Huy turned his mind to the report with difficulty. Mutemwia's scribe glided out of the shadows at her words and settled beside her feet. He opened his palette, and in a moment the sound of burnisher against papyrus brought Huy entirely to himself.

"I have become reasonably proficient in reading and writing Akkadian, and Minister May's scribe seems content with my atrocious accent," he replied stiffly. "Paneb has brought my report for your appraisal, but I would like to summarize it. I have recommendations to make."

"Good." She sat, drawing the folds of her sheath across her invisible knees. The ankh on its silver chain slid sideways to swing gently between her thigh and the floor. The scribe dipped his brush in his black paint and waited. Paneb also waited, not for the report but to record any conversation that would surround it.

"The Scribe of Recruits is honest and capable in his responsibilities to the army and navy," Huy began. "The officers clearly respect him and he is able to speak the language of the barracks with the common soldiers. However, in bringing a fresh eye to the fortification of the northern Delta, and in visiting the garrisons along the Horus Road, I noted some concerns that did not necessarily escape the Scribe's attention but—"

Amunhotep interrupted him. The King had emptied his wine cup and was now leaning back in his chair with arms folded. "You don't need to defend the ability of my Scribe of Recruits to do his job efficiently, Uncle. Why do you think my Mother the Regent promoted him? If you are going to hedge your assessment of the state of my northern borders with an unwarranted concern for your nephew, I'm not going to be able to trust what you say. Where does your first obedience lie? Do you think that there is a conflict between loyalty to Egypt and loyalty to family?"

Huy looked at him, startled. *He's growing up at last. One day soon he will equal his mother's shrewdness.* Huy gave up any attempt at diplomacy. "Amunhotep-Huy expressed a fear to me that you may be planning to rob him of his rank. Because you had ordered him not to discuss deployments or anything else connected to Egypt's military forces, he assumed that you were about to give me his position."

"The arrogant idiot. If I choose to demote him, I will do so. Am I not both Horus-in-the-Nest as I wait for my sixteenth Naming Day and the Incarnation of blessed Amun? And who is he?" He uncrossed his arms and held out both hennaed palms to face Huy. "Enough! My Mother the Regent refuses to convey preferment on anyone, noble or commoner, who is not able to perform the tasks of the office to which they aspire. The only exceptions have been the members of your family, Uncle Huy, and even then, although their promotions were commanded in order to induce you to leave Hut-herib, they have been given the titles and tasks equal to their talents. That includes your nephew, rough-spoken though he is." He refolded his brown arms.

"My son is entirely correct," Mutemwia said. "If we decide to send Amunhotep-Huy away, then we will. Please proceed."

"I apologize," Huy offered. "Very well. My first area of concern is the staffing of the garrisons along the Horus Road into Rethennu. Most of the soldiers stationed in them are mercenaries. During rotations they are free to go home to Rethennu, Tjehenu west of the Delta—there are even a few whose families live in Zahi, beyond Rethennu. I've watched them with the many foreign herdsmen returning home along the Road. There is an acquaintance between them. If they belong to the same tribe, there is amity. Unfortunately, it was the wrong time of the year to observe the relationship between them as the herds are driven into the Delta, but I'm willing to wager that whole families slip past the garrisons without being added to the tally. Judging by my comparison of the lists compiled during the spring months of Peret and the hundreds of foreigners I saw drifting away from northern Egypt, the inventory is scanty at best. The garrison officers cannot oversee their portions of the Road all the time. Your Majesty might be advised to think about the history lesson that dealt with the occupation of Egypt by the ancestors of these same tribesmen. Take native soldiers from our five military divisions and rotate them through the garrisons. The guarding of the Horus Road is our only protection against enemies from the east. No desert gives them pause as it does in the west. Nor is there a Great Green as there is to the north. The Horus Road is necessary, but it is a weak link in our defences."

He paused and drank from the water Nubti had quietly placed by his hand. Mutemwia's scribe put down his brush, flexed his fingers, and selected a new one. Neither the King nor the Regent spoke.

"I learned that Your Majesty already supplies soldiers to both the city of Byblos and the Amurru to strengthen our northeastern flank," Huy went on. "I suggest that you consider opening diplomatic negotiations with the chieftains of not only Zahi but also the Shinar in northern Zahi, and the Katna, Niy, Senzar, Kinanat, and Nukhashshi. All of them are small tribes living within the Bend of Naharin, the region between the two great northern rivers. All of them could be either conquered or suborned by Mitanni. Egypt enjoys friendly relations with Mitanni. Its King imagines himself equal in every way to you, Amunhotep. Egypt and Mitanni have trade agreements with each other. Mitanni is now a kingdom to be reckoned with. Two

Osiris-Kings conquered it and exacted tribute from it, but the tribute has become nothing more than a traffic of goods between our two realms. If Mitanni chooses to expand, it will engulf those little tribes. Better to prepare for such an eventuality. Send their petty chieftains gifts—gold, papyrus, linen. Invite them here so that they may see Egypt's power for themselves. Mitanni must not grow." Huy's voice had become a croak and his nerves were screaming for opium.

"Is that all, Huy?" Mutemwia asked as Huy drained the water jug and Nubti whisked it away to be refilled.

Huy shook his head. "One more thing to try your patience. You doubtless know that after Ptahmose and my nephew left for the southern sepats, I toured the garrisons and naval stations along the northern shores of the Delta. I talked to many captains, including Naval Troop Commander Nebenkempt and Hatmesha, who was your father's Standard Bearer on his ship *Mery Amun* and who commands two hundred and fifty marines. He is an extremely talented naval officer and deserves to be promoted. It was pointed out to me that shipments of copper from Alashia are often either late or do not arrive at all because of the pirates infesting the Great Green between Alashia and the coast that reaches from northern Zahi to our own beloved Delta. Nebenkempt and Hatmesha both agreed that Alashia needs Egypt's help. So far the pirates have not dared to attack our coastal settlements, but they grow in strength and daring. I suggest permitting both nobles to begin serious battle training for the sailors and marines under their authority, and a letter to the ruler of Alashia from you, Majesty, assuring him of Egypt's assistance. We need his copper. That is all." The jug of water had reappeared. Huy drank again, then sat slumped in his chair. The day had been long and fraught with emotion. All he wanted to do was to take his poppy and go to sleep.

"Thank you. I am aware of Nebenkempt's value and his future connection to your brother Heby's family as the father of Amunhotep-Huy's proposed wife Henut-nofret." Mutemwia leaned forward and put a hand briefly on his knee. "Your assessment is of great value and we will consider your advice. Now we will speak of the King's marriage contract with Tiye."

Amunhotep groaned. "Must we do so now, Mother? Uncle Huy looks exhausted and my head is beginning to ache. The Mitanni ambassador is doubtless an important man, but his general conversation is boring, and apart from his vast thirst for the sermet beer our women love, he is uninteresting. I've taken in every one of Huy's words and tomorrow you and I will go over them. Let me play sennet with Nubti and then go to my couch. For once I am actually weary before the horns sound midnight."

Mutemwia ignored him. "I want you to take control of her education and well-being, Huy, as you did for my son. Examine her tutors for their suitability to teach a Queen. Add whatever subjects to her schooling you deem necessary. I thank the gods that Yuya was enlightened enough to allow her to study with her brothers. Talk to her servants and dismiss any whom you do not like. She is to have no scribe of her own. If she wishes to dictate, she must use one of the harem scribes and her letters must be turned over to you for reading. Confer with Userhet regarding her care. He is young but a talented Overseer of the King's Harem. Tiye's mother is a student of all forms of protocol and is of course sharing an apartment with her daughter. She has many titles. Her voice is remarkable. She is Chief of the Entertainers of Amun and Singer of Hathor, among other things. She was raised in the King's Harem and will be quite at home there. Get to know her."

Amunhotep grunted. "King's Harem! The women in there belonged to my father, including Neferatiri and my bothersome sister Iaret. She's been sulking ever since word of my contract with Tiye was announced. I told her I'd make her my second wife, but she swore at me and then told me that as she has royal blood in her veins unlike that Mitanni upstart Tiye, she would be Chief Wife no matter when I married her." He grinned wryly. "There's no spite like a woman's spite. I have no desire to go anywhere near the harem."

For the first time that night Mutemwia laughed, but she quickly sobered again. "I warned you that Tiye's foreign blood would cause trouble," she said to Huy. "My fear is that Iaret will attempt to force a marriage with the King's blood-uncle Prince Amunhotep and then do her best to foment a war. Watch her carefully, Huy. The Prince has retired to his estates as he wanted to do, but his visitors must be noted and his correspondence opened."

So the old fear is still alive in you, Huy thought. *Perhaps in both of you. I understand now why I am not permitted to go south for Anhur, but I resent it just the same.* He stood and bowed, feeling stiff. He was still very thirsty. "I am Your Majesty's loyal servant," he said to Amunhotep. Then, turning to Mutemwia, he inclined his head. "I will do my best to comply with all this, but you have placed a heavy responsibility on my shoulders."

"I've only just begun to make use of you, my dearest brother." She came up to him and, rising on tiptoe, kissed him on both cheeks.

I gave up the right to order my life as I chose, he thought as the silver vultures decorating her brow touched him as briefly as her soft lips. *She calls me brother, the most affectionate term used between lovers. Does she see me as a man, then, in spite of the restriction the god has placed upon me, although she knows about it? Or is she clumsily throwing me a crumb of sweetness after loading me with so many tasks? I do not think so. When I examine our history together, I see only a warm companionship restricted solely by the difference in our stations.*

"Seneb will examine you tomorrow morning," she told him. "Go now. Take your poppy. I shall see you in the Office of Foreign Correspondence after the King's hour of audience."

Huy did not bow again. Nubti was already holding open one of the high double doors. With Paneb behind him, Huy bade the steward a good night and passed through.

Out in the passage, Perti and his guards assembled quickly. *She has left her perfume on my skin,* Huy thought as they set off on the short walk to his apartments. *Lotus for nobility, Narcissus for simplicity, Henna for beauty. Gods, I'm tired!* In his bedchamber, Tetiankh waited with warm water to wash the paint from his face and opium to ease him into sleep, but Huy did not sleep. Mutemwia's instructions became little more than noise in his head as Anhur took form in his mind's eye, his big hand resting on the hilt of his sword, a smile of greeting lighting his face. Towards dawn Huy at last fell into an uneasy sleep, but sorrow and nostalgia imbued his dreams and he was glad to wake just as the sun lipped the eastern horizon.

Physician Seneb was waiting to assess the state of his health before he had even eaten the meal Tetiankh set beside him, and Huy succumbed to the man's poking and prying while the bread cooled and the fresh, almost scentless aroma of the fruit piled on Huy's dish made his mouth water. At last Seneb stood away from the couch. "Great Seer, your muscles are full of tension even though you are only just awake. You must take a massage every evening before you sleep, and continue to observe one day of fasting a week. Is the amount of poppy I have allowed you each day enough?" Tetiankh cast the man a sour look and slammed the lid of the chest from which he had lifted Huy's clean loincloth and kilt.

"I suppose so," Huy admitted slowly. "My appetite for the drug seems to wax and wane depending on the difficulty of the tasks before me, and I've Seen for no one lately."

"If you need more, your body servant must come to me. You must find the time to exercise, Master. You have a remarkably youthful body, but it needs care. Swim, practise with your bow, take out a chariot—do something. Now please dismiss me."

Huy thought his request for dismissal ridiculous seeing that he himself was given no choice as to whether or not he wanted to consult the man, but he nodded, and Seneb bowed and went away.

He walked to the bathhouse and had Tetiankh quickly wash and oil him. The King would be beginning his daily audience soon, and Huy wanted to use the time to dictate a letter to his old friend, the priest Methen. Paneb and Ba-en-Ra were waiting for him when he returned. Huy sat before his cosmetics table, and Tetiankh braided his hair and kohled his eyes while he spoke to them. "Go to the Ladies Thuyu and Tiye in the harem and tell them I'll meet them this evening," he ordered his Chief Herald. "Ask Tiye whether she wants me to go to her or if she would prefer to come here. Find me wherever I am and give me her answer. Paneb, take a dictation."

As the body servant's capable hands smoothed and wound his perfumed tresses into a thick plait, Huy talked to Methen through Paneb's swift brush. *I had no time to spend with him as we passed Hut-herib. I have no time for Heby, living so close to me here in Mennofer. Ishat's children are becoming strangers. My letters to Merenra, in charge of the estate, are limited to inquiries regarding the need for gold and the well-being of the few servants left there. I have not asked whether my parents' home is occupied and being properly tended. I am desperately trying to cling to everyone dear to me while the past gradually slips away. How long will it be before nothing remains but formality?*

He arrived at the Office of Foreign Correspondence just as the King and his mother were being seated. Amunhotep greeted him cheerfully. "Good news from Weset, Uncle Huy. Kha and the twins are at work already. The Berseh and Tura mines have already been reopened for repair, and Kha sent me the plans for the changes and additions I want at Ipet-isut, including a new shrine for Amun's barque. Demolition has begun on my father's sandstone court. Hori wants to tear down the little temple to Amun in the Southern Ipet and begin something much more grand. I've given him the permission he needs. Treasurer Nakht-sobek will protest, but since I now know exactly how rich I am, I shan't care." He turned to May, waiting politely to begin the business of the day. "Give the Seer the diplomatic letters to read to us. Paneb, this is not for you to take down."

Huy's scribe bowed and went to stand in the doorway through which a ray of mid-morning sunlight was streaming brightly golden. May's scribe settled onto the floor near Huy. May passed Huy one of the clay tablets from the small mountain on his desk. Mutemwia began to smile. Out of the corner of his eye, Huy could see her red-hennaed mouth curve upward as he bent over the now-familiar script.

To my brother the great King Ka-nakht Kha-em-ma'at I pros-trate myself seventy times seven in profound gratitude for the quantity of gold you sent to me. May you reign for millions of years. Ask what you will of me and I shall comply. I beg Your Majesty to send more gold so that I may better equip my soldiers who patrol the border against the barbarous Kheta to the north. Know that the ruler of the Kheta who sits in the city of Hattusas does not love Egypt as I do. If he asks of you, send him no gold. I eagerly await a word from your august lips. Artatama, Supreme King and Chieftain of Mitanni.

Amunhotep laughed as Huy fell silent. "What a sly old fox he is! He pressures us to remember how kind he was to my uncle Prince Amunhotep and he thinks that in warning us against the Kheta we will tremble in our sandals! Well does he call me Strong Bull, Appearing in Truth! The Kheta are no threat to the might of Egypt!"

"Not yet," Mutemwia agreed, "and we are certainly not going to send Artatama more gold. However, I have pondered your suggestion regarding the petty tribes infesting the Bend of Naharin, Huy, and there's much sense in it. Arrange introductory letters to their chiefs, and whatever gifts you think appropriate. What else, May? Give the tablets to Huy."

In the afternoon, Huy retreated to his apartments. He knew that he had acquitted himself well in the Office of Foreign Correspondence. He was becoming increasingly aware of the size and scope of Egypt's holdings outside her borders, and of her often convoluted dealings with other independent nations. He supposed that the King's early education had included such important matters. Amunhotep was certainly familiar with the situation surrounding each missive Huy had read aloud. Indeed, His Majesty knew more about the history and culture of such far-flung countries as Arzawa, away to the northwest, or Assur, straddling the eastern arm of the two great rivers sheltering the Bend of Naharin, than he knew about the border defences of his own dominion. Huy was surprised at Mutemwia's ignorance of the situation governing Egypt's borders, and wondered if his nephew was at fault. Had his reports as Scribe of Recruits not been clear and succinct enough? No matter. The Queen would quickly remedy her lack. Before he took to his couch for the customary sleep, Huy heard from Ba-en-Ra. Tiye and her mother would attend Huy in his reception room after the last meal of the day.

They arrived accompanied by Userhet, the Overseer of the King's Harem, as well as an impossibly handsome young man hugging a large cedar box and introduced as Thuyu's cosmetician, two female body servants carrying cloaks and spare sandals, two scribes, and a crowd of harem guards. Respectfully but firmly, Amunmose shut them all out in the passage but for the two aristocratic women, their female attendants, and one scribe. Huy would have liked to ban Tiye's monkey also, a tiny, white-faced creature perched on her shoulder and clinging to her hair with one fist while scratching its genitals with the other. It bared its pointed teeth in a rictus of obvious dislike at Huy as he performed a deep obeisance and indicated three gilt chairs set around his inlaid ivory and silver table. Amunmose and Paroi were swiftly and unobtrusively setting a choice of wines, nuts, and fruit on its gleaming surface. The monkey immediately used Tiye's hair to swing onto the table, and snatched up a handful of the precious almonds. Tiye pried them away from it, all but one. The monkey promptly palmed the nut into its mouth.

Thuyu had seated herself gracefully—straight-backed, feet together, hands folded decorously in her white lap. "I am told that the House of Yuya owes its latest elevation to you, Great Seer Amunhotep," she said, thus giving Huy, as her social inferior, permission to speak. "Please sit and tell me about it." She was smiling, her immaculately kohled eyes with their blue-tinted lids warmly inviting. Her dark wig with its dozens of long braids had not a hair out of place. Delicate necklaces of small bevelled gold hoops were strung around her tall neck, each circle hung with a golden likeness of either the goddess Hathor with her sweetly curving cow's horns or Min the lettuce-eater, a type of Amun who once a year became a god of orgiastic licentiousness.

Of course, Huy thought in the moment before he answered her. *She is not only Chief Singer of Amun but Chief Singer of Hathor also. She presides over the music of Min's primary temple at Ipu and that of Amun at Ipet-isut as well. This is a very intelligent and influential woman.* He took the remaining chair. "Please call me Huy," he replied. "I'm sure that your daughter has related the details of her Seeing to you, noble one. Because of the vision, I was pleased to recommend a marriage contract for her with His Majesty. She is now Great Royal Wife, and will of course be fully a Queen when Amunhotep reaches his majority." The King's name had come easily and unconsciously to his tongue. A brief expression of pain crossed Thuyu's face but was instantly repressed. She had noted his glance.

"Forgive me, Seer Huy," she said. "Even my husband Yuya, Prince of Ipu, is not permitted to address the King with such familiarity. I should have remembered that your long and very close relationship with His Majesty has given you such a privilege." There was no animosity in her expression. Her gaze moved to the table. At once Amunmose stepped forward. "You have irep nefer nefer," she said. It was not a question. "Pour me a cup. Tiye, would you like wine?" The girl nodded.

Irep nefer nefer, very good wine, was one grade below the very best vintage to be had. Huy, not wanting to boast, kept silent as the dark red liquid cascaded into two cups. Thuyu thanked the steward, lifted her cup, and sipped at its contents daintily.

"I am here as my daughter's chaperone until she moves into the Chief Wife's apartments," she continued. "I was raised in the harem, Seer Huy, before I was given in marriage to Yuya as a special favour. The greatest danger to her there is the fever that seems to run rife as the Inundation rises. If necessary I will want to move her, either to the harem by the lake in the desert at Mi-wer or to your estate outside Hut-herib." She sipped again, placed her cup carefully back on the table, and inclined her head slightly in Huy's direction. "Her Majesty the Regent has already told me that Tiye's care is completely in your hands. I am pleased. The King has benefited greatly from his annual stay in your house and I anticipate nothing less for Tiye. My only request is that she is never allowed to be alone with any man other than the King."

Tiye herself had said nothing while this conversation was proceeding. She had been feeding grapes to the monkey one at a time while it perched on her shoulder. "And you, Great Seer," she put in now, "I want the freedom to be alone with you whenever I want. The King doesn't particularly like me, so you must tell me everything about him. Stop it, Prince Rascal!" The beast was patting her cheek and chittering in her ear.

Huy crooked a finger at Paroi. "Take this animal into the passage and give it to Perti to watch." The under steward reluctantly wound its leash around his wrist and lifted it with both hands, holding it as far away as possible as he approached the door. "Now perhaps we may talk without distraction," Huy went on. "Lady Tiye, I am available to you whenever you wish to see me, but I beg you to leave Nib-Nib and Prince Rascal in your quarters!" Looking into her face, he wondered if she had brought the monkey along to annoy him or her mother. "I shall come to the harem tomorrow to learn the routines of your days and I shall attend your lessons with you. I warn you that if I see a need for changes, I shall make them and you will accept them quietly." Thuyu nodded.

Tiye's eyebrows rose and her mouth twisted. "I'll learn far more about being a Queen if you let me attend *your* routines. I should be with the King at his daily audience and with you as you move from minister to minister."

Huy paused before replying. Her comment had surprised him. His encounters with her so far had been between an annoyingly persistent, even rude young noble and his exasperated self. "You should certainly begin to spend time with His Majesty, but that will be at his choosing, not yours or mine," he told her. "If your mornings are spent outside the classroom, you will have to study in the afternoons instead."

She shrugged. "I shan't mind. May I learn to use a bow and arrows? It would be good exercise for me. I need to swim also."

Thuyu made a tiny sound of distress but otherwise remained silent. *There is going to be a battle of wills between her and me,* Huy thought, not without humour. *I wonder if Amunhotep is going to be strong enough to stand up to her when necessary. What if his dislike for her becomes hostility and her light dismissal of him turns into indifference?*

Thuyu delicately cleared her throat. "When you have caught up with your general studies, you will be giving your attention to learning the correct deportment for a Queen. Not only must you gain the King's respect, but the members of the court and the foreign delegations must recognize in you the invisible aura that surrounds a goddess. You can't elude your father's guards and run around the palace gardens with Prince Rascal and Nib-Nib anymore. Your father is now the King's Master of the Horse, Lieutenant Commander of the Chariotry, and Chief Instructor of the King in Martial Arts, as your grandfather Yey was. He will not allow you anywhere near the training ground. You silly girl! You hold the highest rank of any woman in Egypt. Even I must bow to you. Do not squander this authority in foolish displays of self-will."

Huy expected an outburst from Tiye, but it did not come. After a moment she took her mother's hand. "I know that you're right. At night on my couch I think about what it means to be a Queen and I seem to be in the middle of a wonderful dream. But then I remember that I can't go hunting for spent arrows in the bushes behind the barracks with Ay anymore, or play in the dirt beside the river with Anen and Ramose." She pursed her lips and met Huy's eye. "I am used to the freedom of life in a rich and aristocratic household, Seer Huy. It seems to me that the life of a Queen is not free at all, and I am a little afraid."

"I'll arrange for you to visit the Regent privately, in her apartments," Huy promised. "Remember the vision, Tiye. Atum intends the Queen's crown for you. There is no need for fear." At once his mind filled with images: Tiye and an unknown King, a misshapen figure standing beside her in the blazing heat of an unroofed inner temple, her face harsh, her expression closed. But as the conversation became general and Huy's guests got up to leave, that picture faded and another took its place. He had told Tiye that she had nothing to fear, but he wondered whether she and her parents had considered a threat from the thwarted Iaret. And what of Neferatiri, the late King's Chief Wife? She had made no overtures to Prince Amunhotep; Mutemwia's concern in that matter had been almost entirely allayed. The King himself had not cared much for her and never mentioned her in Huy's presence, but might she not be brooding over the latest turn of events with her attention turned to a marital alliance with Amunhotep? A sexual relationship between the two was unlikely but not impossible. However, the true worth of such a marriage contract lay in the power and prestige it would bestow upon the Queen. Was she greedy and ambitious?

Huy sighed as he bowed the women out and Paroi closed the door behind them. He had scarcely spoken to Neferatiri since moving into the palace. She had graced him with a few words in passing as she made her way from the women's quarters. *I must spend tomorrow in the harem once the foreign correspondence has been dealt with,* he thought, standing irresolute for a moment in the middle of his reception room. *I must greet and question everyone. I must obtain the personal histories of all of them from Userhet, make sure that Menkhoper, Scribe in the House of the Royal Children and the King's tutor for many years, is prepared to educate his newest charge, talk to the captain of the harem guards, the physicians who tend the women, the food tasters. I must either place a spy among Iaret's and Neferatiri's staff or ask Mutemwia to introduce me to the servants in her pay and ask to see their regular reports.* He felt both overwhelmed by the new responsibilities being placed on his shoulders and privileged to be bearing them.

For several days he performed his duties in the ministerial office with May and the royal pair, spending the rest of his time in the women's quarters. The river continued to rise, and its increasing height was celebrated with feasts almost every evening. Huy took those opportunities to become familiar with the ambassadors stationed permanently in Egypt. On the whole he liked them. He began to regularly attend the King's morning audiences, watching and listening in particular to the representatives of the foreign tribes and nations paying an annual tribute to Egypt in exchange for their autonomy. The emissaries from Keftiu, Alashia, and the other entirely free countries with which Egypt had trading agreements were polite, well-educated men who understood Egypt's eminence in the world. Their dealings with the King and the Regent were tactful when arguing on behalf of their masters, reverential when approaching the Horus Throne, and knowledgeable when discussing some thorny matter with the ministers involved. They treated Huy with deep respect, seeming to understand intuitively that his influence with the King, always strong, was growing. Huy was aware of this himself. More and more often he appeared in the Office of Foreign Correspondence to be told by Minister May that Their Majesties would not be attending and the letters must be answered by Huy himself. He and May began to present the daily report together.

Towards the end of the month, when Egypt was preparing to

celebrate the Feast of the Great Manifestation of Osiris, Huy and May walked into May's office after the morning's audience to find Tiye and her scribe already there. Both men bowed profoundly, Huy with a pang of anxiety. But Tiye was smiling at them, the downturned mouth that gave her face a deceptively displeased look lifting in greeting and lighting those hooded blue eyes. A band of blue lapis flax flowers encircled her head, emphasizing the dark red gleam of her shoulder-length hair. A soft white sheath fell in graceful folds from her neck to her gold-thonged sandals and was belted to her skinny waist with rectangular pieces of lapis set in gold. In spite of her naked arms, fingers, and earlobes, she was a strikingly extravagant sight. Once again Huy was struck by the atmosphere of latent force she exuded. The usual ray of hot but fleeting sunlight pouring through the open doorway was resting briefly on the almost transparent drape of the linen, and through it Huy could see the slight curve of her calves. The scribe had risen to perform his obeisance before sinking cross-legged to the floor beside her chair, his palette across his naked knees. Huy thought him very young.

"Great Seer Amunhotep, Noble Minister May, this is my personal scribe Anhirkawi." She waved at him. "My new tutor Menkhoper recommended him to me. He comes from the office of the noble Nebmerut, the King's Seal Bearer. So far I haven't used him much, but I intend that to change." Her smile became a wide grin, the scarlet henna on her lips making her small white teeth gleam. "Great Seer, His Majesty and the Regent have given me permission to accompany you each day as you go about your duties, as I told you earlier I wanted to do. Actually, I asked Amunhotep first. He laughed and thought my request was funny, but I remembered your advice and kept my temper. Besides, he wasn't being nasty. The Regent said that you must approve, though. Do you approve? I'll try not to be a nuisance."

"Well, in that case you'd better call me Seer Huy," Huy replied heavily. "You do understand that Anhirkawi may not take down any official correspondence for your private use and I may occa-sionally ask to see his records?"

"Of course." She wriggled further into her chair and folded her arms. "I really want to call you Uncle, as the King does. After all, according to my marriage contract, I'm already Amunhotep's wife, so his relatives have become my own, even though we don't share any blood. I think you'd better call me Tiye, at least until the Queen's crown is set on my head." Without waiting for an answer, she swung her gaze to May. "I know that you are very busy," she said to him, "but I want to borrow the scribe of yours who taught the Seer Akkadian. I must learn the language if I am to understand the problems you encounter in the world of diplomacy. I don't dare approach the ambassadors yet—I'd betray my ignorance, and they'd expect nothing more from a woman, even a noble one. But one day I intend to surprise them, and the King as well."

Astonished and touched, Huy studied her. *She's desperately trying to cultivate not only the delicacy of a genuine tact but also a rather engaging humility. The girl who was so loudly rude to Perti is being quickly reshaped by her new circumstances. By Menkhoper's sensitivity to his pupil's character also, I'm sure. Perhaps even by her mother's civilizing influence. Menkhoper tells me that this embryonic Queen has a sharp intelligence and learns rapidly as long as she has an interest in the information she's being asked to absorb. At least she's leaving her annoying pets in her quarters. But does she throw off her new manners with relief, together with the jewellery and fine linen, when she returns to the harem?*

May was speaking. "Of course you may borrow my scribe, Lady Tiye. As for your attendance to hear the business of my day, I apologize, but I must have a scroll of permission from Her Majesty Queen Mutemwia."

"You're afraid that I'm really a gossip and will spread the King's negotiations all over the palace." She grimaced and rolled her eyes. "My request has scandalized my dear mother as well. She thought I wasn't serious when I brought the matter up with you, Uncle Huy. Well, I see that I must prove myself." She slid off the chair. "At least send me the scribe this evening, Minister May. I wish to master Akkadian at once. Come on, Uncle Huy, let's leave. Where are you going now?"

Anhirkawi slid the lid of his palette closed and stood. May bowed.

"I've been summoned to Her Majesty's quarters," Huy replied, "but you, dear Tiye, will hurry to the classroom, where your fellow students are already busy. Do you share any lessons with the King?"

"A couple. We are wading through the interminable complaints of the Eloquent Peasant. I think Menkhoper has chosen them for Amunhotep to make sure that he really does understand the justice of Ma'at, but if I were the Osiris-King Kheti Nebkaura the Third, I'd have ordered the man muzzled and then gone and got drunk. Menkhoper's very patient with my own complaints and I've never seen him use his willow cane on Amunhotep as any other teacher would sometimes do, even though Amunhotep can be mulish sometimes. There's no hiding behind position in school."

"You do spend a little time with the King otherwise."

"I'm sure you are aware that I do. We play board games, but he quickly gets tired of me. I think he's bored but also secretly amused by me. Well, at least his dislike for me seems to be fading." She pulled Huy to a halt and pointed up at the blue circlet on her head. "This and the belt were gifts from him after the marriage contract had been signed and sealed. He said that I was now entitled to wear the hair of the gods even though I wasn't yet fully a Queen. I don't think that any of it was his idea. Her Majesty the Regent overlooks absolutely nothing." They walked on until the way branched. There she took his hand. "Uncle Huy, I want to tell you everything I think and feel and do," she said earnestly. "Your reputation as an honest man is growing among the courtiers, and you've treated the wives and concubines in the harem with respect. But I don't always want what I tell you to get back to my new husband or his mother or my father." She gave a mock shudder. "The gods forbid! My father still thinks I'm nothing but a spoiled brat! Can you promise to keep my secrets?"

Huy scanned the homely yet oddly compelling little face. "I can, providing what you confide in me does not endanger the King in any way. You honour me. I look forward to your daily company. I'm sure that the Regent's scroll will reach May early tomorrow."

Scribe Anhirkawi was waiting behind them, just beyond earshot. Tiye leaned close to Huy, and suddenly he could smell cardamom with a faint undertone of myrrh. The choice of such a strange and distinctive blend for perfume seemed bizarre, even shocking, on such a young girl.

"I became a woman six months ago," she half whispered. "I'm grateful that Amunhotep hasn't given sleeping with me one thought, because I'm certainly not ready to relinquish my virginity just yet. But what shall I do if he begins to find me attractive? Is he old enough to have a concubine in the harem? I've tried to find out, but my questions must be so discreet that they're incomprehensible. Do you know anything?"

"The Regent has told me that as yet His Majesty shows no interest in sex," Huy answered her as steadily as he could. Both her confidence and her candid question had taken him off guard. "If you sense an interest in you on his part and you have no wish to respond to it, then divert him. I rather think that such a ploy will soon come to you quite naturally, Tiye. But one day you must accept the privilege of his advances."

She raised her eyes and grimaced, a habit Huy was becoming used to, and bidding him enjoy his day she gestured imperiously at her scribe and disappeared into the dimness of the passage. Huy followed slowly. He had a great deal to consider.

Mutemwia was sitting and dictating to her scribe when Huy was admitted and performed his reverence. She waved him to a chair and Ameni, her steward, glided forward to offer him the customary refreshments. Huy shook his head. His morning dose of poppy had set up an ache in his stomach that had prevented him from eating the first meal of the day, and he still had no appetite. He waited, absently breathing in the faint redolence of lotus and henna flowers infusing the air. Presently the scribe put aside the papyrus on which he had been working, set a fresh sheaf on his palette, and began to burnish it.

Mutemwia nodded a greeting to Huy. Although her face was painted and her black hair oiled and braided, she was still dressed in one of the loose, long-sleeved shifts she favoured and her feet were bare. "I didn't attend the daily audience this morning, Huy," she said. "I trust that it went smoothly."

"The reports were thin and no one was very attentive," Huy responded. "Osiris's feast approaches and of course it means a holiday for all. Tiye was waiting for May and me when we entered his office earlier."

"I know. I've already sent May the written permission he needs. I'm very pleased with her progress. Tell me, has anyone in the palace requested a Seeing from you?"

"No, Majesty. Tiye's was the last hand I took. Were you wondering about Iaret and Neferatiri?"

Their eyes met in perfect understanding. Mutemwia hooked

her toes under a nearby stool and pulled it towards her. "Not really. Both women are closely watched and their letters read. They are full of innocuous gossip. Do you miss the exercise of your gift?" She set both her tiny feet side by side on the stool.

"No," Huy said at once. "The only headaches I suffer from now are the ordinary results of daily pressures. Seneb tells me to work my body, but I can't find the time to do so."

"In the future you will be forced to delegate your authority to your assistants. You have sent gold and a promise of other goods to the petty tribes within the Bend of Naharin."

"You know I have." Huy began to be puzzled at the turn the conversation was taking. "You ordered me to do so yourself. I want to establish trade and treaties with them before Mitanni does."

"Good. I want you to turn your attention to the Delta now. I'm giving you the position of Scribe of Recruits. Do what's necessary to strengthen the borders, clean up the careless listing of foreign herdsmen wandering into and out of Egypt, reorganize the manning of the garrisons—anything else you deem necessary for our continued safety. The army and navy are yours also."

So Amunhotep-Huy's fears were justified, Huy thought rapidly. *Now what do I do about family loyalty? What do I owe my nephew? Certainly not a debt that would have me refusing this rank. His life is obviously in no danger, but what of his livelihood? He intends to marry very soon …*

"You need not worry about Amunhotep-Huy." Mutemwia's dry tones cut across the beginning of Huy's silent dilemma. "I've decided to promote him to Vizier. For several years he's travelled to every sepat with Ptahmose. The governors know him. So do I. He's a harsh man. He'll take a fist to a lazy servant, bully his underlings until they do what he expects from them, face down army officers and navy captains, but his devotion to the Horus

Throne is absolute. In that respect he is entirely trustworthy."
She smiled faintly across at Huy. "Surprising, isn't it? His allegiance also extends to every lesser King's son. Part of a Vizier's
responsibility is to distribute land and revenues to those men,
depending on their proximity to the throne. Your nephew knows
the lineage of every one of them. He will neglect his wife and
mete out punishments more severely than is warranted, but he
will die before betraying anyone with a drop of royal blood in
their veins. Is it because he himself comes from peasant stock and
must prove himself? I don't think so."

"He will provoke enmity among the governors," Huy said
slowly. The Queen's assessment of Amunhotep-Huy's character
had taken him by surprise. "He lacks Ptahmose's tact, his cour-
tesy and civility when dealing with the noblemen."

"Perhaps so, but he is frank and honest. It will do the governors no harm to have to deal with the King's representative in a
different way. My son and I have already made the appointment.
We are sending Ptahmose south to reopen the old palace and
prepare it for occupation. We want to be in residence there
before the end of the season of Shemu."

"Amunhotep wants to escape the immediate reach of the
priests in charge of all the temples to Ra in his many guises." Huy
knew this at once. "He also wants to be seen to be allied more
closely to Amun. Weset has always belonged to Amun."

"It makes us relieved and happy, doesn't it, my Huy?" She bent
forward, pulling the shift down around her ankles then resting
both palms on the tops of her feet and her chin on her linen-clad
knees. It was an artless, girlish gesture so at variance with the
complexities she had been discussing that Huy was momentarily
powerless to reply. "Weset also sits in the centre of the country,"
she continued, uncurling and sitting back. "We will be easing the
load we have placed on many of the ministers. You don't know

the Egypt of the south, do you, Huy? You've never been farther than Khmun, where you went to read the parts of the Book of Thoth guarded there. Weset is a mighty city, alive in a way that Mennofer, with its heavy bureaucracy and its ancient traditions, can't be, and the desert to either side of the river, beyond the cultivated fields, has its own beauty."

"It's close to Nekheb, isn't it?"

"Very close. You will be able to take offerings to Anhur's tomb with Thothhotep during the Beautiful Feast of the Valley." With visible reluctance she signalled Ameni. "I must dress and visit Yuya. How will you spend the remainder of this day?"

Huy rose. "First to my duties in the harem and then to Amunhotep-Huy's office. Mutemwia, I don't know whether or not to thank you for my new tasks."

"Ameni, please summon Tekait." Mutemwia pushed the stool away with one foot and, rising, came swiftly to Huy, placing both hands flat against the golden sa amulet he always wore on his chest and looking up into his face. "When I do not see you, my day is incomplete," she said. "I listen for your voice as I come and go through the corridors. I look for you among the crowd of courtiers and ambassadors and boon-seekers at the time of audience. Sometimes I want nothing more than to return to the nights when you and I sat in your office with one lamp keeping the shadows away while we spoke together of everything the future held for us and for my little son. I hold the reins of Egypt in my hands, many reins, and I must be always vigilant in my control. I am more than pleased to place one of those reins in your grasp without any worry. So is the King. To him you are the true God's Father, although the honorary title goes to the men of Yey's family. Do not die, dearest brother!"

For answer Huy laid his own large hands over her warm fingers and, bending his head, kissed her gently on her hennaed lips. "I love you also, Mutemwia," he said quietly, "and our deep friendship over the years has bridged the gulf of blood and station between us. Yet I am also your servant, and Amunhotep's, and I shall remain so until I am summoned to stand in the Judgment Hall and lay my heart upon Ma'at's scales. Now dismiss me. Tekait is hovering and glaring at me."

Mutemwia laughed and let him go, and with a bow he went out into the passage and set off to the harem with Perti and his guards ahead and Paneb at his heels. He could still feel the softness of her mouth against his.

8

THE OFFICE OF THE SCRIBE OF RECRUITS was oddly peaceful when Huy walked through the open doorway with Paneb behind. The floor had obviously been recently swept, the surface of the large desk scoured, and as far as Huy could see, the shelves lining the walls and holding boxes full of scrolls had been dusted. Amunhotep-Huy was alone, sitting behind the desk with his arms folded. On seeing Huy, he stood and bowed. "Scribe of Recruits."

"Vizier."

The younger man did not invite Huy to take a stool. He gestured widely, a sweep of his muscular brown arm that seemed to take in not only the office but the whole dusty expanse of the parade ground outside as well. "It's all yours, Uncle. Everything you'll need to know is in the boxes. I'll lend you my scribe for a few days. I suggest that you put him together with Paneb so that Paneb may become familiar with the complications of the task."

Huy felt his irritation rising and firmly pushed it down. *Amunhotep-Huy is justifiably happy. If he seems full of self-importance and condescension, I'm not surprised. I pray that Mutemwia has made the right decision in giving him the Viziership.* "Thank you for the advice, and congratulations on your advancement," he said. "Will you miss the men you have worked with for so long?"

Amunhotep-Huy shrugged dismissively. "I suppose so. I've

known many of them since I was a boy, studying under Irem. But this new position puts me on a superior footing to Henut-nofret's father, and that's worth losing a few acquaintances for."

It took Huy a few moments to remember that Henut-nofret was the name of Amunhotep-Huy's wife-to-be, and that Naval Commander Nebenkempt was her father. *Superior in office but not in blood,* his thoughts ran on. *You resent your own father and me because we were not born into the ranks of the nobility. Why can't you just be grateful for the wealth and honour you enjoy?*

"I'm glad the court's moving to Weset," Amunhotep-Huy was continuing. "It'll be easier for me to control the various dealings and procedures within the sepats when my office is in the centre of Egypt." He came briskly around the desk. "I must consult with Ptahmose before he goes south, and he's eager to leave Mennofer before the Inundation becomes too high. As it is, I expect he'll be forced to travel by land after a while. I'll see you at my wedding feast next month, Uncle. The King has agreed to attend." His mouth curved briefly in a cool nod to polite convention, then he was gone. Huy heard him shouting for his scribe.

Paneb had walked forward and was running his eye over the inscriptions painted on the ends of the boxes crowding the walls.

"Find the names and histories of the army and navy commanders first, Paneb," Huy ordered, sinking into the chair Amunhotep-Huy had just vacated. "Read them to me. We might as well begin with all the King's officers."

That evening, Huy could not sleep in spite of the massage Tetiankh had given him and the larger dose of poppy he had requested. His body was exhausted, but his mind was full of the information he and Paneb had discussed and he was not able to dismiss any of it. Lying on his side, he watched his body servant come and go as he put away Huy's jewellery, removed the bowl of scented water and the cloth he had used to wash Huy's face, returned to set out a loincloth and a freshly starched kilt for the morning, checked the height of the wick in the lamp beside Huy's couch, and gathered up Huy's limp kilt and smudged loincloth. With the laundry in his arms, he bade Huy a good night and the door closed softly behind him.

Tetiankh has grown old, and I haven't noticed. The realization came suddenly into Huy's thoughts, cutting through the demanding clamour of titles and responsibilities. *How is it that in all the years he has served me I haven't seen him age? The joints of his fingers are swollen. He seldom smiles in my presence because to do so would seem improper, but on the rare occasions when he does relax such formality, his face breaks into a myriad of lines. He is always on his feet. Do they give him pain?* A wave of panic flushed through Huy. *I should retire him to the estate at Hut-herib, let him spend the rest of his life sitting idly in the shade of the house and gossiping with Merenra or Kar, my bad-tempered gate guard, while they drink beer and watch the vegetables grow. How old is he? How old am I? Gods, he and Amunmose are the only servants remaining to me from our days on the estate. Amunmose is in his prime, but you, Tetiankh, my beloved body servant, although I have never heard you complain, do you struggle through the duties of each day and long for rest?* Huy found himself sitting on the edge of the couch, his heart pounding. *You came to me with the others hired by Hut-herib's Mayor to care for Ishat and me and the miraculous estate given to me by the Osiris-King Amunhotep, the second of that name, our present Pharaoh's grandfather. We were so happy there, all of us. Young and strong and full of hope for the future in spite of the arduous work Ishat and I undertook for the god. Atum. Atum, who preserves this body of mine, who has placed in me an awareness of the future as something accessible, and with that awareness has come a curious blindness to the ravages the passing of time leaves behind. I have considered these things before but vaguely, idly. Why have they come to me now with such force?*

Dragging his sheet with him, wrapping it around his waist, he went to the door and opened it. Tetiankh was already asleep on his mattress just outside. The rest of the apartment was dim and quiet. Huy crossed his reception room and, coming to the garden entrance, opened it and stepped outside.

At once, even before Captain Perti turned and bowed, Huy could smell the increased humidity. The river was rising and would bring with it annoying clouds of mosquitoes as well as the blessed assurance of yet another deposit of fertile silt to replenish the parched fields. Fleetingly he reminded himself to keep a very close eye on the health of the children in the harem as he answered Perti's reverence. "Don't you ever sleep?" he asked his guard.

Perti smiled and jerked a thumb at his companion soldier. "Our watch ends just before dawn, Master. Then we are relieved. Are you unable to rest? Shall I summon your steward?"

Huy glanced swiftly into the peaceful dimness waiting for him. "No, thank you, Perti. I'm neither hungry nor thirsty. I want to wander among the flower beds for a while. Without an escort." Perti nodded his understanding reluctantly. Tying the sheet more tightly to his body, Huy went forward.

Very soon the semi-darkness closed in behind him, the air softly benevolent on his skin, bearing the faint scent of winter flowers. There was no wind. The trees stood motionless, dim pillars ending in darker tangled masses partially obscuring Huy's view of the stars as he looked up. The moon sat at the half, its grey light barely reaching the earth. Huy knew that soldiers from the Division of Amun stood at intervals along the surrounding wall, but they were a distance away. The palace gardens, of which this was a small section, were vast. Huy walked slowly on, his troubled thoughts moving from the work he and Paneb had done that afternoon, to an aging Tetiankh, and back again.

He was scarcely aware of a slight rustle in the shrubbery to his left until it came again more loudly. With a lightening of the heart he came to a temporary halt, not wanting to interrupt some nocturnal creature enjoying the night even as he was. He was about to move on again when he saw something emerge from the denser blackness between the boles of two tall tamarisk trees and come slinking towards him. At first his mind refused to recognize it. For one long second he stared at it stupidly as it came shambling on, its yellow eyes fixed on his face, its rear legs bent in a manner that Huy, even in his growing alarm, knew to be entirely natural. About eight paces away from him it stopped, sank onto its lean haunches, and emitted a series of barks that sounded eerily like high-pitched laughter.

Terror seized Huy. He tried to turn and run but found himself unable to flee. *Perti, you must have heard those unearthly shrieks*, he called silently, desperately. *Help me!* But no sound of hurrying men came from the direction of the palace. Again he tried to force his legs into retreat, but they remained rooted to the grass. The hyena went on staring at him impassively. There seemed to be no message in its gaze, no threat. It appeared to be waiting. Gradually Huy's fear began to subside. *There was one in my estate's garden long ago, hunting mice among the cabbages*, he remembered. *Khnit had traded for it in the marketplace, wanting to fatten it up for servants' food. I made Anhur get rid of it. But there was another. It came to me as I had disembarked from my barge and was preparing to enter the house, and it came close to me and sat, even as this one is doing, and it seemed to be warning me, reminding me. Of what? My duty to Atum, to the understanding of the Book of Thoth? I have not thought about the Book for many weeks, nor of standing before the mighty Imhotep, Seer and Physician, in the Beautiful West, while my lifeless body was being taken to the House of the Dead in Hut-herib. I had been struck in the head by Sennefer's throwing stick and had toppled into the lake fronting Ra's temple. I drowned but did not know it because at once the Judgment Hall was behind me and the Paradise of Osiris all around. Imhotep had a scroll across his knees, but he was stroking the hyena nestling beside him. He asked me then if I would be willing to read and decipher the Book of Thoth, and I, innocent twelve-year-old child that I was, agreed. Then Atum breathed new life into my corpse and I woke on an embalming slab in the House of the Dead. The Book of Thoth. Forty-two scrolls on which the creator-god Atum dictated all laws pertaining to the creation of the cosmos, the world, nature, man and the animals, magic, and the next world.*

Standing there in the middle of the night, unable to stir, eye to eye with a desert scavenger that had somehow crept through the outskirts and then the heart of the city, evaded the palace soldiers, and finally made its way almost to his door, Huy knew how long it had been since he had given any attention to the task his younger self had agreed to undertake. *If Atum has sent you to threaten me, it will do no good,* Huy spoke to it dumbly. *When has there been time for me to ponder the contents of the sacred Book? There will be even less opportunity now that I've been appointed Scribe of Recruits. Do to me what you must, you unclean eater of offal. I will not resist you.*

Yet something was nagging at him, something that should have been obvious, and he cast about in his mind for what it might be. He saw himself outside his previous home, watching Anhur's men try to catch the first hyena that had appeared. He saw the second, its black eyes gleaming at him a moment before it slid under the closed gate of his domain and disappeared. Black eyes. But the hyena blinking in the brilliant light of the Beautiful West had watched him lazily with yellow eyes. Here, even through the uncertain light, he recognized the same golden shine. "It is you, isn't it?" Huy whispered. "Atum has sent you to me, but why?"

As if in answer, the hyena rose and began to pace unhurriedly towards him. Its eyes never left his face. Once more Huy tried to tear his feet free of the ground, but the effort failed. *Very well,* he thought resignedly. *I will accept this beast as your emissary, Great Neb-er-djer, Lord to the Limit, and endure whatever punishment you have decreed for me. Lately the Book of Thoth has become a fleeting memory, a single facet making up the woven cloth of my past. For that I am sorry.* Nevertheless, he could not repress a shiver of fear as the animal came to a halt right before him. Now he could smell it, an odour both sweet and pungent that forcibly reminded him of something else, something he could not place. He clenched his fists and waited. The hyena opened its mouth. Gently it took one of Huy's tightly curled hands and began to open his fingers with its teeth. Its limpid eyes closed, and Huy could have sworn that it was purring like a contented cat. He held his breath. Then it began to lick his palm, its warm black tongue quivering with what Huy recognized as pleasure. Amazed, he dared to touch the top of its head once with his other hand. The bristles between its ears pricked him. Presently it closed its mouth and sat back. For the last time its eyes met Huy's in a mild, almost friendly glance, then it turned and loped quickly away.

Huy gave in to a fit of trembling. He looked at his palm, still wet with saliva, and that same aroma rose from it to his nostrils: orchard blossoms, a whiff of honey, and underneath the sweetness a very faint stench of infected flesh. He wanted to wipe his hand on the sheet tucked around his waist, but somehow knew that he must not. Tentatively he lifted a foot. It came clear of the grass. Weakly, as though he were recovering from a long and debilitating disease, he began to retrace his steps. High up in the palace wall he saw the lamplight from his bedchamber shining dully through the slitted clerestory window to be rapidly lost in the darkness beyond. He could not make out the forms of Perti and the guard, nor hear any of their conversation.

Black tongue, he thought as he went. *Egypt's hyenas have black eyes and pink tongues. Atum sent that denizen of the Beautiful West to let me know that in spite of my neglect of the Book of Thoth, he is satisfied with me. I am proceeding within his will, and all I need to do is continue the work assigned to me.* All at once his step faltered. Suddenly he knew where he had inhaled the beast's peculiar smell before. The sacred Ished Tree exuded it, the Tree of Life planted in Iunu at the dawn of creation by Atum in the place where the temple of Ra would later rise. Every High Priest of Ra had been responsible for tending it since then. Huy had happened upon it by accident. He had been a very young student at the temple school, had become lost on a forbidden foray into the area between the temple itself and the high wall enclosing the whole precinct, and had found himself in the Tree's holy presence. So the hyena had indeed come to him from the blessed country beyond the gauntlet of the Judgment Hall where every heart was weighed. Strength began to flow back into Huy's body. He was smiling as he greeted his soldiers, entered his apartment, and, carefully avoiding a still-slumbering Tetiankh, reached his couch. At once he fell into a deep, satisfying unconsciousness.

IN THE FOLLOWING SEVEN MONTHS, Huy fixed his attention almost exclusively on strengthening the defence of the Delta and the Horus Road and reorganizing the divisions of the army and navy in that area. Occasionally he consulted the King and the Regent regarding his decisions, but on the whole they left him alone to work. He soon discovered that the most powerful men in charge of Pharaoh's military had been appointed by the Osirisone Thothmes the Fourth, Amunhotep's royal father, in return for some favour to the Horus Throne or to assure their loyalty.

Huy understood why his nephew had not dared to interfere with these arrangements, but he himself had no such qualms. He was loved by the King and trusted completely by the Regent.

On his assuming the tasks of his new assignment, Mutemwia had made it plain that he was allowed access to her quarters at any hour, and every courtier knew it. There had been a clamour of sycophants and boon-seekers outside Huy's apartment door at the start, but both Perti and a sharp-tongued Amunmose had dealt with them. In any case, Huy was seldom there. He and Paneb often ate and slept in the office of the Scribe of Recruits. Huy's heralds Ba-en-Ra and Sarenput moved constantly between the city and the forts and garrisons of the Delta and the Horus Road, and Huy himself spent many weeks with the officers of both the army and the navy in spite of the Inundation that rose, turned Egypt into a vast lake, and subsided once more. Huy scarcely noticed it except as a nuisance to be negotiated. Free to make what appointments he wished, Huy named Nebenkempt Overseer of All Ships of the King, giving him supreme control over the navy. Amunhotep-Huy's new father-in-law had been a Naval Troop Commander for some time and had captained the royal ship *Kha-em-Ma'at*, Living in Truth, under the last two kings.

By the end of Pharmuthi, the last month of the spring season of Peret, when the crops in the fields were thick and green, Huy was able to present a series of reports to the King of which he was justifiably proud. A new force of military police now patrolled the northern coast to repel any attempts by the Lycian pirates to infiltrate the Delta. They also protected the customs houses along the coast and at the western entrance to the Horus Road, where both goods and foreigners entered Egypt. All merchandise, especially tribute coming in, that was not consigned to His Majesty was taxed. Huy, appalled at the greed and laxness of the officials appointed to oversee this essential service, had dismissed them all and filled their posts with junior officers from the army who were answerable in turn to their superiors. The influx of easterners continued steadily. Some of the foreigners were herds-men, but many had come to Egypt with their families to work and were distributed to assist common farmers. Mutemwia had appointed Kha-em-hat as the King's Personal Scribe in Huy's place. He was a cheerful, capable young man Amunhotep had known since they were children together in the harem. Everyone called him by his nickname, Mahu. Huy had been ordered to See for him. Indeed, Huy had decided to Scry for every man he himself wanted to place in a position of authority. Consequently he often moved through the days bearing not only the burden of his post but also an appalling pain.

He soon discovered that Egypt's vassal states to the northeast were divided into three administrative areas governed by Egyptian nobles responsible for Canaan, Kumidu, and Simurru, an area encompassing Amurru along the coast almost as far as the land of the Amorites, who abutted the kingdom of Mitanni. Huy had met none of them; he had begun his tour of the Delta while Ptahmose journeyed farther east. Huy could easily see that the efficiency of those three governors was vital to Egypt's northern security. Accordingly he requested authority over them from Mutemwia, who granted it without hesitation. For some time they had reported to Khaemwaset, an aristocrat living on an estate just outside the town of Per-Bastet, close to the start of the Horus Road. Huy found him affable, knowledgeable, and health-ily wary of any unverifiable information coming out of the east. Khaemwaset readily agreed to send Huy regular and comprehen-sive accounts of his charges.

So at last Huy felt satisfied with the reforms he had initiated. The defence of the Delta was strengthened. The Delta estuaries were closely watched. Taxes and customs duties had been reformed. The Horus Road was now heavily patrolled, and the means to arbitrate any disputes arising between native land-owners and the herdsmen needing the lush grassland had been established. Huy had even answered an appeal from a contingent of foot soldiers patrolling the Horus Road. They had asked that their numbers be increased as a deterrent to the Nemausha, a nomadic people roaming the eastern desert and occasionally deciding that the animals and other possessions belonging to travellers along the Road should be shared with them.

The more changes Huy was forced to make, the more he wondered at his nephew's incompetence. It was true that many of the orders he sent out with Ba-en-Ra or Sarenput would have exceeded the limits of an ordinary Scribe of Recruits' mandate, that because of his closeness to the King and Mutemwia the power of his influence was greater than Amunhotep-Huy's had been. All the same, there was much the younger man could have done but that he had overlooked. Huy did not know how Amunhotep-Huy was faring as Egypt's new Vizier. Nor did he care.

The physician Seneb had accompanied Huy on his many visits to the Delta, doing his professional best to alleviate the worst of Huy's headaches and fatigue. Now all that was left were the monthly reports to arrive from the many overseers Huy had appointed. He returned to the palace exhausted but relieved that from now on all he had to do was keep a finger on the pulse of the complex he had created. He had sent three boxes of scrolls covered in Paneb's precise script to Mahu for the King's informa-tion and had then crawled carefully onto his couch, eyes throb-bing, skull feeling as though it would burst, and the familiar nausea associated with intense pain roiling in his stomach.

He did not get up for two days. He slept almost constantly through the first and had wanted to resume his palace duties on the second, but Seneb would not allow it. "Besides, as you know, Queen Iaret goes to her tomb in ten days, Great Seer, and only the most pressing business of government is being dealt with," he said. Huy had been about to drink the fresh grape juice Tetiankh had brought. Putting the cup carefully back on the tray, he sat still, waiting for the physician to leave. Then he summoned Amunmose.

The chief steward bustled in at once. "According to Seneb, you're supposed to stay on your couch today, but you might as well be up and have Tetiankh dress you. The Lady Tiye is waiting to see you, tapping her foot and bothering Paroi, and both Their Majesties will be here later this afternoon. Mayor Heby asks for an evening visit. You were away for the celebration of your Naming Day on the ninth of Paophi. He and your nephew Ramose want to bring you a gift. Paneb has a letter for you from Thothhotep."

Huy hushed him with an impatient gesture. "You're giving me another headache. Tell me about Iaret. All I received was an official notification of her death from King's Personal Scribe Mahu. What killed her?"

Amunmose tutted. "There were the usual fevers in the harem during the Inundation. Iaret succumbed rather quickly. A pity, really. Rumour had it that the King was about to name her second wife." He turned to the door. "If you don't need me, I'll continue with the inventory of the household's goods. Mutemwia wants everyone in Weset by the end of Mesore, so Paroi and I have only a scant four months to get everything done. Less, really—all the general holidays get in the way. No servant will work then. Who do you want to see first, or will you get dressed and come out? I must say, you still look very unwell."

"I'll speak with Tiye. Thank you, Amunmose." *Iaret succumbed rather quickly.* Huy mentally shrugged off the implication of those words.

The girl entered immediately and, dragging a stool to the couch, bowed briefly to Huy before sitting down. "I've missed you in the Office of Foreign Correspondence, Great Seer. I've known that you've been in the palace occasionally, but then you'd be gone again. I've needed to talk to you. I love my parents, but to them I'm a child, a pupil, a light dabbler in the weighty affairs of government until my interest wanes, and their only worry seems to be that I may somehow fail to live up to my position as a Queen. I can't speak to them of my fears. If I try, they just become more anxious. Queen Mutemwia invites me to share my confidences with her. She's beautiful and gracious, but very powerful. I'm afraid of her, of what she might do with whatever I tell her, and that makes me awkward in her presence. Ever since you made me apologize to Captain Perti, I've respected you. I trust you. I'm glad you're here for me to run to. I suppose you want to know all about Iaret."

You can still surprise me, little one. Your arrogance remains, and your self-will, but already you are determined to do more than simply fulfill your duty. You may not use those words to describe the ambition to yourself, but you have the seeds of a sane intuition that will serve you well in the years to come. Atum, you chose well for Egypt. "I've been told that she died of fever," he replied carefully, "that it was particularly virulent this year. And what of Queen Neferatiri, the late King's Chief Wife? I've heard no word of her since she was returned to the harem. Did she survive?"

Tiye grimaced and rolled her kohl-rimmed eyes. "That dried-up old prune? What demon could ever be bothered to infest her with a fever? She's nearly thirty years old, after all! She petitioned the Regent to allow her to retire to an estate she owns outside the town of Nefrusi somewhere. I think she invests in the crops from the famous date palms around the city of Khmun. Mutemwia gave her permission. Anyway, Amunhotep would never marry her. She'd probably be unable to produce a Horus-in-the-Nest."

"Iaret?" Huy prompted.

Tiye fixed him with a direct stare. "So you haven't heard the rumours. That perhaps I poisoned her, or conjured against her out of jealousy. The Queen told me not to respond and the gossip would soon die away, but it's been very difficult for me to hold my tongue. Gods! I do get tired of not being able to blurt out whatever I like." She crossed her legs and lifted her shoulders up to her ears in a purely childlike gesture that set her golden earrings swinging, then she folded her hands together and rested them demurely on her lap. "But I can do just that when I'm with you, can't I, Uncle Huy?"

Huy nodded. "And did you poison Iaret, or conjure against her?" he asked gently. "Ma'at would not approve, not at all, but I would understand."

"Understand and keep my secret, but absolutely not approve either!" The smile that lifted the downturned corners of her hennaed mouth beamed out. "I didn't like Iaret and I know that the King didn't like her either, even though she was going to be his second wife. She complained about everything. But I swear before Amun himself that I did her no harm. The fevers began early. Queen Mutemwia ordered me removed to the harem at Mi-wer by the lake for my safety, but I begged her to let me and my mother go to Father's estate instead. So that's where we went. I was very bored. You were away, the tutors weren't allowed near me, and Father wouldn't let me enter the palace to attend either the morning audiences or the daily discussion of the dispatches. I didn't see the King for several weeks."

Something in her tone alerted Huy. "You missed him. You're discovering his many qualities."

"Hardly." She made as if to run her fingers through the sheen of her dark red hair, felt the golden links of her circlet, and held an orange palm up to Huy instead. "I haven't spent enough time with him for that. When we are together we argue, but he seems to like it. He laughs and doesn't get annoyed. No, Uncle Huy. I like the shape of his eyes and the fullness of his lips and how deft his hands are, how they betray no hesitations. If I told my mother those things, she'd twitter with delight and talk about the physical pleasures of marriage."

"I won't twitter, but I'm pleased. I'll be attending May tomorrow morning to hear the dispatches. How is your study of Akkadian progressing?"

"Very quickly." She rose and smoothed down her sheath. "May's scribe continued to come to Father's house and I had nothing else to do but learn those symbols. Plain, aren't they?" Leaning forward, she kissed Huy's cheek. "I feel safer now that you're here," she said, and went out, a thin, still slightly awkward figure bearing herself with a dignity that Huy, with a pang of protective affection, realized he hadn't seen in her before.

After the noon meal he slept, and woke feeling almost well again. He had Tetiankh bathe and dress him, noting more sharply than ever before the body servant's swollen knuckles, the fumbles he tried to hide, his slowness in standing after tying Huy's sandals. On impulse Huy caught his hand. "Tetiankh, your responsibilities have multiplied since coming here. I require your attention far more often than I ever did in the more relaxed days on the estate. I would like Amunmose to find an assistant for you—unless, of course, you want to retire."

"Retire, Master?" Tetiankh frowned, and Huy knew that he had been correct in his offer. There was no shock or indignation in the man's response. "It's true that I'm not as capable as I used to be. I need more rest than the pace of your life allows, but I'm proud of my privileged position as your body servant. I was angry when Physician Seneb took away from me the preparation and administration of your poppy. It was at the command of Queen Mutemwia, you know."

"I had suspected as much."

Tetiankh withdrew his hand. "I have kept the secrets of your bedchamber for years, Huy. The care of your personal belongings and especially your body has been my sole vocation since the Mayor of Hut-herib deposited me on your estate. I do miss those happy years. I miss the Lady Ishat. So many memories, Master! You are quite right—I ought to retire. Part of me longs to return to the peace of the estate, but I hate the thought of abandoning you into another man's keeping. I will stay if you will allow me to choose an assistant and train him myself. You are relieved, I see."

Huy hugged him, ignoring his recoil against such a breach of propriety. "I am relieved. Selfishly so. I ought to have given you this choice before we moved here. Now find my gold and carnelian earrings, Tetiankh. The King will be arriving at any minute."

Once seated in his reception room, Huy called for Paneb. "I have time to hear the scroll that arrived from Nekheb. Read it to me, Paneb, and don't sing it. I don't approve of the accepted monotone taught to scribes."

Unperturbed, Paneb broke the unstamped wax seal and unrolled the papyrus. "'To my dear Master, greetings,'" he read. "'Know that I have considered the request that I return to your employ with both longing and dismay. My mind often strays to the day you approached me in the heat and dust of the market-place and changed my life forever, and the desire to rest once more under your kindly wings is strong. However, the dismay I would feel if I left Anhur is greater than that desire. I take flowers and food offerings to him almost every day, and I sit outside the entrance to his tomb and talk to his ba. I go into the goddess

Nekhbet's temple and pray for him. Thus I am comforted. Besides, there is much activity taking place just to the east of the town, at the mouth of one of the valleys where a desert route from the gold mines of the far south ends. A new shrine to Nekhbet will rise there. The white cord has been stretched and the foundations sunk. I have spoken with one of the architects named Hori. He says that he has met you. He tells me that the King and all his court will be moving to Weset soon, and Weset is only a few miles downstream from me. I yearn to see you then. Please forgive me. Your friend and servant Thothhotep, Scribe.'"

A day for unexpected memories, Huy thought rather sadly, watching Paneb let the scroll roll up and set it aside, his face quite correctly bearing no expression.

"Do you wish to reply to Scribe Thothhotep, Master?"

Huy shook his head. "There's no point. Thothhotep can be stubborn when she wants to, and she has good reason to stay where she is. I'm content with your proficiency, Paneb, and even if Thothhotep had accepted my plea I have quite enough work to keep three scribes busy. Get ready to note down any salient points of my conversation with the King and Queen Mutemwia. They will arrive at any moment." *I feel suddenly restless,* Huy told himself as Paneb melted into a good scribe's place of anonymity. *It's been years since I drove a chariot, but today I want to feel a set of reins in my gloved hands, or a bow, or even the heft of a well-balanced spear. I'll have Ba-en-Ra or Sarenput go to the noble Yuya and arrange something for me tomorrow.* Huy knew that his need for movement was a response to the unwanted surge of memories filling his mind, as though the sweat of his body might dilute them, force them to flow back to where they came from.

Behind him, Amunmose was opening the doors and around Huy his servants were falling to their knees. He did so also, pressing his nose to the reed mat under him and stretching out his arms in worshipful submission. *Arbiter of my fate*, he thought as he saw her tiny jewelled feet come close. He was not addressing the King.

In the evening, he greeted his brother with joy. They embraced fondly and at once settled themselves knee to knee in the soft lamplight of the reception room. Huy took his nephew Ramose's chin and smiled into the boy's alert face. "So, Steward in the Mansion of the Aten at Iunu," he teased, giving him the title Mutemwia had granted him, "are you giving your mother Iupia any more grey hairs?" *How different he is in every way from his half-brother the Vizier*, he thought as Ramose grinned back. *Everything about him is captivating.*

"I do hope not, Uncle. I'm doing well at school and that pleases her. I'm learning everything I can about the Aten so that when I reach my manhood at sixteen and go to Iunu to take up my tasks there I may serve the Regent well."

Huy looked at him curiously. He himself was fully aware that Mutemwia had given Ramose the appointment so that she could have a spy among the Aten's priests. The King's father had been well on his way to angering both the Atum and Egypt's saviour god Amun by detesting Amun's priests and openly preferring to worship the sun in all his hypostases, particularly Ra as Aten, the light as distinct from Ra as heat. Fortunately, Thothmes the Fourth had died before the cosmic balance of Ma'at had been put in true peril, and Mutemwia was determined to restore the correct equilibrium. Did Ramose know what his loyalty to the Queen would entail?

"Speaking of my twelfth Naming Day, you forgot it." Ramose sank to the floor and settled his back against his father's legs. "The first of Athyr, remember? We didn't forget you, though, Uncle. We have a gift for your fifty-first Naming Day. I passed it to Amunmose. You can examine it later. Anen, what are you doing? Come and sit beside me."

The younger boy, who had been earnestly talking to one of the guards, approached Huy, who rose at once and bowed. Tiye's brother lowered his head politely. "Great Seer and Scribe of Recruits."

"Noble Anen."

The child pursed his lips and cast a sidelong glance at Ramose. "I'm a Prince now, the Prince of Ipu. My father holds so many titles that he gave that one up. Ay will inherit all the others one day." He waved Huy back into the chair with a carelessly natural gesture and slid down beside his friend. Graceful and delicate of body, he reminded Huy of Thothmes, who had been small for his age at school but had made up for his size with a sturdy wiriness. This boy, Huy reflected, seemed overly fragile. He could easily understand Ramose's protectiveness. *There must be at least two or three years between them*, his thoughts ran on under cover of the general conversation, but judging by the Prince's comments his intellect was as sharp as his sister's.

Both boys were drinking pomegranate juice and helping themselves to the honeyed sweetmeats Amunmose was presenting.

Heby sat back and sipped appreciatively at his wine. "Syrian, Huy?"

"No." Huy smiled across at his brother, noting with an inner wrench the spider lines fanning across the temples, the slight bowing of the naked shoulders, the pouch of flesh hiding Heby's belt. *We no longer look alike, Huy reflected glumly. There was a time when we shared the virility and attractiveness of a manhood in full bloom, but Heby ages whereas I remain the same. No greyness, no sagging skin, no diminution of either intellect or physical strength except that caused by the strain of the Seeing. Atum has placed me beyond the grasp of time. He waits for me to discover the final solution to the meaning of the Book of Thoth, and his patience is an impersonal, relentless thing.* The eyes of the hyena came flooding into

Huy's mind, its golden gaze fixed on him as though it could go on staring at him serenely forever, and with a violent inward force he drove the vision away. "No, it comes from Alashia, Heby," he explained. "A gift from the King of that island for directing our navy against the pirates. Do you like the flavour?"

"It's different." He drank again and set down his cup. "I'm going to miss having you so close, Huy. I've given up my position as Mayor of Mennofer so that I'd be able to concentrate on my duties to Amun's cattle, and being Overseer of Amun's two granaries here in the north is no happy boat trip either. Obviously Iupia and I will be staying on. I've commissioned an architect to design us a house outside the city, even though Amunhotep-Huy will be going to Weset with the court and before long Ramose will be taking his place at Iunu." He gave Huy a rueful smile. "I'll be sorry to leave our little house and our noisy, dusty street, but Iupia's been nagging me for years to build something she considers more appropriate to my titles." He glanced down at Ramose and Anen, sitting cross-legged on the floor and chattering away to each other.

"I remember the day you married her," Huy put in. "I sat under the one scrawny sycamore tree in your tiny garden, drinking date wine with Thothhotep and watching your guests. You were still only Chief Scribe to Ptah's High Priest here in Mennofer then, and Iupia was the daughter of an aristocrat. Now you're a King's official and so am I." He paused, holding his cup in both hands and gazing down at the red liquid. He could see his distorted reflection in it, the image trembling slightly. He looked back at Heby. "Both the past and the future are ephemeral," he said slowly, "and even the present, which we seem to inhabit endlessly, is a lie. Yet we dare to speak of where we will be in five or ten years' time. Heby, we will still be in the present and still thinking that the moment lasts forever."

"Why are you, the Great Seer, suddenly fretting about the passing of time?" Heby held out his cup and Paroi stepped forward at once to refill it. "It's the move to Weset, isn't it? You don't want to go." He took a mouthful of wine and smacked his lips.

"Her Majesty keeps increasing the amount of work she piles on me," Huy replied. "On the one hand, I am blessed by her trust in me and my abilities. On the other, I have a strong sense that once in the south the load I carry will increase. I've spent my whole life so far in or near the Delta, Heby. All my memories are here. Weset means the beginning of a completely new life. It's not that I don't want to go. Something waits for me there, a final test of my loyalty to Atum. He has not put me to any test since I failed to stand against the King's father, but I've told you that he has promised me a last chance to redeem my cowardice. I saw a hyena in the garden." He had always shared the details of his strange existence with his brother. Now he related his encounter with the magical beast. Heby drank and listened, but it was young Anen who spoke up when Huy fell silent.

"You say that the hyena in the garden came to you from the Beautiful West, yet hyenas belong to Set, god of darkness and chaos, and they hate lions, and lions are the rays of the sun striking the earth, Ra and the Aten, golden and beautiful. Then how can there be hyenas in the Beautiful West?"

The words had tumbled out eagerly. Anen had risen to his knees and was holding the gilded arm of Huy's chair. As Huy turned from Heby, he saw a red flush creep across the boy's delicate features.

Anen sat back on his heels. "Forgive my presumption, Great Seer. I know I have offended good manners in eavesdropping on your words. I learn much that way, but Father punishes me for the habit."

"It is a bad habit, but a good way for a boy to learn of adult things, Prince," Huy responded gravely. "However, along with stolen knowledge must come the resolve to keep what one over-hears to oneself. As for hyenas in Paradise, all I can say is that I saw one there but it was unlike the vermin the peasants fatten up and eat. Perhaps there is a place for the followers of Set in the Beautiful West. Who can say?"

"There must be, because some of the members of my family, having foreign blood, are red-headed, and yet we were born in Egypt and worship the King and the gods with every loyalty. The red-headed, and those who must use their left hands for every-thing instead of their right, belong to Set. So the priests say."

"You need not fret about it, Prince. Set is not evil, he merely loves turbulence."

Anen looked solemn for a moment. Then he nodded. "Thank you for informing me of this, Great Seer. Our tutors do not mention Set very often. According to your definition of the god, my sister Tiye used to be one of his followers. She enjoyed making turbulence. But since His Majesty has married her, she resembles a devotee of the goddess Hathor. She has begun to care about love and beauty and doesn't tease me anymore or set her goose Nib-Nib to chase my brother Ay."

I wonder if Tiye knows how closely she's watched by these intelli-gent eyes, Huy thought with amusement. *The Prince would make an excellent little spy for Mutemwia.*

Anen touched him briefly and reverently on the knee. "Great Seer, will you Scry for me? I would like to prepare myself for my future."

"I would be honoured, Prince, so long as your father agrees. Have him send me a letter."

"Thank you, Great Seer." Anen scrambled back to his friend. Huy watched him go with affection. His scrupulous politeness reminded Huy even more strongly of Thothmes, who would apologize for being in your way if you stepped on his toe. *He'll be staying in Iunu to go on governing his sepat. I really only have three good friends apart from Heby: Thothmes, Ishat, and Methen. I'll be reduced to trying to stay close to all of them by letter. In spite of my intimacy with the King and Mutemwia, the bonds of true friendship cannot exist. Either one of them has the power to destroy me. As for Amunhotep's ministers, I am already superior to many of them. And Atum? Anubis? One does not make friends with gods who enjoy far more supremacy over one than the King himself.*

"Huy, you should be very pleased when you look back over your life and see how far you've come," Heby was saying to him. "Why do you seem so glum?"

"Perhaps I am not grateful enough," was all that Huy replied.

Later, after his guests had left and the household was settling down for the night, Huy sat in his office and read the reports from Naval Commander Nebenkempt, who requested that the building of more ships be considered; the noble Khaemwaset, governor of the three northeastern provinces, who had received a plea for heavier border patrols from the Assistant Governor who controlled Simurru, the area that included Amurru; and the officer in charge of the soldiers guarding the Horus Road. He and his men had been involved in a skirmish with the marauding Nemausha, killed a handful of them, and chased the rest back into the eastern desert. The scroll from Khaemwaset was more troubling. Amurru stretched along the coast. It bordered the land of the Amorites, and the land of the Amorites directly abutted the kingdom of Mitanni. Huy already knew from the foreign correspondence he dealt with that Mitanni was growing in population and prosperity. Governor Khaemwaset seemed to believe that Mitanni might be preparing to assimilate the tribes of the Amorites. Therefore a greater Egyptian military presence along the Amurru-Amorite border might ultimately be beneficial. *Mitanni would certainly become aware of such a move*, Huy thought as Paneb waited at his feet with brush poised. *There will be protestations of wounded trust from Mitanni's King, although he'll certainly be aware of the reason behind it. I wonder if Mutemwia would consider a complete Egyptian occupation of the Amorites. Of course Nebenkempt must have more ships if he needs them. The shipwrights of Nekhen and Nekheb are our best. Nebenkempt can send both mayors a list of what he needs.* The idea of Nekheb, a city he had never seen, brought Thothhotep's face floating into his mind. It remained there while he dictated the necessary letters and reminded Paneb to make copies of the reports for the King and file the originals. The niches from floor to ceiling in Huy's office were filling up rapidly.

Having dismissed Paneb, Huy had almost reached the haven of his bedchamber when Amunmose materialized out of the shadows, barefoot and clad only in his loincloth. He was holding a roll of papyrus. "I know that you're anxious for your poppy and your couch, Huy," the steward said, "but I knew you'd want to open this. The seal's imprinted with the symbol of the Heq-at sepat. I'm assuming it's from Governor Thothmes or the Lady Ishat." He handed the scroll to Huy. "I'm off to my mattress," he finished. "Sleep well."

Huy entered his room with a light heart. He had not received word from either of his friends since the beginning of the month, and even before he came to a halt in the middle of the floor he was breaking apart the red wax. Quietly Tetiankh began to undress him, lifting the earrings from his lobes, pulling off the wooden frog always used to fasten his braid and setting it down on the cosmetics table, unhooking the silver necklet that tinkled as he laid it aside. The scent of lilies wafted to Huy from the bowl of hot water set ready for him, but for once he was unaware of the aroma.

"It's not from Thothmes or Ishat, it's from Nasha!" he exclaimed. "She apologizes for using the Governor's stamp. Or rather, she doesn't." He stood still while Tetiankh washed the paint from his face, then sat, and while his feet were washed he silently scanned the letter.

"Dearest adopted brother, omnipotent Seer, and stern controller of the army and navy," Nasha had dictated.

I am using Thothmes' seal totally without compunction so that you will open my letter at once. I hear of the King's move to Weset with indignation. I am so very bored, rattling around Father's estate all by myself, and no one has thought to invite me to Egypt's most exciting city. Therefore I have decided to invite myself. I intend to live with Amunnefer until your beautiful new house is built. Yes, brother of mine, everyone knows that you detest living in the palace and the King has promised you a private estate of your own. Such news filters down in mysterious ways from Thothmes' servants to mine. If I receive no bleat of protest from you, I shall appear in your reception hall with all my chattels on the day you move in. Otherwise I am in danger of lying about in a drunken stupor for the rest of my days and facing a very unfavourable weighing in the Judgment Hall when my heart at last rests on the scales and will not balance Ma'at's feather. Darling Huy, please do not refuse me this. Signed by my own hand, the Lady Nasha, the month of Pharmuthi, Year Two of the King.

Huy began to smile. He let the papyrus roll up, set it beside the water bowl, and, climbing onto his couch, drained the vial of poppy set ready for him and lay down. At once Tetiankh began to apply the nightly oil and honey to his face. "She wants to come and live with me when the King has finished building our new house," Huy said. "I'd like that very much, Tetiankh. She and I have been close friends since I was a boy staying on Nakht's estate with Thothmes and her sister Anuket. Nakht is dead now, and Thothmes is the Governor of the Heq-at sepat in his place, with Ishat and his children to keep him doubly occupied. Anuket is dead too. Nasha is very much alone. She ought to have married. The gods know she had many opportunities to do so." He rolled over and Tetiankh began his regular massage.

"Forgive me for offering my opinion without being asked, Master, but it has always seemed to me that the Lady Nasha preferred your company to that of any other young man. She will be a good companion for you."

"How tactful you are! I spent years besotted with Anuket. I've always loved Nasha as the sister of my best friend and we've always been easy with one another. I assume that Anuket's husband, the noble Amunnefer, has already agreed to house her. I'm anxious to meet him again and inspect the poppy fields outside Weset that we ventured into together. I've never seen them, although the crop has helped to make me a very wealthy man. I'll consider Nasha's request." *Even if I'd wanted her instead of her sister, that perfidious little witch Anuket, I wouldn't have been able to make love to her,* Huy's thoughts ran on. *I have been impotent by the will of Atum since I returned to my body and found myself in the House of the Dead, more years ago than I care to remember. Nasha herself will be somewhere in her fifties. She's older than Thothmes. We shall be two old people bent over a board game and yawning while Nut swallows the sun and our couches beckon.* The vision was so distasteful that Huy murmured aloud. Tetiankh's sure touch faltered and then continued. Huy fell asleep before the massage was over.

Three weeks later, on the fifteenth day of Pakhons, the month marking the beginning of the harvest season of Shemu, Iaret was accompanied to her husband's tomb by Amunhotep, Mutemwia, Overseer Userhet and the other harem administrators, many of the women she had come to know during her stay there, and two hundred paid mourners who wore the blue sheaths of custom, wailed pitifully, and often stooped to place soil on their heads. Huy did not attend the funeral, but he heard the women's keening gradually fade as Iaret was carried away from Mennofer's House of the Dead. *Apart from the King's blood-uncle Amunhotep and his mother Mutemwia, he has no relatives left,* Huy mused as he sat in the garden under the dense shade of a cluster of sycamores and watched the glittering liquid from the gardeners' leather buckets being carefully poured onto the thirsty flower beds. *Last year Amunhotep's half-sisters Amunemipet, Tiaa, and Petepihu succumbed to—what? Was it the fever that consumed them, or something worse? Has Mutemwia been coldly weeding out any contenders for the Queen's crown but for the choice she rightly believed I would make?* The possibility was both flattering and horrible. *But she promised me once that she would never offend against Ma'at,* Huy reminded himself. *Her control over every aspect of government is absolute, but even if it wasn't, I saw no guile in those wide gazelle's eyes of hers when she vowed always to live according to the dictates of the goddess.*

Away to Huy's left, a donkey hitched to a cart laden with huge water barrels twitched its long grey ears and stared patiently ahead. Obviously, even though the fifteenth of every month was a public holiday, it was necessary for the gardeners to continue tending the vast royal acres. Shemu would grow hotter. The river's flow would grow sullen, its height reduced, and the farmers' fields would become dusty expanses spidered with deep, dry cracks. But the many tributaries of Ta-Mehu, the Delta, would enable the peasants to keep the land moist, the orchard trees healthy, the grazing for the King's herds lush and green. *What will*

Shemu be like at Weset, far to the south? Huy wondered, leaning back on one elbow and watching birds alight close to the gardeners in the hope of catching a worm. *So relentlessly hot that no one at all can work?*

He saw Tetiankh emerge from his apartment door, step between Perti and his soldier, and start across the lawn. He was followed by a younger, shorter man in a crisp white kilt who seemed vaguely familiar. Huy's heart sank as he sat up. Tetiankh was supposed to be resting along with Huy's other servants. The two men came in under the shade and bowed.

"A pardon for disturbing you, Master, but I am taking the opportunity today to present to you my choice for the position of assistant body servant." He stepped aside and gestured. "This is Kenofer of Sumenu. He has been an assistant to the keeper of the bathhouse closest to your apartments and is accomplished in the art of massage. He knows the properties and uses of every oil available in Egypt. He wishes to better himself."

"So that's where I've seen you, Kenofer of Sumenu. And where's Sumenu?"

"It's a town a very few miles south of Weset, Master," Tetiankh said hurriedly. "Many important men belong to the ruling Sobek family there. Our Treasurer, Nakht-sobek, comes from Sumenu. Kenofer knows the area well and can answer any questions about it you may have."

Huy was touched by Tetiankh's obvious concern that his choice should make a correct impression. He looked the younger man up and down. Kenofer met his eyes without a sense of either obsequiousness or challenge. He had pleasant features, an important consideration in a servant who would be closely attending an employer returning to a bedchamber exhausted and needing the unobtrusive care of a face projecting nothing more than a welcome tranquility.

"Have I ever been under your hands?" he asked.

Kenofer shook his head. "No, Great Seer. Tetiankh would not have allowed it."

"True. Have you a family?"

"No wife yet, Great Seer, but my parents and brothers still live in Sumenu."

"Why would you want to serve me, Kenofer?"

An engaging smile spread across Kenofer's rather solemn face. "A body servant is his master's best source of gossip," he said promptly, without a shred of embarrassment. "He hears in silence and he carries what he hears to his master. If it is merely a rumour, he says so. If it is a truth, he says so. I have heard many things, urgent, stupid, fanciful, out of the mouths of my betters as they stand on the bathing slab or lie on a bench waiting for my hands. I have ignored them all."

"So you secretly mock your superiors?"

Tetiankh made a tiny whimper of protest. Kenofer shook his head. "Not so, Great Seer. I spoke clumsily. I ignore what is said because my knowledge of the working of the court is limited. What sounds urgent, or stupid, or fanciful, may be of the greatest importance to a master I have yet to find and tell."

"Does he think a silence must be filled? Does he want to natter on about nothing?" Huy asked Tetiankh, then he waved them away. "It doesn't matter. Tetiankh, he's on trial for the next three months. Train him well."

Both men were beaming as they bowed themselves away. Huy lay back in the soft grass and, folding his arms across his chest, gazed contentedly into the lacy foliage above him. The King would send for him later, he knew, but for now he had nothing to do. He was happy.

9

OVER THE NEXT FEW WEEKS, the palace gradually emptied of courtiers and servants. At first Huy did not notice the less congested corridors or quieter nights. Then the daily business of the audience hall became sparse as the ambassadors left Mennofer together with the administrators who did not need to present daily reports. Huy was sometimes able to don a leather helmet and gloves and take out a chariot in the company of Tiye's father, Yuya. So far Huy had had little to do with the Master of the King's Horses. As Egypt's most senior noble, Yuya commanded great power. Huy wondered whether Yuya resented his influence with Amunhotep, but nothing in Yuya's manner suggested it. Out on the desert to the west of the city the two men raced each other, the small, light chariots making easy work of the arid terrain. The balance and skill Huy had learned at school came back to him and he welcomed the healthy ache of muscles no longer accustomed to such strains.

Once, they were accompanied by Yuya's elder son Ay, a handsome youth a year older than his sister Tiye. Ay took the reins while his father stood protectively behind him on the wicker floor of the vehicle. Ay gave Huy the deference his position at court required, but Huy read the suspicion he had not found in Yuya behind the boy's grey eyes. "Ay loves me very much," Tiye had said of her brother. "He used to lie to Father and take the punishments meant for me. But now of course I behave myself with decorum, and Ay has no need to shield me from anyone. He and I are firm friends. I have you to protect me now, Uncle Huy." Huy understood Ay's coolness towards him if its root was mere jealousy, and was grateful that Tiye had another champion besides himself. He made a mental note to get to know the young aristocrat.

Userhet and the majority of the harem attendants sailed south with the women Mutemwia had chosen to take up residence in the new palace. Tiye and her mother did not go with them. They returned to Yuya's estate to wait until the King himself left Mennofer.

In the lull before the final emptying of the palace, Huy reluctantly attended Amunhotep-Huy's wedding feast, held in Heby's tiny garden. "It should have been celebrated on Nebenkempt's estate," Amunhotep-Huy grumbled as he joined Huy, who was standing in the thin shade cast by the house. "Look at this crowd, crammed elbow to elbow! Father ought to have moved into something larger a long time ago. I can imagine what my new father-in-law is thinking!"

"He's probably thinking of Heby's wisdom in continuing to live close to his responsibilities as Mennofer's Mayor," Huy replied. "Commander Nebenkempt is no spoiled court dandy. Your father is building a new house by the river now that he's relinquished control of the city. How is your own project progressing on the lake?"

Amunhotep-Huy's scowl deepened. "His Majesty has ordered me to take my new wife there and oversee the erecting of the house myself for a while. He said that as my first tour of the sepats as Vizier won't take place until after the harvest, I should concentrate on making Henut-nofret happy. She does love

Ta-she." His expression softened briefly as he craned to see her through the press of jewelled and perfumed bodies. Huy had shared a few pleasantries with her earlier. She was undeniably beautiful and well bred, but shy, almost timid. Huy did not think she would be happy with his cantankerous nephew.

"I don't think His Majesty wants me in Weset," Amunhotep-Huy finished sourly. "I'm his most senior administrator now. How will he consult with me if he's almost at one end of Egypt and I'm stuck miles out in the desert at the other? Ta-she is a magnificent lake. The town of Mi-wer on its banks is surrounded by lushness. But I won't enjoy spending my time harassing my architect and sailing with my wife for long."

He left abruptly, pushing his way through the guests, and Huy watched him go. *Why did you make him Vizier, Mutemwia?* he asked silently. *He has almost no tact, surely a vital asset for any high official, and too quick a temper. The governors will not like dealing with him. I don't believe that you suffered a lapse in judgment when you took the position of Scribe of Recruits away from him.* With relief Huy saw Nebenkempt threading his way through the fluttering linens.

"I'll be captaining the *Kha-em-Ma'at* to Weset next week, Huy," he called as he extricated himself and stepped into the shadow. "Thank you. The last time I did so was for the King's father."

"It's your prerogative." Huy smiled. "Will you find it more difficult to see to the affairs of the navy from Weset? At least you and I will be close to Nekheb, where the new ships are being built. Incidentally, with the King residing permanently at Weset, we must talk about reorganizing the placement of the divisions." They fell into an easy discussion of their several responsibilities, eventually sliding to the sparse grass and putting their backs against the wall of Heby's house. Paneb, unobtrusive and ever-present, had reached for his palette, but Huy shook his head. The hour was precious, time spent with a man who was fast becoming a friend, and neither of them looked up until the throng began to thin and Henut-nofret approached. The men scrambled to their feet and Huy bowed.

"Mother has had a room prepared for Amunhotep-Huy and me at home, Father," the girl said. She was flushed, Huy noted, and her words were slightly slurred. "We will leave for Ta-she in the morning. Amunhotep-Huy is saying goodbye to his family." She executed an unsteady bow to Huy and retreated.

Nebenkempt laughed. "There's nothing quite as pleasant as a heket of beer on a hot day, although Henut-nofret prefers getting drunk on grape wine. Well, Scribe, it has been a momentous and joyful occasion. I pray they will be as contented with each other as my wife and I have been." He embraced Huy and started away.

Huy wanted to catch his arm. *If there is trouble, come to me,* he wanted to say. *If Henut-nofret needs escape, tell me first and not the King.* Illogically, he felt a need to defend the honour of his family. He had not forgotten his nephew's agreement that family loyalty, if it did not collide with one's duty to the King, came before all else.

"I love my son, but I fear that little Henut-nofret will not be strong enough to curb his tendency to bully everyone he can." Heby's voice seemed to echo Huy's own thoughts. He turned to find his brother beside him. "Now that Amunhotep-Huy's a Vizier, he's no longer inferior in station to his father-in-law," Heby went on. "I'm afraid it means trouble for that sweet girl. Nebenkempt has been very generous in his gifts to the pair of them, and of course if she ends up divorcing him she'll take it all back when she goes. Amunhotep-Huy won't be pleased." He blew out his lips. "Why am I worrying about all that now? Habit when it comes to my children, I suppose. Tell me, Huy, when are you leaving Mennofer? The Queen tells me that you'll be travelling on *Kha-em-Ma'at* with her and the King." He slung an arm around Huy's shoulder. "Don't disappear back to your lair just yet. Come inside. You and Iupia and I will pick at the remains of the feast and share the gossip. After all, I won't be seeing you again for some time."

Inside the house, the lamps were being lit, giving the modest rooms a cozy glow. Iupia was sitting back being fanned by her body servant, who was waved away as the two men entered.

"Thank the gods that's over," she said. "Prahotep, bring us date wine. My stomach is upset." Heby's steward nodded and withdrew. "Ramose is spending the night with Anen on Chief Rekhit Yuya's estate," she continued as Heby and Huy sat. "As Prince of Ipu, Anen will be heading south, and Ramose is going to miss him a great deal. We have the house to ourselves, Heby. It'd be a lovely night to drift on the river under the full moon, with you also, Huy, but I'm just too tired. Tomorrow we must make the short journey to Hut-herib for the Beautiful Feast of the Valley, and offer food and prayers to your parents."

With a jolt, Huy remembered that the Feast was always celebrated at Payni's full moon. The tombs of the deceased were blessed with incense, and families would gather outside the sealed entrances to eat and commune with their dead relatives. *Next year I shall join Thothhotep in venerating Anhur, while Heby does his duty for our parents Hapu and Itu. What will next year bring? I wonder.* He accepted the wine Prahotep was pouring for him, and drank. As always, it began to settle his stomach. Iupia too seemed to find it soothing. The conversation became agreeably comfortable and spasmodic, the idle comments of three weary but contented people.

Huy finally took his leave and was carried back to the palace in his litter. *Mutemwia won't leave until the Beautiful Feast is over,* he mused drowsily. *I'll make the overnight journey to Hut-herib with Heby and Iupia tomorrow and visit my estate afterwards. It will be my last chance to greet Merenra and all my old servants, and perhaps sit in my garden surrounded by memories. If Physician Seneb is waiting to poke at me tonight, I'll send him away. All I need now are opium and sleep.*

The King readily gave Huy permission to go to Hut-herib for a couple of days, and after the poignant ceremonies at his parents' tomb Heby and Iupia returned to Mennofer. Huy hurried to his estate. The old gate guard, Kar, still sat in his mud-brick shelter by the gate above Huy's watersteps, and greeted him with a nod and a grunt. Steward Merenra and the members of Huy's staff who had been either too old or merely unwilling to take up positions in Huy's palace household stood bunched together in an excited group, smiling and bobbing as Huy, Paneb, Ba-en-Ra, Tetiankh, and Captain Perti with his contingent of soldiers walked the short distance to the house. The walls had been freshly whitewashed, Huy noted with approval. Neat rows of vegetables and flowers filled the garden. Amongst the stand of mature date palms lining the little canal running from the river to the edge of the plots, the stalks of the henna plants Huy's last gardener, Seshemnefer, had been allowed to cultivate for his own profit looked bare and ugly. Seshemnefer harvested the flowers and sold them to the dyers. Huy was pleased to see that he still did so—or someone did, on Seshemnefer's behalf. Seshemnefer and his wife Khnit, Huy's cook, had been sent to oversee the estate on the shore of lake Ta-she that the Rekhet had deeded to Huy in her will. Huy had never seen it.

The steward Merenra dismissed the staff and approached Huy, who embraced him. "It all looks the same," Huy said as they broke apart. "Even the shadows dappling the garden are familiar. I almost expect Ishat to emerge from the rear door with a scroll in her hand and beckon to me." He spoke gruffly, on a surge of emotion, yet a part of him noted his surroundings with an unanticipated objectivity. The estate was a good deal smaller than he remembered, and as he entered the house itself with Merenra behind him his sense of mild dislocation grew. Every room was spotless, and standing at the head of the stairs leading to the upper floor, Huy's previous house servant Ankhesenpepi was waiting for Huy's praise, an anxious expression on his face. Huy gave it warmly and walked to the far end, where one could step over the low sill and stand on the roof, his glance darting into the bedchambers as he went.

"I ordered the lion skin burnt, Master," Merenra was saying as Huy turned to retrace his steps. "It became infested with beetles. I know that it was a gift from our King's grandfather, but I couldn't save it."

"It doesn't matter. Neither Ishat nor I liked it. I see that the servants are using the upper rooms. That's good. Tell me, Merenra, have you any news of my parents' house?"

"Your uncle Ker's foreman lives there with his family. He keeps it in good repair. I assume you still have no communication with your aunt and uncle? Neither is in good health."

"They're both aged." Huy spoke indifferently. His uncle had paid for his education at Ra's temple school in Iunu until his accident. Both Ker and his wife Heruben, believing that he had been possessed by a demon after Methen carried him home from the House of the Dead, had shunned him completely and transferred their support to Heby. Huy had been unable to forgive them. He had desperately needed the comfort of his relatives, but only his mother had continued to trust and love him.

He was silent as he went back to the tiny reception hall. *This place overflows with memories, but it no longer calls to me with nostalgia. I'm no longer the young man full of hopes and visions who lived* here so happily with Ishat. I've changed, become less innocent, less hopeful, and my visions have been curbed and channelled by order of the King and his mother. Only the mystery of the Book of Thoth remains unsullied by the passage of time, its solution still beyond my reach, its message still waiting for me to discover. Atum will not be satisfied until that enlightenment comes to me. He sighed. "'Let us call Light first—but known only through darkness,'" he quoted aloud from the Book.

"Master?"

Huy came to himself. "Everything is as I left it," he said to the steward. "Thank you, Merenra. Is there anything you need? Is the amount of gold I send you regularly for the estate's upkeep enough?"

He shared a cup of barley beer with Merenra in the garden before he left. They reminisced idly. In a mood approaching desperation, Huy strained to recover something of those days, a pure emotion that would temporarily nudge aside the inner self he had become, but he took his leave knowing that the ghost of his younger self would drift through the pretty rooms and linger in the garden forever, inaccessible to the Scribe of Recruits and adviser to the Horus Throne.

A WELCOME AND SURPRISING FAMILIARITY wrapped him round as he and his attendants entered his palace apartments. Amunmose met him at the door. "A message has come from the Regent, Huy. We leave Mennofer on the second of next month. If your craft isn't large enough to accommodate your household goods and servants, I'm to let Nebmerut know. You'll be on the royal barge Kha-em-Ma'at together with Tetiankh. You'll need a cot, bed and body linens, oils and cosmetics, and of course plenty of poppy."

"Has anyone told you what our accommodations will be like in the old palace at Weset?" Huy wanted to know.

Amunmose made a face. "No. Apparently the complex is very large, much larger than this, because the Osiris-one Ahmose Glorified, Egypt's saviour, renovated and restored it after it had fallen into ruin under the rule of the vile Setiu. He removed a wall that had stood between his estate and the old palace and incorporated the two. But that was a long time ago. We'll see what Architect Kha has been able to accomplish in the time he's had to make the place habitable."

"Are there gardens?"

Amunmose shrugged. "I don't know. I assume so. There's plenty of desert out behind the protecting walls, though. Or so I've heard. It sounds terrible—dry and hot and dead compared to the blessed Delta. Why the Regent wants to drag us all down there, I can't imagine. Rakhaka will have your evening meal ready for you in about an hour. Paneb has reports for you to read. Oh, and gardener Anab begs not to be left behind when we go."

Mutemwia's decision to move south is sound, Huy mused as he walked into his bedchamber. *Remove Amunhotep from the influence of Ra's and the Aten's priests, show a closer alliegance to Amun, and enable the ministers to function more easily from the centre of Egypt. Besides, by all accounts, Weset seems to be attracting large numbers of people seeking a greater prosperity.*

His new body servant, Kenofer, had just lit the lamp beside the couch and the room was filling with the pleasant odour of fragrant ben oil enriched with essence of lilies. He came forward bowing, a smoking taper still held in one hand. "Welcome back, Master. I trust that your visit to Hut-herib was satisfactory. I have taken the liberty of opening your shrine and cleaning the interior. I—"

Tetiankh, who had followed Huy, shushed the young man fiercely. "The sole purpose of a good body servant is to learn every preference of his master and then to not only provide what is wanted but anticipate what his employer may not even be aware that he needs. In silence, Kenofer! In silence! He looks for no thanks! He does his duty unobtrusively and quietly!" He turned to Huy. "I apologize for my assistant, Master. He is obviously slow to learn!"

Kenofer fell to his knees and put his nose to the mat. Huy laughed.

"Get up, you idiot," he ordered. "Undress me and find me a fresh sleeping robe. I'll eat on my couch. Tetiankh, find Paneb. I'll dictate a letter to the Lady Nasha while I'm waiting for my food."

Tetiankh went out. Kenofer scrambled up and hurried to one of Huy's tiring chests. Huy saw that he was eager to speak but had wisely decided to keep his mouth closed. *I shall miss you, Tetiankh,* Huy thought sadly as he took the chair beside the couch. *I have said farewell to many friends over the last few years. I fear I shall see many more fade into old age and retirement. Thothmes, Ishat, don't change! Don't die! The loss of you will be too hard to bear.*

Kenofer had at last found what he was looking for and was laying the soft folds of a sleeping robe across the foot of the couch. He stepped to Huy and stood waiting. Huy rose, all at once glad to be back in these few rather anonymous rooms where the constant comings and goings of the hundreds of inhabitants set up a background hum that never ebbed. *Until now,* Huy thought as Kenofer reached reverently to undo his jewelled belt. *Now this tumultuous heart of my country's power has been gradually falling silent, and soon only insects, mice, a few servants, and guards will remain to watch the rays of sunlight crawl down the walls and across the dusty floors to dissolve in the pink, ephemeral mists of Ra's setting. He will vanish into the mouth of the sky goddess Nut unremarked by royal eyes. Even though his devouring may be seen from the streets of Weset, neither the King nor the Regent will notice it. The attention of the Incarnation of Amun and his royal Mother will be fixed elsewhere.*

On the second day of Epophi, the last inhabitants of the palace left Mennofer, their skiffs and barges strung out along the surface of the river like a long, multicoloured snake. The bank between the city and the water was thick with quiet citizens watching them go.

"They feel deserted," Tetiankh remarked. He and Huy were leaning on *Kha-em-Ma'at*'s gilded rail as the city slid by. "It has been hentis since a King ruled from Weset."

"They'll soon recover their pride. Mennofer's wharves will always be busy with trade and tribute." Huy turned to look along the wide deck and past the cabin. The royal colours of blue and white fluttered from the tall flagpole in the stern, and beyond it a forest of oars dipped and rose as far back as he could see. The river was very low. The current flowed sluggishly towards the Delta, but its force was still sufficient to battle with the summer wind coming out of the north. Every sail was filling, and every oar was out. Somewhere behind him, his servants and his chattels were following, lost in this vast mass departure. In spite of the steady breeze, the morning was hot. A large canopy had been erected against the wall of the cabin and another attached to the prow. The cushions and mats strewn under them were empty as the travellers lined the rails to see Mennofer sink below the horizon. Mutemwia's body servant Tekait was vainly struggling to hold a sunshade over her mistress's head. Mutemwia ignored her. The King had joined Nebenkempt in the prow as he was speaking to the helmsman on his high perch, the huge tiller tucked under his arm as he leaned down to listen. Steering the "Living in Truth" between hidden shoals and other unseen obstructions was doubly difficult at this time of the year.

Shemu used to be the battle months, Huy thought as the southern suburbs glided slowly by. *Our history records a southern revolt against Egyptian control at the Appearing of every succeeding King, followed by the assembling of troops, the interminable march into the furnace of Wawat and Kush, the inevitable subduing and punishing of the barbaric tribesmen. So far I haven't had to consider the eventuality. Are the troglodytes waiting until Amunhotep comes of age and receives the Pshent? If I were a chieftain, I'd have fomented rebellion as soon as his father died, while Amunhotep-Huy was still Scribe of Recruits. In a couple of years Amunhotep will indeed receive the Red Crown and the White Crown. But perhaps when word that Weset has again become the home of the Horus Throne trickles down into Wawat, it will prompt the uprising I'm certain will come. Sometime on this voyage Nebenkempt and I must plan a strengthening of the forts below the Cataracts, particularly Buhen.*

"What ponderous thoughts are consuming you, Uncle Huy? Why are you frowning?" The voice was Tiye's. She had come up beside him and was squinting into the bright sunlight, the silver ankhs hanging from her earlobes tangled in her wind-whipped hair. More silver ankhs encircled her neck and held the linen sheath close to her narrow waist. Her arms were bare, but she wore several ornate gold, red jasper, and lapis rings. Huy thought fleetingly that they entirely dwarfed the embryonic grace of her fingers. Winding itself sinuously between her ankles was a small grey cat with blue eyes and black tufts to its sharp ears. It peered up at Huy disinterestedly, sat down on one of Tiye's sandal-clad feet, and lazily began to wash itself. A servant had followed Tiye and was trying to extricate the earrings from the girl's tousled tresses.

Tiye jerked her head. "Leave me alone!" she snapped. "Here. Take Lord Claw away and brush him if you've nothing better to do!" Snatching up the cat, she thrust it at the servant, who bowed awkwardly and hurried away. Tiye graced Huy with a brilliant smile. "That's Heria, my very own body servant. The Queen appointed her. Up until now my mother's women have seen to my care. I liked that arrangement, but apparently now that I'm a King's wife, even if it's in name only so far, I must have a full complement of household staff. I'm to have my own apartments in the new palace. Did you know? Steward, scribe, permanent guards, all of it." She grasped Huy's arm and stood on the tips of her toes. "I have no say in who they are," she went on in a low voice. "Pass the rod of your judgment over them, will you please, Great Seer? I have nothing to hide from Mutemwia, but all the same, I resent being spied on. Oh, damn these stupid earrings! Mother made me wear them today and she wouldn't let Heria braid my hair. She didn't say so, but I know she wants Amunhotep to see it flowing free and be dazzled by such beauty as I have. She didn't bargain on a stiff wind. I can hardly wait until my authority is greater than hers!"

"Is she not on board?" Huy gently began to free the ankhs, Tiye's perfume of mingled cardamom and myrrh faintly reaching his nostrils.

"No, thank all the gods! She's back there somewhere with Anen and Nib-Nib and Prince Rascal. Father and Ay are travelling by land with His Majesty's horses. The Queen didn't want her here with me anyway."

"Did she not?" As always after spending a few moments with Tiye, Huy ceased to notice the hooded eyes, wide nose, and downturned mouth that removed the girl from the ranks of the physically beautiful. Her presence alone became increasingly beguiling. One wanted to find and embrace, or at least pin down and define, what one sensed was an elusive quality composed of intelligence, vivacity, and independence rendering her well-nigh irresistible.

"No. Neither did Amunhotep." Holding the mass of her dark red hair back with one hand, she glanced over the side of the boat to where the forest of oars dribbled small streams of glittering water as they rose, and left swift eddies as they sank again. "We must put into a convenient bay before sunset to give the poor sailors a rest," she commented. "I have never camped in a tent. Will I enjoy it, do you think? Will you make sure that I'm well guarded? When you were young, you walked from Iunu to Hut-herib, didn't you? Was it fun?"

Huy met those large, heavily kohled blue eyes without astonishment. "No, Lady Tiye, it was not fun at all," he replied.

Later, he called Tetiankh, had him braid Tiye's hair, then joined Mutemwia under the cabin's canopy, where she was drinking beer and picking at a dish of grapes, fat ripe figs, and blackcurrants. "There are Mennofer's pistachios, and walnuts too," she offered as Huy lowered himself beside her in the welcome shade. "Amunhotep took the dish of almonds with him, though, when he went to sit under the prow." She laughed. "He was comfortable here beside me until he saw your body servant tying the tips of Tiye's braids. Then he moved. Look at them, Huy."

The King was reclining easily on one elbow, his face raised to Tiye, who had sunk cross-legged beside him. Her back was to the watchers, but Huy saw that she was saying something to Amunhotep that lit up his smile.

"They are becoming quite companionable," Mutemwia said. "They play board games together and argue about the dispatches, of all things! It distresses Thuyu. She believes that such conversation is not ladylike, but I see in Tiye a Queen who will be more than a wife to my son. He's used to discussing matters of state with a woman. By the time Amunhotep is crowned, Tiye will have taken my place as an adviser and guide under your supervision." Deftly she pulled a cluster of grapes free of its stem. "Work has begun on your new house," she told Huy. "I want you to be happy at Weset. I ordered Kha to put one of his assistant architects on the project. Kha has selected the site himself, by the river and surrounded by your own poppy fields. Thus you will have the privacy and quiet you desire." Selecting a grape, she slid it between her hennaed lips.

"Your Majesty is kind." He watched the muscle along her jawline flex as she crunched the grape pips between her strong teeth.

"Not really." She picked another grape from her open palm. "Weset will be our permanent home, all of us. I can't have you moving to Sumenu or Aabtu because you're unhappy." The piece of fruit vanished into her mouth. Sumenu was approximately twenty miles south of Weset, between the city and Nekheb, Huy reflected silently, and Aabtu, where the head of Osiris was buried, lay a little farther away than that to the north. "In the meantime, your apartments in the old palace are ready for you." She smiled across at him, her kohled eyes squinting against the bright sunlight in spite of the billowing canopy under which the two of them sat. "You will be living between the King and myself so that you will be easily accessible to both of us. I shall occupy the original Queen's quarters until Tiye receives the vulture crown. Kha tells me that all the rooms are large and cool." She dropped the remainder of the grapes back onto the platter. "I want you to be happy, Great Seer," she repeated. "There is much work ahead of you."

For a moment they were both quiet. The low murmur of other conversations mingled with the sound of the wind-ripped flag and the low, rhythmic tones of the officer calling the beat to the oarsmen. Tiye's high, spontaneous laugh came floating across the deck. A grinning Amunhotep had taken both her braids in his hands and was pulling her head from side to side. As Huy watched, Tiye reached towards Amunhotep's brown ribs. The King recoiled, and both of them began to hurl bantering insults at one another.

"They are learning to touch one another without the risk of a rebuff," Huy remarked. "I shouldn't be surprised at how quickly they've become friends. After all, Atum has willed their union. But I'm amazed at their increasing ease with one another."

"So am I." Mutemwia held up a cup and immediately her chief steward, Ameni, filled it with water. "I think it pleases my son to discuss the business of each day with a female other than his mother. Tiye has no authority with which to challenge his own supremacy."

"Not yet," Huy responded thoughtfully. The King had thrown an arm across Tiye's shoulders and was whispering something into her ear. "He is secure in his dominance as someone older and more knowledgeable than she. But Majesty, that disparity is closing fast. Tiye has a genuine interest in the practices of government. Any immaturity she displays belongs to youth and inexperience, two handicaps that will disappear quite naturally in time."

"She is suspicious of me, my network of spies, my power over Amunhotep. If her suspicion turns to jealousy, we will have a problem. I want her to trust me." She drank a mouthful of water, took the square of linen Tekait swiftly held out to her, and dabbed her lips.

"Yet you yourself quite rightly trust no one," Huy reminded her, "and Tiye sees her position as precarious in spite of the marriage contract. She's ambitious, Mutemwia. Already she understands that wearing the Queen's crown when the time comes will not guarantee her a place in the King's affections or allow her a share in the making of royal policy. She must capture the one and strive to make herself indispensible to the other. It's an enormous undertaking."

Mutemwia was holding the cup cradled in both hands. Her head went down over it. Huy could no longer see her face. "I confess that I'm the one feeling the stirrings of jealousy when I see them together," she said without looking up. "Since the vision of my son's future came to you by accident all those years ago, I have been consumed by one aim: to see him mount the Horus Throne. I have ordered everything in his life to that end, from the details of his education to the gradual fostering of a necessary self-discipline within his character. My life has belonged to him alone. All my thoughts, my plans, have been concerned with little else but the gradual unfolding of his destiny." Now she glanced up, and Huy saw her eyes filling with tears. "Tiye will take my place. Atum has decreed it. I shall be put out to pasture like a chariot horse too old to be driven into battle." Carefully she placed the linen she still held beneath each eye so that her tears would not carry kohl down her cheeks. "I struggle against the antipathy I feel for Tiye, her common ancestry, her plainness," she continued in a low voice. "I resent the intelligence in her that will rival my own. Amun help me, Huy. I would never have considered myself so petty."

Huy quickly scanned the deck. Tekait and Ameni, although their attention was obviously fixed on their mistress, were politely out of earshot. Tetiankh was still hanging over the railing some distance away.

"Tiye cannot appropriate the love and respect Amunhotep reserves for you alone, Mutemwia," Huy said quietly. "She cannot miraculously become a part of the memories you and Amunhotep share. You've always known that the time would one day come for you to relinquish the administration of Egypt to the King. Indeed, you have worked patiently and subtly towards that goal for many years. I believe that young Tiye is learning to be worthy of taking your place. She looks to you and to me to help her. Are you willing to deprive Amunhotep of a source of comfort and good advice once you go into the Beautiful West over an emotion as base as jealousy? Such a weakness is beneath you."

"You're right, of course." She sighed and held out the now-stained linen for Tekait to retrieve. "It's this present upheaval. I have many capable stewards and administrators handling our move from the Delta to the south, and in his letters Kha assures me that the tasks of building and restoring are proceeding without hindrance, but until I disembark at the watersteps of the old palace and walk through it to my own quarters I shall not be at ease."

"Tiye needs you," Huy told her. "She needs both of us. Let's make sure that this beloved country of ours will be ruled by both a wise and capable King and a Queen worthy of her crown."

Mutemwia did not reply. Settling a pillow at her back, she relaxed against the wall of the cabin. "That, my dear Seer, is a great deal to ask," she said after a long moment, and closed her eyes.

It took the cumbersome flotilla almost a month to reach Weset. Each late afternoon the barques and skiffs put in against a secluded stretch of the western riverbank. The ramps were run out, fires were lit, linen was collected and washed, the oarsmen spread their blankets out and dozed, and as night fell a simple meal was cooked. Tents were set up. Amunhotep and his body servant had one to themselves, guarded by soldiers appointed by Huy from the Division of Amun. Mutemwia and Tiye shared the other. Huy had declined the offer of any covering. Over the protests of a scandalized Tetiankh, he chose to sleep in the open, leaving his tent to Amunmose, Paneb, and Ba-en-Ra, who had travelled in Huy's own boat behind the King's and Mutemwia's staff.

Perti took up a position beside Huy, sinking cross-legged onto the sparse grass and placing his sword across his knees. "I can sleep during the day, Master," his answer had been to Huy's objection. "It seems that no matter where we tie up, we're discovered by curious villagers. I don't want them close to you."

Huy found the presence of his captain comforting. He lay listening to the vast crowd gradually settle into a welcome quiet occasionally interspersed with a snore or a cough, his eyes on the multitude of stars above him glimpsed through a latticework of drooping leaves. It seemed to him that as the ships slowly moved farther south, the air became increasingly dry. The sweet-smelling humidity of the Delta was being replaced by an odourless atmosphere that seemed to deepen the sky and sharpen the multitude of white points glittering overhead. Mesore, the last month of the harvest, was almost upon them. They had floated past mile upon mile of empty irrigation ditches lined with dusty palms within whose boundaries the peasants laboured, the golden stalks of emmer wheat and pale stems of barley swaying and collapsing before their scythes. An increasing number of fields already lay denuded, the surface of the soil cracking under the relentless heat of the sun.

This Egypt is ugly, Huy thought on the few occasions when he left the shelter of the canopy to stand at the deck rail, hot to his touch. *Everything is barren. I did not know that the face of my precious country could be so harsh. The villages seem empty. Even the animals are sheltering from the power of Ra. In the Delta his strength is muted, but out here he is pitilessly omnipotent. Once Nut has swallowed him and the breath is no longer fiery in our lungs, we feast on blue-black grapes and the sweet, juicy fruit of the nebes shrub. We scoop out the pink flesh of figs and dip fresh dates and reremet fruit in honey, and it is as though these foods are conjured by a magic that has formed them out of nothing, out of the emptiness of death itself. Small wonder that eating reremet fruit becomes more prevalent at this time of the year. Mandrake makes us drowsy, amorous; it diverts us from the fear that seeps towards us from the desolation on either side of the river. Will Isis cry? Will the gods permit yet another Inundation?*

The nights were blessedly temperate, however. Huy slept soundly, waking to eat the profusion of fruits Rakhaka provided for him and Tetiankh offered, and rising to join in the communal prayers to mighty Amun before the tents were struck and the interminable journey continued.

On the twenty-eighth day of Epophi, the King's helmsman began to negotiate a wide bend to the east, and Mutemwia joined Huy by the rail. "We approach the holy city of Weset," she said, smiling. "At last, Huy! I believe that we should be able to hear it as soon as we curve back to the south. I've enjoyed having nothing to do for weeks, but the King and Tiye are increasingly bored." She had spent most days dressed informally in the loose robes she preferred, but now her filmy white sheath was heavily bordered at the hem, neck, and shoulder straps with a succession of silver scarabs. Her headdress was plain, however, a thin silver circlet with the god of eternity, Heh, resting on her brow. As usual she wore little jewellery. Two blue faience rings shaped delicately like cornflowers blossomed from her fingers, a thin silver band made up of ankhs dangled from one tiny wrist, and red jasper pellets glowed on her sandals. Her steward Ameni held a white linen sunshade over her and Tekait waited, a large ostrich feather fan in both hands, to cool her.

Amunhotep and Tiye were sitting on stools under the canopy. Both were staring silently ahead, obviously weighed down by the full splendour in which they were clad. The cobra and the vulture, the royal uraeus, lifted majestically from the band of Amunhotep's blue and white striped helmet. Nebmerut, Seal Bearer and Senior Scribe of Protocol, sat at his feet cradling the silver chest containing the Pshent, the Red and White Crowns Amunhotep would not wear until he attained his majority, and the symbols of his supreme authority, the Crook and the Flail. Amunhotep and Tiye were heavily painted, the thick kohl surrounding their eyes glinting with gold dust. Tiye's wide belt was made up of golden ankhs, and hanging from it in front were several representations of a Queen's totem, the vulture goddess Mut, each bird clinging to the one beneath it by glittering talons, each folded feather of the great wings limned in dark blue lapis. More vultures in gold and lapis swung from her ears. The vulture headdress of a Queen completely hiding her hair held a shen sign of protection in each golden claw in front of and just below her ears. Its golden neck and lapis-beaked head reared above her forehead. Its green turquoise feathers swept back.

"Long before we left Mennofer, I very carefully chose what they will wear when they disembark," Mutemwia went on. "Amunhotep must be immediately seen as Amun's obedient son and Tiye as the god's divine consort, Mut." She turned to Tekait. "Bring me a stool under the canopy. I don't want to sit on cushions dressed like this." She left the rail and entered the shade.

Huy turned back to watch the eastern riverbank. Its aridity had begun to be replaced by thick stands of acacia and tamarisk bushes, sycamore trees and palms, the growth broken at intervals by wide stone watersteps where boats were tethered. Small groups of people had gathered by the water, and as Huy watched them kneel at the sight of the imperial flag and then slowly drift astern, he suddenly became aware of a sound that must have been growing beyond his awareness, a constant low rumble.

Tetiankh appeared at his elbow. "Judging by the intensity of noise, every citizen of Weset's sepat has gathered here to welcome the King. Listen to the undercurrent of excitement, Master! We have almost rounded the bend. Soon we shall see them."

The prow of *Kha-em-Ma'at* was slowly turning to the south. Nebenkempt's voice rang out, issuing a flurry of commands to the helmsman. For a while the boat held to the centre of the river, and now the banks on either side were hidden under a vast throng of jostling, shouting people trying to kneel as the gilded vessel drew abreast of them. But the crowd was too thick to allow most of them to perform their reverence, and Huy watched the frantic struggle with a pang of apprehension.

"Many of those in front are being tumbled into the water," he said. "How many more are being crushed? As Scribe of Recruits, I sent a message to Weset's Mayor some time ago, warning him to anticipate this chaos and requisition enough soldiers to keep order."

"It would have taken a full division of all five thousand men to maintain control of this multitude," Tetiankh replied. "And look, Master! They have been deployed around the city's water-steps and along the river path right to the gates of the palace compound itself. We have begun tacking to the eastern bank at last."

Huy glanced up to where the helmsman was forcing the great steering oar to respond to Nebenkempt's curt directive. Weset's watersteps drifted past. Huy could see almost nothing of the city itself for the double row of soldiers straining to hold back the eager throngs behind them. However, above their heads a forest of pillars was limned sharply against the blue-white heat of the sky, telling Huy that he was passing Amun's home, the sacred temple of Ipet-isut itself, and a short while later *Kha-em-Ma'at* came smoothly to rest against another set of steps. Above them on the stone apron, a solemn group of officials obscured the lower portion of the tall wooden gates leading into the palace precincts. Here the sound of the crowd, forced back a good distance, was muted.

Nebenkempt's sailors sprang to run out the ramp. Guards quickly lined it. The waiting dignitaries bent and then folded onto the ground, the acolytes carefully holding up their censers so that the smouldering grains of frankincense should not fall out of the cups. Huy inhaled its gently wafting smoke with pleasure, watching as Commander-in-Chief Wesersatet bowed himself aside and the King and Tiye, with Mutemwia behind them, stepped onto the ramp. Amunhotep bade the group of bent backs to rise. Ptahhotep, newly appointed High Priest of Amun, signalled to his we'eb priests, and the welcoming and sanctifying blend of bull's blood and milk made shallow pink puddles on the warm stone.

"You may speak," Amunhotep told him. Huy did not miss the note of impatience in the King's voice and neither did his mother. Mutemwia's fingers spasmed briefly against her thigh. One bead of sweat was trickling down Amunhotep's temple. *He's hot and uncomfortable,* Huy thought, *but it doesn't matter as long as he keeps it to himself. Today he must show no weakness.*

Ptahhotep inclined his shaven head. When he looked up, his heavily kohled eyes were smiling. "Mighty Amun of the Double Plumes welcomes his son and Incarnation to this, his greatest city. All Weset, indeed the whole Uas sepat, is in festivity. Amun eagerly awaits Your Majesty's presence before him in his sanctuary."

"Of course. And I am eager to pay him my homage and present him with such gifts as I have brought. Maani-nekhtef!" The Chief Herald approached and bowed, and looking beyond him along the empty river path the soldiers had cleared, Huy saw other boats being tied to the mooring posts. Many other ramps had already been run out. "Order my Treasury Overseer Nakht-sobek to Ipet-isut with the many offerings I have prepared for my father Amun," the King continued. "He is to wait for me there in the outer court." Stepping from the ramp onto the dampness of milk and blood, he pulled Tiye's arm through his and gestured to his litter-bearers. "We will have the curtains closed as we go," he announced. "The citizens must surely have had their fill of my royal person by now. Ptahhotep, walk beside me. Mother, Uncle Huy, send for Architect Kha and have him ready to guide me on an inspection of the palace. And I shall want much beer."

"He acquitted himself well," Mutemwia remarked in a low voice to Huy as Wesersatet and his men surrounded the litter. Huy nodded as it was lifted and the entourage moved off. Now that the sacerdotal ceremony was over, he felt suddenly tired and slightly homesick for his rooms in Mennofer. Perti and Mutemwia's guards were waiting, and just beyond them two soldiers unfamiliar to Huy were standing one to each side of the massive gate and watching Mutemwia expectantly. *The sentinels of this entrance,* Huy decided. *How many more does the compound have?* He sighed, and surprisingly Mutemwia laughed.

"Occasionally you must actually earn the gold and preferments showered upon you, Great Seer!" she teased him gently. "Seal Bearer Nebmerut is waiting to escort the Horus Throne to its place in the new audience hall, and the royal regalia grows heavy in his arms. Let us begin."

It was a curious invitation to walk forward, Huy thought, but he understood it perfectly. At the Queen's word the gates swung slowly apart, and Huy caught his breath.

A short distance beyond them, the entrance was blocked by another huge gate even now being swung open, its two components catching the sun as they moved and throwing out flashes of brief intensity so blinding that Huy was forced to close his eyes. "Electrum!" he breathed. "The Osiris-one King Ahmose must have been richer than we can imagine in order to provide his artisans with such a wealth of silver and gold!"

Mutemwia shook her head. "It was not always so. Have you forgotten your history lessons, Huy? Years went by when he, his brother the Osiris-one King Kamose, and his father, brave Prince Seqenenra, were so poor that the women of their family denuded themselves of all their valuable things so that the war against the occupying forces of the vile Setiu might continue. But in the end Ma'at triumphed, the gold coming north from the mines of Wawat and Kush began to fill the royal coffers instead of increasing Apepa's treasure, trade was re-established, and the Royal Treasury was ours once more. This gate was the Osiris-one's first expenditure. Amunhotep's grandfather had the wooden gates built because the men guarding the old palace became tired of persuading the curious populace using the river path to stop gawking and move on."

The gate now stood open. Mutemwia glided through and Huy followed. *Apepa. I do remember him from my boyhood lessons. He was the Setiu foreigner from Rethennu whose ancestors usurped the Horus Throne. Both Prince Seqenenra and King Kamose were slain in the war of deliverance they were forced to wage against him, and since then the evil serpent of the Duat has carried his name.*

But Huy's musings fled as he paced after the Queen. The area between the gates and the pillars of the palace's main entrance was surprisingly vast, an inviting expanse of well-watered, shaded grass dotted with trees, large ponds on which lily and lotus pads floated, and paths that left the main avenue to disappear beneath the spreading branches of sycamores and the thick but tiny leaves of the tamarisks. Clusters of acacia bushes abounded. There were no blooms, of course; the end of Shemu was only a month away. But Huy could imagine this glorious area bursting into colour— the pink tamarisk flowers, the delicate acacia blossoms, white here in the aridity of Egypt's south where the bushes cultivated for their gums and medicinal remedies were hardier than those of the Delta with their yellow flowers—and, permeating it all, the sweet, heady flower perfumes rising from the beds. He was pleased to see his lame gardener, Anab, already hobbling out of sight in the company of a man who must be one of the many servants tending these arouras. Huy turned his attention to the palace itself.

The white pillars, the outer walls, the welcome dimness of the entrance hall, were covered in a riot of colourful scenes. Heavy purple grapevines curved sinuously upward. Red-feathered birds fluttered in the green forest of many trees whose trunks descended to meet the cool yellow tiles of the floor. Fruits, breads, and vegetables cascaded from offering tables set within stylized temples above whose pylons the names of the gods were painted in black and enclosed in cartouches. Servant girls in short, transparent linen lifted jugs from which dark wine poured into golden goblets held out by jewelled and kohled diners. Animals seemed to wander from panel to green panel, and fish swam in a bilious blue river. The smell of fresh pigments hovered in the air, and Huy wondered how recently Weset's artists had finished restoring these glorious depictions of life before hurrying back to their modest homes. Glancing up, he saw that a huge rayed sun filled the centre of the high ceiling.

At the far end of the hall, a square doorway beckoned. Beyond it Mutemwia took a few steps and halted, and Huy moved to stand beside her. To their left a wide dais ran from wall to wall. Doors had been set to right and left behind it, almost invisible in the sweep of solid gold comprising not only the one wall but the other three also. Into each one the likeness of a victorious King Ahmose had been hammered, his sandalled stride reaching the floor, the raised axe in his hand only inches from the ceiling. Around the lintels of the doors into and out of the audience chamber his name and many titles had been incised.

"Amunhotep wanted them left alone." Mutemwia gestured at them briefly. "He wants every ambassador and visiting dignitary to be reminded of what happens to foreigners who dream of conquering and enslaving us."

"This place will awe everyone, particularly when the lamps are put in place and lit," Huy replied as Nebmerut and his perspiring servants went past carrying the shrouded Horus Throne. "The sprinklings of pyrite throughout the dark blue lapis of the floor will glitter constantly. This royal house is more spacious and opulent than the palace at Mennofer. The ministers should be overjoyed to be working here."

The throne had been lowered reverently onto the centre of the dais and Nebmerut, having set a guard around it, had disappeared through one of the small doors at its rear still carrying the ornate chest holding the Pshent, Crook, and Flail.

"According to Kha, the ones who arrived earlier are already pleased with their offices. He's waiting for you, Huy. My steward Ameni will escort me to my quarters." Acknowledging Huy's bow, she left the room trailed by Tekait and her entourage. It took a long time for them to pass through one of the doorways at the far end.

With a lightened heart Huy saw the King's Chief Architect striding towards him. Kha was smiling broadly, his blue eyes merry. The hall was gradually filling up with people. Officials, army officers, servants, a few priests, milled about with a sense of aimlessness that Huy knew was temporary. Tomorrow would see a return to the smooth organization of an administration known as the most powerful and efficient in the world.

"Great Seer Huy, I greet you with all respect and affection!" Kha exclaimed as he came up to Huy. "Her Majesty has ordered me to acquaint you with this magnificent place and to make any changes to its design you may desire for your comfort. My sons asked me to convey their greetings to you also. I hardly see them anymore. They are as busy as I. Hori has gone south to Nekheb to see to the completion of Nekhbet's temple, and Suti spends all his time carrying out the additions to Ipet-isut His Majesty requested." He gestured widely. "The Throne Room of Senwosret Is Observing the Primeval Hill. When His Majesty returns from Ipet-isut, I must show him his new home, but for now, come with me!"

As they went, Huy began to realize what a monumental task of restoration his friend had accomplished. Having studied architecture himself, he knew how much time each part of the project had required. "It hasn't been necessary to enlarge any of the rooms," Kha told him. "As you can see, the ceilings are lofty and the clerestory windows carefully placed to direct only the morning sunlight into these airy spaces. Mainly bricklayers and artists laboured here." He laid a hand on Huy's arm and brought him to a halt. "I am giving you so many details because Her Majesty Queen Mutemwia warned me that if you see anything amiss, anything at all, you have her authority to change it through me. Now we come to the royal apartments and your quarters between them."

The two men wove their way between the laden servants crowding the wide passage and coming and going through two open doors to their right and one imposing admittance directly ahead. Armed guards had already taken up their station there, and as Huy followed Kha through one of the other doors, both Perti and Amunmose hurried to greet them with bows. Huy found himself in a reception hall at least twice as large as the one he had left behind in Mennofer. The vibrant scenes of domestic life on its walls glinted where details had been etched in gold. The floor, or what Huy could see of it beneath the clutter of boxes, chests, and pieces of furniture, was made up of yellow tiles that took on a tinge of blue as they disappeared towards the centre. Facing Huy were open double doors through which he could see a small pond, some grass, and a couple of sycamore trees, all suffused with the strong, blinding light of the south.

"Master, I've made an inspection of these rooms and I was about to set a guard before seeing the rest of my men settled into their own new quarters," Perti said. "It will be easier to keep a watch on you here than in Mennofer. The garden is all your own and is walled, with only a small gate leading into His Majesty's precinct." He smiled. "I shall be co-operating with the senior officers of the Division of Amun, and Commander-in-Chief Wesersatet of course. May I proceed?"

"And a good thing too," Amunmose grumbled as Perti and his soldiers left. "Perti has been poking his nose into every cranny and the servants have been tripping over his men. Tetiankh and Kenofer have set up your couch and are unpacking your personal belongings. Rakhaka has been allowed a portion of the kitchens all to himself. Naturally, he's found plenty to grumble about." All at once the steward's dazzling grin lit up his face. "I sense that there has been much happiness in this palace, Huy. I believe that you also will be happy here." Bowing again, he turned to where Paroi was urgently gesturing. Paneb and Ba-en-Ra were engaged in a close conversation, sitting out of the way with their backs against the far wall. Huy slipped out into the passage with Kha.

"Come up onto the roof," Kha said. "From there you can see the whole compound, and much of the city."

It took them a long time to walk through the palace and out to the rear, where steps clung to the wall. By the time they had climbed over the lip of the roof, Huy's eyes had adjusted to the unrelenting glare of a sun at its zenith, and he found himself facing an expanse dotted with wind catchers of various sizes that funnelled the prevailing north wind of summer into the rooms below. Some of them sat beside modest doorways with stairs obviously leading down into the second storey. But one of the wind catchers, clearly recently repaired, rose next to a low opening filled with bricks and rubble from lintel to sill. Huy, fully aware of Kha's abilities, asked him why this doorway remained as it was.

"It's said that the steps are haunted," Kha told him. "At least, I assume that there are steps inside, connecting this doorway with another blocked aperture below. His Majesty forbade me to touch any of it. The story is that a Prince of Weset often used that stair to come up here and pray or think, and sitting in the shade of that wind catcher he was attacked and grievously wounded. Later he died in battle. His Majesty insists that the Prince was the Osiris-one Seqenenra, he who began our revolt against the vile Setiu, and at that time the palace was a dangerous ruin. Whatever the truth is, we know that the Tao family lived there." He pointed to where a long, low building sprawled close by. "King Ahmose, Seqenenra's son, had the wall between the two removed, and it was he who accomplished the first major restoration here. But he would not unblock the stair up which his father's betrayer may have crept, and neither must we." He laughed. "I was a very lazy student of history and was beaten many times because of it. All I cared about was designing in brick, wood, and stone. I have expanded the Taos' old estate. It will house the women, except for Queen Mutemwia, of course, and later His Majesty's Consort. Look to the south. The ministers are very pleased with their new offices …"

He went on describing the scene directly below, but Huy, after passing a swift gaze over the vast royal acres with their protecting wall surrounding him, looked beyond them. The river was a thin brown ribbon waiting for the Inundation, still over a month away. On the west bank the scattered mortuary temples and tombs of the dead could hardly be distinguished through a haze of beige dust hanging suspended over a waste of barren, churned sand. Beyond them a serried range of cliffs shivered in the heat.

Here on the east bank, outside the green and watered confines of the palace grounds, lay the city of Weset, spreading out of Huy's sight to north and south, a bewildering accumulation of narrow dirt streets, jumbled houses, shrines, markets, all wrapped in the same thin pall of summer motes, yet murmurous with brisk life. It seemed to Huy, as the city's muted clamour reached him, that the pulse of Weset's heart beat more rapidly than Mennofer's dignified pace. *Here the past exists as a foundation to be built on,* he thought suddenly, *not sunk into with an excess of awe.*

"I have already begun drafting the plans for the King's new palace over on the west bank," Kha was saying, and Huy's attention returned to him with a jolt. "It will be a long time before the laying of the cord, and perhaps by then His Majesty will have changed his mind. Senwosret Is Observing the Primeval Hill is a beautiful and harmonious place."

Once back at the entrance to Huy's apartment, Kha invited him to dine and then took his leave, and Huy answered the salute of the familiar soldiers to either side of his door and went in. Quiet enveloped him. His tables and chairs sat peacefully on the spotless floor, where the central motif, a cluster of blue water lilies, was now revealed. The far door leading to the garden was closed. The air was cool and smelled faintly of lotus oil. Walking towards one of the doors on his far right, he glanced inside. His couch had already been dressed in clean white linen. One of his lamps, together with a jug of water and a cup, sat on the small table beside it. His tiring chests were lined up neatly against one wall, and against the other his shrine to Khenti-kheti, totem of the Delta town of Hut-herib near where he had been raised, stood open, a long-handled censer lying beside it.

As he hesitated on the threshold, there was the brisk slap of sandals on tiles behind him and he turned to see both Tetiankh and Kenofer approaching, accompanied by Seneb. Both body servants looked tired, but the physician's newly shaved skull gleamed and the black kohl around his eyes had obviously been freshly applied. "I have your midday dose of opium, Great Seer," he said, "and by the Queen's order I am to give you a complete examination. I have not done so since you left Mennofer."

Huy nodded curtly, reached for the drug, and drank quickly, welcoming its familiar bitterness.

"Amunmose has gone to the kitchens to taste your noon meal, Master," Tetiankh told him. "It will be here directly. You might wish to eat it while it's hot." He cast a disapproving glare at Seneb. "Scribe Paneb waits for your attention with letters."

For answer, Huy stepped towards the couch. "Hurry up and get this over with, physician. The food can wait. I'm not hungry. Kenofer, tell Paneb to bring the correspondence as soon as Seneb leaves. No, not you, my dear Tetiankh," he added as the man turned away. "Your service was at an end when I left Mennofer. You've trained Kenofer well, and now it's time to take the gold I've given to you and go home to your family. We've already said our goodbyes." His smile took the sting out of his words.

Tetiankh hesitated, then bowed. Kenofer had already disappeared. "Caring for you has been the habit, and the pleasure, of my life, Master, and I am reluctant to relinquish my duties. But you are right. I trust that I leave you in capable hands. Farewell."

Huy returned his bow with an inward pang of regret. Seneb had begun to surreptitiously tap one hennaed foot. Huy swung back to his couch and began to remove his sweat-stained kilt.

Later, bathed and clad in clean linen, he sat in his imposing new reception room with Paneb before him and his Chief Herald Ba-en-Ra a polite distance away, waiting for instructions. Paneb's palette lay on the ivory-inlaid table beside him together with a box full of unsealed scrolls. "I have taken the liberty of saving you time by reading these, Master. Naturally, their contents remain with me in the strictest confidence. Shall I begin?"

Nasha had written that she had managed to secure a small suite of rooms for herself and her servants in a house not far from the palace. "Anybody who is anybody is rushing to move to Weset, and lodgings are scarce," she said. "Who knows—I might even find myself an agreeable husband in this arid, rather horrible city. Please use your authority, O mighty and powerful Seer, and get me an apartment inside the royal compound. I am impatient to see you."

"Make a note of her request," Huy said. "Next?"

Thothhotep's letter was warm and full of news. "I see a great deal of Architect Hori," she told Huy. "Since Anhur's death I have been at a loss for something to do, and Hori often employs me as an assistant scribe. The work is easy and the progress being made on the erection of a new temple for Nekhbet very interesting. Are you well settled into the palace yet?" *She doesn't urge me to visit her,* Huy thought as Paneb set her scroll aside and picked up another one. *That's good. She is becoming less lonely.*

"Prince Amunnefer wishes to show you your poppy fields as soon as possible," Paneb said. "The present crop was sown during the last month of Akhet and this year's opium has just been extracted. A yield of superior quality, he says. He invites you to a welcome party in his house tomorrow."

"Send Herald Ba-en-Ra. Tell the Prince that I'm most eager to greet him once again and to see the fields for myself at last. If Their Majesties have no need of me, I shall meet him tomorrow morning. Use your own words, Paneb. No dictation is necessary." *Amunnefer,* Huy mused. *A good, kind man once married to a vain and selfish woman. Anuket. I can speak your name to myself without a single tremor, and even the boyhood memories of my passion for you have no sting anymore. How was your heart weighed in the Judgment*

Hall? I wonder. Did Ma'at's scales balance after all? "Anything else, Paneb?"

"Your brother has sent you a sack of pistachio nuts harvested from Ra's temple gardens, with a brief letter wishing you well."

"Good. Now prepare your palette. As Scribe of Recruits, I'm summoning all army and navy commanders to Weset to discuss the changes in troop strength and deployment this move south has demanded. The policing of our northern borders with the Great Green and east with the tribes of Rethennu and beyond must increase. Don't include Prince Yuya, though. As Master of the King's Horses, he holds no rank outside the royal household." *Nevertheless, I must deliberately do my best to cultivate the man's acquaintance,* Huy's thoughts ran on as Paneb gathered up the scrolls and bowed himself away. *His foreign blood notwithstanding, he is an Egyptian aristocrat and father of the future Queen, and Tiye is close to her brother Ay. I need their confidence.*

That night, in spite of his regular dose of poppy, Huy could not sleep. It was his first night in a strange place. The shadows on the walls of his bedchamber moved in unfamiliar ways as the flame within his night light guttered. He was aware of the hundreds of rooms and mazes of passages cocooning him in walls through which no sound seemed to penetrate. He was acutely conscious of his position between the young King on one side of his apartment and Mutemwia on the other. He did not know where Tiye was—probably asleep in the Tao's refurbished estate, safely installed with her mother and her new servants. Huy lay on his back gazing up at his starry blue and white ceiling. He poured himself water from the jug Kenofer had set ready for him, and considered waking the young man for a game of sennet, but immediately rejected the idea. He was too restless for board games. In the end he got up, put on the kilt he had worn all afternoon, and let himself barefooted out into his garden.

Softly greeting the guard on the door, he stepped onto the dry grass and walked away from the deep shadow of the palace wall. The moon was three-quarters full, casting a dim, pallid light that barely reflected in Huy's little pool, and the darkness under the trees was thick. Nevertheless, the sky was a dense mat of stars, clearer and sharper than anything similar seen in the Delta, where the humid air created a mist that veiled the heavens. The air here was dry and almost scentless, with a barely perceptible whiff of the desert that stretched immeasurably far on either side of the river beyond the thin and somehow precarious spread of both city and cultivated fields. *It embraces the tombs on the west bank,* Huy thought. *It is as arid and lifeless as the desiccated bodies lying in their coffins. I can sense its voice beneath the muted rumble of the city, timbreless, eternally self-sufficient, unchanging, as cities rise and wane and men are born, flourish, and are eventually carried into the House of the Dead.*

A puff of wind found him, lifting his tangled mane of hair and pressing the kilt briefly against his thighs. He had wandered to the wall dividing his garden from that of the King and was about to turn back when he heard a low laugh followed by a string of quiet words, and paused. He recognized the voice. It was answered at length by another—deeper, more masculine. Huy could not make out what was being said, but he stood still and began to smile. *The vision you gave me spoke true, Anubis,* he said silently to the jackal god who had become his guide and often his taskmaster. *Amunhotep and Tiye are talking together quietly, intimately, under the cover of a hot summer night, and I am happy. Everything is going to be all right.*

PART TWO

10

CHIEF STEWARD USERHET bowed profoundly as Huy, with Paneb behind him, walked into the Queen's apartments and settled into one of Her Majesty's gilded chairs. Paneb lowered himself to the floor at Huy's knee and began to prepare his palette, the small sound of the burnisher against his papyrus faint but discernible in the quiet air. The room was empty but for Userhet, who glided past them to take up his station just out of earshot against one of the walls. Slowly Huy inhaled the faint, spicy aroma of the perfume Tiye still wore, a distinctive blend of cardamom and myrrh that enveloped her and remained hanging, an invisible cloud, wherever she had been. The room was empty and still but for an occasional gust of the hot night wind out of the north, coursing through the low, unshuttered window. It was the middle of Mesore.

Throughout the country, the last of the harvest was being hurriedly reaped, grain scythed, fruit pulled from tree or vine, honeycomb lifted, oozing golden and sweet, from the hive. Here in Weset the heat was unrelenting. Dust pervaded every corner of the city. The fields straggling along the river's eastern bank were already fissured by deep cracks. The palm-lined canals were dry. At first Huy had been appalled and depressed by such aridity, but in the twelve years since he had sailed south with the court he had learned to endure it. Nevertheless, the return of the New

Year was celebrated here with a greater fervour than the dwellers of the Delta could understand. The river was due to begin its life-giving rise in about two weeks, and the prayers of the populace had become clamorous with entreaties to Isis for a fresh outpouring of her tears and to Hapi for an Inundation teeming with fish.

Twelve years, Huy mused. How rapidly the time has slipped away! Weset has burgeoned into one of the largest and most vibrant cities in the world, the centre of an empire I have forged for my King. At its heart the golden outer skins of its stone buildings are visible for miles around. Its citizens enjoy the influx of a constant supply of goods from every nation eager to befriend a King who could crush them with a wave of his hand if he chose to end their precarious autonomy. My countrymen flood Kush and Wawat as far as the Fourth Cataract. Gold cascades into the Royal Treasury every day. Amunhotep desires, and out of all this wealth the things he desires at once acquire substance. What he desires most is the beautifying of his domain, and I have spent the better part of these last years in fulfilling his wish. Apart from the projects begun before he was crowned, my hand has been on the raising of every monument, every statue, so that wherever I go I see a memory of those times. A few are not particularly pleasant. Working with Amunhotep-Huy on the restoration and adornment of Ptah's temple at Mennofer was difficult. I became Vizier in his place, but he was given the control of Ptah's temple as Overseer of Works in the temple of Nebma'atra-United-With-Ptah, and Overseer of Priests. I can understand why the King wished himself to be seen united with the creator-god, but I have never understood why he elevated my bad-tempered nephew to a position of such power in Mennofer. Was it Mutemwia's decision, a ploy to keep Amunhotep-Huy firmly fixed in one place? He drove his craftsmen with whip and harsh tongue, and at that time I had not been given the authority to replace him.

In any event, after six years of labour the temple stood ready for Prince Thothmes' obligatory term as a Priest of Ptah, and how he complained at the prospect of leaving the south! Huy smiled at the recollection of the boy's mutinous face, so like his father's at that age. The ceremonies in Mennofer had taken all day, and it was an exhausted court that had straggled to the barges sitting low in the depleted river and gratefully headed for home. Huy was still tired. His body servant Kenofer had scarcely finished washing the grime of travel from him when the Queen's summons had arrived. Clad in a clean kilt and little else, he had left his servants to unpack his belongings and made his way with his scribe, a few soldiers, and Captain Perti to Tiye's spacious apartments on the second floor of the palace. Custom had taught him patience. The Queen would appear when she was ready. In the meantime he, like Chief Steward Userhet and Paneb, waited without anxiety.

The events of this year have left me with a miasma of sheer weariness when I remember them, Huy's thoughts ran on idly. *Amunhotep's demand for more temples, more sacred statues of himself and the other gods, has grown almost frenetic. He seeks to leave more monuments than any other pharoah before him, and in doing so he wishes to eclipse the lies and near apostasy of his father. He wasn't happy when every oracle he consulted told him that his very first, precious son must be named Thothmes. He wanted the baby called Ahmose after the country's great emancipator. Yet the Prince is a sturdy, intelligent nine-year-old boy with the promise of greatness in his eyes. Tiye refused to believe me when I touched his warm, sweet-smelling skin and predicted his death.*

Huy unconsciously sighed aloud and Userhet glanced his way. Huy shook his head, correctly interpreting the steward's unspoken question. *Both the King and the Queen have deliberately put my warning out of their minds,* Huy told himself. *Amunhotep bends over the architect's drawing board and I bend with him. Kha, Hori, Suti, Men the Master of Works and Overseer of Sculptors—all of us with one aim: to beautify the country and glorify His Majesty. I have built a temple to the crocodile god Sobek Lord of Bakhu, complete with a statue of the deity lovingly embracing Amunhotep. The temple of Thoth at Iunu has been refurbished and a great statue of a baboon placed before it, to help the sun to rise. The little shrine Kha and I designed to honour the creator-god Khnum on the island of Tent-to-Amu at the First Cataract is begun. Likewise a House for Horus Nekheni Lord of Nekhen opposite the temple to Nekhbet, farther south of Weset, where Thothhotep used to live.* All that toil, and myriad smaller tasks as well.

Huy, not without a mild inner misgiving, had received orders that His Majesty would like to see himself increasingly depicted with the female members of his family. Bes, the dwarf god of all pleasures of the flesh, and Taurt, hippopotamus goddess of childbirth particularly venerated by women, had begun to adorn the palace walls, furniture, and cosmetic items, reflecting the King's increasing preoccupation with his dozens of acquisitions inhabiting the House of Women. The goddess Hathor, mother, wife, and daughter of Ra himself, held sway. As the Eye of Ra, she also protected the god. Her name meant "House of Horus," and as such she provided a womb in which the King, as the embodiment of Horus himself, could feel secure. Yet Amunhotep was fully aware of Hathor's other aspect, the vengeful and savage Sekhmet, who had unleashed a bloodbath upon the country at the behest of Ra, angered by the lack of respect humankind had shown him. If Hathor-Sekhmet had not been deceived into drinking beer dyed red and subsequently become drunk, she would have destroyed everyone. Amunhotep had often pointed out to Huy that he drew his strength and many of his powers from the goddess's aggressive vitality. Huy had not commented. He disliked the subtle aura of femininity that now seemed to diffuse from every room and hall of the palace. Nor did he appreciate the many hours he had spent designing the statues of the King that now stood in virtually every temple. Over a thousand of them proclaimed him as the beloved son of Ra, or Hathor, or Sebek, or the sky goddess Nut, or Amun himself, emphasizing not only his divinity but also his equality with them.

Huy had mastered the language of diplomacy long ago. His nephew Ramose was now a senior scribe in the Treasury. An aging May still presided over the Office of Foreign Correspondence, and he, together with Huy and the Queen, maintained a firm yet tactful hold on the country's vassals and trading partners. The Khatti and the kingdom of Mitanni required more careful handling. Both principalities exerted a strong influence on the petty tribal regions around them, and neither Huy nor the Queen desired the wastage of a war. The King showed very little interest in any foreign negotiations unless they concerned the cementing of an alliance with a marriage. Babylon, Assur, Zahi, Arzawa, circled Egypt in obedience, and the provinces of Katna and Nukhashshi, properly belonging to Mitanni, wisely preferred a cautious liaison with Egypt.

Then there were the deaths. Five years ago the King's uncle, walking his fields, had died suddenly at the age of forty, an event that had surprised Amunhotep, who had virtually forgotten his relative. Huy and the Queen had quietly removed their spies from the Prince's household and generously endowed his funerary temple. In the end he had been an honest man who had endured a melancholy fate, and Huy pitied him. Heby also was gone, his beautified body lying deep within the tomb he and Huy had prepared together for the members of their family. Huy had stood outside it with Ramose and a weeping Iupia while Amunhotep-Huy, as Heby's elder son, performed the Opening of the Mouth. He and his father had agreed on very little, but all the same he was pale and his voice trembled as he spoke the time-honoured words. Huy had no doubt that his brother's heart would balance on Ma'at's scales. Heby had been respectful of the gods, kind to his wife and sons, and resolute but fair with his underlings. His titles and responsibilities had passed to Menkheper, who became Mayor of Mennofer. Amunhotep-Huy was now Royal Steward at Mennofer, Overseer of Priests, and Overseer of Works in the temple of Nebma'atra-United-With-Ptah, in charge of the reconstruction and embellishing of Ptah's home. The pompous designations fooled no one, least of all Amunhotep-Huy himself. The King did not want him at court. Mennofer was his place of exile, and he bitterly resented the task he had been set.

The wound of Heby's passing was still fresh in Huy, but not as agonizing as the death of Ishat, and at that memory Huy grunted and closed his eyes. He heard Userhet stir again, a tiny whisper of linen in that silent place, but Huy ignored him. Ishat at sixty-two, her dear, familiar features lined and crumpled with age, her hands stiff and painful, her body, that lithe and graceful body, thickened and slowed by the multiplying years. Thothmes had sent a panicked message to Huy begging him to come to Iunu, sure that his best friend could somehow defeat the god who waited invisibly to take Ishat's hand and lead her into the Judgment Hall, but Huy had no power to heal this, the woman who had always meant the most to him, and in spite of his secret hope, Thothmes knew it. She lay cradled against her husband's breast, her children to either side of the couch, her hand resting between Huy's as he knelt beside her. There was no point in trying to See for her; her only future now lay with Osiris in the Beautiful West. Huy had been fully aware of the presence of Anubis at his back, the god motionless and patient, his measured breath barely perceptible. Ishat had been without the energy to speak, yet she smiled, her sluggish glance moving from Huy's face to the being standing behind him.

"You see him, don't you?" Huy had said, his voice heavy with tears, and she had nodded, struggling to form words. Huy hushed her, squeezing her fingers. "I love you, my Ishat," he managed. "The years we spent together were the happiest I've ever known. You need not fear the scales, and I pray that I too may be found blameless by Ma'at so that I may embrace you once more under the branches of the sacred Sycamore Tree."

He felt his own well-being as an insult then, the scant physical evidence of his years an affront to those with whom the passing of time had dealt with its usual harshness. The awareness that Atum had decreed his survival until his service to the god was over brought him no comfort. The children, adults though they were, clung to each other with tears. Thothmes laid his cheek against the crown of his wife's tousled head, and as Ishat's eyes turned upward towards him she sighed, went limp, and died. *Now let me see her as she was.* Huy had spoken fiercely and silently to the jackal god as Anubis stepped to the couch and bent over it. *Give me a glimpse of her youth and strength, her clear eyes full of mirth or hot argument or thoughtfulness, her black hair gleaming suddenly as we passed from the shadow of our house into the full glare of a summer afternoon!* But Anubis did not even glance his way, and Huy found himself with face pressed into the rumpled sheets and the palm of Ishat's lifeless hand still warm against his mouth.

He did not wish to remember what followed: the constant ache of bereavement, he and Thothmes locked together in a flood of grief and loss whenever they met, the terrible seventy days of mourning while Ishat's body lay gutted in the House of the Dead. Her funeral simply underscored Huy's deep sense of abandonment. All he wanted to do was escape to his tiny estate outside Hut-herib where he and Ishat would always be young and full of an innocent hope.

Two years ago, Amunhotep had decreed the construction of a temple at Hut-herib as a mark of gratitude to Huy. It was to replace the smaller edifice Huy had visited many times. He and Methen, Khenti-kheti's priest, had formed a strong bond over the years since Methen had found Huy naked and half deranged outside the House of the Dead and had carried him home to his parents. Methen too was now dead, and by royal command Huy had become Overseer of the Priests of Horus-Khenti-kheti, a title Huy stubbornly refused to acknowledge although he added the supervision of the new temple's architects and stonemasons to his already crushing list of duties. Huy made sure that Men, who had worked under Kha and his sons, was promoted to Overseer of the Works of the King, and as such Huy thankfully left the project at Hut-herib in his care. Men's reports on his progress were terse and satisfactory. Amunhotep had decided that the new temple should be dedicated to both Horus and Hut-herib's crocodile totem. Huy had not objected; indeed, he had not cared. The assurance of the King's continued love and trust for him was the true gift.

Construction had at last begun on Amunhotep's new palace on the west bank, away from the dense and clamorous sprawl the city of Weset had become. The King's funerary temple had also begun to rise under Huy's control. It was to be a vast edifice of gold-plated sandstone walls depicting the King celebrating his jubilee festivals in the company of the gods and his family. It was to have silver floors, and an avenue of stone jackals would lead from the river to its entrance. Amunhotep did not say so, but Huy suspected that the King had chosen the jackals not only because this was to be his funerary temple but also in deference to Anubis the psychopomp, who carried the words of Atum to Huy, his Seer.

Huy had Seen for the King many times since arriving in Weset, and the King had prospered. His habit was to consult Huy and his mother when any decision was to be made, but Mutemwia, in her mid-forties, preferred to devote her time to running her many lucrative business concerns now that her son had the benefit of two wise advisers, Huy and his Chief Wife Tiye.

At the thought of Tiye, Huy felt himself tense. He had made sure to ingest a larger than usual amount of opium in preparation for this meeting, with the now inevitable consequence of a nagging pain in his stomach, but the thirst for even more of the drug came rushing at him from the image his mind presented. Six years ago, during a time of upheavals in the administration and a burst of frenetic building projects that rendered Huy both harried and extremely exhausted, the King had sent for him. It had been evening. Huy had attended the daily morning audience as usual, gone from there to the Office of Foreign Correspondence with Tiye, returned to his own office to dictate a mountain of letters answering questions from Hori, Suti, and Men, among others, ate hurriedly with Nasha, who now organized his household together with his two stewards, worked on the plans for the temples of Sobek, Khnum, and Horus at Nekhen, and consulted on the quarrying of quartzite for the colossal statues of baboons to grace Thoth's temple at Iunu. He had been too tired to eat the last meal of the day, and had been drinking a cup of wine while listening to a regular update regarding the state of his opium crop when the summons had come. The King's chief steward, Nubti, a little more bent, a little more wizened, but as keen-eyed as ever, had brought it himself. Gliding forward with both Captain Perti and a glowering Paroi in the rear, he reached Huy's chair and bowed, handing down a thin scroll to Huy's Chief Scribe Paneb. Huy nodded reluctantly for him to speak.

"Great Seer, I bring a command from His Majesty that you should accompany me to his apartments at once. The scroll bears the same invitation. His Majesty requires that everything to do with this matter be officially and correctly recorded."

Huy's eyebrows rose. "As you can see, I am tired and ready to retire to my couch," he replied. "Can this discussion not wait until tomorrow?"

Nubti bowed again, this time with an air of apology. "Great Son of Hapu, I see the marks of weariness on your face," he said gently, "but His Majesty expects you at once. Be pleased to follow me. I have a litter waiting."

Huy's heart sank. He knew that he was not alert enough to either match wits with Amunhotep's obstinate nature or weigh some vital administrative consideration. "Nubti, may I not send my humble regrets to the King?" he tried. "I am truly of no use to him tonight."

Nubti's expression did not change. He merely stood quietly, looking at the floor. After a moment Huy hauled himself out of his chair, called for his sandals and a cloak, and, beckoning to Perti and Paneb, followed the steward out of the room.

The night was calm. A slight breeze stirred in the expanse of opium fields surrounding Huy's house, bringing the faint odour of river growth to his nostrils. The sky, as always here in the south, was startlingly clear and brilliant with stars. The constant rumble of the mighty city came muted to Huy as he and Paneb slid into the first royal litter. Perti pulled the curtains closed, and at the same time Nubti's voice gave the order to proceed. The litters swayed forward.

It was some distance to the palace compound, and Huy fell into a doze as the bearers left his guarded arouras, skirted the wide canal that provided both access to his home and water for his precious crops, and set off north along the river path. It had been six years since Huy had walked into the palace quarters allotted to him, and two since he had moved into the large house he had been allowed to commission in the centre of the poppy fields he and Amunnefer owned. He did not begrudge the extra time it took for him to reach the palace each day. The small but important distance of separation between himself and the endless activity in the royal domain had brought him a peace not unlike the contentment he had shared with Ishat on his estate outside Hut-herib. He had been accorded a privilege many of the King's ministers did not share. He was still Uncle Huy to Amunhotep, and Mutemwia continued to afford him the affection of a beloved brother. Huy was blessed, and he knew it.

Paneb woke him as the litter was being lowered carefully to the ground, and together they walked across the palace's lofty reception hall behind Nubti, their sandals whispering on the shrouded lapis floor, Perti's leather belt creaking gently as he brought up the rear. The room was empty, its brooding dimness lit by two lamps on tall gilded stands whose fragile glow was soon lost in the vast reaches. The surroundings were entirely familiar to Huy. Every morning he stood on the dais beside the Horus Throne, hearing reports and petitions with the King, offering advice, instructions, admonitions, but this vacant half dark disturbed him. It seemed to him that as the bustle of the day faded, the past had come sliding in to fill the void, bringing the whispers of long-dead courtiers, their pale faces glimpsed briefly out of the corner of his eye as he paced through the duskiness. Thinking of the sealed stair leading up onto the roof, the memory of the tragedy with which its stale air was imbued, he shook his head and hurried on, the sight of Nubti's misshapen spine a reassuring link with the present.

Huy's apartments had been situated between the King's on one side and Mutemwia's on the other. Now they were occupied by

Chief Herald Maani-nekhtef. The corridor leading to Amunhotep's double doors was lined with soldiers from the Division of Amun. Several servants in the royal livery of blue and white were loitering by the stool where Nubti usually sat and decided who should be admitted. He had never turned Huy away. At Nubti's approach the servants bowed and moved aside, for he was an important man in his own right, and at the sight of Huy they bowed again. Nubti rapped on one of the doors. It was immediately opened by Nubti's under steward, who remained in the passage. So did a watchful Perti. Nubti gestured, and Huy and Paneb walked into the King's private reception room.

It was empty, but a cheerful flood of light poured across its blue and white tiled floor from a doorway on their right and at once Amunhotep's voice invited them to approach. To Huy's surprise the young man standing by the ornate couch was fully clad, his white kilt glinting with gold thread, his sturdy arms heavy with silver and carnelian bracelets. More silver rested across the impressive musculature of his chest. A loose white bag wig covered his skull, surmounted by a small silver uraeus. Both the Lady of Dread and the Lady of Flame had red carnelian eyes that glared balefully at Huy, but Amunhotep smiled and beckoned him closer. The air in the room was redolent with the King's perfume, rosemary, and a lingering whiff of something Huy could not place. The sheets on the couch were rumpled and the blankets disordered. Obviously Amunhotep's evening had been spent pleasantly.

"I was washed and repainted for this occasion, Uncle Huy. I wear silver in anticipation of your promise that the floors of my as yet unbuilt funerary temple will be paved with it." He flicked at one long silver earring and grinned. "There's more silver than gold in the Treasury now. Did you know? But of course you did— you were responsible for the trading agreements that put it there.

Your nephew delights in telling me how every day my wealth grows larger. I'm fond of Ramose. He has an amiable disposition as well as intelligence, unlike that bad-tempered stepbrother of his who keeps order with his whip. I disapprove. Why his wife stays with him I can't imagine. However, I digress." He passed a critical eye over Huy. "You look terrible, Uncle, and I can't make use of a dead man. Get more rest."

Huy did not respond. *He's at the height of a glorious maturity*, he thought with a spurt of love and pride. *For twenty years his mother and I have nurtured and disciplined him, and here's the result: a pharaoh of power and good judgment, not to mention good health.*

Amunhotep must have seen something of Huy's musing in his eyes. His grin widened into a warm smile. "I love you also, Great Seer. Paneb, sit there beside Nebmerut and prepare your papyrus."

Huy had barely noticed the King's Chief Scribe and Seal Bearer. Nebmerut was a taciturn man of indeterminate age whose presence was often overlooked, a trait Amunhotep valued in a Chief Scribe.

"Uncle, you may take the stool." Mystified, obedient, Huy sat. He was entirely unprepared for the King's next words. "You have strengthened the buffer states of Canaan, Kumidu, and Simurru between us and Mitanni." It was a statement, not a question.

"A long time ago, Majesty. Governor Khaemwaset presided over the three Assistant Governors responsible for those three areas of Amurru. He has since retired, but the replacement I appointed is extremely efficient. He sends me regular reports."

Amunhotep began to pace. "Last year, Assurubalit made a nuisance of himself with a flood of letters complaining about the treatment his messengers received." Again, it was an assertion of fact.

"Yes. He wanted to be recognized with dignity as the King of Assur. I took the liberty of composing a few titles for him when I dictated a reply, and promised gold in exchange for a treaty. A treaty with him was not really necessary—Wesersatet and the army could have squashed him like a bug—but a mutual agreement cost you nothing, Majesty, and perhaps preserved Egyptian lives, not to mention equipment and food. Besides, it allowed Assurubalit to save face."

"Last year, you were forced to reassure the King of Alashia that trade between his island and us would not be threatened by the marriage alliance I wanted to make with Katna."

"It took many letters and much tact to satisfy both King Azizi of Katna and our old and very valued partner in Alashia."

"You did not approve of my marriage to this foreign woman."

"You know that I did not. You endangered our relationship with Alashia."

"Yet as always your diplomatic ability resulted in our ultimate benefit."

"Queen Tiye and I spent many hours arguing it to a successful conclusion. Majesty, what is in your mind? Have I displeased you in some way?"

Amunhotep stopped pacing in front of Huy and folded his arms. "On the contrary. Everywhere I look I see the results of your guidance within and without this blessed country. Even Kush and Wawat can at last be considered one peaceful Egyptian province under Viceroy Merymose, yet another able administrator of your choice. You have made me an empire, dear Uncle Huy. I trust you completely. Paneb, Nebmerut, wet your brushes and write. From now on, the Son of Hapu will be mer kat."

Momentarily stunned, Huy stared up at the handsome painted features. Mer kat was not a title. It denoted a position of unique authority, bestowed so rarely that Huy could not remember the name of the last mer kat unless it might have been Imhotep himself, healer, architect, and Seer. *Like you, peasant,* a voice whispered inside him. *Like you. And do you not deserve this final accolade? Total supremacy over every facet of Egyptian life. Total power to do what you will. Pharaoh is the divinity, but you express his desire, commissioned to act without ever consulting him. You will rule Egypt.*

"But surely this honour should go to Yuya, your Chief Rekhit, Amunhotep," Huy said huskily. "Or to one of the Queen's brothers. Ay and Anen—"

"Are estimable men," Amunhotep finished for him impatiently. "Both have their strengths, and as for Yuya, he has so many titles already that my food gets cold while he's being announced. You have always refused the titles I've wanted to honour you with, but mer kat is not a title, Uncle—it is a state of being. A mer kat is above everything and everyone alive in the country. Are you keeping pace with this, my little scribes?" He was happy, excited, his kohled eyes shining, arms unfolding to spread wide. "Well, Great Seer? Will you be my mer kat and thus free me to hunt and drink and visit my House of Women every day? You virtually run Egypt anyway. I might as well make it official."

Huy was recovering from the shock, but his heart still raced. "If I accept, I shall be universally feared," he pointed out, rising. "Every administrator, every priest, will know that he is at my mercy."

"Your mercy instead of mine!" Amunhotep laughed. "This is not only a great idea, Uncle, it's a huge joke as well. Imagine the faces when the news is announced at audience tomorrow!" Then he sobered, grasping Huy's shoulders. "I have thought long and hard about this. I have prayed. I have talked it over with my Mother. She agrees that you are eminently well qualified to govern. You must say yes. I am your King and I command it."

But what of the Queen? Huy wondered, looking into the King's earnest brown eyes. *What will Tiye say? Does she already know?*

Amunhotep kissed him lightly on one cheek then enveloped him in a crushing embrace. "Well?" he pressed.

Huy stepped out of the King's arms and bowed. "I will accept this great honour," he heard himself say. "I am humbled by the supreme trust you're putting in me, Majesty, and I promise that it will not be abused." He felt weak as well as exhausted, as though, paradoxically, he had carried a weight that had just been taken from him.

"Good! Then tomorrow morning will be my last audience! But you may come to me at any time, dear Uncle. Now get up, Paneb, and leave with your master. Make a copy of all that has passed here and make sure that it is deposited in Weset's House of Life together with Nebmerut's scroll. Huy, send Nubti to me on your way out."

Huy bowed and backed towards the door. He wanted to put a hand on Paneb's shoulder for balance, but pride forbade it. Wordlessly, he signalled to Nubti and the door slammed closed behind the chief steward. Perti approached, and at the sight of him Huy repressed an absurd desire to cry. The litter was still waiting for him just beyond the pillars of the palace's entrance, and he and his little entourage returned silently to his house through the warm serenity of a southern night.

That had been six years ago, and under his hand Egypt had prospered. Its citizens went about their business in safety. The floods of the Inundation did not fail to leave behind a generous deposit of silt that produced thick and healthy crops. The borders, tightly patrolled by officers personally selected by Huy, were secure. Riches continued to stream into the Royal Treasury from every corner of the empire and spill out to eventually benefit the majority of the populace. An exuberance of building projects throughout the country proclaimed the omnipotence of the gods and the King's eminence as the most powerful sovereign in the world. Egypt, and Amunhotep, was envied. Petty and not so petty princelings swamped the Office of Correspondence with pleas for alliances, trading agreements, and protection from enemies real and imagined in exchange for a surrender of auton- omy and an Egyptian Governor complete with a division of Egyptian soldiers. Foreign ambassadors crowded the reception hall every morning with requests and complaints. Even the new Khatti ruler Suppiluliumas had sent an envoy, although the man presented nothing but his credentials. He always stood at the rear of the hall, watching and listening. Huy made sure that his letters home to his King were opened, read, and resealed. The Khatti underling responsible for their safe delivery was generously compensated by Huy for his perfidy, but the messages contained nothing of interest, merely descriptions of the palace, and the courtiers and administrators, and general comments on Egypt's continued growth and wealth.

"Suppiluliumas snatched power by sacking the capital city of Hattusas and murdering his predecessor," May pointed out to Huy one morning as they waded through the usual mound of scrolls. "He's entirely ruthless, Great One, and the extent of his holdings is larger than the Kingdom of Mitanni. He has asked nothing of us. Why not?"

"Because he hopes to take it all anyway one day," Huy had replied. "But according to our spies, he is still a long way from consolidating his control of the land. I'll have the Khatti border with Mitanni and Arzawa strengthened, and we'll continue to watch this barbarian closely."

Egypt's governors and administrators soon realized that the decisions of their new mer kat were informed and just. Their mistrust of him slowly died. Indeed, if they had paused to consider the matter, they might have imposed Huy's features instead of Amunhotep's beneath the smooth height of the

Double Crown. The King was still in evidence, hunting lions or lesser game out on the desert with his retinue, and the men in charge of governmental affairs knew that at any time the King could override Huy's policies. But he never did. Huy, with the steady support of Queen Mutemwia, laid his hand upon the country, and it flourished.

But Queen Tiye was another concern. According to Nasha, who in spite of her age still managed to not only run Huy's household amicably with Amunmose and Paroi but also visit the House of Women for hours of gossip and wine drinking, the Chief Wife had hotly protested Huy's elevation to mer kat. Her father Yuya was an aristocrat and thus far more worthy of such a distinction. Her brothers Ay and Anen were princes. The Seer, regardless of his qualifications, was a commoner and had no right to direct the fate of the whole country. Her husband had listened to her unmoved. He had not reminded her of Huy's long and excellent record of advice, or of her own affection for him, or of his rare and extraordinary relationship with Atum, the mighty Neb-er-djer, Lord to the Limit. When she had run out of words and had fallen into a flushed and angry silence, Amunhotep had said simply, "I have spoken," and had ignored her until at last she had flounced out of the room.

Now, on this sixteenth day of Mesore, in the quiet, hot dimness of her great reception room, Huy waited for her. He did not expect her to be prompt. The good manners in which both her mother and Mutemwia had instructed her no longer applied to him. She was not foolish enough to be outright rude to him, even in private, but she treated him with a coolness that hurt and exasperated him. The reason had little to do with his absolute authority, he knew. Her anger over that had been short-lived, particularly as neither her father nor her brothers had seemed offended by Huy's elevation. No, it was one of his

Seeings that had begun the rift between them, and Huy was sorry.

At last the double doors were flung open. Guards held the doors wide while others moved swiftly to scan the shadows. Huy rose and Userhet strode forward. Servants carrying tapers began to disperse, and at once lights burst forth from the many tall oil lamps scattered about. Heria, Tiye's body servant, disappeared in the direction of the square aperture leading, Huy knew, to the Queen's bedchamber, carrying an ornate cosmetic box and a spare pair of sandals. By the time Tiye had entered the room and seated herself opposite Huy's chair, the woman had returned with a footstool. Tiye's scribe Anhirkawi bowed to Huy and then went to the floor beside Tiye, opening his palette. More servants approached carrying a silver tray, a ewer, two silver cups, and a silver dish piled with little cakes.

In spite of his exalted rank, Huy had to wait for the Queen to speak. Heria knelt, lifted the royal legs, and lowered them onto the footstool. A cat appeared from somewhere, stretching and yawning, and sprang lightly onto Tiye's lap. Automatically her ring-encrusted hands began to stroke its sleek grey spine, but Huy kept his attention fixed on her painted face. The servants, but for Anhirkawi, drew away to stand against the walls. Silence fell. Finally Tiye sighed. "Mer kat."

"Empress."

"The Horus-in-the-Nest is now beginning his obligatory term as a priest of Ptah in Mennofer under the guidance of your nephew."

"Yes."

"They tell me that the restoring and beautifying work on Ptah's temple overseen by Amunhotep-Huy is finished, and is completely satisfactory."

"Yes."

"Under your guidance a new mausoleum for the sacred Apis bulls has begun construction, the new Palace of the Dazzling Aten continues to rise on the west bank, and His Majesty's funerary temple will have floors of solid silver rather than the more plentiful gold. You are a busy man. May tells me that you have also put the Assyrians in their place."

"Majesty, your attention is constantly fixed on governmental offices," Huy replied with an air of patience he was far from feeling. "You know all this and more. In particular your familiarity with the affairs of foreigners is prodigious. Even as a girl you loved the negotiations into which May entered. Almost every day you, Queen Mutemwia, and I gathered to work with May in the Office of Foreign Correspondence. Is there something pressing that you need to discuss with me?"

"Need." The creases beginning to etch permanently into her face from nose to mouth deepened. "Need is a dangerous word, mer kat. Or rather, the prospect of its alleviation can be seductively dangerous." She snapped her fingers and held up the cat. Huy could hear it purring. At once Heria materialized, took it gently, and disappeared. Tiye laid hennaed palms flat on the drape of the gold-shot linen across her thighs. "Because of you the King need not concern himself anymore with the administration of this country. He hunts, he frequents the House of Women far too often, and he has begun to drink too much."

"I watch him as carefully as you, Empress. I have loved and served him since he was a little boy coming to Hut-herib to stay on my estate. I agree that he is becoming somewhat profligate in his tastes, but he still requires my reports every week and is far from ignorant regarding the state of his realm." He hesitated, then plunged on. "Placing the cloak of responsibility around my shoulders six years ago was a relief to him. You wished to assume ultimate power instead of me, but you are certainly aware that the country would never accept a female mer kat. Empress, yes. Supreme ruler under the King, no. Amunhotep looks about him, and all is well. Egypt has never been richer or more secure. He has royal daughters and a handsome Hawk-in-the-Nest ..." Huy realized his mistake at once and mutely cursed himself, but he was beyond exhaustion and he ached with the desire for his evening dose of poppy. *Need,* he thought grimly. *Even I, Egypt's supreme Overseer, have needs, dear Tiye.*

"Who is already nine years old and in full health," she cut in. "I have made sure that he is never alone, and two physicians examine him every day. Only you, His Majesty, and I know that Atum has decreed his death. Or so you said when you Saw for him." Her mouth turned down. "Every other oracle predicted a long life full of successes. Everyone but you. And what of my daughters, mer kat? Death for every one of them, according to you. Could it be that Anubis is greedy for their souls or that Atum himself has decided to visit a punishment on Egypt's ruling house for some reason unknown to us? Or perhaps the gift of Seeing has deserted you and you have resorted to lying." She had leaned forward, the scorn in her voice all too familiar.

"We have walked this ground before, Empress. Why must we do so again? I have never lied to you, and in your heart you know it. You need me to See for you again, don't you? Why?"

Her hands came up to cover her face, then she sat back. "My physician tells me that I am pregnant again," she said dully. "I have given my King four daughters but only one son. He has other wives, Huy, some of them barbarian, foreign. I remain his friend, his most intimate companion, and the bedmate of his choice, but if I continue to produce daughters he will be forced to legitimize any one of his other women so that he may have more sons. The Horus Throne must be protected. One Hawk-in-the-Nest is not enough, particularly as you have predicted an early death for my darling Thothmes." One hennaed palm rose briefly to cover her mouth, a gesture betraying such desperation and defencelessness that Huy was shocked. "Forgive my harsh words," she begged. "They are spawned from fear and bitterness, two emotions I disdain but which seem to dog me all too often of late. Userhet! Come and pour us wine. It is shedeh, your favourite, Huy. Or would you rather have beer?"

Huy wanted neither. Tiye's fingers shook as she raised her cup, draining half the red liquid before cradling it on her knee. She was very pale. Userhet had disappeared. "Please See for me now, tonight," she begged. "I can't sleep without a word from you." The earlier hostility had vanished, but it would come back, Huy knew sadly. It always did.

"I will do as you wish," he said, "but you must dismiss your scribe and send for Paneb, who will take down my words as usual."

At a sharp order from Tiye, Anhirkawi uncurled from the floor, bowed to both of them, and waited in front of one of the double doors until a soldier let him out. At another command Userhet followed him. There were several minutes of quiet. Tiye had apparently regained most of her poise. *Either that,* Huy thought, eyeing her carefully, *or the pomegranate wine is unusually potent.* She sipped occasionally and gazed at the dimness of the far wall. *You no longer trust my visions,* Huy's thoughts ran on, *and yet what I said to you is true. In your consciousness I lie in order to preserve my position as mer kat, but deep in the recesses of your ka you know perfectly well that no one else will give you certainty. In spite of your crown, your life as a woman has been hard. You bore your children in rapid succession—Thothmes, Sitamun, Henurtaneb, Isis, and now the baby Nebetah, one female after another—and in spite of your youth and health you have begun to fear the damage each long pregnancy might be causing in that tireless body of yours. To*

*make matters worse, I tell you that your beloved children will soon die,
and only Sitamun will temporarily escape the Judgment Hall. If I had
spoken fully of Sitamun's disastrous end, what would you have said?
Would you have bowed in humility to the will of Atum? Not the girl
who came to my palace apartment in Mennofer all those years ago and
demanded that I See for her. Not the young woman who constantly
thwarted her mother's attempts to turn her into an ideal wife for a
King. Yet your intelligence and candidness won Amunhotep's heart
and mind, as Atum required. It is a hard thing to let go of one's
offspring, my Tiye, but if you are to maintain control of your husband
you must overcome the fear and bitterness of which you spoke. Don't
you know that I am the one person in the whole of Egypt who requires
nothing of you at all?*

"Sitamun," she said suddenly. "Her estate yielded well this
year? She remains in good health?"

"You have my reports, Empress. As the Overseer of the
Princess's holdings I decide what crops must be sown and I see to
the care and disposition of her herds. She prospers. Her tutors tell
me that she has little interest in her studies but she enjoys watching her brother take his chariot lessons."

"Now that Thothmes is in Mennofer, she will have to find
other means of entertainment." Tiye's tone was waspish. "You are
in charge of her education, mer kat. Hire new tutors if necessary,
but Sitamun must learn to care for something other than the
glamour of the chariot."

"She's only eight, Tiye. She cares that she closely resembles
you."

"That is hardly an accomplishment."

Huy was saved from replying by a flurry of movement at the
door. Paneb came forward with his usual unhurried pace, knelt
before Tiye and touched his forehead to the tiles, and at her
word sat up and crossed his legs. Quietly he opened the drawer

in his palette and said the prayer to Thoth as he prepared to work. Huy leaned forward, enfolding Tiye's hand in both of his. For a moment their eyes met. Huy could not read her expression, but he noted that before her blue-dusted lids closed, her left eye was slightly bloodshot. The hour was late. Clearly she was as tired as he.

"A remarkable woman, isn't she, mer kat?" Anubis was leaning his folded arms negligently against the back of Tiye's chair, his jackal snout inches from the top of her bowed head, the golden kohl sweeping around his eyes glinting dully in the flickering lamplight. Thin gold chains slung across his chest winked at Huy, emphasizing the oiled blackness of the god's skin. Thick golden bracelets crowded each strong wrist. "She's given our increasingly dissolute young King five children in the space of nine years, all of whom but Sitamun will die before they reach maturity, yet she fights to keep a flame of hope burning inside her. Perhaps this one will be different. Perhaps this time the gods will reward me with a son who will survive to inherit all the wealth and power the Egyptian empire offers. An empire that you created, mer kat. How unfortunate that you are not a pharaoh with an able son! If anyone deserves to rule Egypt, you do, and your progeny after you. But wait! How foolish of me! You already rule Egypt, don't you, mer kat, even though no son walks the halls of the palace behind you." He laughed, a hoarse animal bark, lips drawn back from two rows of glistening white teeth.

Huy waited. He was well used to these goads and had stopped reacting to them long ago. Anubis unfolded his arms and, roughly grasping Tiye's head, lifted it so that Huy could look directly into her closed face. Her breathing remained even. Her eyelids did not even flutter. "She wants you to tell her that a male child inhabits her womb," Anubis went on harshly, "but the seed she carries is death, Great Seer, more death than you or she can possibly imagine—the eclipse of Ma'at and the destruction of this blessed country. A Queen, but worthy to be a King, is she not? And she knows it. She will indeed give birth to one, and then let Egypt beware!"

To his horror, Huy saw that the god was weeping. Tears were slipping over the lustrous fur of his doglike face and falling onto Tiye's dark red hair, and where they landed, small uneven circles of grey appeared. Her features were aging also, the folds more pronounced, the corners of the mouth turned down in an expression of cruel petulance. Huy had seen her like this once before. Frantically he searched his mind, until with a savage gesture Anubis let go Tiye's head and seemed to fling something at him. A familiar vision blossomed: Tiye and a royal man Huy did not recognize standing side by side in a place that resembled the inner court of a temple except that the roof was missing and scorching sunlight flooded the place. Huy could feel its heat, but more than the physical discomfort, it carried with it a sense of desolation so strong that he cried out.

"You chose to ignore this prophecy, didn't you?" The image vanished. Anubis straightened. "The happy scene preceding it was altogether too convenient, wasn't it? A way for Egypt's Great Seer to demonstrate his wisdom, his closeness to Atum, his infallibility. Tiye as a Queen? A commoner like yourself elevated to the pinnacle of the aristocracy, and, moreover, at the will of Atum himself? How deliciously improbable, and what a challenge, to force those around you to agree!"

"It was not like that," Huy protested—but it was. He vividly remembered the anxiety the vision had caused him and the relief he had felt when the scroll on which it was written had been sealed and stored away. He did not think he had been as arrogant at the time as Anubis had described him, but he had certainly pushed for a betrothal between Tiye and Amunhotep on the strength of only half the message the god had provided.

"Yes, it was like that," Anubis hissed, lips raised to reveal his pointed teeth. "And now Atum commands you to undo the harm your conceit has caused. All these years, Son of Hapu, all these years as a Seer, so many visions granted to you, and you still have not divined the difference between what is inevitable and what may be changed."

Only a god can do that, Huy wanted to object. *Such a subtlety of understanding is far beyond the reach of any Seer, no matter how able. None of the visions accorded me held the slightest hint that the events I saw were not predestined.*

Yet there were moments of doubt, weren't there? a small voice inside him answered. *Times when the visions were fulfilled in unexpected ways or their events transferred to someone other than the petitioner. Then I was troubled.*

"But not troubled enough," Anubis said. He stepped back, and at once Tiye's features smoothed. Colour returned to her hair and she took a slow, deep breath. "We have great sympathy for you, Huy," the god continued. "Your intentions have been good. You made a choice in the innocence of youth when you stood before Imhotep in the Beautiful West and agreed to read the Book of Thoth. You could not have anticipated everything your decision implied, yet when you realized that the task of Seeing had been thrust upon you, you were obedient in spite of your rebellious desires. Atum, Thoth, Ma'at—we all know what you have lost and what Egypt has thus gained. You rule her well." Once more the god's jackal lips lifted, this time in a smile. "But you are human, you will die, and unless you find a way to disinherit the boy the Empress carries, all your work will have been in vain. Amunhotep is your tool. Use him."

Huy had opened his mouth to ask just how the King might be

used when he realized that his head was pounding, the god had gone, and Tiye was pulling her fingers out of his grasp.

"Well?" she said. "Did Anubis tell you the sex of my child? I am not afraid to hear it, Huy."

Yes you are, Huy thought, watching her eyes. *And my fear at the knowledge is now greater than yours.* "You are carrying a male child, Majesty," he said.

Her face lit up. Clapping her hands, she called the guards on the door to summon Userhet, and picking up her cup, she drained it quickly. "Good news!" she exclaimed. "Great news! Thank you, Huy! Amunhotep will be overjoyed! Now we must have more wine to celebrate!"

Huy shook his head, then winced. "Forgive me, Tiye, I must go home to my opium and my couch."

Immediately she sobered. "Of course. You are in pain. You may go. Userhet, escort the Seer to his litter."

The steward had come up to Tiye's chair. Now he offered Huy his arm, and gratefully Huy took it, struggled to his feet, sketched a bow, and, followed by Paneb, escaped into the corridor, where he leaned against the wall.

"Perti, have my litter brought here—I can't walk through the palace tonight. Userhet, go back to your mistress."

He wished that Kenofer had accompanied him. The body servant would have been ready with Huy's drug, but Huy had been unprepared for a Seeing. He was thirsty for water. Already the familiar black and white pattern was forming in front of his eyes, blocking his sight. By the time he and his attendants reached his house, he could not see at all. But before he allowed Kenofer to administer the opium and then undress him, he dictated the sum of his encounter with Anubis to his scribe. As always he remembered every word said, every inflection. Paneb would seal the scroll and place it in the chest with the accounts of all the other royal Seeings. Then Huy took the tiny ball of raw opium and stood while Kenofer removed his clothes, washed him, and helped him onto the couch. He could neither sleep nor think. He lay curled in upon himself like a child while the night wore away.

11

THE KING WAS CAUTIOUSLY PLEASED with Tiye's news. "You didn't see an early death for the child, I suppose?" he said to Huy as they stood together outside the entrance to Amunhotep's tomb. "Must I order the masons to hew yet another room out of the rock below in sorry anticipation of a second son's demise?" He waved a commanding arm at the gaping hole behind them. "I'm beginning to think that I've offended the gods in some way, although I can't imagine how. I've poured gold and manpower into their glorification throughout Egypt. I've been obedient to the laws of Ma'at. What else can they expect of me?"

"All I know is that the Empress will give birth to another boy," Huy replied. "Atum will not show me his fate until I'm able to touch him."

"As the harbinger of constant bad news, are you becoming as suspicious of Atum's prognostications as I am, Uncle?" Irritably, Amunhotep waved away the cup of water a servant was offering. "You've given Thothmes the title of Troop Commander and allowed him to begin drilling the soldiers stationed at Mennofer in his spare time away from Ptah's temple. A sensible position for the heir to the Horus Throne. Can it be that you doubt the prediction of his early death?"

"All I know is that the Prince won't see his twenty-first year,"

Huy answered. "And no, Majesty, I'm sorry, but I don't doubt the word of Atum. I continue to See for many of the courtiers with the accuracy the god provides."

"Tiye insists on coddling the boy," Amunhotep said testily. "Two physicians and even a guard in his bedchamber, even though she's aware of the years ahead that have been allotted to him. Hopefully another son in the nursery will set her mind at rest. It will certainly do so for me. A second male child strengthens the possibility of a peaceful succession."

Not according to Anubis, Huy thought moodily. *Your marriage to Tiye was a mistake of my own arrogant making, and I'm commanded to undo the harm I've done. But how? How may I use Amunhotep to do so? All these deaths to come, are they the result of a marriage that wasn't meant to be? Will Atum wipe all trace of this royal family from Egypt's sacred history?*

"Wake up, Uncle. You're not even listening to me." Trailed by his entourage, Amunhotep began walking towards the scattered piles of bricks not far away. His sunshade bearer hurried to catch up to him. "Let's see what progress is being made on my new palace. Already I can imagine the magnificence of my finished funerary temple, but why are the labourers working so slowly on this?"

"Because you keep changing the architects' plans and driving poor Hori and Suti to distraction, not to mention Men, the Overseer of Works. They're also responsible for the ongoing construction of your funerary temple, *and* Amun's temple at the Southern Apt."

"A beautiful tribute to Amun and myself," Amunhotep said. "Your design is glorious and harmonious, and the avenue of holy sphinxes lining its short distance from Ipet-isut very grand, but it's been twelve years since its foundation was laid and still it isn't ready to be consecrated. Everything slow slow slow! I'm impatient to take up residence on this side of the river, away from the noise and stench of Weset. Hurry them up, Huy."

"I can if Your Majesty will stop interfering and leave my architects alone."

Suddenly Amunhotep's infectious grin broke out. "And will you forbid Anhur to take me fishing and send me to my room if I disobey?" He laughed. "Very well, dearest Uncle, I leave my future comfort in your hands. Let's get out of this infernal heat. I want my couch."

They boated across the river, now at its lowest ebb, and parted, the King to his apartments and Huy to his house. His bearers were waiting, sprawled drowsily in the sparse shade cast by the tired trees lining the canal to the palace's entrance. Huy left the curtains of his litter open as he was carried the short way to his house. The river path, dusty and deserted at that time of the day, soon began to run between the river and the poppy fields that formed a protective area around Huy's estate. Here the bearers paused to allow Huy to answer the challenge of the soldiers before turning towards his sheltering wall through the desiccated plants. Their appearance was deceptive. Leaves yellow, dry stems bent towards the arid sand, they looked dead, but Huy knew that the precious drug had already been harvested from the pods and the seeds carefully collected to be sown the following spring. Guarding the arouras against thieves was a boring necessity, and Huy and Amunnefer made sure that the men stationed on the perimeter of their lucrative venture were amply compensated.

Two gates gave access to Huy's domain. One faced north into the poppy fields and the other spanned the canal leading from the river and running past the house to the luxuriant garden beyond. Now, in the middle of Mesore, the canal was dry. The guard on the northern gate admitted the litter, and soon Huy was alighting under the pillars that fronted his reception hall.

Amunmose emerged from the shadows and bowed. "Paneb has gone to his afternoon sleep but wants you to be prepared to deal with the seven scrolls on your desk this evening, Master," he said, following Huy as he entered the coolness of the great room. "Kenofer is also asleep on his mat before your door but begs to be woken if you need him. The Lady Nasha has not returned from the house of the Lady Thuyu. Captain Perti—"

Huy hushed him with a wave of his hand. "Everything can wait until I've rested. Get to your own couch, Amunmose. For once I'll be eating the evening meal here at home, so tell Rakhaka, will you?"

Removing his sandals, he set off across the long expanse of the hall, glad to feel the slight chill of the white and blue tiles against the naked soles of his feet. It took him some time to reach the hot breeze of the open passage beyond and the guarded stairs leading up at right angles to the chambers above. Most of the administrative business inherent in his position as mer kat was conducted in the many offices adjacent to the palace, but sometimes matters of a delicate nature were dealt with here, in his home, where his reception area was deliberately designed to create a diffidence in the officials who appeared before him at the foot of his dais. Amunhotep had insisted that the imperial colours be apparent in the house. "You are the extension of my arm and the chosen companion of the gods," he had said flatly. "My brother, my uncle, my beloved Seer, the only man I trust completely. If anyone is privileged to live amid the blue and the white besides myself, it's you, mer kat." So Huy's staff were kilted in blue and white, the flags flying from his skiffs and barges also sported the colours of a royal house, and Huy himself wore striped blue and white linen ribbons plaited into his long braids. The palace servants, the common folk he encountered coming and going, would kneel and prostrate themselves when he passed, and long ago Huy had given up trying to prevent their extreme homage. "The people know who rules Egypt," Amunhotep had casually stated in dismissal of Huy's protest. "They're expressing their gratitude for the lives of peace and plenty you've given them, that's all. You're concerned that you're appropriating my prerogative, Huy, but I'm not troubled in the least. This matter is of no importance." Thankfully, Huy's personal staff did no more than bow to him occasionally as they pursued their duties.

His under steward, Paroi, passing the foot of the stairs, nodded as he disappeared into the lower labyrinth of the great house. Huy nodded back, mounted the stairs, and at last stepped over a snoring Kenofer and turned into his own door.

The body servant had lowered the reed slats covering the one window Huy had insisted upon when the house was being designed. It was uncommon for a bedchamber to have more than a small clerestory transom just under the angle of the wall and ceiling—often there was no window at all—but Huy had not liked either trying to fall asleep or waking up in complete darkness. He still remembered tumbling into the utter blackness that had swallowed him when at the age of twelve he had been brutally attacked, and he preferred the discomfort of increased heat and the white sunlight filtering through the blind in the afternoons to a resurgence of that memory. Kenofer had placed fresh linen on the huge gilded couch and a silver dish of wrinkled figs beside the water jug on the bedside table. A clean loincloth and kilt lay on the lid of Huy's tiring chest, waiting for Kenofer to dress Huy for the evening's activities. A pair of earrings and several bracelets had been set beside the copper mirror on Huy's cosmetic stand. Everything was as it should be, as it always was at this time of the day, yet Huy paused.

Some time ago, he had begun to wear the spicy perfume extracted from the small greenish-yellow flowers of the plum trees that grew freely in the sandy soil of the south. He had reached an age when almost every other scent either reminded him of those he had loved and lost to the Judgment Hall or else impelled a vivid memory, sometimes pleasant, sometimes distressing. Such moments could not be avoided, but surely it was not necessary to carry the constant recollection of Ishat or his mother or even Anuket on his own body. He disliked the brown fruit produced by the particularly unlovely, spiny, thorn-covered tree, but the odd scent of its flowers suited him. The perfume was kept in a blue faience bottle in his cosmetic box, and although it was firmly stoppered, the aroma always imbued the air of the room, mingling with a trace of the frankincense he often burned before his shrine.

Now, standing just inside the entrance, he became alert, his nostrils flared. Another odour, so faint as to be almost undetectable, was hanging in the close stillness, and he had the immediate feeling that he was not alone. His first brief thought was of Anubis, his mind swirling with images of fur and black skin, but the god carried the scent of myrrh with him as well as the odour of his body, and the air Huy was drawing into his lungs was unrelievedly rank. An animal had found its way upstairs, perhaps a pampered palace feline that had followed him home or, worse, a rat from one of the grain silos at the bottom of his garden. Paroi was engaged in a constant battle to poison them.

Carefully, Huy surveyed the room. His couch stood on four legs and there appeared to be nothing under it. Neither was there movement under the cosmetic stand or the gold and ivory table in the centre of the floor, and the chair drawn up to it was empty. The ornate golden shrine holding a likeness of Khentikheti, crocodile god of Huy's natal town, was closed, and with a growing sense of unease Huy's attention became drawn to its double doors incised with Khenti-kheti's long snout and bulbous eyes. Inside the shrine, Huy knew, the god himself sat benignly, scaly tail curved around his stubby feet, waiting for the doors to open in order to receive Huy's daily obeisance. Or did he? Huy glanced quickly into the thin shadows around the shrine. Nothing stirred, yet that distasteful odour was intensifying, edging out both perfume and incense. As Huy hesitated, the horrific conviction grew in him that Khenti-kheti no longer occupied the shrine, that something corrupt and tainted now squatted in his place, and that on no account must he open those little doors. But the idea was ridiculous, preposterous, belonging more to the realm of nightmares than to a hot, sleepy Weset afternoon.

Angry with himself, Huy resolved not to wake Kenofer. He took one determined step towards the shrine, and as he did so he caught a movement out of the corner of his eye. He knew that his couch had been empty a moment before, but now an animal sat on his sheets staring at him imperturbably, its yellow eyes slitted, its pink tongue hanging motionless from its wide black snout. The fur covering its hide was stiffly bristled, ugly, and doubtless sharp to the touch, Huy thought in the second of shock before he recognized it. *But you touched it, didn't you, Imhotep?* he said to himself. *You stroked its spine as it sat beside you, tame and contented, while those yellow eyes regarded me with solemn self-containment. This is no ordinary hyena. This creature has come to me from the Beautiful West. Why?*

He took another step. The hyena did not move. "What are you doing here?" Huy whispered. "Did Imhotep send you? Is there a message from Anubis?" At the sound of his voice it blinked, and rising on its thin haunches, it stretched. Then, to Huy's dismay, it jumped to the floor, shambled towards him, and began to rub its body against his leg. The feel of it, rough and coarse, filled him with such revulsion that he cried out and stumbled away, and almost at once Kenofer's tall form filled the doorway, already winding a crumpled kilt around his waist.

"Master, what's wrong?" he asked, coming swiftly to Huy. "You're trembling! A dream? No. I see your couch is undisturbed. Are you ill?"

Huy scanned the room, hysteria not far away. There was no sign of the hyena, but he fancied he could smell its breath, a stench of warm, rotting offal. *But that's wrong?* his thoughts ran on. *The celestial hyena had no odour, gave off no evidence of animality. The earthly hyenas become imbued with the stink of what they eat.* Going to the couch, he bent. His sheets still bore the imprint of its forepaws and its narrow buttocks.

"Come here, Kenofer," he ordered tersely. "Look down. What do you see?"

Kenofer's hands went automatically to smooth the already uncreased white linen. "Nothing, Master. At least, nothing but the sheet. What am I supposed to see? Did the washerman leave a stain?"

"No. What do you smell?"

Kenofer's dark eyebrows rose. He inhaled noisily. "Stale incense and your perfume," he told Huy. "I can have the room washed down with vinegar if those odours are beginning to bother you."

Huy could still see the indentations. They seemed to mock him, and the skin of his bare calf was crawling with the feel of that abrasive pelt. "Have my couch stripped and the bedding washed again. I need to be thoroughly bathed at once, please, Kenofer. While you're attending to me, your assistant can be making up the couch in one of the guest rooms and I'll take what's left of the afternoon sleep there. I'll want poppy. Meet me in the bathhouse."

The body servant nodded and vanished quickly into the

passage. Huy followed him almost at a run, turning right and hurrying along the wide hallway to the head of the stairs leading down to the privacy of Huy's sumptuous bathhouse. Ahead was the guarded entry onto the roof. *Soldiers everywhere*, Huy thought as he fled down the steps, *but no human being could have prevented what just happened to me. Gods, I feel dirty, besmirched inside and out! If I could vomit up the filth I can almost taste as well as smell, I would, and then drink nothing but water and vinegar until I was cleansed.* Reaching the damp floor of the bathhouse, he tore off his clothes, jewels, and sandals and flung them away, tripping over himself in his haste to get onto one of the bathing slabs. There were several in the large, enclosed space. A generous seat ran around walls alive with depictions of naked men and women raising their arms to cascades of water, sailing in reed skiffs on a river choked with silvery fish, drinking from brimming cups offered to them by Hapi, god of the Nile, himself. Bowls of natron, flagons of scented oil, piles of linen towels, ivory combs, even ribbons and hair ornaments for needy guests, rested neatly about. Beyond the doorway opposite the stairs leading up into the house, a secluded area contained a firepit for heating the washing water, and benches high enough for Huy's masseuses to knead the maltreated bodies of overindulgent guests. The luxuries and comforts of Huy's estate rivalled those of the King's palace itself, but today Huy stood alone with his eyes closed and his teeth clenched, as nude and defenceless as the most destitute of Amunhotep's subjects.

Tensely, he waited for Kenofer and the purifying water. *Purifying, yes*, his thoughts ran on under the chaos of his fear. *I have been sullied and I don't know why. I sensed no taint in the hyena Imhotep was caressing. Everything in that blessed place was free of pollution. Yet today its touch contaminated me, as though it had come to give me some terrible ukhedu and if I look down at my leg I will see a suppurating wound. Why? Those steady yellow eyes were full of intelligence. Did they hold a message I was unable to decipher?* In spite of the humid warmth of the bathhouse, he began to shiver.

Kenofer entered briskly, clean linen over his arm, and fetching hot water and a generous amount of natron, he proceeded to douse Huy, scrubbing him expertly from the waist-length ropes of his hair to the soles of his feet and then rinsing off the salts several times. Huy watched the grimy water splash from the stone slab onto the slanted tiles and disappear through the drainage hole in the floor. Wrapping him in linen, Kenofer picked up a jar of oil and led him outside to one of the empty stone massage tables. Huy did not resist.

Lying under the man's firm control, eyes closed, he felt the panic leave him. *Atum is merely using the hyena to drive home my obligation to deal with the Empress's unborn son,* he told himself calmly. *There is a perversion I must correct so that Ma'at may remain whole, so that my spinelessness will not make her bleed as it did when I stood before the King's grandfather and my courage failed me. But surely the mere sight of the beast would have been enough. Why was it allowed to wipe the filth of a mortal being against me? Why not a moment of encouragement from the Blessed Realm? Do the hyenas in the Beautiful West need food, and if so, what do they eat?* An answer so outrageous formed in his mind that he grunted aloud, and Kenofer's hands were stilled. *They eat the fruit of the Ished Tree.*

No! his mind clamoured. *Surely not possible, even in Paradise! No living person, not even Ra's successive High Priests who guard and tend the Tree, is allowed to consume the crop that falls to the ground. It's gathered and burned every year. But those humans and sacred animals who have passed through the Judgment Hall, those who are justified, what new rules and laws apply to them? A hyena in the kingdom of the undying might very well be an unblemished object of veneration, whereas here they are fattened for food by the poor and regarded as necessary scavengers by the rest of us. But if venerated, why? If free to eat the fruit of the Ished Tree, why?* No instant response came to him. Kenofer had resumed his task, and Huy did his best to give himself up to the man's healing touch.

That evening, he slept in his own room on freshly washed sheets. By now he was used to the one acute disadvantage of his long years of addiction to the opium, an almost constant nagging discomfort in his belly that often prevented him from eating, but after the massage his appetite had returned and he was able to consume a large evening meal. Milk and date wine or date juice ordinarily served to give him some relief, and Steward Amunmose made sure that those liquids went with him as he hurried from morning audiences to administrative offices to building sites, but for once he closed his eyes with appetite sated and stomach at peace. Nor did he dream.

On the following day, when he, Hori, Suti, and Men stood on the western bank of the river, under the thin protection of their white linen sunshades, looking towards the King's embryonic funerary temple, Huy saw the hyena again. Beside the men was a churned hole where a landing stage would be erected and a canal dug for Amun, who would cross the water in his Divine Barque from Ipet-isut in order to visit the temples of the Osiris-kings during the Beautiful Feast of the Valley in Payni. Amunhotep had requested an avenue of jackal statues in honour of Anubis to run on either side of the waterway to the concourse before the as yet unbuilt entrance to his great funerary temple. The whole area seethed with busy workmen.

"How many statues are finished?" Huy asked Men. "These foundations are ready. And what about the draft your father submitted to you regarding the layout of the temple, Hori? Is it final, or has the King been meddling with it again?"

"The sculptors at Swenet tell me that they have almost completed their charge, and I've sent a flotilla of barges south to collect the statues," Men replied. "My son Bek will supervise the loading. I'm not happy with this canal, though, Huy. I don't think it's deep enough."

"The major plan is finished, mer kat." The higher voice was Suti's. Huy could still not tell them apart until one of them spoke.

Hori was squinting at his brother, kohled eyes narrowed against the sun. "The King can play with the details all he wants. It'll be some time before the interior begins to take shape. The One wants the design to make sure that all but the innermost sanctuary will be flooded during the Inundation. Father isn't happy with the strain such an annual occurrence will put on the building's foundations, let alone the numerous royal statues."

Huy blew out his cheeks. "Kha must simply find a way to cope with Amunhotep's wishes." Huy peered ahead at the lively anthill. Between the chaos that was the birth of the King's funerary temple and the hot beige cliffs shimmering beyond it, the temples of other dead pharaohs rose out of the churned sand as though the desert had spewed them up an eternity ago. A little to the left, the temple of the Osiris-one Thothmes the First sat a distance apart from that of his unfortunate son Thothmes the Second, husband to the upstart Queen Hatshepsut, whose far more glorious monument lay tightly against the Cliff of Gurn, far to Huy's right. Almost directly ahead was Thothmes the Fourth's sacred structure, looking as ancient as the others although it had barely been finished before that King met his end, a death Huy did not grieve in the least. He wondered whether anyone brought prayers and offerings to the priests caring for him or for his father Osiris Amunhotep the Second, with his small edifice to the north. However, Huy smiled as his gaze moved over the large temple that followed. Many times his dear friend Thothmes had made the long voyage from Iunu to present gifts and petitions to his hero and namesake Thothmes the Third, warrior and empire builder. After Ishat's death Thothmes had turned over most of the chores of the sepat's government to his elder son Huy and had become something of a recluse, although he and Huy corresponded regularly as they had always done. Looking at the Osiris-one's funerary shrine gave Huy a swift pang of longing for his friend's face, and he was about to turn away when he saw a familiar shape sitting beside one of the foundation pits for the jackal statues halfway between himself and the King's future forecourt. It was motionless, its blunt head turned towards him. There was a threat in its very stillness.

Hori pointed. "Look at that!" he exclaimed. "A hyena, right where one of the avenue's statues will be placed! This is an undesirable omen. Perhaps the gods do not approve of our designs for the King's temple, Suti!"

So the others can see it also, Huy thought. *Therefore it belongs to this world, a creature of the desert with perfectly ordinary black eyes.* Yet the relief he ought to have felt was missing. He knew with a dull certainty that it was not here as a sign of the gods' favour. *Its presence is for me alone,* his thoughts ran on. *A warning, and a reminder of what must be done. But gods, I cannot, I absolutely will not, murder the Empress in order to destroy the child within her.* Just the word *murder,* lucid and pedestrian, caused him to break out in a nervous sweat. *Must I pray for a miscarriage, an event that would surely distress Amunhotep and drive Tiye into despair?*

"Oh, look!" Hori repeated. "It's washing its face as though it were a cat!"

Huy watched as the pink tongue caressed one of its forepaws and the limb passed up the coarse fur of its cheek and over its ear. *Even this gesture is a message,* Huy realized. *I must cleanse my craven soul—but how?* The hyena got up and shambled away towards the narrow shade of the temple's foundation blocks, and Men turned to toss the scroll in his hand towards the basket his servant held.

"We'd better go south and inspect the latest progress on the King's new palace," he said. "It's not far, but I don't fancy walking in this heat." He signalled to the group of litter-bearers. "I want the canal to the river finished before the Inundation so that all my men and equipment can be floated to the site. Carts and donkeys trudging through the sand slows everything down."

The men got into their litters and immediately drew the curtains against the ferocity of the sun. Huy did so unconsciously, blind to the discomforts of the day. The Empress's son would be born sometime in the middle of Phamenoth. *I'll be sixty-four by then*, he reflected grimly as his bearers laboured to keep a steady footing, *and Atum is still not finished with me. Neither is the King. Do I dare to approach Mutemwia with the grim knowledge I possess? To whom may I turn for guidance regarding the damning decision I must make?*

In the end, he kept his own counsel. What he was contemplating was outright treason. Mutemwia would hear him, understand, and absolutely forbid him to take any action. Worse, she would no longer trust him. To unburden himself to the King was simply unthinkable. Amunhotep was already delighted that a second son would ensure the continuation of his royal line. Neither Thothmes nor Nasha, both of them old and partially infirm, could offer him a way out of his dilemma. A mer kat had no friends. The totality of his power set him irrevocably apart from every other citizen. His relationships with the country's many ministers and governors were cordial but bounded by the reserve inherent in his vastly superior station. His word was law, and he dared not undermine his position. He was sufficiently in control

of Egypt's welfare that to endanger his status would be to endanger the country itself. The perceptions of those relying on his
judgment must not change.

From then on, a hyena began to shadow him, sometimes an
earthly animal loping behind him as he was carried through the
choked streets of the city, following him from audience hall to
administrative offices to the homes of the nobles, or squatting
out of reach of the many lamps in Huy's reception hall at his
feasts, or, worst of all, watching him from a dim corner of his
bedchamber once Kenofer had seen him onto his couch and
closed the door. Since Hori had remarked on the beast in the
vicinity of the King's funerary temple, no one seemed able to see
the thing stalking Huy. Only in the privacy of his own room did
the ugly creature stare at him with the unblinking yellow eyes of
Imhotep's tame hyena in the Beautiful West. After a sighting
among the opium poppies one morning and a command to Perti
to drive it away with a hail of stones, he had stopped acknowledging its presence. Perti and his soldiers had searched the field
for its misshapen grey body in vain, and on that day Huy realized,
with a mixture of horror and resignation, that he alone was being
haunted. Occasionally Amunmose reported to him that the
house servants had swept up several hard white balls of hyena
feces. Slabs of poisoned meat had been set out, none of which
were ever disturbed.

At first Huy attempted to speak to the animal in spite of his
fear that it would respond by rubbing itself against him again, but
it never responded, merely continuing to observe him dispassion-
ately. Nothing drove it away—not pleas to Khenti-kheti or
entreaties to Atum or any of the desperate attempts to engage
Anubis's sympathy during Huy's increasingly infrequent Seeings.
Anubis had expressed a fleeting pity for Huy only once. Huy had
not expected any help from the jackal god himself, but he had

become frantic enough to beg an end, if not a suspension, to the persecution being inflicted on him. Anubis ignored his frantic request. In the end, by having Kenofer double his evening dose of opium, he was able to fall asleep under the gaze of those expressionless eyes, but sometimes they followed him into his dreams and he would wake, sweating and sickened, to the same calm regard.

The Sopdet star appeared in the sky. The Inundation began amid the usual universal rejoicing. Huy, haggard and feeling demon-ridden, fought to carry out his many responsibilities with a sanity he was far from feeling. Apart from his household staff, Queen Mutemwia was the first to notice his condition. With her lifelong interest in the affairs of state she often attended the morning audience always conducted by Huy, and one hot morning in Paophi she accosted him.

"You are very sick, mer kat," she said without preamble. "How are you afflicted?" Her glance went to the sa amulet on his chest and the shield provided by the two rings the Rekhet had made for him many years ago, the gold and red jasper Soul Protector with the hawk's body and the head of a man, designed to prevent any separation of soul from body until the proper time, and the golden Frog of Resurrection with its blue lapis eyes. "Have you become careless in wearing your talismans?"

"No, Majesty, of course not." Huy forced himself to meet those dark, intelligent eyes in their nest of wrinkles. "I believe that I'm temporarily beset by an evil neither Atum nor Anubis will remove. Therefore I must conclude that it is for my own good." The temptation to tell her everything was very strong, but Mutemwia was no fool; sooner or later she was bound to arrive at a deduction that would be far too close to the truth for Huy's liking.

Her gaze sharpened. "What form does this evil take? Why do you feel that it plagues you to your ultimate benefit? Does it weaken your ability to rule Egypt competently, dear mer kat?" Her eyes had softened with concern.

Huy shook his head. "No. I understand it, Majesty. It often invades my sleep. I become tired, but it does not enter my soul. Exorcism is not the answer. Only the passage of time will bring me relief." *If I can solve this appalling dilemma. If I can find a way to give the god what he demands.*

Mutemwia sighed. "If you didn't consume large amounts of poppy, I would recommend kesso root and ginger to help you to remain calm," she offered. "As it is, those remedies will have no effect on a body saturated with opium. Are you sure you don't wish to confide in me, my old friend?"

Huy shook his head. "You would be the first to know what ails me if I could speak of it," he replied. "Pray for me, Majesty, and do not worry. I shall find a resolution in time."

Bowing, he left her, walking to his customary appointment at the Office of Foreign Correspondence trailed by his entourage. Every knee was bent at his passing. Every nose touched the ground. *Resolution,* he thought resignedly as he went. *What resolution, great Atum? How am I to redeem myself?* He could find no answer.

12

ON THE FIFTEENTH DAY OF PHAMENOTH, the third month in the season of Peret, Tiye gave birth to a healthy son. When her labour began, all work in the palace ground to a halt. The nobles and officials gathered outside her thick double doors, their servants laden with food and drink, cosmetics, stools, and board games to keep their masters fed and occupied. The corridors leading to the women's apartments became choked and noisy as the hours passed. Huy, after inquiring of Chief Steward Userhet regarding the Empress's progress and leaving one of his servants to keep him abreast of the news, intended to escape to the tiny apartment where he sometimes stayed if the pressure of his work became too urgent. He did not get far. A royal herald accosted him as he, Paneb, Kenofer, and Perti were hurrying away from the passage leading to the royal quarters.

"His Majesty asks that you join him in his private suite," the man said, bowing. "He wishes you to be close by when the birth of his son is announced."

For answer, Huy nodded and turned reluctantly towards Amunhotep's rooms. They were almost adjacent to Tiye's, and a few steps brought him to the wide double doors now standing open. Through them came a thin haze of incense smoke and the subdued murmur of several voices. The guards saluted Huy, and one of the King's under stewards rose from his stool and reverenced him, hands on his linen-covered knees and back bent. Gesturing to Perti to remain outside, Huy entered the spacious area beyond. As soon as he was noticed, a silence fell. Huy briefly scanned the lowered heads. Ptahhotep, High Priest of Amun, Steward of Amun, Overseer of the Priests of Upper and Lower Egypt, was arrayed in full regalia, the leopard skin draped over one shoulder and secured to his waist by the thin links of a golden chain. Not only Fanbearer on the King's Left Hand, he was soon to be appointed Mayor of Weset. Huy had amassed a comprehensive secret file on Ptahhotep. He liked the man, but that did not prevent him from listening carefully to the reports of his spies. Ptahhotep held a long censer and beside him an acolyte carried the box containing the pellets of frankincense.

Chief Treasurer Sobekhmose, son of the previous Treasurer Nakht-sobek, stood by the open doors to the King's garden, an intermittent breeze stirring his immaculate linen, and with a spurt of pleasure Huy recognized his favourite nephew, Ramose, limned in the glare of sunlight beyond. *Ramose, Treasury scribe and steward in the Mansion of the Aten at Iunu,* Huy thought briefly, warmly. *Twenty-five years old, and your half-brother thirty-four. You miss Heby as much as I do, don't you? Does Amunhotep-Huy also honour his father's memory?* As if the unspoken words had conjured up the man, Huy's travelling gaze met the unmistakable shape of his older nephew's shaved skull, and paused. Even in an attitude of veneration, Amunhotep-Huy's posture managed to convey the antipathy he had always felt towards his uncle. For the thousandth time Huy wondered why Mutemwia had insisted on making Amunhotep-Huy a Vizier, although it was true that Amunhotep-Huy was punctilious, even overly so, when conducting the land transactions that were a part of his responsibilities. *Was it perhaps a matter of keeping a volatile personality close by while making sure to include him in the favours she bestowed on all the members of my family? Why make an enemy when you can create a loyal subject?*

With a terse word, Huy released the company from their obeisance and moved farther into the crowd. Quiet conversations began again. Stepping into the respectful space surrounding the King and his mother, Huy bowed deeply. The Queen's perfume, the combination of lotus, narcissus, and henna essences in satke oil she had worn through all the years he had known her, made him feel immediately comfortable, and he smiled at her while waiting for her to speak first, as was the custom. Mutemwia was now in her middle forties, but unlike the majority of women of her age, her body remained naturally slim and her gestures as artlessly graceful as ever. The henna dye with which she disguised her increasingly grey hair gave it a reddish-orange tinge, and her cosmetician now widened the sweep of kohl around her dark eyes to hide the spreading wrinkles, but she continued to choose the simple jewellery and unadorned linen sheaths she preferred. In spite of the encroachment of the years, Huy noted as both she and the King bade him stand upright, her intellect was as sharp as ever. Generally, she and the Empress both agreed with Huy's decisions regarding foreign and domestic policy. Both took a keen interest in all aspects of the country's affairs. But when they disagreed, their arguments could be loud and heated, although they knew perfectly well that ultimate authority rested with Huy.

Mutemwia returned Huy's smile. "I have such faith in your prediction for this birth that I've sent Chief Herald Senu north to Prince Thothmes in Mennofer with the news that he will soon have a brother. Indeed, I suppose by the time he arrives, the baby will already be sleeping in his crib." She snapped her fingers. "Ameni, bring the Seer a goblet of wine. We shall drink to the wisdom of Ma'at!"

Huy took the cup Mutemwia's chief steward offered and raised it, drinking solemnly and catching the King's eye over its rim.

Amunhotep grinned. "I thank all the gods for this son. If Tiye gave birth to yet another girl, we'd all be hiding from her rage. I'm waiting for word from Nubti that my new son has produced his first cry. Dear Uncle Huy, what reward can I possibly give to the man who already has everything?"

Briefly his arm went around Huy's shoulders before he turned to give his attention to the Empress's father, and he and Yuya began to discuss the latest addition to the royal stables. Huy lost interest. Mutemwia was softly joining Ptahhotep's chant as a fresh billow of incense smoke hazed the room. Huy was about to sidle towards the open doors and escape when he felt a hand on his arm. His nephew Ramose, with Anen beside him, bowed.

"I haven't seen you since my father's funeral, Uncle," Ramose began. "I've been busy in the Aten's temple at Iunu. I wish the Queen would relieve me of that stewardship and move me closer to you and Anen at Ipu. The reports I send her have been boring and repetitive so far. But I thoroughly enjoy your letters."

Huy reverenced Tiye's younger brother, thinking as he did so how vital and alive these two friends were. Anen had inherited his father's blue eyes and the reddish sheen to his hair along with the good looks the Empress lacked. He was also free of her quick temper.

"I trust you are well and your enterprises are prospering, mer kat," Anen said politely, and Huy was free to answer.

"All is as it should be, Prince, and I'm sure that the district of Ipu flourishes under your hand. I saw your brother in the corridor outside the women's quarters. He seemed preoccupied."

"Ay's wife is pregnant and unwell," Anen told him. "She would request a Seeing from you, but she fears the result. Ay is worried."

"My amiable half-brother will also become a father again next year," Ramose put in dryly. "Naming his existing son Ay against the advice of the priests was a crude attempt to curry favour with your family, Anen. Honestly, Uncle, I've done my best to remain close to him. Father would have wanted it. But to my shame, I make most of my visits to his estate while he's away on the tours of the Vizierate. I like Henut-nofret and I admire her loyalty to him."

"You're talking about me, Ramose." Huy's elder nephew had come up behind him, obliging Huy to step aside. Amunhotep-Huy carried with him a strong cloud of jasmine perfume. He bowed deeply to Anen. Huy's head began to pound at once as he unwillingly inhaled an aroma he hated.

"We were speaking of your good fortune in anticipating the birth of another child," Anen half lied. "You must be very pleased, Vizier."

"I am, Prince," Amunhotep-Huy agreed curtly, shooting a suspicious glance at his brother's face. "My son Ay is already able to crawl, and shows a growing intelligence. His grandfather Nebenkempt, Commander of His Majesty's Naval Troops, comes often to my house to play with him."

Huy sighed inwardly. Nebenkempt was one of his close friends, and both men knew that it was only the Naval Commander's rank and the King's favour that prevented Amunhotep-Huy from treating his wife as roughly as he treated his servants.

"I hear that the King was so delighted with your work on the temple of Ptah at Mennofer, he allowed you to erect a statue of yourself next to his, within the sacred precincts," Ramose said warmly and also, Huy reflected, with a moment of guilt.

Amunhotep-Huy's chin rose. "Not only does my likeness stand beside His Majesty's, but the meals set before that of His Majesty are placed respectfully at my feet by a we'eb priest when the divine force of royalty has taken its fill," he said proudly. "Ptah's worshippers give obeisance to the King as they gather in the outer court. They reverence me also." *And I deserve their veneration*, his tone implied.

"An honour indeed." Prince Anen nodded. "Apparently your glorification of Ptah's holy house exceeded even the King's expectations." He turned to Ramose. "Let's find Userhet and inquire how my sister is faring and then get something to eat. I'm very hungry."

Immediately Huy and his older nephew bowed. Ramose hugged Huy and gave his brother a quick smile, and the two friends moved into the throng. Huy supposed that Amunhotep-Huy would swiftly melt away also, but glancing at him, Huy saw that he was frowning and chewing his lip.

"There's something Ptah's High Priest asked me to tell you, something he thought you'd find interesting," he said. "He gave me the message months ago, and he said it wasn't important enough to send with a herald. You and I meet so seldom that I completely forgot about it, but speaking of my statue has reminded me. My statue beside a divinity," he went on proudly. "The power of our god and King enfolds my likeness and I share in his reflected glory. Oh, this is so annoying!"

Huy watched and listened, bemused. Amunhotep-Huy folded his arms. His sandalled foot began to tap. Huy was about to suggest that he might go away and consider the matter elsewhere when Amunhotep-Huy's brow cleared and he rolled his eyes.

"Of course! Now I remember, and it's no wonder I forgot— such an unimportant piece of information. During the temple's restoration, the House of Life had to be emptied, and the archivists took the opportunity to inspect every scroll and update the records. Apparently an ancient scroll was found wedged behind the much larger one that listed every High Priest of Ptah since the temple was first built. Ptahmose wants you to travel to Mennofer and inspect it. He thinks it confirms Imhotep's term as one of Ptah's High Priests. Imhotep's tenure there has always been suspected but never proved. I believe that's all. Does it have a special meaning for you, Uncle? You've gone pale. Here. Drink your wine."

Stupidly, Huy looked down at the cup he still held. His hand had begun to shake. In an uncharacteristic act of kindness Amunhotep-Huy folded his own hands around Huy's and helped him lift the goblet to his mouth. Huy gulped thirstily at the violet liquid. His throat had gone dry.

"Thank you, my nephew," he managed. "This news is indeed of great concern to me."

"I can't imagine why." Deftly Amunhotep-Huy removed the wine from Huy's trembling grasp. "You're the only person with permission to sit down in His Majesty's presence. Let me find you a stool."

But Huy was already recovering. He shook his head and smiled into the other man's face. "I'm fine now, and I must send word to Ptahmose at once. Take my fond greetings and congratulations to Henut-nofret regarding her latest pregnancy. I would like to visit both of you soon. Thank you again for your care of me, Amunhotep-Huy."

Immediately the customary expression of smooth detachment fell like a mask over the man's painted features. "The well-being of the mer kat is essential to us all," he replied evenly. "Just send to me when you would like to grace our home." He bowed perfunctorily and was soon lost to view in the crowded space.

Affection, pity, and annoyance warred briefly in Huy and then were swept away on a wave of sheer excitement. A hidden scroll had emerged from the darkness of uncounted hentis, a scroll regarding the man who was now worshipped as a god. *Regarding?*

Is it too much to hope that the hieroglyphs on the ancient papyrus were painted by the great Imhotep himself? Are they even legible after so long? And, oh gods, are they the key to the puzzle of the Book of Thoth? The final entry I've always suspected to be missing?

Huy began to weave his way purposefully towards where the King now sat, Seal Bearer and Chief Scribe Nebmerut on the floor beside his chair, intending to ask Amunhotep's consent to leave, but there was a sudden commotion by the doors and a path magically appeared for Chief Steward Nubti. Amunhotep sprang to his feet.

"Majesty, you have been blessed with a son," Nubti announced. "The Empress begs for your company."

Amunhotep gestured peremptorily to Huy and, without waiting for an answering bow, hurried through the doors and into the passage beyond. Tense with frustration, Huy followed. How many hentis had that scroll lain in dust and darkness before being pulled into the dimness of the temple's House of Life?

The doors to Tiye's apartments opened briefly and the King, his scribe Mahu, Mutemwia, and Chief Steward Nubti, together with Royal Seal Bearer Nebmerut, disappeared inside. Huy, bringing up the rear, caught a brief glimpse of Tiye's mother, the Lady Thuyu, dishevelled and obviously preoccupied, performing her obeisance before the doors closed again. An expectant silence had fallen among the aristocrats and their various servants waiting outside. They drew away from Huy as he found a place by the wall. Coolly, Kenofer reached behind one of them, picked up his stool, and set it down for Huy, who sank onto it gratefully. He had no idea how long he would have to wait before as mer kat he would be commanded to inspect the little Prince and sign his name over Nebmerut's seal, beside those of the hereditary lords required to attest to the royal arrival. *Fortunately I won't be asked to See for the baby at once*, he thought, his eyes on

Perti's sturdy spine where the soldier had taken up his station in front of him. *I have a day or two in which to compose myself. I have a strong inkling of what Anubis will show me, and how will I summon up the courage to approach Tiye and Amunhotep with the truth?* After a while a subdued conversation resumed around Huy, but he did not hear it.

The sun was about to set and a gloom was creeping into the crowded corridor by the time the doors were again flung open and the aging but still imposing figure of Chief Herald Maani-nekhtef appeared, flanked by Chief Harem Steward Userhet and Seal Bearer Nebmerut. "The Queen and Empress Tiye, beloved of Mut, divine wife of Amunhotep hek-Weset, Neb-Ma'at-Ra, Ka-nakht kha-em-Ma'at, Great of Strength, Smiter of the Vile Asiatics, has been delivered of a son." Maani-nekhtef's clear tones rolled over the weary throng. "Let Egypt rejoice! Let her citizens bring offerings of thanksgiving to mighty Amun, father of our King! Approach, noble ones, and recognize your Prince! Do homage to him, and set your illustrious names upon the scroll of legitimization!"

The men surged past him. Huy followed more slowly. As the pre-eminent power under Pharaoh, it was his right to be the first to acknowledge the baby and sign the scroll, but he walked through the spacious antechamber and into Tiye's sleeping room reluctantly. The air was hazed and fragrant with the incense still wisping from the cup set at the feet of Bes, fat-bellied dwarf god of fertility and safe childbirth, who was grinning complacently through the smoke. The birthing stool had already been removed, and Tiye lay propped up on her couch, the baby in her arms, her women around her, and a beaming Amunhotep beside her. Huy bowed respectfully to her mother Thuyu, who gave him a frosty nod in response. Thuyu had never warmed to the man she saw as a usurper of her husband Yuya's place at the King's side. Long ago Huy had given up trying to win her over. Tiye's body servant Heria had obviously just finished washing her mistress and was reaching for a comb on the littered bedside table. Anhirkawi, Tiye's scribe, cross-legged on the mat by the couch, was opening his palette. Huy sensed relief in the purposeful activity around him.

Seeing him, Tiye waved him forward while the cream of Egypt's nobility waited impatiently behind Commander-in-Chief Wesersatet's unspoken warning. Huy knelt at Tiye's elbow, and after kissing her hand he glanced at the boy. Red, wrinkled, and hairless, the tiny being was asleep. Bundled in spotless linen as he was, Huy could see little but his head.

"Don't touch him, not yet," Tiye said. "He already has the protection of onions dipped in honey tied around his waist, and as soon as you predicted a son for me I commissioned an amulet from a lector-sau at Amun's temple to place on his wrist. I want you to See for him before the seventh day when the seven Hathors come to predict his fate. Their pronouncements will be unimportant, because you will See everything, Huy." She winced as Heria found a knot in her tousled red hair, then smiled up at her husband. "I know you're eager to send out the heralds. Give Egypt a few days of holiday in honour of your second Prince."

Amunhotep bent and took her head, pressing it tightly against his gold-hung chest and then carefully smoothing his son's tiny brow. "I adore you for this amazing accomplishment, my Tiye," he exclaimed. "Rest now, and enjoy your triumph." He strode away, pride and confidence in every step. The assembled mass knelt as he passed. The doors slammed shut.

Tiye waved Heria away. "Bring me a small dose of poppy," she ordered. "I ache and I'm sore." When the servant had gone, Tiye put her face close to Huy's. "Last night Amunhotep dreamed that a serpent had slithered into his beer," she murmured. "It's a good omen, as you know. It means that his heart will overflow with happiness. But I dreamed that I was drinking beer, gulping it down with a terrible thirst that would not abate. Suffering will come upon me, Huy, terrible distress going on and on. You have the ear of the gods. How may I avert this thing?"

Huy thought quickly. "There's no suffering as acute as the pains of childbirth, Majesty," he said, matching her quiet tone, "and more often than not it increases in intensity and seems endless. Don't fret over this dream. Suffering has already come upon you and continued for many hours. The meaning of the dream is true, and has been fulfilled, and is gone."

Her expression cleared. "Of course. How wise you are! Now please, mer kat, after you set your name to Nebmerut's scroll, have that ghastly statue of Bes removed. I didn't want him here in the first place, but my ladies were insistent. I've endured his fat belly and the tongue hanging out of his grinning mouth for long enough. Let Hathor preside over our dancing and merry-making instead, and drive away the evil spirits!" All at once she yawned. "As soon as the rest of them have done their duty, I shall take my poppy, hand over my miraculous Prince to his wet nurse, and sleep for a very long time." Planting a kiss on his cheek, she dismissed him, and he rose gratefully to his feet and moved away from the couch.

His first look at the child had filled him with a sense of fore-boding that stayed with him as he gave orders for Bes's removal, gathered up his entourage, and sought the privacy of his litter. Full night had now fallen. The stars were clear in a velvety black sky and the air was pleasantly warm. Weset's inhabitants were still wandering about the streets. The combined noise of their thou-sands followed Huy as he left the palace precincts and turned south towards his house, the litter-bearers carrying him through the city's outskirts and beyond, to the guarded poppy fields. As usual his escort was challenged. As usual Perti answered curtly, and before long Huy was walking into the blessed familiarity of his vast reception hall. Paroi met him with a lamp and accompanied him to the communal room that lay between his bedchamber and Nasha's apartment, offering him food and drink before leaving him to settle into the plain cedar armchair with its matching footstool he most preferred. He dismissed Paneb, and Kenofer took up his post within earshot by the door.

Nasha looked across at Huy and smiled. "You're back early," she commented. "So was I. Nebetta's party bored me. She should restrict the use of her skills to her official profession as a singer in Isis's temple. Catching up on the news is difficult when one must listen politely to yet another ode devoted to His Majesty's glory and composed by the singer herself." Swilling her wine, she drained it, licked her lips, and set the cup back on the table between them.

It had been several years since she had fingered her burgeoning girth, gazed with distaste at the faint spidering of broken veins across her cheeks, and regretfully decided to restrict the amount of wine she drank. Two cups at social gatherings and only one each evening when she was forced to stay at home were all she allowed herself. Huy, remembering Anuket's disastrous addiction to wine, had admired Nasha's self-discipline. Her waistline had slowly shrunk. The veins in her face had been replaced by a myriad of delicate laugh lines around her eyes and of smiles around her generous mouth. She was now sixty-six, and as full of acerbic wit as ever. She had never curbed her tongue when confronted by the babble of a fool, and expressed herself with such a consistently intuitive perception that Huy had come to rely on her as a trusted intimate. She had never reminded him of her sister Anuket, Huy's great love, but often her walk and gestures brought Thothmes, her brother, to mind.

"Egypt has another Prince, Nasha." Huy broke the small silence that had fallen. "The astrologer-lectors will decide whether this evening was a lucky third to the day and therefore auspicious for the baby or not. I think they'll choose to call him Amunhotep after his father and grandfather."

"His birth is no surprise," Nasha commented. "You forecast it months ago. But it troubles you, Huy, and you won't tell me why." She shot him a shrewd glance. "You often find comfort in unburdening yourself of the weight of government, and I hold many of your secrets. This child has haunted you from the time he was conceived. There's something dark in his future, isn't there?"

"Yes." Huy hooked one foot under the stool, pulled it towards him, and lifted both feet onto it. "Atum has not yet shown me exactly what it is, but in some way it concerns the fate of Egypt herself." He watched the play of lamplight glide across the moonstones on the thongs of his sandals. "The less you know, dear Nasha, the safer you will be if Wesersatet comes to question you."

"Huy!" She reached for her cup, remembered that it was empty, and crossed her arms over her breasts in an involuntary gesture of self-protection. "You make it sound as though you are contemplating something reckless that will bring danger to us here! You are mer kat! You can do anything without fear of retribution. Your word is law. You are not accountable for any deed other than blasphemy against the gods or the King." Her grip on herself loosened. "Egypt is under the shelter of both, as long as her citizens honour the laws of Ma'at. I've known you almost all my life. There's no one in this blessed country more honest than you, or less likely to violate Ma'at's statutes. So what on earth are you talking about?"

"I don't know. I'm not sure." He leaned back and signalled to Kenofer. "Find out from Paroi whether Rakhaka has stored any lotus petals steeped in red wine, and if he has, bring us enough for one cup each," he ordered. His attention returned to Nasha. "Break your rule for once," he said wryly. "The infusion of lotus will make us both very happy."

Her kohled eyebrows rose. "Your permission is my excuse, mer kat, but pouring good wine down your throat is a waste."

"The wine's a waste, but the wine-soaked lotus petals are not. Added to my nightly dose of poppy, they might give me a sound sleep for once."

Paroi, Huy's under steward, had obviously been preparing for bed when Kenofer approached him. With freshly cleansed face and bare feet, he served them himself before padding back to his own quarters. Huy and Nasha sat on, talking with the ease of long aquaintance. Both avoided the subject of Egypt's baby Prince. By the time Nasha stuck a finger into her goblet and tried to extract the limp and saturated lotus petals remaining, she was giggling at nothing. Huy, mildly stimulated, took it firmly from her. "If you suck them, they'll be bitter," he told her. "Go to bed, Nasha, and get a massage in the morning. You'll need it."

Obediently she gathered up the folds of her yellow sheath, kissed him on the cheek, and unsteadily made her way across the shadowed room. Her door opened and closed behind her. Huy was alone. Getting up, he retraced his steps through the house, and emerging into his garden he walked a short way across the grass. The sod was damp through the labour of his gardeners. The noise of the city had been reduced to a constant drone. If he listened carefully Huy could separate the various sources of the sound, but he had no interest in the daily life of Weset, or in its nightly pursuits either.

He lifted his face to the breeze and closed his eyes. *It's coming out of the west, Isis's wind, flowing over the City of the Dead, stirring the growth on the banks of the river and finding me here in the safety of my own domain. Isis, faithful wife, loving mother, surely there is pity in your tender heart for me, for my young King, for the tiny scrap of irreplaceable life just born!* In the deeper darkness of his high defensive wall a guard coughed briefly, and with a sigh Huy swung back into the house. *There are six days left before the seven Hathors make their pronouncements, and I could be summoned to See for the child on any one of them. There is no time to hurry to Mennofer and return, but I simply must travel to Ptah's temple as soon as possible. The answer to every riddle I've pondered lies there—I'm sure of it. I'll See for the Prince, but I won't speak of the vision. Not yet. Tiye won't understand, but the King will. The Book of Thoth comes first.*

The astrologers wasted no time in proclaiming that the boy should be called Amunhotep, and long before the six days were over Huy received an official summons from the King to look into the baby's future. Amunhotep seldom issued orders to his mer kat anymore, so Huy knew that he must obey at once. Speaking briefly to Nasha, Amunmose, and Paroi, who were discussing household affairs, he took Paneb and Perti with a contingent of soldiers and was carried to the palace.

It was the seventeenth day of Phamenoth, the morning air hot and still. Everywhere along the river, Huy knew, the farmers and their peasants would be out in the fields inspecting the barley, precious flax, emmer, and hemp for signs of ripening. Later in the season the fat purple and green grapes would be plucked, the marshes of the Delta combed of the reeds and rushes that offered a hundred uses, the clover cut yet again to make semu. Huy, tense with apprehension, allowed his imagination to feed him with memories of great piles of the plant waiting to be bound for forage, the almost unbearable gusts of fragrance the acres of his uncle's flowers exuded as he walked past them on his way to Hutherib, the tang of crushed mint from his mother's herb garden. Here in the south the odours of growing things were more ephemeral, quickly thinned and then dispersed by the desert winds. *I'm homesick for my youth. I want to be waiting by the orchard hedge for Ishat to appear, with our house behind me and Father away at work among Ker's glorious perfume blooms and Mother on her knees by the tiny pool, weeding her cabbages and melons and humming to herself.*

His litter had emerged from the poppy fields and onto the public path that ran beside the river and into the city. Huy pulled the curtains more tightly closed. Perti began to call the usual warning: "Make way! Make way for the King's mer kat!" Sounds drifted past Huy—snatches of conversation, the soft thud of a donkey's hoofs on the sandy track, the laughter of a group of children running past. *I'd give all my wealth to be somewhere else in another time, to be free*, his thoughts ran on. *Terror is looming in the nursery of the palace, invisible evil waiting for me to give it the power of form. I know it. After my moment of cowardice before the Horus Throne and the Osiris-one, our King's father, Atum was merciful. There would be another chance to right the wrong I had done. Today that chance will at last be offered, and I am deathly afraid of the things the god will show me, in what dreadful manner I will be required to rectify both my weakness and the conceit in which I interpreted the vision of Tiye to suit my own vanity.*

He heard his escort challenged, felt his bearers step onto more solid ground, and soon he was being set down. Perti opened his curtains and held out an arm for assistance. Huy glanced up at him as he left the litter and stood straight. *You refused Wesersatet's offer of promotion within the ranks of the royal Division of Amun for my sake. You are no longer the talented young soldier in whom I placed my safety, yet you still command my guards, and now you control the vast web of spies you and I placed throughout Egypt and beyond when I first became mer kat. I am as loyal to you as you are to me, and the King sleeps more peacefully because of you.*

"Mer kat? Master?" Perti said quietly, and Huy came to himself.

"Let the bearers wait under the trees," he said. "Bring all my escort with me, Perti. By now the palace guards understand that they may not be prevented from entering. Paneb, are you ready?" His scribe nodded, and surrounded by Perti and his soldiers they crossed the broad concourse and walked between the pillars into the cool spaciousness of Pharaoh's reception hall. Few people were about, but their reserved conversations still echoed softly against the lofty star-spangled ceiling. They knelt in homage to Huy as he passed.

It took him and his men a long time to arrive at the tall guarded doors beyond which were the women's quarters and the nurseries. Userhet rose from his stool and bowed. "His Majesty, the Empress, and Queen Mutemwia are waiting for you, mer kat. They are in the anteroom to Prince Amunhotep's nursery, where there are refreshments for you. I am to assure you that His Highness fed well this morning and Royal Physician Seneb has pronounced him healthy."

Huy nodded. "Let us in, then, and announce me."

Userhet gestured at the guards, the heavy cedar doors swung open, and Huy and Paneb passed through. Huy did not particularly like small children or the harem. Its corridors were narrower than those in the main body of the palace. Many doorways fronted their lengths, the rooms beyond them each occupied by one of the King's concubines or one of his foreign acquisitions. Huy was familiar with most of the foreign women. They had been acquired as part of various official agreements between the Horus Throne and its vassal states or those petty kingdoms greedy for gold, linen, and papyrus and wise enough not to challenge Egypt's superior power. The alien princesses on the whole were arrogant and demanding, noisily claiming their royal rights over the King's native women and threatening to send letters to their relatives complaining of their treatment in Egypt. Userhet occasionally consulted with Huy over some particularly delicate situation within the harem if it might endanger an advantageous treaty. Otherwise Huy stayed away from the shrieks of children and the nattering of the adult residents.

Leaving Perti and his guards outside the door, Huy waited to be admitted. Userhet knocked, and at once Nubti opened for Huy and Paneb. Beyond, in the rather cramped anteroom, Huy bowed respectfully from the waist, arms extended in worship. Paneb performed a full prostration.

"Rise, Scribe Paneb," the King said immediately. He was smiling. So was Tiye, her eyes expectantly on Huy, her gold-ringed fingers wound about each other on her scarlet lap. She and the King were sitting close together, a table loaded with wine and sweetmeats in front of them. Amunhotep was cradling an ornate silver cup in both hands, a previous New Year's gift from Yuya, Huy remembered, and by the slight glazing of his dark eyes as he slumped back in his chair Huy could see that he was drunk.

Your appetite for the grape is growing, my dear Emperor, Huy thought as he approached them. *I can sympathize. By making me Egypt's ruler, you've left yourself nothing to do but commune with Amun in his sanctuary on behalf of this country, flaunt our wealth and strength before ambassadors and foreign dignitaries, and pursue the delights of hunting and women, in both of which you excel. Your intelligence was obvious from the first day you arrived to stay with me on my estate outside Hut-herib. So was your wilfulness. I'm sad when I see the erosion of aptitude and self-discipline in you.*

He glanced at Mutemwia. She was not smiling, and her glance as it met Huy's was sombre. Her chair had been placed a little apart from the others. She was leaning slightly away from the chair's back, her spine straight, knees together under the drape of white linen falling to the floor. Her bare arms rested along the gilded arms of her seat, but they were not relaxed. *Your unflagging determination to see your son on the Horus Throne has brought you to this day, Mutemwia,* Huy's thoughts ran on. *You decided that the vision that came upon me when he reached up and grasped my finger all those years ago was your turning point, a sign from the gods on which you built an entire destiny for your son and yourself. So did I. We grew as close as possible given my peasant blood, and I came to trust your knowledge and intuition. Instinct is warning you that this Seeing will be no happier than those I reluctantly gave to the rest of the King's children, including the Hawk-in-the-Nest, Thothmes. You sense what I know and dread. The fate of Tiye's little Prince will be more terrible than an early death.*

"Please don't ask us to leave the room," the King joked, still smiling. "You like to conduct the Seeings in privacy, with your scribe beside you, but I beg you, my Uncle, let us stay! My son lies through there." He waved towards the open doorway on Huy's right. "Userhet will place his stool between us and the nursery, and I promise you we will not make a sound."

Huy considered briefly. He knew that Amunhotep could make the request a command. He also knew that he himself would be obeyed if he insisted on being alone with the Prince. Amunhotep had not outgrown the early training towards compliance and respect for Huy first instilled in him. He loved and trusted his adopted uncle, and Huy loved him back. *You've never been the problem, Emperor,* he said silently. *It's the Empress who wishes to wrench the control of Egypt out of my hands.*

"I'm honoured to be given the choice, Majesty," he answered. "I shall perform the Seeing perfectly well if you wish to remain where you are. The work may be long or short, I don't know, but I do ask for silence."

The King gestured sharply, a servant opened the outer door and summoned Userhet, and Huy turned towards the inner room. As he did so, a wave of desperation swept over him. *Poppy,* he thought. *Poppy poppy poppy. I hope Mutemwia has remembered that I'll need it as soon as I'm finished.*

Two women and an older man went to the floor and then rose as he and Paneb walked quietly towards the crib. Huy, in spite of the apprehension that was filling him, exclaimed in delight. "Royal Nurse Heqarneheh! It makes me happy to see you still occupying the position you held when the King was a child! You've aged well."

"So have you, Great Seer." The two men embraced briefly. "I have three sons and a noisy household of my own just outside Weset. The eldest will inherit the title of Royal Nurse when I retire and is already learning his future duties as my assistant."

"Those in his care will be fortunate indeed if he's anything like his father." Huy moved regretfully away. "I would like to spend an evening reminiscing over all the months we spent together during the King's stay at my house."

"So would I. I remember how much he enjoyed fishing with you and Anhur. How is the captain of your guard?"

"He died. I miss him a great deal, but his replacement has many of his qualities. I must travel north soon, but when I return you will feast with me."

The women had been watching the conversation nervously, and as Heqarneheh left the room they hurried to follow him. Userhet was already half blocking the doorway. At last Huy turned to the crib.

The baby had been so quiet Huy assumed that he was asleep, and he was shocked to bend over the crib and see two solemn eyes looking up at him between a tuft of brown hair and a swaddle of spotless linen. *Most babies show excitement at the sudden appearance of an adult face above them. Their legs kick. Their arms wave. They gurgle and smile. But of course this royal offspring is too young to do more than stare up at me.* He heard Paneb settle onto the floor beside him. The palette rattled softly as the scribe began to assemble his tools. Prince Amunhotep did not even blink at the sound. He continued to regard Huy impas-sively. *Children of this age are incapable of displaying emotion,* Huy thought, annoyed with himself. *They sleep, they wake hungry and cry, they sleep again. I am imagining an indifference in this baby's steady gaze.* Carefully he reached in and loosened the swaddling. He felt a strange disgust as the baby moved in response to his action, a reluctance to touch the child, something he simply must do if he wanted to See for him. After a short struggle a pair of thin arms appeared, the hands impossibly tiny to Huy, the fingers delicate and beautiful. Those light brown eyes remained fixed on Huy's face as Huy offered one of his own fingers, expecting the baby's fist to curl around it, but with a barely heard mew Prince Amunhotep turned his head away sharply and his hands flailed. *He knows,* Huy thought in shock, *but how can that be? How can he be afraid of me, this mindlessly animated piece of flesh?* Gently but firmly Huy imprisoned the baby's forearm, his thumb and index finger curling around it. At once the child became still.

"Are you ready, Paneb?" Huy asked, but it was not Paneb who answered.

"Paneb is ready, but clearly you are not," the familiar voice remarked. Deep, rough to the point of hoarseness, its tones were redolent with animality. It was standing so close to Huy that he could smell its perfume, the sacred myrrh, mingling with the faint but pungent odour of its skin.

"Anubis," he whispered. The jackal god smiled. Although he dared not turn to see the long furred snout, Huy had an instant image of sharp white fangs being bared in a semblance of mirth, and a pink tongue. A gust of kyphi incense invaded his nostrils.

"I have not had the pleasure of your company since you Saw for Tiye's last disastrous effort to produce another boy for her husband," Anubis said. "Poor Tiye! Empress of most of the world yet less fortunate than the servant woman with a dozen robust sons painting henna onto the soles of her feet." The exotic timbre of his speech was rich with sarcasm. "But look, Great Seer! What is it that you are clutching? Could it be the insurance Amunhotep has prayed for?"

"He is a good King and Tiye a fine Queen," Huy managed. "Do not make fun of their sorrow, Mouthpiece of Atum. I See for this child in obedience to them, but without hope. I love and pity them." With a mixture of horror and a strange kind of relief Huy felt the god's black hand come to rest on his shoulder. Out of the corner of his eye he was able to glimpse the golden rings adorning each finger and a glitter of more gold from the thick bracelet encircling the sinewy wrist.

"I know you do," Anubis said quietly. "Well actually, you love the King and Queen Mutemwia. Most of your pity, as well as your hidden anger, belongs to the Empress. She does not deserve it. You should be turning it upon yourself." Huy's shoulder was gripped in a sudden and painful pinch and then released. "Who knows how many healthy little princes might be causing havoc today in the women's quarters if Amunhotep had not been persuaded to marry Tiye? You need not respond. Under your hand my beloved Egypt has prospered, and Atum is pleased. You are a talented mer kat."

Huy had no intention of responding. He knew that there was worse to come. But Anubis fell silent. Huy could feel the god's warm, feral breath on the back of his head. He waited.

Presently Anubis sighed. "You have been considering how the

Empress's reputation might be sullied, how the King might be persuaded to send her home to her illustrious parents and elevate one of his other wives in her place. But you already knew that you had done your work all too well. Amunhotep would not have given her a second look if you had not deliberately thrown them together at every opportunity. Now he is hers. Although his sexual appetite is becoming legendary, her fire in bed gives him more pleasure than any concubine and her frank, intelligent conversation still delights and intrigues him. He is alternately comfortable and stimulated in her presence, and she will make sure that she maintains her hold on him. In spite of your disastrous blunder in forcing them upon each other, she is a woman to admire. Besides, you fool, as long as she was pregnant with the promise of another Prince, did you imagine that any scheme of yours could pry them apart? Too late, Great Seer. Too late!" The throaty undercurrent of the god's tone degenerated into a snarl. "This human spawn will bring Egypt to the very brink of destruction! See what you have done!" Suddenly Anubis was facing Huy, his furred lips contorted, the snarl becoming a fierce growl as he bent and thrust his black hands into the crib. Jerking the baby upward, he threw it at Huy. "Here! Take it!" he spat. "See what is coming, and tremble under the weight of your responsibility!"

Shocked and unprepared for the god's actions, Huy let go of the Prince then managed to catch the bundle, stumbled, and would have fallen if Anubis had not seized him by one of the braids lying on his chest and pulled him upright. Huy looked down, expecting to see himself clutching the boy, but his arms were empty. He was standing in the middle of a wide paved road facing a high walkway that joined the building on his left to another on his right, at the rear of a restless crowd whose murmurs held an undercurrent of impatience. The stone flags under his feet were hot. So was the top of his head. Looking about, squinting against the glare of an unforgiving sun, he saw flags, mighty pylons, wide paved streets, the dazzling limestone walls of more buildings. Trees flourished everywhere, seeming at first to be lushly green, but as Huy tried to find something recognizable in all this magnificence he realized that the palms were drooping, their crowns thin, many of their leaves brown and brittle. *It must be summer, perhaps the month of Mesore, because it's obvious that the Inundation has not yet begun. But where am I?*

He did not think that he had spoken aloud, but the man standing next to him answered. "Come up from Kush or Wawat, have you? Working under one of Pharaoh's governors there? You must have been away from Egypt for a long time. This is Akhet-Aten, the City of the Horizon of the Aten, and that"—he pointed to a wide aperture high up on the walkway he and Huy were facing—"is the Window of Appearing. The King stops there every day as he walks between the Palace and his House with the Queen and their princesses, and lets the people see him. Often he throws down gold collars to his ministers and commanders."

"Gold collars? You mean the Gold of Favours?"

"I suppose so." The Gold of Favours was bestowed only rarely on those who had shown particular bravery in battle or had served the King in some exemplary way. "I wish he'd pray to Isis and beg her to cry," the man continued, "but every petition now must be addressed to the Aten. The King has forbidden the worship of any other god."

Confused, with a growing fear, Huy began to sweat. "What month is this? How long has it been since the last Inundation?"

The man gave him a pitying look. "The sun has obviously addled you. It's the beginning of Paophi. Egypt should be a huge lake by now, but the flood hasn't come. We used to dedicate nine days to Hapi the god of the river during Paophi and Athyr. Not anymore. No wonder Isis and Hapi are punishing us. It was the same last year. At least His Majesty makes sure that no one living in Akhet-Aten goes without food or beer."

"What of the rest of Egypt? Without the water and the silt there can be no new crops, or silage for the cattle!"

The man shrugged. "Not my concern. When Pharaoh closed the temples throughout the country, he brought all the stored treasures and grains here. We'll be fed, and eventually the flood will come again. You must have noticed the low level of the river, coming up from the south."

Huy was speechless. The sweat of dismay as well as heat was now trickling down his spine and temples. Lifting the hem of the blue kilt in which he now found himself dressed, he wiped his face. As he did so, a roar went up from the throng. Huy followed their gaze. A group of people now filled the window. Several very young girls clad in transparent white linen and loaded with jewellery were whispering and giggling to each other, painted palms to their mouths. A very beautiful woman wearing a coned headdress and a white sheath of many small pleats with similarly pleated voluminous sleeves stood closely to the left of a man with the most curious deformities Huy had ever seen. His face was fine, even noble, with its sweep of straight nose, its almond-shaped eyes and long chin, but beneath the loose feminine sheath he wore Huy could see that his chest was shrunken, his belly low-slung and protuberant, and his thighs distressingly fat. He appeared to have a pair of female breasts, their prominent nipples ringed in orange henna. His head was covered by a blue bag wig. He sported a wide gold necklace, and his arms and fingers were heavy with gold.

Huy's attention moved to the woman on his right. He studied her carefully, all at once alert. She was familiar to him. Her heavy eyelids glistened with dark green paint, and the black kohl surrounding her eyes and sweeping across both temples was equally thick. Her sheath and similarly pleated sleeves were bordered with silver sphinxes. The ringlets of a formal wig fell almost to her waist. Her jewellery was beyond price: electrum bracelets, rings of amethyst and lapis lazuli, and an ornate sphinx pectoral made entirely of purple gold from Mitanni. One of her wrinkled breasts was bare, obviously a nod to fashion, as one of the much younger woman's high, painted breasts was also unselfconsciously revealed. But it was the older woman's headdress that puzzled Huy. Ornate and weighty, its polished disc flashed in the strong light. The two horns of Hathor curved around the disc and its two tall golden plumes seemed to quiver in the burning air. "The Empress's crown," Huy muttered. "Then where is the Emperor? I know that face. I've seen it before. Deep lines to either side of a downturned mouth. Sharp, watchful eyes. Authority …"

The man leaning out of the window had begun to speak, his voice a light treble, like a woman's. "People of the Holy City! Today is blessed in the history of Egypt. Today the Empress graces us with her august presence. Today also, as a mark yet again of my favour towards him, the noble Pentu receives the Gold of Favours from my hand. Pentu!" A man came swaggering to kneel beneath the window, his arms upraised to catch the shower of gold that would come. "This is the third time, is it not?" the man in the blue bag wig continued.

"It is indeed, Most Munificent One!"

"For your devotion to the Aten, for your sacrifices and prayers, I make you a Person of Gold!"

Huy watched aghast as the malformed figure began to strip himself of his jewellery and toss it down to the man below. *Sacrifices and prayers? And the third time this Pentu has been given so rare and precious an award? What is happening here?* The older woman in the long wig and Empress's crown leaned towards the man next to her, grasping his arm and speaking rapidly into his ear, her face a mask of anger.

"The goddess is not pleased," Huy's companion remarked. "She arrives today from Weset to find her husband-son displaying himself rudely like any commoner, and debasing one of Egypt's most hard-won honours. Amusing, is it not, Seer Huy? Titillating perhaps?"

The voice had become deeper. Huy swung round. Anubis's black jackal's eyes met his. The god's muzzle was slightly open, and as Huy watched, a pink tongue emerged to moisten the furred lips.

"We are both clad in blue, the colour of mourning," Anubis went on. "Now why is that? Why do I grieve, and wait for you to recognize your own anguish? Why have I been standing in Set's temple, inhaling the smoke of the sacred kyphi that rises in Set's sanctuary? To beg my brother, the god of chaos, to have mercy on Egypt, or to bury her under the sands of her deserts? No. I would have done so, but Atum wishes to wait and see what his chosen Seer will do with this final chance to avert the blasphemy of Akhet-Aten and its decadent inhabitants. Look at her, Huy! At last she knows what she has done! At last she prays for a pardon that the gods will not give her! Look at her!"

His rising voice boomed back at Huy, echoing against the pure lines of the buildings fronting the avenue, but the crowd was watching Pentu and his gold walk towards a chariot that waited for him, and the man framed by the wide window went on waving and smiling at the people below. The older woman had stepped back into shadow, and suddenly Huy saw her in his mind's eye, standing beside this same man in a roofless temple where the sun beat down on them with relentless heat and a hot, greedy silence surrounded them. He knew the vision. Its details lay rolled up and neatly sealed in his office. It composed the second half of a Seeing he had performed years ago for Tiye.

Tiye. The older woman was Tiye. But who was the creature at her side?

"Who indeed?" Anubis hissed. "Perhaps if you had solved the meaning of the Book of Thoth, this future would be nothing more than the fragment of a fantasy blown through your mind and vanishing as you walk from your fine house to your waiting litter-bearers." He stepped forward and placed both black palms against Huy's cheeks. He had begun to weep. Glittering black tears slid down the fur of his face to splash on the pavement in front of Huy's feet. "You have the power to make all this a lie," he whispered. "Go north, Seer Huy—and hurry! Destiny is waiting for you in Ptah's House of Life. Go now, and tell neither Amunhotep nor his wife what cursed thing your hand is holding until you return to Weset."

The god's face began to fade, became as transparent as thin linen, and Huy found himself staring at a blank wall through cool, dim air. At once his head began to pound. Turning to place both hands on the edge of the crib and steady himself, he realized that he was still holding the baby's tiny forearm. With a grunt he let go, lost his balance, and slid to the floor. At once Paneb set down his palette and Userhet left his stool and came hurrying. Carefully both men lifted Huy and helped him take the few steps to where the steward had sat.

"Bring poppy quickly," someone ordered. Huy sank onto the stool and bent over. One of his feet felt damp. Seeing a small grey stain on it, he touched it, and his finger came away wet.

"Anubis's tears," he croaked. A cup appeared and he grabbed it, draining the contents with a prayer of thanks to Atum for the creation of opium and passing it back. He closed his eyes. A silence fell. Huy could feel the tension of waiting all around him, but he did not move until his pain became a dull throb. Then he asked that Paroi be summoned, and aided by his scribe and his under steward he was able to rise and approach the King.

"Well, Uncle?" Amunhotep demanded sharply. "What have the gods decreed for my beautiful new son? Will there be another early death, or will he outlive Thothmes and ascend the Horus Throne? Just give us one or two words. Then you must rest, and come back tomorrow to tell us every detail."

"Help me to kneel," Huy half whispered to the men who were holding him upright. When he felt himself reach the floor, he forced his arms to extend with palms up in the attitude of reverence and supplication.

"No!" Tiye exclaimed. "Not again! I will not have it!"

Huy turned his palms down, a quick gesture of rebuttal. "Majesty, you need not fret. Before I can impart the result of the Seeing, I have been commanded to travel north to Mennofer. I may not tell you anything at all until I return. I am sorry."

"Why Mennofer, Huy? Why does Anubis want you to go there? Can you at least tell us that much?" The voice was Mutemwia's. Huy raised his face to her with difficulty. She was leaning forward almost double and looking straight into his eyes.

"I must find the end of the Book of Thoth and solve its mystery before you may hear the words of Anubis," he blurted. "It lies in Ptah's temple. I must keep my counsel until then." Despair filled him as he tore his gaze from hers. Amunhotep was staring at him and frowning. Tiye's cheeks had flooded with colour and she was tapping the arms of her chair with all ten furious fingers.

"How long will all that take you, mer kat?" she snapped. "Even if you leave immediately, it will take you a month to reach Mennofer. Did your vision show you exactly where the scroll or scrolls are? How long it will be before the final secret is revealed? We won't see you for months. Months! Who will administer this

country while you are gone? Will you take hundreds of officials
and heralds with you?" Her tone was biting. "I respect the gods,
but this is too much!"

You want to call both me and Anubis liars, but you don't dare, Huy
thought as she swept up a silver goblet, her hennaed hands
shaking with rage.

"Peace, Tiye." Amunhotep left his seat, and with both strong
arms he pushed Paneb and Paroi aside and hauled Huy upright.
"Go home and sleep, and come to me tomorrow so that we may
discuss the tasks to be done while you are away." He seemed to
be sobering rapidly. "Most of them can be accomplished from
Mennofer. Make use of the palace there if you wish. We will wait
patiently for Atum's word regarding our Prince. Thank you, my
old friend."

It was a gracious speech. Gratefully, Huy returned to the care
of his men. Nothing further was said. Together they and Huy's
guards walked slowly back to the waiting litter and the blinding
heat of afternoon. While the little cavalcade made its way to
Huy's estate, he lay still on his cushions, tensed against every jolt.
Before Kenofer eased him onto his couch, he dictated his vision
to Paneb, giving the scribe the usual instructions regarding its
safekeeping. Paneb bowed himself out. Huy fell into a drugged
sleep.

13

HE WOKE WITH A SENSE OF DREAD and lay staring at the ceiling. His dreams had been muddy, unlike the lucid fantasies the poppy usually gave him in sleep, and his body felt heavy. He did not shout for Kenofer, who would be waiting for the summons outside the door. Instead he forced himself to review the Seeing he had performed for Prince Amunhotep. Now that he was no longer a participant in it, being buffeted from one shock to another, he was able to examine several details he had overlooked at the time. As he did so, his trepidation grew. There had been no Inundation for two years according to the man who had stood beside him, a sure sign that the gods were exacting a terrible punishment on Egypt and her King. The misery caused by just one season without the life-giving spate of water and silt had taught the country's governors and High Priests to store grain against the famine that would ensue. Huy had been told that the King in his vision had closed the temples and denuded them of their gold and the contents of their silos as well, so that the inhabitants of Akhet-Aten would suffer no want. But what of the rest of Egypt's citizens? Had the people been commanded to worship the Aten and no other? If so, it was no wonder that the gods, especially Egypt's great saviour Amun, were offended and Ma'at herself wounded. Uneasily Huy remembered the Seeing in which Ma'at's blood had spattered the ground between the two of them. Her pain had been his fault, the result of one act of weakness on his part. The King in this latest Seeing had committed many terrible sacrileges. Who was he?

"The goddess is not pleased." Anubis's distinctive voice came back to Huy. "She arrives today from Weset to find her husband-son displaying himself rudely like any commoner ..." Perhaps Anubis was referring to the beautiful young woman clinging to his arm? Huy unconsciously began to count the number of white stars painted on the ceiling above him. Yes. Yes. That conclusion was logical, sane. There were few lines to mar the misshapen King's face, and the giggling, scantily clad girls seemed very young. They were not behaving like palace servants. His daughters? So the strikingly lovely woman would be their mother and the King's wife. Chief Wife? Goddess? No, not goddess. The ceremony at the Window of Appearances presented a semblance of formality, yet it was Tiye who stood on the King's right and stared out over the crowd, her harsh features grim. On the King's right. And it was Tiye who was wearing the great Empress's crown with its disc and horns, Tiye who had turned and hissed something angrily into the man's ear. If Tiye was "the goddess" arrived from Weset, was her husband Amunhotep still living? Was the peculiar man beside her one of her relatives? But no. Only a King could bestow the Gold of Favours, and besides, neither Ay nor Anen, her brothers, even remotely resembled this ... this ugly thing. Cursed thing. *The cursed thing.* Huy's body tensed under the sheet and he began to count the stars more quickly, desperate to keep at bay the conclusion his mind was inevitably forming.

"her husband-son ..."

"the cursed thing ..."

With a groan, Huy forced his eyes away from the ceiling and sat up, gripping his raised knees. Anubis had called the baby "the cursed thing your hand is holding." Prince Amunhotep, Tiye's son. Her husband also? Her future husband? If so, then what unimaginably terrible reason could have impelled her to break one of Egypt's strictest laws? A Hawk-in-the-Nest might marry one of his sisters in order to legitimize his claim to godhead and therefore to kingship. The pure blood of godhead had always flowed through female royalty. But a Queen, indeed any female citizen, might on no account form a sexual relationship with a son, let alone marry one. To do so would upset the delicate balance of Ma'at and bring hardship and ruin to Egypt. Two years of drought ...

Huy's thoughts ran on. *Why, Anubis? Why an act of such profanity on Tiye's part? Can this vision be averted?* The answer came to Huy at once, not from Anubis but from his own mind. *What I saw will be the result of my own failure. It's too late to go back, to prevent His Majesty from marrying Tiye, yet somehow I must make sure that this Seeing proves false. But how?* Before his mind could put forward a logical answer, he shouted for Kenofer. "Poppy and a cup of milk," he ordered as his body servant appeared. "No food. My stomach is on fire. And send Amunmose to me as soon as possible."

Kenofer hesitated. "Master, Physician Seneb wants you to limit your intake of the poppy. It is damaging your stomach and destroying your appetite."

"I know. Seneb refuses to understand that I rely completely on Atum's protection against the more pernicious effects of the drug, and he will uphold me until he doesn't need me anymore."

"That may be so, but Master, you're in your sixty-fifth year. Surely—"

Huy left the couch and stood. "Please hurry, Kenofer. The poppy will not kill me, and my welfare does not depend on Seneb. Make sure there's hot water for my bath."

Kenofer nodded reluctantly and went away. Huy began to pace the confines of his chamber. It seemed a long time before Chief Steward Amunmose knocked on the door and bustled in carrying a tray. Huy drained the cup of milk offered to him, and then swallowed the poppy.

"The water in the bathhouse has been kept hot for you." Amunmose returned the empty cup and vial to the tray and peered at Huy. "You still look drained," he remarked. "You do know that there's a better way to take your opium, don't you, Huy? Governor Amunnefer recommends it—straight from the harvest in its brown form."

"I know. But I'm afraid of its strength, Amunmose. I cope reasonably well as matters are, and only prescribe the raw poppy to those for whom I See if their pain warrants it." *You also are being ravaged by the inroads of time, my dear steward,* Huy said to him mutely. *You were a voluble, cheerful young man, quick on your feet, always ready to share a joke. You're still voluble and cheerful, but age is gradually leading you to the day when crossing from your chair to the door will be as huge an undertaking as a journey to Punt.*

"Very well." Amunmose set the tray down on the small ebony table to one side of the door and looked at Huy inquiringly. "Kenofer said that you wanted to see me."

"Yes. I intend to leave Weset and move into the palace at Mennofer as soon as possible. As my chief steward, the organization of this is your responsibility. I want you with me in Mennofer, Amunmose, not Assistant Steward Paroi, who must stay here and see to my affairs while I'm gone. Talk to Chief Herald Ba-en-Ra. He must accompany me, of course, and provide other heralds. As his second-in-command, Sarenput can arrange the conveyance of messages to me from the administrative offices here. Trying to govern this country from the north will be a nuisance, but it can be done. After all, kings and administrators did so for hentis before me. I want my own cook also. Rakhaka will grumble, but he's to have no choice."

Amunmose's kohled eyebrows rose. "Is this move to be permanent?"

"No. I'm convinced that the last portion of the Book of Thoth has been found in Ptah's temple, and I must see it at once. We'll stay in Mennofer until all of it has finally become clear to me."

"That miserable nephew of yours told you about it, didn't he?" Amunmose said. "I've heard that the restoration and additions he oversaw for Ptah are wonderful. How strange, that he of all people should be the one to place the Book's final solution in your hands!"

"Strange indeed. Go about your business, Amunmose, and I must be bathed and present myself before Their Majesties. The prospect of my imminent departure does not sit well with either of them, particularly the Empress." *At least I am spared the necessity of reciting the events of Prince Amunhotep's Seeing to them,* Huy thought as he made his way down to the bathhouse. *Atum himself wants that moment postponed, and I am profoundly grateful.*

He had reached the confluence of several passages and was about to turn down the one leading to the heavily guarded royal wing of the palace when Chief Steward Ameni rose from a stool and swiftly approached him. Bowing, he indicated an open door through which a beam of strong sunlight lapped at Huy's feet. "Her Majesty Queen Mutemwia asks that you briefly attend her before proceeding to the King's apartments. She will not detain you for long, mer kat. Follow me."

Captain Perti hesitated, Huy nodded at him, and surrounded by his soldiers Huy took the few steps out into the garden, squinting into the bright day. Not many residents of the palace were about. Ministers and lesser officials would be in their offices, beginning the duties of the day. The Minister of

Foreign Correspondence, Vizier Amunhotep-Huy, Treasurer Sobekhmose, together with their assistants and scribes, would have concluded the daily affairs of the morning audience over which Huy himself usually presided and would be preparing their reports and recommendations for him. The ambassadors resident in Weset would be dictating the letters to their lords and chiefs that were clandestinely brought to Perti for reading and copying before being passed to the heralds. *I'll have to leave Perti behind if I want to retain control of all foreign communications,* Huy thought as he threaded his way through intermittent shadows cast by the many varieties of trees dotted everywhere. *That solves the problem of our control outside Egypt. But who can shoulder the many and complex duties inherent in the governorship of this country? The King makes broad policy; he cares little for the dozens of decisions required every day to carry it out.*

Mutemwia was sitting on a mat at the base of a spreading sycamore, her attendants around her. Seeing him come, she gestured and the women scattered. Huy signalled to Perti and went on alone, bowing as he entered the welcome shade, and the Queen patted the grass beside her. She was not smiling. Huy folded near her feet and drew up his knees in a motion he recognized a moment later as self-defensive. His arms went around them.

"Neither Amunhotep nor Tiye understand why they must wait to hear the god's prediction for the baby," she said, "but I do. I remember your long struggle to untangle the mysteries of the Book, the frustration you lived with almost every day. The end of the task you took upon yourself all those years ago must come before all else. But I'm deeply troubled." She laid a hand lightly on his arm. "I know you far better than either my son or his Empress. They saw your refusal to divulge the details of the Seeing as a simple obedience to the command of Atum, but I saw more. Shock and dismay, mer kat. Anubis showed you something terrible, didn't he? Something even worse than the death of a royal heir. Since yesterday I have been imagining one future disaster after another." Clasping her fingers together, she placed them in her lap. Her gaze, when it met Huy's, was composed. "You told us that, unlike Prince Thothmes, this child will not die young. Did you lie?"

"No, dear Majesty. I neither lied nor distorted the truth." He resisted the urge to shift his position, smooth down the braids lying against his collarbones, loosen the tiny stud holding the earring against his lobe, anything to lessen his growing tension.

Mutemwia leaned towards him. "Is he to be maimed in some way, then? Or perhaps you were distressed because he will not rule well when the Double Crown is placed on his head? Will there be an unsuccessful palace revolt against him? Will Egypt suffer under his hand? What? *What?* You and I are almost as close to one another as brother and sister, Huy. Can you not relieve me of this anxiety?"

Now Huy did move, swaying onto his knees and bending forward with head lowered in a gesture of submission so that she could not see his discomfiture. Her guesses were unpleasantly close to the truth. "Majesty, if I were allowed to unburden myself of this Seeing, I would have hurried to approach you before any other. You and I share a mutual respect and understanding in spite of the gulf of blood between us. But I dare not defy Anubis's clear directive. Forgive me."

She was silent for a while. With his face inches from the sweet-smelling grass, the idle conversation of her women drifted over him. A bird screeched angrily in the branches above and flew away with a rustle of dry leaves. The gold border of her sheath was a bright blur on the periphery of his vision. Presently she sighed.

"Given your honesty, there could be no other answer," she said. "In the meantime, I must try to quell my gloomy conjectures and get on with my duties as best I may. Will you at least promise to come to me first when the god's ban on your tongue is lifted?"

I could do so, Huy thought swiftly, *but what if she forbids me to attempt to reverse this country's grave destiny for fear that my action may endanger her surviving grandson? And what action are you planning anyway, mer kat? All your desire is bent on sailing to Mennofer, examining the scroll, solving the one puzzle that has obsessed you since your thirteenth year. Have you any idea how Egypt's fate is to be averted?* "The contents of the Seeing belong to His Majesty the Emperor first," he said carefully. "He alone must weigh its importance. Believe me, Mutemwia, I would rather dissect its message with you than with Horus, indeed already I wish that I could call upon your insight and calm astuteness. However, I also must follow a diversion, and the vision must wait."

"Very well." She signalled that he might rise. Huy stood, taking the graceful hand extended to him and kissing it lightly. "Go and mollify Their Majesties before you embark for the north. I wish you success in the culmination of your quest. Send me scrolls of your progress, and may the soles of your feet be firm. I love you, dear friend."

I love you also, Huy thought as he bowed and walked into the dazzling heat of mid-morning. *There is no one whose advice I value more, but I have a growing suspicion that no advice will be able to save me from the solution Atum expects. I thank the gods that I need not ponder the matter for weeks to come.*

To Huy's surprise and relief, his interview with Amunhotep and Tiye did not take long. Both of them seemed to have accepted the necessity of his absence. Amunhotep, entirely sober, grudgingly agreed to attend the morning audiences and make decisions together with Chief Royal Treasurer Sobekhmose and Seal Bearer and Chief Scribe Nebmerut. "Everything will be sent on to you, though," he said. "It's a nuisance, Uncle, to tie up the majority of my heralds in running to the Delta and back, but there's no choice. Why don't you just ask that the scroll be brought to you here? I'll provide an escort for it of as many soldiers as you like."

"It may be in a very fragile condition, Majesty," Huy replied. "Having it carried south, no matter how carefully, might irreparably damage it. Besides, I doubt if Ptah's archivist will allow it to leave his care." He spread his hands. "You own Egypt, Amunhotep," he pressed. "All of it is yours under Ma'at. You're entirely capable of taking the reins of government from my hands for a few months, even though—"

"Even though your hunting dogs and concubines will have to amuse themselves," Tiye broke in firmly. "Huy has had no rest from the demands of government since you made him your mer kat. What emergency could possibly arise that can't be dealt with by you and Huy's advisers, my love? Anyway, when was the last time Huy made a personal request of you? Let him go." Her kohled eyes met Huy's then slid away.

You see this as an opportunity to sample the taste of real power, don't you, my Empress? Amunhotep will quickly tire of morning audiences and long meetings with the ministers, but you will not.

"Well, what if you die of some accident or disease?" Amunhotep grumbled. "Then Tiye and I will never know the substance of the vision regarding my little Prince."

"It resides with my scribe Paneb. If I die, you may immediately request it from him."

"The gods will not allow you to die, mer kat. Not yet." Tiye was leaning forward. "Now acquaint His Majesty with any current business in which you are engaged, then go with our blessing."

The brief exchange was over. Huy, bowing himself out, felt a pang of possessiveness towards the many complex duties he was relinquishing into the Empress's greedy hands, but the emotion was quickly submerged under a flood of anticipation. He was temporarily free.

HIS BARGE PULLED AWAY from his watersteps just before sunset, followed by the two vessels carrying his servants and belongings. He intended to sail downriver until he had rounded the bend that took a leisurely sweep eastward before the water returned to its northerly flow and the bustle and noise of the city was behind him. The month of Phamenoth was almost over. Egypt's fields lay carpeted with newly sprouted green crops, its canals still largely full. The river below Huy flowed gently toward the north. Huy, leaning on the rail, watched the sky gradually darken and the stars appear. Nasha's perfume drifted up to him. She was sitting on a stool by his side, stirring occasionally, hands folded in her lap. Huy had rightly assumed that she would want to travel as far as Thothmes' home at Iunu. He was eager to see his old friend but did not regret the fact that he would be disembarking at Mennofer, a full day's journey south of that city. Ramose had also begged to be included in the flotilla. He was returning to the Aten's temple at Iunu, where he would perform his overt duties as a steward and prepare his customary private report for Queen Mutemwia. *He and Nasha will be good company on the long journey,* Huy reflected. *They will prevent me from becoming too preoccupied with the task facing me. How good it is to be away from the demands of the court!*

By the time Huy stood beside his litter on the palace's watersteps at Mennofer and watched his barge continue north, the Inundation had begun. It was the middle of Pharmuthi. A full month had slid by since Weset had sunk below the horizon. His other boats were being tethered to the posts sunk at the foot of the steps. In a moment the ramps would be run out and servants and goods would begin to file along the edge of the guarded canal, across the vast concourse, and into the emptiness of the labyrinthine residence.

Huy had decided to occupy whatever quarters lay closest to the Temple of Ptah, in the southern palace apartments, so he could easily reach the temple without his litter. The Fine District of Pharaoh was surrounded by a high and sturdy wall and bisected north to south by another wall sealing off the palace from the ancient White Walls, the Citadel, and the large District of Ptah. Two canals met the outer main wall. The northern waterway ended at the edge of the stone forecourt leading to the palace's main reception hall. The second, farther south, ended at the bisecting interior wall, and was intended to accommodate those privileged worshippers arriving by skiff. There was a gate and a short paved avenue leading directly under Ptah's entrance pylon and into the wide outer court. All Huy had to do was walk to the head of the canal, go through the gate, and take the few steps to reach the towering pylon. He neither knew nor cared whose rooms were filling with the chaos of unloading under Amunmose's sharp eye. They were larger than his previous apartment, with a garden between the outer doors of his reception room and the inner wall cutting through the precincts, and a massive cedar door that protected him from the reverential comings and goings along the god's canal. Even though the King was not in residence, soldiers guarded every entrance and exit. The palace at Mennofer was ancient and sacred.

Quelling the urge to send a message to the temple immediately, Huy took Perti with him and escaped from the temporary chaos in the apartment to find the captain of the guards. He did not hurry. The huge building was blessedly quiet, the corridors dim, the air untainted by the scents of human occupation. *No distasteful aroma of jasmine carrying its weight of unhappy memories,* Huy thought, listening to the echoes of his and Perti's sandalled feet against the walls they were passing. *No need to thread my way through a constant press of servants and courtiers, acknowledging bows and greetings, my mind full of a dozen tasks to be accomplished before I can retreat to the cramped quarters that were assigned to me here. My full attention will go to the scroll. The baby Prince's Seeing will be relegated to the verge of my consciousness.* But his spurt of exhilaration was short-lived. He was midway along a wide, dusky passage when he thought he heard the sound of a faint scrabble behind him, and his nostrils filled with the acrid whiff of a wild animal. Gripping Perti's arm, he came to an abrupt halt.

"There's something following us," he said. "Some kind of a dog. I caught its odour briefly. Listen." He wanted to turn around, to see one of the greyhounds the King used for hunting emerge from the gloom at the far end, but he did not dare.

Perti was scanning their surroundings. Finally he shook his head. "I smell nothing, and if an animal was trailing us, we would have known about it sooner. I can walk back, Master, but I think it's just the sheer emptiness of this place distorting the noise of our feet and our breathing."

Huy did not answer him. They set off again at a brisker pace. Huy's spine prickled. *So even here, where I've come in obedience to the will of Atum, I am to be shadowed,* he thought with an anger tinged in fear. He was very glad to emerge from the palace into bright sunlight and the tug of a hot wind.

Perti escorted him back to the apartment before leaving to order the necessary new duties for the soldiers now under his command, and closing the wide doors behind him with a moment of inner relief, Huy beckoned Amunmose. Much of the disorder had disappeared and the reception room was quiet.

"Rakhaka and his staff have gone to the kitchens to prepare a meal," Amunmose said in answer to Huy's question. "He's grumbling about the distance he and the food must travel, but then he always finds something to complain about. Your couch is dressed and your chests unpacked. Amun and Khenti-kheti have been placed in their shrines. I've spread the servants out in the other apartments along this corridor. Kenofer's gone to see that the nearest bathhouse is ready for you. I don't know what happened to the wine jars, but I dare say someone will appear to tell me before long." He grinned. "I'm going to enjoy being the only chief steward in residence, Huy. Do you need anything?"

"Yes. Find Paneb and Ba-en-Ra." He went to the nearest chair and sat.

Amunmose sketched a bow. "I gave them separate quarters. Paneb already has a pile of papyrus from Weset for you to deal with." He hurried away.

The doors to the little garden were open and guarded. Huy looked past the two broad-shouldered soldiers to the dazzle of sun-drenched growth beyond. The grass was yellowing. *Amunmose must find a couple of men to water it each evening,* Huy thought, but behind the thought was a sudden anxiety. *A hyena could easily slip past my guards and come in if I don't keep the doors shut. It could pad through the reception room, find my bedchamber, be squatting on my couch and waiting for me.* He stirred. *But no. Doors open or closed mean nothing to the creature Anubis controls and Imhotep caresses, the emissary whose message I'm unable to comprehend.* He was glad when his scribe and his herald came purposefully towards him over the blue and white tiled floor.

He dictated a polite letter to the archivist of Ptah's House of Life, warning him that he would be present to examine the scroll the following morning, and gave it to Ba-en-Ra to deliver at once. Then with a lighter heart he turned his attention to the number of scrolls Paneb had placed on the table beside him. *Tomorrow I will see the end of a long and troubling journey*, he told himself, listening to Paneb read while his excitement mounted. *High Priest Ptahhotep is in residence at Weset. As one of Amunhotep's Fanbearers he has little time to spare for his duties to Ptah here in Mennofer. A good thing—I have no desire to discharge what would have been a necessary obligation to acquaint him with my findings, seeing that the scroll belongs to his temple. Dealing with the archivist will be annoying enough.*

He slept poorly that night, waking often on the unfamiliar couch to lie and listen to the deep silence of empty corridors and dark, untenanted rooms. He half expected to hear the scrabble of animal claws against the tiling of his floor before feeling the weight of a lean body settle beside his knees, but the shadows remained still. Each time he returned to consciousness the ache for more poppy woke with him, but he was used to this particular demand, a craving that had now become constant, and he was able to cocoon it within thoughts of the scroll. When he heard Kenofer cough and rustle as he rose from his pallet outside the door, Huy got up, wrapped himself in a sheet, and went to greet his bleary-eyed body servant. The sun had not yet risen.

Huy was tempted to order a larger dose of poppy than usual, but refrained from doing so for fear it would make him sluggish and blunt his faculties when the scroll was placed in his hands. *I should not be allowing myself this extreme anticipation*, he thought as later he made his way to the nearest bathhouse, where Kenofer waited. *The only evidence I have that the last words of the Book of Thoth will unroll before me is the fact that Imhotep is rumoured to have served as High Priest in Ptah's temple. I should be cautious, doubting, ready for disappointment.* But he was unable to stem the flow of euphoria quickening his heartbeat.

Returning to the apartment, he forced himself to eat a small

amount of bread and cheese, had Kenofer dress him in the sumptuous kilt, sandals, and jewellery he would have worn to any New
Year's celebration under the King's gaze, and taking Perti and a
small contingent of soldiers he walked across the garden and out
through the gate, and turned left to where Ptah's short canal lay
glittering in the morning sunlight. He had declined Paneb's offer
to accompany him and had left his own scribe's palette behind.
"If the scroll is a part of the Book of Thoth, I won't need the
contents written down, thank you, Paneb," he had said, "and if it
isn't, I have no interest in whatever it might contain."

He did not open a conversation with Perti, who according to
protocol had to wait for his master to speak first, but Perti seemed
to sense his preoccupied mood and simply matched his stride as
they accompanied the canal and were soon walking through the
pylon and into the temple's vast outer court. Here Huy paused. A
flow of white-sheathed young women carrying sistra was emerging from the inner court and hurrying to where an untidy heap of
sandals lay. Behind them came the three musicians who had
joined the dancers in welcoming the god to the advent of a new
day, and a priest stood just within the smaller court and watched
them. A flood of chatter had broken out, but as the girls became
aware of Huy and his escort it died away. One by one they slipped
past Huy with bows and were gone. The priest was already striding towards him with a smile of welcome.

"Mer kat! I received your message and passed it on to our
archivist, but there was little time to send a reply, and besides, we
are all at your immediate service for as long as you are studying
the scroll." He halted and bowed. "I am Neb-Ra, Second Prophet
of Ptah. My father was Second Prophet before me. I was little
more than a child, but I remember your illustrious brother the
noble Heby on his frequent visits to the temple during his years
as Mennofer's Mayor." He had begun to shepherd Huy and the

soldiers towards the entrance to the inner court. "If you will wait here, I will fetch Archivist Penbui, and also bring the servant I have assigned to see to your needs. Your personal guard is not really necessary—the temple guards are all well-seasoned men. But of course if you want them to attend you outside the House of Life, they will be cared for. No, do not remove your sandals. The doorway you see just this side of the inner court leads to the passage that will take you past the priests' cells and on to the House of Life. Stand in the shadow—the morning is becoming hot." With another bow, he disappeared.

Huy turned to Perti. "I don't think there's much to fear from the temple's staff. All the same, I'd like familiar faces outside the House. I may be here all day, or you and I may be straggling back to the palace in a matter of moments." His stomach gave a sudden lurch, and he could feel his heart throbbing against the soft linen of his shirt. *Very soon*, his mind whispered. *Very soon …*

The man who had already performed several deep bows before he came up to Huy was clad in a voluminous white gown. The brown leather sandals on his wide feet had obviously been mended several times. His only piece of jewellery appeared to be a tiny golden ankh earring no larger than the lobe where it rested. His scalp was shaved. Extending both naked arms, he gave Huy a final reverence, and lifted a face seamed with age but dominated by a pair of merry brown eyes.

"Keeper, I think I know you," Huy said. "Have we met before?"

"No, mer kat, but my brother Khanun was Keeper of the House of Life at Thoth's temple in Khmun. He spoke of you often when we met. He was pleased to receive your letters."

"Of course. I became fond of him on the occasions when I was forced to read the portions of the Book stored at Khmun. He was very kind to an unhappy boy. I promised to impart the meaning of the Book to him, but as yet I have not solved the riddle. Is Khanun still alive?"

"Unfortunately not, noble one. If the scroll in my care belongs to the Book, perhaps you will tell me the meaning so that I can include it in my prayers to Khanun."

They had approached the door, gone through it, and were walking side by side along the open-roofed passage, Perti and the soldiers behind. Suddenly, on a wave of nostalgia, Huy missed his old friend, Khenti-kheti's priest Methen, and his little cell in the god's modest precinct at Hut-herib. A grand new temple to Huy's first totem was rising on the foundations of that original shrine. Huy had personally chosen the architects and stonemasons who were to bring his vision to life, and construction had begun four years ago. It was a tribute to the god's priest as much as to Khenti-kheti himself, but Methen was dead, and most of Huy's devotion to the project had died with him. *I need you beside me now,* Huy said silently to the man who had carried him home from the House of the Dead and been his protector and mentor from then on. *You of all people deserve to be the first to receive Thoth's wisdom. Nothing and no one can replace you.*

"The scroll," he said abruptly. "You've unrolled it, Keeper Penbui?"

"Of course." A group of acolytes had appeared and were pressing themselves against the rough wall of the passage in order to let Huy and his entourage pass by. They managed to bow, and Huy nodded to them, remembering his days as a boy at Ra's temple school. "As Chief Archivist I am expert at the handling and restoration of ancient papyrus."

"So the scroll is indeed ancient? Is it in need of restoration?" The question was vital and in asking it Huy felt his throat go dry. The previous scrolls the Book comprised had been in perfect condition.

Penbui smiled across at him. "The papyrus has darkened with age but is not in the least brittle, mer kat. I was able to unroll it easily."

A dozen more questions sprang to Huy's mind. *What of the hieroglyphs? Are they as ancient as the papyrus? Could you decipher any of them? How thick is the scroll?* Instead he said, "Is it proven that Imhotep was once a High Priest of Ptah here in Mennofer?"

"But of course." Penbui had come to a halt before the closed doors of a long stone building that seemed to stretch all the way back to the high wall sheltering and surrounding the whole precinct of the temple. "We treasure several of his works to do with the use of magic, and a couple of his original plans for his King's monuments. You didn't know this?"

"No. Tell me, Keeper, do any of the hieroglyphs on the scroll match Imhotep's hand?"

"Perhaps," Penbui replied cautiously. "I am not sure." He pulled open one of the doors. "Let us go in, noble one. I have prepared a table and chair for you and set out the relic. Do you require the skills of a scribe? I see that you have not brought your own."

"No, thank you, Keeper."

Penbui looked at him curiously then stood aside, and Huy entered Ptah's House of Life.

The smell surrounded him at once, the slightly musty scent emanating from the thousands of books stored in the row upon row of alcoves and mingling with the odour of dust, stone, and ink. Huy paused, inhaling it with pleasure. It spoke to him of the schoolroom, of the slow learning of a scribe's discipline, of knowledge imbibed and mastery hard-won. The air was still, cool, and quiet. The only illumination came from thin shafts of sunlight slanting down through the clerestory windows a long way above his head. Not far into the great room stood a table which held a plain oil lamp and a bundle that caught at Huy's breath. Beside it a piece of carpet lay ready for the scribe Huy knew he would not need. A smaller table a step away had been covered with a linen cloth, two jugs, and two clay cups. Penbui had also paused. *As though we are paying homage to something sacred,* Huy thought, his eyes on the larger table where the treasure waited for him. *This moment is the culmination of all my years of struggle with the Book's mysteries, enduring Anubis's scoffing and, worst of all, carrying guilt and a sense of my own inadequacy day and night like a load of mud bricks I could not send tumbling to the ground.*

At an unspoken word the two men walked forward and Huy rounded the table to stand looking down on his prize. "The other volumes were encased in soft white leather," he said, his voice falling flat in the motionless atmosphere.

Penbui shook his head. "No white leather, mer kat, and no wax seal either. Just a cedar box, warped and cracked with age and lack of care. One of our artisans is making a new box for it, but of course if you determine that it is indeed a missing part of the Book of Thoth it must be honoured with a sheath of white bull's hide. In that case I pray that the One will allow it to remain under Ptah's protection."

"I shall urge His Majesty to do so." Huy drew up the chair and sat, a gesture of dismissal.

Penbui bowed. "The jugs contain water and wine. A servant will be outside the doors to bring you whatever you need." He hesitated, and in spite of his tension Huy smiled inwardly. He had never met an archivist who did not hover over his charges like a goose with her goslings.

"I promise I will not bring either water or wine over to this desk," he said, "and if I need to consult some other text you might have here, I will send for you. I have one request: a bowl of water, a dish of natron, and a fresh square of linen so that I may wash my hands should they become sweaty."

Penbui flushed, then smiled broadly. "My apologies, Master, for being a fussy old man. Your servant will bring the things I have omitted. I was somewhat flustered at the prospect of your presence here."

Huy smiled back and watched Penbui flit through the half door. It closed quietly.

My dear Keeper, I am probably older than you, Huy thought as the silence crept around him. *I exist in a limbo of timelessness by virtue of Atum's desire. Shall I be released now, today, with the meaning of the Book revealed clearly to me at last?* He sat waiting, palms flat on the surface of the table to either side of the scroll, and presently the door opened to admit a laden servant who bowed to Huy and set water, natron, and two linen cloths beside the clay cups with the smooth precision of long practice. Bowing again, he left, and Huy was free to touch his prize at last.

As he held it gently in order to turn it, he was enveloped in a glorious yet slightly sour aroma he recognized at once. His ears filled with the whisper of leaves brushing against each other and he was a youth again, sitting under the branches of the sacred Ished Tree that grew at the centre of Ra's temple, the first volume of the Book of Thoth lying under his terrified fingers. "Time ..." the tangle of moving shadows sighed as his younger self sat with eyes fixed on the far wall, afraid to look down at what lay on the palette resting across his folded knees. "Time ..." Huy shook himself, and hooking his fingers carefully under the lip of the papyrus, he drew the scroll open.

He had not seen the delicate, almost painfully beautiful script since he had read what had appeared to be the last volume of the Book just before his fifteenth Naming Day, but he recognized it at once and his heart gave a thud and began to pound in his ears. The language was archaic, but as before he was able to follow it with ease. *This is real,* he was thinking deliriously even as his gaze skimmed the characters. *I was right, Methen. The Book lacked finality. Will it now reveal a practical application for its convoluted and obscure wisdom? Will I see it, perhaps even experience it, for myself?* He wanted to unroll the scroll all the way in order to discover whether the equally familiar hand that had penned so many explanations for him in the past might have done so again. But he took a deep breath and returned to the beginning.

I Thoth, the Heart of Atum, now set down the Bridge of
which I am a part.
It is Ra who rests in Osiris; it is Osiris who rests in Ra.
Secret, mystery, it is Ra, it is Osiris.

Three gods are all the gods: Amun-Atum, Ra, Ptah, who
have no equal.
He whose name is hidden is Amun, whose countenance is
Ra and whose body is Ptah.
Amun-Atum, Ra, Ptah, Unity-Trinity. His image can never
be drawn, nothing can be
taught of him, for he is too mysterious for his secret to be
unveiled, too great and
too powerful to be approached ... one would fall dead at
once if one dared to pronounce
his secret name ...
He who began the becoming the first time. Amun-Atum
who became at the beginning,
whose mysterious emergence is unknown. No Neter had
come before him who could
reveal his form. His mother who made his name does not
exist. A father who could
say "I engendered him" does not exist. It was he who
hatched his own egg. Powerful,

mysterious of birth ... God of gods, who came from
himself. All the divine entities
became after he commenced himself.
He who manifested himself as heart, he who manifested
himself as tongue, in the
likeness of Atum, is Ptah, the very ancient, who gave life
to all the Neteru.
The King is all Neteru, the divinities, the hypostases of
Atum which are
his limbs. The King becomes in becoming.
The soul of the master of heaven is born, and shall become.
Come then Ra in thy name of the living Khepri ... illumine
the primordial darkness
that Iuf may live and renew itself.

Holding the papyrus firmly open, Huy glanced up for a
moment. *Thoth is indeed curving back to the beginning as the last
scroll I read said he would. He is restating the contents of the first four
scrolls, putting the difficulties into concepts that might be easier for a
reader to understand. He wants to be understood because he is Atum's
heart, and the Lord of Ra's Bau. So far I find no problems. Amun-
Atum enunciates, he speaks from his heart. Ptah takes this vital word
and materializes the Neteru, the great archetypes. And of course, as
the High Priest of Ra at Iunu told me once, Ra himself is not the sun,
not light, but penetrates the sun, and lights the primordial darkness so
that Flesh may live and renew itself. What Flesh? And what darkness?
Of the Nun or the twelve houses of night? How odd it is, and yet how
right, that I should be sitting here at the end of my long search, considering matters that became familiar to me even before I left my school!*
His gaze returned to the scroll.

Horus who protects Osiris, who fashions him by whom he
    himself was fashioned,
Who gives life to him by whom he himself was given life,
    who perpetuates
    the name of him by whom he himself was begotten.

The King is liberated from the humanity which is in his
    members ...
Horus receives him between his fingers, he purifies him in
    the lake
    of the jackal, he brushes the flesh of the royal double.
Oh arise! You have received your head, your bones are
    reassembled, your members
Are rejoined to you. Shake off the dust!

I am Iuf, the soul of Ra. I have come here to see my body in
    order to inspect
My image which is in the Duat.

Come then to us, thou whose Flesh sails, who is led towards
    his own body ...
The sky is for thy soul, the earth for thy body ...
Illumine the primordial darkness so that the Flesh may live
    and renew itself ...
Thou art he who becomes, he who metamorphoses himself
    towards
    the east.
The soul of the Master of Heaven is born and shall become.
The King returns to the right hand of his father ...
Akh is for heaven, kha is for earth ...
Thou livest now, flesh, in the earth.

Again Huy paused. *So Ra, the divine principle of light, becomes Iuf, flesh. At this point I think I'm losing my grasp of what I'm reading. Akh is spirit, my spirit. Kha is my body. I have the feeling that all I can do is allow my memory to absorb the words and try to understand them later.* He read on.

To me belongs today and I know tomorrow.
Who is this?
Yesterday is Osiris and tomorrow is Ra.
O Isir! Thy mouth is opened for thee with the thigh of the
    Eye of Hor ...
    with the hook of Upual ... with this metal born of Set,
    the adze of iron,
    with which is opened the mouth of the divine entities.
My mouth is opened by Ptah with celestial iron
    scissors ...

I have come to you, Osiris. I am Thoth, my two hands
    united to carry Ma'at.
Ma'at is in every place that is yours ...
You rise with Ma'at, you live with Ma'at, you join your
    limbs to Ma'at, you make
Ma'at rest on your head in order that she may take her seat
    on your forehead.
You become young again in the sight of your daughter
    Ma'at, you live from
    the perfume of her dew.
Ma'at is worn like an amulet at your throat, she rests on
    your chest, the
    divine entities reward you with Ma'at, for they know her
    wisdom ...
Your right eye is Ma'at, your left eye is Ma'at ...

Your flesh, your members, are Ma'at ...
Your food is Ma'at, your drink is Ma'at ...
The breaths of your nose are Ma'at ...
You exist because Ma'at exists ...
And vice versa.

There was a great deal more. The scroll was thick, and Huy was tempted to hold it open by placing the clay cups on it, but the fear of harming it kept him in his seat. He read steadily, so absorbed that he was unaware of the passing of time until at last he saw the words;

There, where everything ends, all begins eternally.

Nothing more was presented in that exquisite hand, but following a portion of blank papyrus Huy saw a scattering of words written in a way he recognized as identical to the clarifications that had been added to each of the Book's scrolls he had seen. *It's you, Imhotep, I know this is you, and I wish I'd brought my palette with me because, although every word of the Book itself sinks perfectly into my memory, your additions fade with time, a proof that the author of the Book is indeed Atum, dictating to Thoth.* Stretching until his spine cracked, he glanced out into the shadows of the extensive room. The thin rays of light illuminating the uppermost tiers of stored scrolls had gone and the small, high windows themselves showed only diffused patches of bronze sky. *I've been sitting here all day,* Huy thought with a shock. *I'm neither hungry nor thirsty, and the dose of poppy I always take at noon still rests in Perti's leather bag.* Suddenly oppressed by a weight of fatigue, he looked down, concentrating on the commentary the great Imhotep had penned so many hentis ago.

The King is Ma'at on earth. He spans the gulf beween earth and the Beautiful West. His limbs are the hypostases of Atum and he is the living Ra as Iuf, Flesh, as Horus himself, one of the mighty three. The heb sed not only renews the King's strength, it transmutes him. These words of Atum confirm it. It is the sacred heb sed that gives him the limbs of Atum and the Flesh of Ra. This is the way the King truly becomes a god.

Huy lifted his hands and the scroll rolled up with a tiny whisper. *Heb sed,* he breathed on an audible sigh of sheer tiredness. *A day on which every King performs the rites of regeneration, ceremonies established hentis ago in the darkness of the deep past. We think of it simply as the replenishment of his vigour. We believe that every Hawk-in-the-Nest becomes divine when he ascends the Horus Throne. But what if that is not true? Was the heb sed designed by Atum to do so much more? Have I found the practical application of all I have puzzled over through the years? The Book tells of creation, the beginning of magic, the becoming that resulted in the formation of the Neteru, the growing multiplicity of everything living on the earth, the holiness of Ma'at whose precepts we are commanded to follow. But until now, until the words contained in this last precious chapter, the Book did not speak of the nature and sanctity of kingship. Is this the culmination of all that has gone before since Ra-Atum filled the void of the Nun with his becoming? Does the King truly emerge from the heb sed as a unique being? I can't think about this anymore today.*

He rose stiffly, walked to one of the double doors, opened it, and stepped outside. At once his men and the temple servant with them scrambled up to bow. A pleasant, warm gush of air embraced Huy. Half the sun had already disappeared into the mouth of Nut, and the light was slowly changing from hot bronze to a delicate pink. Huy addressed the servant. "Tell your master the archivist that I have finished with the scroll and that I shall want to consult with him tomorrow. He may replace it in its box now, and leave it there. You are dismissed."

The man nodded and left. Huy beckoned Perti and together they began the short walk out of the temple grounds, along Ptah's canal, and through Huy's garden gate, the guard behind them. At the door to the apartment Huy released his men. "I'll send for you tomorrow," he told Perti. "The temple staff fed you, I hope."

"They did, Master. They wanted to bring you food also, but I took it upon myself to forbid them."

"Good. Go now." *I'm both thirsty and very hungry,* Huy realized as he entered the apartment and Amunmose came sweeping towards him, *but as yet I don't crave poppy. How strange.* "Get me hot food and a jug of beer," he said as his steward came up to him. "I'll eat and drink and then see to the dispatches in my room."

Amunmose bustled away and Huy turned to Kenofer, hovering at the door to Huy's bedchamber. All at once the full importance of the day burst upon him and he paused. *I have done what no one else has done since the time of Imhotep,* he marvelled without any sense of pride. *Indeed I know that I am simply standing in the wake of a great man worshipped by many. What else might Atum require of me now that the Book is complete?* A vision of Amunhotep's latest son appeared in his mind's eye, and firmly he thrust it away. "I've time for a massage before Rakhaka stops grumbling and cooks for me," he said to his body servant. "I've been sitting all day." Kenofer bowed briefly without speaking. *He's learned to be quiet at last.* Huy smiled to himself as he entered the room and sought his chair. Kenofer knelt and began to remove his sandals.

14

HUY DID NOT FALL ASLEEP until the coming dawn was a barely discernible lightening in the gloom around him. He lay on his back in a state of peaceful calm, hands behind his head, eyes open to the invisible ceiling, while he allowed the Book of Thoth to unreel slowly and steadily through his mind. Its elaborate concepts did not distress him, and he was able to form his own thoughts behind the words. *If Imhotep is correct, the Book is proof that every Pharaoh who performs the heb sed emerges invisibly transformed,* he reflected. *We have paid lip service to the idea for so many hentis that the wonder of its implication has become commonplace. The King dies, is beautified, and ascends to ride in the celestial barque among the stars with the other Neteru, who welcome him as an equal. But is he? They are archetypes, but the heb sed metamorphoses him so that he becomes Horus, Ra-Harakhti in his guise as Iuf, the Flesh of Ra. "The soul of the Master of Heaven is born and shall become," says the Book. Atum-Ra is gestated, cocooned, and born protected by uraei. The Neteru, the divinities, are the hypostases of Atum-Ra. Therefore they participate in this activity. From the rites of the heb sed the King becomes truly holy. "Come then, Ra, in thy name of the living Khepri … that Flesh may live and renew itself." As a god greater than everyone else but Iuf in the celestial barque,* Huy mused. *Greater than Wepwawet the Opener of the Ways, who stands in the front, or Sia, Knowledge, or the Lady of the Barque. Only the Great Neter Iuf stands in the central shrine, with Hu, the Word, behind him. Where does the transfigured King stand?*

His thoughts remained serene. *Tomorrow, Archivist Penbui will acquaint me with the procedures of the heb sed, but I now understand the meaning of the Book from Egypt's birth, through all the complex modes of material creation infused with magic, to the rituals that make every King unique. The Book is a material and spiritual history of Egypt, clear to me at last, and Atum's desire for this blessed country is finally revealed. I feel its resolution to the core of my heart. It will be my honour and privilege to tell Amunhotep.*

And *what of the baby Prince?* his mind whispered. *The present Horus-in-the-Nest, ten-year-old Prince Thothmes, will die. I have foreseen it. Does Atum want his successor in Egypt to be the creature I saw in my vision? Will he grow up to be worthy of the Double Crown, let alone the awesome gift of true godhead? What am I going to do about him? And what of the hyenas, both ghostly and corporeal, that haunt me? Where in the Book is there an explanation for their repulsive and alarming presence? I've always believed that they afflict me for a reason contained within the Book, and they will continue to trouble me until I know why.* Yet even the thought of the hyenas did no more than send a mild tremor through Huy, and at last, his eyelids now heavy, he turned on his side and slept.

He woke late, and before he had even opened his eyes he realized that his strong need for poppy had returned. He sat up, and Kenofer mutely handed him the vial, watching as he tipped the contents into his mouth. "Has any word come from the temple?" he asked.

"I don't know, Master." Kenofer took the vial and set it aside. "Either Amunmose or Paneb will have that news. I did see Paneb earlier, carrying an armful of scrolls. Will you eat?"

"I suppose I should. Bring me bread, beer, and whatever dried fruits Rakhaka is hoarding, and send Paneb to me. We might as well deal with the business from Weset while I eat, and then I'll go to the bathhouse."

Paneb was carrying a reed basket full of scrolls as he bowed himself in. "Do I usually see to such a magnitude of business at home?" Huy said glumly, and Paneb permitted himself a smile.

"Most of these are copies of decisions and directives the Empress has dealt with, Master," he replied, sinking cross-legged to the floor and setting the load beside him. "She has included a letter asking you to go over them and acquaint her with any changes you want made."

"Very astute of her." He waited while Kenofer entered, set his meal on the couch beside his knees, and went quietly away. "Begin reading, Paneb, and do so quickly. I have no doubt that most of Her Majesty's resolutions will agree with those I would have arrived at myself." Ignoring the griping of his stomach as he forced down the food, he concentrated on Paneb's words. *Tiye knows that I'll give every detail of day-to-day government my full attention. Obviously Amunhotep has already grown bored with audiences and receptions and has handed the administration over to her. Where did we go wrong, Mutemwia? Is it my fault or yours that the weaknesses in the King's character have engulfed the early promise he showed? Where is the intelligent, curious child we were at such pains to guide and instruct towards an enlightened rule? Are you as disappointed as I to see the fruit of all our hopes emptying the wine jug in the middle of the morning? Atum did not show me this. Why not? Because he knew I would become mer kat, and thus Amunhotep's laziness and licentiousness would not matter? Because he knew how Tiye's ability to govern would also compensate for her husband's lack? She will continue to consult with me by letter, making subtle deviations from the directions I would have taken, particularly with regard to foreign policy. If I want to retain control of Egypt, I must be careful to tug on the rope holding us together once in a while.* Huy impatiently watched Paneb alternate his attention between his palette and the diminishing pile of curled papyrus, until the scribe put down his brush and flexed his ink-stained fingers.

"Captain Perti received a verbal message from Ptah's Chief Archivist earlier, and passed it on to me," he told Huy. "Penbui will greet you in his quarters at any time today."

"Good." Huy slid off the couch. "You'll have to deal with the correspondence for Weset later, Paneb. I'll need you to come with me to the temple." He dismissed Paneb, joined Kenofer, who had been waiting just beyond the door, and went to the bathhouse. He did not hurry. A sense of formality moved with him, a calm certainty that before Nut swallowed the dazzling heat of Ra that evening all would be made clear, providing Atum willed it.

Later, he had himself dressed simply in a plain white kilt and shirt, still feeling himself surrounded by an aura of gravity, wondering what changes the knowledge he was about to acquire might bring about in him but not really caring. It was enough that he had accomplished what no man save the great Imhotep had done before him. At twelve years old, standing before Imhotep with the Judgment Hall behind him and Paradise ahead, he had not realized the extent of the privilege being offered. He had chosen to read the Book, and in so doing had determined his fate as a Seer and much later as mer kat, ruler of Egypt with no authority but Pharaoh's to gainsay him. *But will he?* Huy dared to ask himself as he began the short walk to the temple with Paneb behind and Perti and his soldiers ahead. *The end of the Book sets down the cryptic means whereby a King truly, actually, becomes a god. It's the climax of Egypt's journey, the reason why Atum chose to enter the Duat of metamorphosis and so began the process of creation according to his desire. Magic,* Huy thought as

Perti opened the garden gate and bowed him through. *Deep, strong, fierce heka pouring from Atum and carried on the breath of Ra to culminate in a man who is transformed into a god by the ritual of the heb sed. But only one man, only a King? Those who have been correctly beautified may live forever in the Beautiful West, but not as divinities. Is there no avenue to godhead for the rest of us? Imhotep has been worshipped as a god for hentis, but at first he was simply one of the beautified, like my parents, like Ishat, like dearest Heby my brother. Did Imhotep set out to become a god by deliberately, perhaps even secretly, performing the heb sed for himself? But would that not have been a blasphemy against Atum? Imhotep spoke to me kindly and patiently as he sat beneath the Ished Tree with the Book across his knees and a tame hyena with golden eyes beside him. Is it that we Egyptians over many hentis have chosen to see him as a god when he is not? Or does Atum intend godhead by ritual for all of us?*

Huy knew, as he and the others turned to walk beside Ptah's canal, that he was not really engaged in the puzzle. He and the archivist would solve some of the mystery, but not all. *And there is still the hyena,* he reminded himself as they passed into the afternoon shadow of the entrance pylon. *That is another matter entirely.*

He left Perti and his men in the outer court, and after asking a passing priest the way to the archivist's cell, he and Paneb made their way along the side of the House of Life to where a large mud-brick house with a modest garden shared the library's rear wall. Penbui himself rose from a stool in the shade by the doorway and bowed profoundly. The face he lifted to Huy was alive with curiosity.

"Yes," Huy said. "The scroll is indeed the final piece of the Book of Thoth. I'm hoping that you will be able to help me make it intelligible. This is my scribe Paneb, who will record our conversation."

"You will share it with me, Great Seer? I'm honoured. Please enter my home. Refreshments will be provided in due course." He ushered them into a room that instantly reminded Huy of the cozy cell occupied by Penbui's brother Khanun at Khmun, although this was larger. Khanun had decorated his walls with bright scenes of everyday life along the river that, though crude, were full of vitality. Penbui's depictions were more expert but expressed a similarly exuberant joy of living that lifted Huy's spirits at once. "Khanun and I shared a love of language and a reverence for knowledge," Penbui said, noting Huy's glance as he took a chair. "Such interests were unusual in two peasant children raised on a farm. I counted myself most blessed to have finally been appointed caretaker to the precious scrolls in this House of Life after many difficult years. Khanun rejoiced in his success also. But we sometimes missed the simple freedoms of our upbringing." He waved at his colourful walls.

"My roots are modest also," Huy told him as Paneb settled at his feet and began to prepare his implements. "Thoth's priests at Khmun seemed alarmingly refined to the young boy I was. I took refuge with your brother. We had much in common. Please sit, Penbui. The recitation will be long. Paneb, this is not a dictation."

The scribe set his palette on the floor beside him. The archivist settled back in his chair, crossed his legs, and rested his folded hands against his white-clad lap. At once a long silence fell. A not unpleasant blend of birdsong wafted through the open door of the house together with a thin shaft of sunlight, but it became muted at once by a weight of stillness that had begun to infuse the dim interior of the reception room. To Huy, with Penbui's gaze fixed steadily on him, it had the quality of the moment just before dawn when a motionless expectancy invaded the world, when everything, even the river itself, seemed to hold its breath. *I have never before recited the Book of Thoth in its entirety, and I do so now, not before kings, nobles, or priests, but before a man as humbly born as myself. Yet it feels right. The flimsy accretions of privilege I have gathered over the years fall away like dead leaves and I am nothing but an instrument of Atum's will.* His voice, when he spoke into that quiet air, was strong and steady. "Up until yesterday it was believed that the Book consisted of five parts, the scrolls divided between the temples at Iunu and Khmun. Now we know that there is a sixth, here in Mennofer. Each part begins with a declaration by Thoth, who took the dictation of the contents from Atum. Thoth lists his own many titles, warns the reader of the dangers to those who dare to study the sacred concepts within, and then proceeds to set down the mysteries. There's no need to go through his introduction to every scroll. I'll recount only Atum's direct words."

He paused. A sudden greed for the poppy washed over him, drying his throat and spasming in his fingers, and for one desperate moment all he could see was the vial hanging in a linen pouch from his scribe's belt. But he fought the dismal familiarity of the desire, and gradually it ebbed under the force of his will. Closing his eyes, he began at the beginning of the very first scroll.

"'The Universe is nothing but consciousness, and in all its appearances reveals nothing but an evolution of consciousness, from its origin to its end, which is a return to its cause.

"'How to describe the Indescribable? How to show the Unshowable?

"'How to express the Unutterable?

"'How to seize the Ungraspable Instant? ...'"

The sonorous phrases rolled off Huy's tongue, filling the room with their mystery and poetry, and as Huy passed slowly from scroll to scroll he felt time itself draw away from him and collapse into insignificance. He was perched on the edge of his cot in the cell he shared with Thothmes at Ra's temple school at Iunu. It was evening. The fresh smell of rinsing vinegar rose from the clean sheets under him. Pabast had been late bringing the lamp. He had arrived at the same time as Thothmes, who was bleeding from a scratch on his calf. "I got between Menkh and the ball," he explained while the servant was setting the lamp on the table between the two couches. "I'll put some honey on it after we've been to the bathhouse. Huy, are you all right?"

Huy, sitting in Chief Archivist Penbui's house reciting the Book of Thoth, could feel again the sore throat that had been a precursor to the fever through which Thothmes had nursed him, could look with an overwhelming love at the features of his friend's youthful face as it had once been. As the remembered scene was played out, its details became sharper and more immediate, until Huy no longer knew that he himself was an old man. Thothmes' worried face as it came close was everything, the yellow lamplight was everything, the incomprehensible words of the very first scroll he had read under the Ished Tree in the centre of the temple were everything as he recited them to Thothmes, there in the sweet safety and predictability of a student's life.

He was plunged into other scenes so vivid and immediate that the self whose words went on effortlessly filling Penbui's room was forgotten. "Undo your braid," Henenu the Rekhet said, and he was sitting in her little house, milk and dried figs on the plain table beside him, the cowrie shells hanging from her waist and festooning her ankles clicking as she ordered her servant to bring oil and a comb. The oil, when it came, gave off a sweet, heavy aroma that made him sleepy in body but alert in mind. He had just finished thanking her for the amulet she had made him, and while she loosened his long hair and began to comb it, he was reciting the few incomprehensible sentences of the Book's fifth part. The odour of the reremet, the mandrake root she had crushed and added to the oil, filled his nostrils as it imbued the comb gliding over his scalp. She was speaking of his youthful rebellion against the gift of Scrying that had accompanied his agreement to read the Book, a gift that had brought with it an unwelcome sexual impotence that he, now fifteen years old, resented with an angry bitterness. He had begun to hate the god who had imposed such an unexpected consequence on him. "It will be better for you if you realize that for you there are no large choices in life," she told him as her hands moved hypnotically through his hair. "Your journey was chosen for you by the gods and by you when you agreed to read the Book. The sooner you accept that Atum rules your fate, the sooner you will achieve the peace that eludes you."

Coming suddenly to himself in the archivist's house, he could still hear the tuneless clacking of the shells she constantly wore to protect herself against the demons she confronted every day in her work. *She was old even then*, he thought as he struggled to return to the present. *She was my touchstone. She loved me, and I, in my selfish, often careless way, loved and trusted both her great spiritual knowledge and her down-to-earth good sense. I miss her. Gods, there are so many people I miss, so many dear ones I've seen carried into their tombs! Only Thothmes and Nasha are left to remind me of my youth, and in spite of my power as mer kat and my ability to foresee the future, I am helpless to prevent their dissolution. Take me back to the hovel I shared with Ishat!* he begged whatever force was separating his memories from the flow of Atum's words streaming out of him. *Put us face to face, not with the imprecision of common recall but as sharply clear as Thothmes and Henenu were!* His sudden need to be with Ishat was a stab of homesickness so violent that it closed his throat, and seeking the next verse of the Book he realized that the narration was over.

He opened his eyes. Small sounds began to take the place of the profound silence that had seemed to seal the room. Intermittent birdsong, the drowsy rustle of leaves stirring in hot puffs of breeze, the brief cough of the servant waiting in the shade outside, began to return Huy and the others to a welcome normality. Paneb stood, stretched, and then resumed his position on the floor beside Huy. Penbui left his chair with some difficulty, walked to the table, poured two cups of water, and offered one to Huy. Both his hands were shaking. Huy drank eagerly.

Penbui went to the door. "We need food," he said hoarsely to the servant who had scrambled up. "See what you can find. There should be roasted gazelle left over from last night's meal, as well as bread, cheese, and plenty of raisins. Don't forget a large jug of barley beer." Resuming his seat, he folded his arms, hunching his shoulders as if in defence, but Huy recognized the gesture as one of supreme awe. "Today I am the most privileged citizen in Egypt," he half whispered. "Today I have heard the words of the great creator-god himself."

Huy did not answer. Drinking more water, he set an elbow on one knee and, resting his forehead on his open palm, closed his eyes again. He was very tired. No one spoke. *Before I give the archivist the words of Imhotep's summary, I want to hear his assessment of the Book. He said that he'd read the last scroll, or parts of it. Did he unroll it far enough to find the great man's conclusion? And shall I tell him about the hyena that haunts me?*

He woke startled from a doze some time later to find Paneb's hand on his arm. "The food is here, Master," he was saying quietly. "The temple kitchens have provided onion and garlic soup. I know that it's probably not as hot as the air outside, but please try to eat it. You need to renew your strength."

Huy looked at his scribe with bleary astonishment. The only conversations he and Paneb had held in all the years of Paneb's service had concerned matters of palace business or Huy's invest-ments in the poppy fields and trading caravans. Paneb, sober, punctilious, and excellent at his profession, had never before stepped beyond the bounds of his responsibility.

"Paneb, you made a joke!" Huy exclaimed.

Paneb moved to the table and, picking up a tray from which an appetizing aroma was wafting, brought it to Huy, setting it carefully across his linen-clad thighs and then shaking out a square of napkin. "Kenofer is not here. Therefore it is my privi-lege to perform his duties." He draped the napkin carefully between the tray's edge and Huy's crumpled shirt and stood back, obviously waiting to serve.

Huy waved him away. "You are not to take over the obligations of my body servant, although you have my gratitude, Paneb. I'm perfectly capable of feeding myself, and I shall indeed eat this wonderful soup. You must eat as much as possible yourself—your task today is about to begin." Lifting the beer mug to his mouth, he glanced across the room at Penbui.

"We could have gone to the priests' dining hall, mer kat," the archivist explained. "After all, the sun is setting and Ptah's servants break their fast early so as to see to the needs of the god at nightfall. But I assumed that you would not welcome the attentions of my fellows. Not today."

Huy took a mouthful of the rich, dark beer. *This is reality,* he told himself as he put it down on the tray and began to tear apart a large piece of flatbread. *These pleasant odours and the clink of Penbui's spoon against his bowl and the murmurs of idle servants' conversation drifting through the door with the shaft of golden evening light imperceptibly lengthening across the tiled floor and being lost in the cool dimness. These things are sanity. These things are everything.* "Thank you, Penbui," he replied. "If you have formed an opinion of all that you've heard, are you willing to discuss it after our meal, or shall we resume this meeting tomorrow?"

The archivist nodded. "I'm eager to proceed with the matter, Seer Huy. We must pray to Thoth and to Atum himself for enlightenment, and believe as we speak that we are correctly stripping the protective concealment from the kernel of an immeasurable and very sacred truth. I am most honoured by your trust."

I feel the weight of this in a way you cannot possibly understand, Penbui, although I wish with all my heart that I could share it with you, Huy mutely addressed the man sitting opposite. *My prayer will not be to either Thoth or Atum. It's Anubis, my guide, my tormentor, from whom I shall beg both his pity and his enlightenment. Surely I deserve a reprieve from a lifetime of his taunts and condescension.*

The three men finished their meal without conversation. *Any polite talk would be frivolous now, even blasphemous,* Huy reflected. *I'd like to go away and be alone, immerse myself in the heka that has always isolated the Book's contents from the ravages of passing time, but magic will not confirm the conclusion Imhotep came to regarding its ultimate meaning. Archivists are steeped in many areas of knowledge. They are expected to understand the value of the information stored in their care. Every citizen is familiar with the ceremony of the heb sed. It usually accompanies a King's jubilee when he celebrates his first thirty years on the Horus Throne and is meant to renew his potency. A fortunate King might celebrate two or even three jubilees. Often the necessity might arise for him to prepare a jubilee long before the stipulated thirty years have passed if there is unrest in Egypt or a dispute to do with the legitimacy of his right to rule. Atum chose to dictate an account of his divine actions from the moment when he metamorphosed himself from the nothingness of the Nun and began the intricate process of creation. Would he have done so for no other reason than to end it with a commonplace ceremony to return full might to whichever Horus is at the pinnacle of Egypt's ongoing existence? Only priests and Pharaoh himself take part in the heb sed. The rest of us cheer an occasion to hold feasts, get happily drunk, and complain about the temporary absence of servants who are also taking the chance to carouse. Imhotep knew better, and the knowing turned him into a god.*

A word of command from Penbui roused Huy and he watched as two servants obediently cleared away the meal's debris. The door closed behind them. Penbui looked across at Huy. There was a pause during which Huy could hear the small sounds of Paneb mixing his ink and applying his scraper to the papyrus. At last Penbui said hesitantly, "Great Seer, what do you want of me?"

"I want us to discuss any passages neither you nor I understand," Huy replied. "They will differ, of course. For example, when I first read the second part of the Book, containing the lines

I am One that transforms into Two,
I am Two that transforms into Four,
I am Four that transforms into Eight,
After this I am One,

I was too ignorant to know that Atum was speaking of bringing order to the chaos of his shadow by means of the pairing of male and female archetypes before he embarked upon the creation of the material world." As Huy spoke of the shadow, he was aware of a growing uneasiness. Imhotep's commentary on Atum's state when he became Light and thus cast the first shadow had always filled Huy with a rootless anxiety that returned each time the words formed in his mind, and today was no different.

Yet the Light cast a shadow,
   grim and terrible,
which, passing downwards,
became like restless water,
chaotically casting forth spume like smoke.

He did not utter them aloud.

"Water, endless space, darkness, and what is hidden," Penbui said. "The archetypes coming together in pairs to form the foundation upon which Atum made everything that is. I heard a wealth of similar beauty in the Book as you recited it, and many pronouncements I only partly grasped before you moved on. The rudiments of the creation account are usually taught to our children before they enter the schoolroom."

"Unless one's parents have no particular interest in such esoteric things," Huy said. "I loved Hapu and Itu, my parents, but like many peasants too occupied with the necessities of survival, they had no time for the luxury of religious edification."

Penbui nodded. "One cannot blame them. Khanun and I were born with a desire for such knowledge and we spent most of our meagre leisure time in the company of our local totem's priest. Fortunately, he did not dismiss us as the children of Pharaoh's cattle!"

Huy smiled across at the old archivist. "Over the years, I've been able to interpret each section of the Book to my satisfaction, but the suspicion that it lacked a final chapter grew in me because its meaning as a whole continued to escape me. Now that you've heard it all, can you hazard a guess as to its ultimate conclusion? Why did Atum trouble himself to dictate it all to Thoth for our benefit? Is it more than a marvellous account of Egypt's formation? Does it describe a journey to be taken, a formula of hitherto unknown heka to be followed, a set of arcane laws, a series of images showing us the Beautiful West? What?" His smile disappeared. He was aware that his voice had risen, his body had become taut; the urgency slowly fermenting in him was at last spilling over, and he could not control it. "I don't want to fill my mind with these things," he went on loudly. "My days and too often my nights also are crammed so full of governmental responsibilities that I fear I will wake some morning and find myself unable to face them. Yet the obligation to grasp the Book's conclusion, to see the purpose of Atum made clear, has oppressed me since I was twelve years old. Fate has led me here, to you," he managed more calmly. "Surely now I may hear a new source of wisdom and so resolve this dire predicament. I am in the Second Duat, trying to keep my head above water, and the darkness around me seems absolute!"

Penbui's look of alarm had gradually given way to one of cautious sympathy under Huy's vehemence. He set his beer down on the table beside him and sat back. "I think you should take the risk of confiding in me completely, Great Seer. If we have come together through the hand of fate, then the result of our meeting must be foreordained. I am only Ptah's archivist. You are Pharaoh's mer kat and I am well aware that your word is law throughout Egypt, yet the gods have laid a burden on you much greater than the weight of the King's cloak around your shoulders. I ask in all humility—let me help you if I can."

"Then tell me what you think." There was a moment of silence during which the man's head went down, and Huy realized that he was praying. Huy waited. *I will not call upon you for enlightenment or anything else, Anubis*, he said mutely to the god who had often taken a malicious delight in answering his questions with riddles. If he was Scrying to determine a cure for some illness or the result of some horrible accident, Anubis would immediately provide a medical procedure, but any other inquiry

Huy had would be met with an insult to his intelligence or an even more complicated enigma. *I owe you nothing,* Huy's sour thoughts ran on. *Time and again you have left me desperate for answers, expecting me to reason through to conclusions only a god might understand. I am not your toy. And if this good man and I are able to succeed in our task, I shall take great pleasure in telling you so.*

Penbui looked up, cleared his throat, and settled himself further into his chair. "With respect to your own great erudition, mer kat, I can say that I am more familiar with the rites and origins of the heb sed festival than any other temple official in Egypt. After all, by custom those rites must be enacted here, in Mennofer. Our kings have almost always ruled from the ancient palace close by, and Mennofer's founding as the country's sacred capital took place so long ago that very few scrolls from that age survive. One of them contains the oldest instructions in existence for the procedure of the festival. The information is here in Ptah's House of Life, but no minister of protocol has asked to study it since the time of the Osiris-one Hatshepsut, she who usurped the Horus Throne from her ultimate successor, our mighty Thothmes the Third, grandfather of our present King. It was after her Myriad of Years, a jubilee celebration she had commanded far in advance of the customary thirty years of rule, that she caused these words to be inscribed on the walls of her admittedly beautiful temple on the west bank opposite Weset: 'I am God, the Beginning of Existence.'"

"What are you saying?" Huy demanded sharply. "That in your opinion a King's transmutation into godhead doesn't truly take place until he performs the rites of the heb sed? That without ever reading the Book, Hatshepsut's minister of protocol deduced as much from the earliest account of the heb sed we have, and that his belief somehow allowed her to have such an unequivocal declaration of her own godhead chiselled on her temple?" A fume of excitement began to uncurl inside him. He felt it as a heat in his belly not unlike the first welcome indication that the poppy had begun its blessed journey through his body.

"We Egyptians are unique in the unquestioned belief that our kings are not only men but gods," Penbui replied. "That through their divinity Egypt continues fertile and prosperous, and that the heb sed renews their divine power to maintain our country's strength. Since the beginning this has been so, and we take every ruler's dual nature for granted—we don't even think about it. But truthfully, mer kat, how many of us really believe in such a thing?" He leaned forward. "We accept the omnipotence of the gods without thought. We pay respectful lip service to Pharaoh as Horus, as Amun, but the usage of hentis has rendered his uniqueness commonplace. If we are naive enough to raise the subject seriously in aristocratic company, we create a moment of mild embarrassment and our fellows politely turn to other subjects of conversation. Do succeeding kings themselves truly believe in their divinity as something other than a nod to Ma'at at best and a foundation for their sense of superiority at the least? The Queen Hatshepsut came to truly believe." He had grown progressively more hoarse with the intensity of his words. Pausing, he quickly drained his beer, dabbed his mouth on the linen laid ready by his now empty plate, pursed his lips in a gesture of apology, and gazed across at Huy. "I'm close to blasphemy, I know, but you asked me for my honesty."

"Yes, I did. The great Imhotep agrees with you. I'm assuming by your answer that you didn't unroll the scroll to its end."

Penbui's eyebrows rose. "No. The script remained consistent for as far as I tried to read it. Are you implying that Imhotep added something to it in his own hand?"

"Someone of erudition added an explanation to almost every chapter of the Book, and I believe that person to have been

Imhotep. See for yourself. He writes, 'The heb sed not only renews the King's strength, it transmutes him ... This is the way the King truly becomes a god.'" They stared at one another in a silence that seemed to reverberate with Huy's last few words. *The King truly becomes a god ... a god ... a god ...*

At last Penbui stirred. "This gives the rites of the heb sed a new interpretation," he mused aloud. "Already I see them differently in my mind. I shall give you the ancient scroll I mentioned earlier to take back to your quarters and study, and if you agree with me that its contents support Imhotep's conclusion, then we Egyptians are uniquely blessed. How Khanun would have loved to discuss these things with us!" He rose with difficulty and bowed. "Be pleased to dismiss me, mer kat. My joints are a little stiff and I need to rest."

Huy also stood and Paneb rose from the floor, sliding the lid of his palette closed with a click as he did so. Huy bowed back. "Thank you for this enlightenment, Penbui. The scroll you lend me will be returned as soon as possible."

"And perhaps you might require my presence again once you have read its contents?"

"Perhaps." The archivist's eyes were shining with anticipation. *How many scholars come to Ptah's House of Life in order to study the vast wisdom accumulated here?* Huy wondered, touched by the man's eagerness. *Surely Penbui doesn't lack for stimulation! But of course this situation is different—a scroll worth more than every other scroll stored in the library, and we two following in the steps of the greatest architect, physician, and magician this country has ever seen. Son of Ptah, Imhotep is often called. Son of Atum also? Is he worshipped as a god because he became one? Did he use the heb sed for himself? Is such a thing even possible for anyone but an anointed King?*

"Master?" Paneb said softly at his elbow, and Huy came to himself, following Penbui out into the last ephemeral vestiges of twilight. He felt suddenly drained and thin, as though some invisible bau had been sent to weaken him, and although the distance to his quarters in the palace was short, he wished that he had asked Perti to have his litter brought. He waited outside the library while Penbui went inside to fetch the document. Perti and the accompanying soldiers waited with him quietly. To Huy it seemed that he, Paneb, Perti, all of them, had battled some mighty storm together and had emerged safe but exhausted.

Responding to Penbui as he returned clutching a cedar box took all the strength Huy could muster. He held out a hand and, after an instant of reluctance immediately quelled, Penbui passed it to him. "Of course, I have made several copies of it," the archivist said hopefully.

Huy shook his head. "I need the original hieroglyphs. Mistakes can creep in by accident and the concepts conveyed be misinterpreted."

Penbui smiled briefly. "Of course. If I were in your place, I'd make the same decision. May Thoth guide your thoughts as you read, mer kat, and I thank you for the many pleasures of this day."

With an inward sigh of relief, Huy turned towards the now dark passage that would return him to his apartment.

He had thought that once the door closed behind him he would be keen to acquaint himself with the rituals concealed within the box, but examining his inner self he found that his curiosity had temporarily subsided, replaced by thirst and an awakening need for poppy. Laying his precious burden on the bedside table, he beckoned a waiting Kenofer. "Undress me. I'm too tired to bother with the bathhouse this evening, but bring hot water and wash me here. Bring a jug of water and a dose of poppy."

When the servant's tasks were complete, Huy dismissed him and composed himself for sleep. The opium, obedient as ever, coursed slowly and langorously through his veins. The lamp by

his couch cast warm shadows that merged with the heavier darkness beyond the flame's reach. Yet Huy did not fall asleep for a
long time. He was not anxious or troubled. Relaxed in body, he
had no particular thoughts as the events of the day passed slowly
and peacefully through his mind. Even the sense of supreme
accomplishment he had expected to feel after a lifetime of
pondering the enigmas of the Book was absent. It was as though
the joys and griefs of the past and the hidden life of the future did
not exist. There was only a calm present, and Huy was
profoundly grateful.

He and Paneb spent the whole of the following day dealing
with a welter of letters from the officials and administrators he
had left behind in Weset. Many of them contained additional
comments in a hand Huy recognized as that of the Empress's
Chief Scribe. "I approved this, but I don't want you coming back
and countermanding my decision, so confirm it," was one such
waspish remark. "I'm told that you worked on these negotiations
for half a year, but I don't like the concessions you have agreed
to make," was another, longer harangue.

The ambassador insists that by your own word Egypt prom-
ises to provide not only the protection of his border with
our troops but also supplies for the creation of three thousand compound bows and the artisans necessary to instruct
the foreigners in their construction. I do not approve of
arming those who may one day turn against us. Is he or is he
not taking advantage of your absence to extract more from
us than you promised to his King? Nothing of this matter
has yet been put to papyrus, an omission that I find entirely
frustrating. If you do not return to Weset soon, I intend to
begin the negotiations over again from the start and more
realistically, unless you can give me good reasons for the

offer you presented. When will you come back? In my opinion you have left me with several administrative problems that are unnecessarily complicated.

Huy answered every query as tactfully as he could without surrendering any of his authority. There was no message from the King.

By sunset, he and Paneb had dealt with the last of the correspondence and Paneb had given Chief Herald Ba-en-Ra a full bag for delivery to the palace at Weset. Ba-en-Ra would hand it to one of the heralds under him. Once Huy had read the scroll regarding the rites of the heb sed and had dictated his own account of its contents to Paneb, he would be free to leave Mennofer, but he was in no hurry to acquaint Their Majesties with the details of his vision regarding the newly born Prince and perhaps be forced to confront them with a solution they would not like. *I'll go north to Iunu, spend time with Thothmes and Nasha, perhaps even go farther and watch the final work being done on Khenti-kheti's temple at Hut-herib. I thank the gods that I'm answerable to Amunhotep and not to Tiye!*

He ate the evening meal in his bedchamber with very little appetite, a tray across his thighs, his attention now fixed on the cedar box, and when he had eaten and drunk what he could he sent once again for Paneb, had Kenofer bring more lamps, and was finally ready to see what the ancient and anonymous author of the heb sed festival had created.

He saw at once that the papyrus was very brittle. Tiny pieces of its edges had broken off and lay on the bottom of the cedar box, and he would have to unroll the thick scroll on a firm surface. Reluctantly he carried it to the room that had been set aside for his office. He had not used that area since his arrival in the palace. It represented the affairs of government from which he had managed partially to withdraw, and he approached it unwillingly, Paneb following. Kenofer brought the lamps, setting two of them on the desk and one on the floor to illuminate Paneb's work before closing the door behind him. Gingerly Huy began to open out the scroll.

The hieroglyphs were in a hand he did not recognize. Tiny and neat, they flowed pleasantly under Huy's gaze, unfolding in a version of dialect less ancient than that of the Book, Huy surmised, and easier to read. "An account of the ceremonies and secret rites composing the sacred progression of the heb sed festival whereby the land is rejuvenated and the King's transmutation affirmed," the opening sentence proclaimed. "It is Thoth who gives the words. It is Wepwawet who ensures the correct performance of every ritual. Thus may His Majesty's mouth be opened to eternity."

Wepwawet, Huy repeated to himself. *A lesser wolf god with a shrine in the town of Aswat. If I remember my lessons correctly, he bears two titles: Lord of War and Opener of the Ways. He stands in the celestial barque with other gods as they convey the King through the Duat and do battle with Apep the serpent and the demons of the dark. We think of him as opening a way in the night, but what if he does a great deal more? He is one of the earliest of our deities, the origin of his powers lost in the past. What if he presides over the heb sed because without him the King's transformation into a god could not take place? Rejuvenation of King and land, yes, but what if Wepwawet in his guise as Opener of the Ways is the only one commanded to form a path along which Atum's transforming magic may travel?* Putting aside conjectures that were futile at present, Huy returned his attention to the scroll.

There were seven solemn rites making up the days of the festival, and as the details of each one unfolded, Huy sank more deeply into the anonymous scribe's descriptions. Every stage of the King's progress towards rebirth had been set out with a clarity and precision that enabled Huy not only to understand and visualize each phase but also to link it directly to passages from the Book of Thoth. One such segment that had always puzzled Huy, coming as it did at the end of what he used to believe was the last portion of the Book, said, "… he has gone around the entire two skies, he has circumnambulated the two banks …" Now it was set firmly into the third stage, when the King lies curled in a small chamber especially erected to be both a tomb and a womb from which he will be reborn. The tiles decorating the space are blue-green. The King is wrapped in a cow's skin representing the womb of the sky goddess Nut, who swallows Ra every evening and expels him each morning. An Opener of the Mouth, a funerary priest, enfolds the King and watches as he crawls into the place where he symbolically dies and from which he will emerge transmuted. Inside the tomb two paired glyphs are depicted representing both halves of the sky, east and west, and both banks that make up Egypt herself on either side of the river. *The same passage from the Book goes on to speak of the resurrected King's triumphant flight once his assimilation with Horus is complete*, Huy realized. *The King is reborn. He has died, and now he emerges from the womb of Nut as Horus himself. The waiting funerary priest performs the Opening of the Mouth ceremony with the Pesesh-kef knife, giving new senses to the young Horus. The King then suckles, eats, and teethes as spells are said to render those activities authentic, but he is still both living and dead until the assembled officials privileged to attend his emergence from the tomb—the priests, sem priests, magicians, and archivists from Ptah's House of Life—shout, "Awake! Awake! Awake!"*

There was more, much more. Some of the rites had to do with a rejuvenation of Egypt herself as the King was reborn, but to Huy, utterly engrossed in the ancient text, the ones carried out in strict privacy were plainly intended to metamorphose a mortal King into an immortal god. Wepwawet, Opener of the Ways, presided over it all from the first solemn procession to the raising of a djed column and the unveiling of new statues of the King scattered throughout Egypt, announcing a renewal of both the ruler and the land.

As the scroll rolled up, Huy finally came to himself. Paneb still sat cross-legged on the floor beside the desk, but his chin rested on his breast. He was asleep. The alabaster lamps were burning brightly. Someone had refilled their oil without Huy's being aware of it. He leaned back, all at once conscious of an ache at the base of his spine, stiff shoulders, and a difficulty in focusing as he scanned the room. The apartment lay resting in a deep silence Huy was loath to disturb, but reaching down, he touched Paneb. Immediately the scribe was awake. "Go to bed," Huy told him. "Tomorrow I'll dictate my thoughts on this matter. Kenofer will be snoring outside the door. Send him in to me as you go."

15

THE FOLLOWING MORNING, Huy set Paneb the task of
copying the heb sed scroll and ordered Amunmose to
have his belongings packed. He sent a herald north
with a warning to Thothmes to expect his arrival in three days'
time, and one to the King explaining his actions. All that day,
while his scribe laboured over the ancient text and a harried
Amunmose shouted imprecations at the servants creating chaos
out of what had been a very fragile order, Huy sat in a corner of
the shady garden and attempted to lay out in his mind everything
he had learned. The Book of Thoth made sense to him at last,
and coupled with the grave procedures of the heb sed festival, the
will of Atum-Ra was finally revealed, not as a pious hope carried
down through the ages and taken for granted by every citizen of
Egypt, but as an unequivocal truth. *Every pharaoh undergoing the
death and resurrection of the heb sed becomes a god. That's why Ma'at
was given to us in the first place,* Huy realized. *That's why adherence
to the harmony of both cosmic and earthly laws she represents is so
vital. Even the King himself must obey them as diligently as every one
of his citizens. He must be worthy of godhead, and we, his subjects,
must give him the same deference Ma'at demands of him. But does
every King merit true godhead? Do the rites of the festival confer transmutation no matter what the character and deeds of royalty may be?
What of the appalling vision granted me regarding the baby Prince?*

Huy groaned softly and Perti, standing guard not far away, glanced towards him. Huy uncrossed his legs, leaned back against the tree sheltering him, and waved at Perti. *If that child grows up to sit on the Horus Throne and repudiates all gods but the Aten, Ma'at will desert us and Egypt will be defenceless,* he thought as Perti turned away. *I've felt the threat ebb and flow over the years. So has Mutemwia. Placing my nephew Ramose among the priests of the Aten's shrine to spy for her signified her concern. But Prince Thothmes is fated to die, and nothing will prevent Prince Amunhotep from becoming the Hawk-in-the-Nest. Nothing, that is, but his death.*

The words were so fraught with horror that Huy pushed them away, deliberately calling his friend's face to mind instead. *I'll be with him and Nasha for the Feast of the Great Manifestation of Osiris on the twenty-second of this month,* he told himself firmly. *There will be good wine and feasting, and the closeness Thothmes and I have always enjoyed, and his son Governor Huy, my namesake, will greet me fondly and be full of local affairs to discuss.* Before the reassuring images he had conjured could fade, he got up and called for a litter. The streets and alleys of Mennofer would be brimming with life and he needed a complete distraction.

He was not sorry to leave the echoing corridors of the old palace. The scroll was returned to Ptah's archivist together with a gift of gold dust for the temple and beer, honey, and almonds for Penbui himself. Perti had officially handed the guarding of the Fine District of Pharaoh back to its permanent soldiers. The rooms Huy and his men had occupied had been emptied and scoured. To Huy, the preparations for departure, grown so familiar to him and his servants through much travel over the years, seemed fraught this time with an entirely uncommon atmosphere of change, *as though,* Huy thought, *we have all been living under a spell, taking the heka into our bodies where it has begun to remake us so that everything we know feels strange.*

At dawn, he stood at the handrail of his barge with Amunmose and Perti as the oarsmen carefully guided the craft into the slowly sinking level of the river. There was no reason why he should feel tired, but all he wanted to do was quickly reach the city he knew and loved and then sink onto the couch in Thothmes' familiar guest room. There was an uncharacteristic ache along his spine, and the knuckles of his left hand throbbed for no reason.

A journey that should have taken a full two days was accomplished in a little over one due to the vigilance of Huy's captain and the efforts of an exhausted crew to keep the craft just within the pull of the central current and free of the shoals hidden close to the western bank. Iunu sat on the river's eastern bank. In the dark small hours of the morning the barge was finally tethered to the sunken mooring poles of Thothmes' watersteps and the ramp was run out. Huy had left his remaining two vessels at Mennofer with the bulk of his staff, and only he, Paneb, Perti, and Kenofer walked towards the two soldiers guarding the entrance to Thothmes' estate. Recognizing him, they both saluted.

"Go quietly up to your master's house and find out if he's awake," Huy said. "If he sleeps, don't allow him to be disturbed— I'll remain on my barge until dawn." Kenofer had been carrying a stool and Huy sank onto it with a secret relief. He himself had been unable to rest as the craft moved steadily north, and now his eyes burned and his back gave him a pang with every movement. He was not sorry at the wait. Slowly he absorbed the well-remembered aura of Thothmes' arouras: the faint, delicate aroma of the flowers Ishat had commanded the gardeners to plant because they bloomed at night, the slightly rank odour rising from the lily-choked ponds and narrow canals channelling water to the vegetable gardens at the rear, and under it all an indefinable scent of grass, palm trunks, and sun-warmed mud brick. The flood was slightly more than two months away from its crest and by then the watersteps and much of the ground around Huy's perch would be drowned, but for now he inhaled his own spate of poignant memories carried to him on the intermittent caress of the soft air.

He would have been happy to sit there dozing for the rest of the night, but before long he saw the pale glow of a lamp draw nearer and a man he did not recognize came to a halt in front of him and bowed. The servant who had been carrying the lamp ahead of him stepped aside.

"Forgive me for speaking first, Great Seer," the man said, "but I have not had the pleasure of serving you before. I am Hay, chief steward in the household of the noble Thothmes."

"Paser is retired? Dead?" Huy glanced into the face above him. *So many administrators look too young to cope with the responsibilities they have assumed,* he thought gloomily, *but the truth is that I'm just too old to remember the weight of accountability I myself used to bear.*

"He died and was beautified several months ago," Hay explained. "My master has been awake for some time and is eager to greet you. Please follow me."

Long before you were born, I could walk this path blindfolded, Huy thought with unaccustomed rancour. *Why would you imagine otherwise? And why am I suddenly filled with this petty resentment so foreign to my nature?* Rising, he obeyed Chief Steward Hay's request.

He sensed rather than saw Nakht's house far off to the left. Thothmes' father had been the Governor of the Heq-at sepat, and at his death Thothmes had inherited the title. Now Thothmes' first-born son Huy lived in his grandfather's house and ruled the district from Iunu, its capital. Nakht, Thothmes' second son, had risen in the army to become commander of the

Division of Ra, and Thothmes' daughter Sahura, married to the
Governor of the wealthy Ament sepat west of the Delta, had
forged a lucrative business in her own right by obtaining royal
permission to share in the profits from the vast natron deposits of
the sepat in exchange for providing the workers with housing,
food, and medical care. She also oversaw the cultivation of
hundreds of grapevines that produced the famous Good Wine of
the Western River. *Ishat, Huy often thought, would be proud of the
accomplishments that have vindicated her own determination to
become literate and her insistence that Sahura be more than an able
household manager.*

At the imposing entrance to Thothmes' home, the doorguard
left his bench to reverence Huy. He had hardly opened the doors
when Thothmes himself came hurrying forward, arms outstretched. "Huy! What a wonderful surprise! Nasha said you'd be
unable to resist the opportunity to visit Iunu again once your task
at Mennofer was over!" Huy's own arms were flung wide and the
two men embraced. Thothmes had always been shorter and more
slender than Huy, but now, holding his dearest friend tightly, Huy
was horrified to feel the jutting bones of Thothmes' spine under
his hands and the outline of ribs against his chest. He was forcibly
reminded of the last time he had greeted Nakht, whose gaunt
body was already ravaged by the wasting disease that had killed
him. Thothmes was barefooted. He was wearing a loose white
sleeping robe. His face, cleansed of all cosmetics, seemed all
jutting cheekbones and deep furrows. As they broke apart, Huy
noticed a slight stoop to Thothmes' narrow shoulders that
brought him a pang of dismay followed at once by a wave of love.

"How long has it been?" he said huskily. "I haven't seen you
since the court moved south to Weset."

Thothmes made a face that instantly returned Huy to their
school days together, and linking arms they moved into the

reception hall. "I've often thought of making the journey," Thothmes said, "but somehow I never did find enough energy to see my house turned upside down and then face those endless miles into desert country."

"I know, and the King would never have released me for anything other than the most pressing emergency. I'm sorry."

"So am I." Thothmes shot him a quizzical look. "Nasha told me why His Majesty finally allowed you to leave Weset. Was it worthwhile, Huy? Is the search over at last?"

"Yes." They had crossed the hall and had come to the foot of the stairs and the passage beside it leading farther into the house. "I need to tell you everything, Thothmes, but I must sleep and eat first."

Thothmes nodded. His brown eyes, still full of the eagerness for life Huy remembered so well, swiftly scrutinized Huy's face. "Hay's been busy preparing for your arrival since your message was delivered. I'm longing to hear the news, Huy, but later. I don't sleep much anymore, but tonight, or rather this morning, I know I'll be able to. Incidentally, I can tell you with great glee that you're showing your age at last, mighty mer kat! I think the gods have finally grown bored with you!"

Smiling, he snapped his fingers at the steward and disappeared into the dimness of the passage. The group scattered to their accommodations. Perti and Paneb shared a room beside Huy's, and a pallet outside Huy's door had been left for Kenofer. As the house settled into the deep hush of the hours before dawn, Huy lay on the familiar couch, drowsily relishing the sense of complete security the city of Iunu and Thothmes' presence had always meant to him. He did his best to stay conscious in order to enjoy the feeling for a little longer, but a profound sleep overtook him and he did not wake until half the morning had gone.

There had always been a sanity to Thothmes' house, compounded, Huy believed, of Ishat's clear-headed honesty, Thothmes' steady kindness, and the blessing of Ra upon a family dedicated to the laws of Ma'at. He felt it most strongly when visiting his friend after a long absence. Today, standing on the slab in the bathhouse while Kenofer scrubbed him with natron, it slowly uncluttered his mind, separating the maelstrom of his emotions from the enormity of the knowledge he had recently gained, so that by the time he lay on one of the benches in the shade outside to be shaved, plucked, and oiled, he was able to order his thoughts calmly.

The noon meal was served in the reception hall, and to Huy's delight Thothmes' sons, Governor Huy and General Nakht, were present. "I couldn't pass up the chance to see you again," the Governor told him. "There aren't many official duties to perform at this time of the year. Of course I'll be busy once the flood's subsided, but until then I can amuse my children and please my wife."

"There's nothing much for a general to do either," his brother remarked, dipping bread into the bowl of garlic-flavoured olive oil on the gilded table by his folded knees. "You're responsible for the distribution of the divisions, mer kat. My soldiers need something to do. Perhaps a little war?" He grinned at Huy before biting into the bread, and in the lift of his mouth his resemblance to his mother Ishat made Huy's heart turn over.

Nasha pointed her spoon at Huy. In her other hand the red liquid in her cup trembled. Over the years her liking for wine had not diminished, and Huy had often marvelled at her body's ability to withstand its long-term effects. Unlike poor Anuket, she was not consumed by the need to seek oblivion in it. Her wit remained as acerbic as ever, and although she was older than Thothmes, she did not look it. Huy had greeted her warmly as he lowered himself to the floor beside her and prepared to eat, noting that her stay with her brother had done her good. Her eyes were clearer and her skin less sallow. Now she was frowning.

"What have you been doing to yourself in Mennofer?" she said sharply. "I've never seen swelling under your eyes before. Did you offend Ptah?"

"I don't think so." Huy's tone was mild. Nasha's concern for him invariably sounded like anger. "I've been reading a great deal, Nasha, that's all."

"Well, you look terrible. Shall we be staying here for long?"

Huy considered. *I should go home. My search has been concluded. Unfortunately, I have no reason to stay in the north.*

"You may stay as long as you like," he replied reluctantly, "but I must return to court once I've talked to you, Thothmes. Their Majesties are waiting for information from me regarding a Seeing I performed before I left. I mustn't keep them in suspense for any longer than is necessary." He wanted to tell Nasha that she would be safer here in Iunu, that once he had unburdened himself to the King and particularly to Tiye his fall from favour could very well be immediate, that the only solution to the problem of the baby Prince he had arrived at so far would mean disaster for him and danger for everyone close to him—but such words could only be spoken in private. Meeting Thothmes' eyes, he read a question there.

Nasha sighed loudly. "I might as well settle in here for a while, and besides, the days when I actually ran your household are over, Huy. You don't really need me. I'll miss my friends in Weset, but I don't fancy a long and uncomfortable journey south just yet." Draining her cup, she held it out to be refilled. Nakht laughed at her, making some caustic remark, and a general babble of conversatin began.

The meal ended happily. Governor Huy and his brother

Nakht took a fond farewell of Huy and left, and Nasha made her way to her own room to sleep the afternoon away. Thothmes beckoned Huy. "Let's go into my office, and someone can bring us something to drink," he said. "I think that what you have to tell me is serious, isn't it, Huy?"

His earnest words and look of concern brought a lump to Huy's throat. *A mer kat can have no friends*, he thought as he followed Thothmes along the passage leading from the reception hall and through to the rear gardens. *He dare not confide in anyone. Therefore I thank the gods for your affection and incorruptibility, my old companion. Without you, my loneliness would be complete. In spite of Anubis's warning I shall tell you everything and ask your advice, because as soon as I describe my vision to Amunhotep and warn him of what must be done, my own future will almost certainly descend into chaos.*

Thothmes turned in at an open door, waited until Huy was inside the room, sent a hovering servant for water and beer, and closed the door firmly. "Now, tell me everything."

So Huy did so, beginning with the discovery of the end of the Book of Thoth, his reading and interpretation of the ancient heb sed rites, and finally, with fear and a secret rebellion, the details of the vision Anubis had shown him. He paused once, when a servant quietly set jugs, cups, and napkins on the desk and then withdrew. Thothmes did not interrupt him. He sat with legs crossed and arms folded, his eyes on Huy's face. Even as Huy spoke, he was thinking how much older and more fragile Thothmes looked in repose. Without the cheerful expressions and gestures that animated him, he resembled his father the last time Huy had seen him, drawing in all his strength to celebrate Thothmes' marriage to Ishat. *Let me die before Thothmes*, he begged to no particular god. *Please don't deprive me of my last true friend.*

After he closed his mouth, there was a long silence unbroken by any sound from the slumbering house. Then Thothmes unfolded his arms and placed them on the desk. "Let me understand this. You believe that the Book together with the rituals of the heb sed actually initiate a magic that indeed transforms a King into a god. He enters the tomb, it becomes a womb, and as he emerges his flesh becomes sacred. Of course, I can accept such a construal. It merely confirms what all of us take for granted. A King and a High Priest are the only people allowed to enter the inner sanctuary of any temple. Each King stands before each god as the embodiment of Egypt herself, and to Egypt as the living personification of each god. I'm glad that you have been allowed to confirm this belief. But what does it have to do with the terrible future you saw when you took the baby Prince's fingers?"

Huy poured himself water, drank it all, refilled his cup, and drained it a second time. His throat was dry and his tongue felt swollen. "If my vision showed me the truth, that child will grow up to destroy Egypt and corrupt the power and sanctity of the Horus Throne," he said roughly. "His brother, the Hawk-in-the-Nest Prince Thothmes, will die. I predicted it. There'll be no one left to wear the Pshent but he. It will be tainted from the moment it's placed on his head. And his body, Thothmes—the vision showed me something very wrong with his body. Everywhere I looked, Isfet. Everything Anubis let me see, Isfet!"

Thothmes sat back. "A harsh judgment, Huy, and perhaps too swift? How can everything in Egypt become so twisted that the whole of the country is in opposition to Ma'at—is Isfet?"

"If the King who represents us to the gods is corrupt, then so is Egypt. He will repudiate every deity but the Aten. He will only worship the Visible Disc. I sensed this danger a long time ago, and so did Queen Mutemwia."

There was another silence, this one fraught with tension.

Thothmes was frowning, his eyes still on Huy's face but his gaze unfocused. Absently he picked up one of the napkins. Huy thought he was about to wipe the sweat from his face, but he unfolded it on the desk and began to smooth it out slowly, obviously unaware that he was doing so. "Is it possible that Anubis showed you a lie? Forgive my presumption, Huy, but you've told me of occasions when what you saw differed from what came to pass—not in the healings you've performed under Anubis's authority, and not in the ultimate fulfillment of fate, but in details that have slightly altered future outcomes. I'm thinking particularly of my mother's death." The thin hands on the white linen were stilled. Thothmes' glance at Huy became direct. "The very first Seeing that took you by surprise when we were still nothing but boys happened when you touched Nasha, remember? You saw a grim destiny for her in the Street of the Basket Sellers—but it was my mother who ended her life under the wheels of a cart in that street. Why?"

"I don't know. I've tried to solve the puzzle many times, to no avail, and Anubis will not help me. Every time it creeps into my mind, I'm filled with doubt. Atum cannot be a deceiver. Neither can Anubis. Therefore something within me causes the distortions." A bleak and all too familiar uneasiness began to creep into his mind, bringing with it an echo of Anubis's voice mingled with the sinister laughter of a hyena. Sitting straight, he forced it away and met Thothmes' brown eyes.

"Is it possible that parts of the vision are false?" Thothmes pressed. "Perhaps the Empress will not be called Goddess, or the city in which you found yourself will turn out to be a future Weset, changed and grown."

"Perhaps," Huy replied unwillingly, "but those changes are not minor aspects of the Seeing. It was so real, Thothmes! All of it!" Abruptly he left the chair and began to pace. "I must negate it, take deliberate aim against its inevitability, conceive a plan that will keep Ma'at safe and Egypt fruitful." He rounded the desk and came up to his friend, leaning over, feeling an uncontrollable grimace of distress contort his features. "It's my fault. I was too ashamed to tell you. The need to test my power resulted in a marriage that set all this in motion, and Anubis warned me that my last opportunity to expunge the worst of my mistakes—my cowardice before the King's grandfather and his father—is now. But I cannot undo what has been done, and only one solution has become apparent to me. If I act on it, I put myself irretrievably beyond a favourable weighing in the Judgment Hall." Stepping away from Thothmes, he lifted the jug of beer and upended it directly into his mouth. "I think I'm damned, Thothmes," he finished, setting the jug back on the desk and slumping into his chair. "Have you any advice for me?"

"I dare not presume to do any such thing," Thothmes said huskily. "All I can do is urge you to pray, and I will also. Would it help you to go to Khenti-kheti's temple at Hut-herib and fast and live in his outer court until he gives you an answer? Or appeal to Ra under whose shelter we spent our school days?"

"Perhaps, but I don't believe so. The coming disaster is mine to avert. The gods know that I alone created it. They will not help me."

"But Huy, there has to be a way out other than a deliberate crime against Ma'at! No god would allow any of us to be backed into a corner from which there is no escape!" He raised his hands stiffly before him as though he could push the whole matter away with his strength.

"You don't ask me the nature of the solution eating at my mind." Huy looked down at his own open palms. "I don't need to tell you, do I? What else would prevent me from acceptance into the Beautiful West? I'm so angry, Thothmes. At Anubis and his arrogance, at my own hubris, at Imhotep for hiding the consequences of my decision to read the Book when I was too young to understand what I was doing. I should have refused the offer and stayed dead!"

Thothmes did not respond. He closed his eyes. A tense quiet fell, during which Huy struggled against a rush of self-pity. The ache in his back had intensified, and all he wanted was to be lying face down on a massage bench with the coolness of scented oil spreading over his skin and his body servant's firm touch. When Thothmes spoke, it was in a thin whisper. "The heb sed metamorphoses a King's mortality into divinity, Huy," he murmured. "Body, ka, khu-spirit, bau, shadow, everything—all the seven parts making up our being, including that of every pharaoh—transformed, every corruption invisibly cleansed away. A god need not worry about damnation."

Huy stared at him. "You're suggesting that I use the heka of the heb sed myself so that I may be recognized as a god? It would be the ultimate act of sacrilege." Horrified, he found himself near to tears. "I can't do it, Thothmes," he said thickly. "I mustn't even think about it. Imhotep came to be worshipped after many hentis because he heard and answered the prayers of those who asked for his help. He earned the godhead bestowed on him. How could I ever achieve such majesty?"

"Many believe you already have," Thothmes said coolly. "You've brought healing to dozens through your gift of Scrying. You've comforted many more by giving them a glimpse into their futures when all seemed dark to them, my darling Ishat included. As mer kat, your policies both within Egypt and throughout the empire have resulted in wealth and justice and peace. You have no idea how truly great you are, do you, Huy? Will the removal of one threat to the future of this country negate every good you've done in the eyes of the gods? I don't think so."

Huy got up with difficulty. His knees felt stiff and obstinate. "Murder, Thothmes. The murder of a child. There—I've said it. What will all my achievements mean against that, when my heart is placed on Ma'at's scales? I love you for daring to make the proposition you did, but it's something I must not even idly contemplate." He walked to the door. "Now I need my drug and a long sleep before the evening meal. Thank you for sharing my load, dear friend."

Thothmes left his chair and, coming up to Huy, hugged him briefly. "Let's hope you're able to put the matter to Amunhotep in a way he can understand. Whatever happens, you have a home here in Iunu with us. We'll eat together later." Rapping sharply on the door, he waited until it opened and then went out, Huy behind him.

Reaching the flight of stairs leading to his quarters, Huy paused and glanced up. The number of steps suddenly seemed formidable. Sighing, he began to climb.

He stayed with Thothmes for a further three days before deciding to return to Weset. With the river gradually sinking, the flow of scrolls from the officials under him had begun to ebb. He could have travelled north to Hut-herib and spent some time in Khenti-kheti's temple and a night or two on the little estate close to the town where he and Ishat had once lived. He had kept it because he loved it. The memories he had made there, both happy and sad, no longer troubled his emotions. He knew that he could sleep well and safely in his old bedchamber, but the servants with whom he and Ishat had shared those years were either dead or in retirement, and the house and garden were being cared for by a couple he had never met. For the first time those inevitable changes reminded him of his age. He had not cared about such a thing before. His many years were not evident in his body, nor had they dimmed his eyesight or deafened him. But all at once, in the space of a few days, his fingers and his spine had woken him to the fact that he was about to turn sixty-five.

On his last morning in Thothmes' house, he was sitting on the low stool in his bedchamber, already dressed and kohled against the sun, so that Kenofer could comb and braid his long hair. Nasha was with him, still enveloped in a rumpled white sleeping robe, sipping from a large cup of purple grape juice and walking to and fro while they talked amicably together. Kenofer's ministrations were no more than a familiar background to their conversation until the body servant exclaimed softly and Huy could no longer feel the comb on his scalp. He looked up. "Is something wrong, Kenofer?"

"No, I suppose not, Master," Kenofer replied slowly. "It's just that I've never seen a grey hair on your head before. Now there are several where there were none yesterday."

Nasha came close. "He's right, Huy," she said after a moment. "Three of them by your right temple. It's about time! You can begin to henna them like the rest of us if you wish. Here." She picked up the copper mirror on his cosmetics table and held it out. "See them for yourself."

"No, thank you. Make the braids, Kenofer, and then finish packing my belongings. We have a long, hot journey before us." Nasha replaced the mirror and wandered out into the passage and Kenofer began to separate Huy's thick tresses. *Three grey hairs,* Huy said to himself. *So I have almost completed the tasks Atum assigned to me and now he doesn't need me anymore. I have been his tool since the age of twelve. Will he allow me an easy slide into death when I have discharged my last obligation? And what of the hyena? Will it become an agent of retribution against me because of what I am condemned to do?*

Kenofer's knuckles brushed the nape of his neck and he almost cried out. "Master, your skin is very cold," Kenofer said. "Perhaps you should consult the noble Thothmes' physician before leaving Iunu." Huy shook his head mutely. Kenofer obviously knew better than to press the issue. He too fell silent.

Huy sent a message to Under Steward Paroi that he was returning to Mennofer and to ready the remaining two barges, one scroll to the King with the news that he had begun to wend his way back to Weset on the river, and one to warn his staff on his Weset estate. Then he ate a hurried meal with his friends. Thothmes asked him diffidently if he would like to visit Ishat's tomb and pray there before he left. Huy declined.

"I have no doubt that she has attained the Beautiful West," he replied harshly. "She has no need of my petitions to the gods on her behalf. Nor will she ever become a vengeful ghost that must be propitiated with prayers and offerings. She waits for you, Thothmes. It's your voice she longs to hear now. Besides," he went on more quietly, "I hope to visit you again before I must stand outside the tomb where she lies and watch you being carried inside it also."

"So you plan to outlive me, do you?" Thothmes laughed at these words he had intended as a mild joke.

Huy smiled thinly. "Believe me, I beg the gods to send me into the Judgment Hall before you or Nasha so that I won't have to suffer your loss, but I strongly suspect that my selfish desire will remain unfulfilled."

He deliberately began to speak of Thothmes' children. The talk became light again, but later, standing at the foot of his ramp while the barge rocked behind him, he pulled Thothmes' small body against his own and held him tightly. For many moments they clung together. Then Thothmes stepped away.

"I know, Huy, I know," he said. "We share the same thought, but I don't want it expressed aloud. If you're forced to flee from Weset, come here, but I have the oddest feeling that the King will understand everything you must say to him. May the soles of your feet be firm. I have always loved you."

"And I you, Thothmes. Don't stay out here in the sun."

Both of them knew that this was a final goodbye. Huy kissed Nasha, walked along the ramp, and, crossing the deck, went straight into the cabin. He did not look back.

Although the southward journey against the current took far longer than the journey north with it, it was still not as long as a trek on the edge of the water would have been. Once deprived of Thothmes' company, Huy's thoughts began to revolve once more around the coming interview with the man who called him Uncle, and he found himself unable to control them. Even when he managed to wrest his mind free, the image of a hyena took their place, so that between dread and repulsion he was tormented. When he slept, his dreams were nighmarish. The world around him during the day—great sheets of murky water, the tops of drowned palm trees, villages baking in a heat that seemed to contain an evil sentience—took on an aura of hostile otherworldliness that distressed him almost as much as the visions haunting him at night. For the first time in years, he requested larger doses of poppy than usual from Kenofer. The drug pained his stomach and took away his appetite, but at least it allowed him more pleasant dreams when asleep and a welcome disconnection from reality when awake. He was surprised—he had not really expected any relief from his dismal state. Normally all the poppy could do was marginally reduce the ache in his head after a Seeing and dull the stabs of anxiety that plagued him almost daily when faced with the load of crushing responsibilities thrust upon him at Weset. Kenofer cautioned him that the supply might run out before he reached home, but Huy pointed out that there were physicians at almost every town along the river and obtaining more would not be difficult. *Atum is doing this*, Huy told himself as he sat on the deck beneath a canopy, his back against the cabin's wall and a flagon of water to hand. *He is returning me to the early days, before I became inured. He is preparing me for what I must do.* The thought was no comfort, but at least, under the continuing influence of the poppy, it did not distress him.

The barges reached Weset on the first day of Mesore. The river was at its lowest. Huy barely glanced at his naked poppy fields as the litter-bearers carried him home. With a mixture of reluctance and pleasure he leaned out to see the whitewashed walls of his house gleaming in the sunlight. Before the litter was set down, Paroi was bowing and offering his hand. Huy took it, and stood.

"Well, Paroi, coming home is a fine thing," he said. "Obviously my message arrived safely."

"Welcome back, Master." Paroi's eyes quickly scanned Huy's face. "Yes, we've been expecting you. So has His Majesty. There's a scroll from the palace as well as several from the various ministries. I opened only the one from Chief Royal Scribe Mahu. Will you eat while your belongings are unloaded and unpacked?"

Huy could see that the man wanted to say more but was tactfully biting back the words. Huy said them for him. "It has been a difficult few months, full of worries and surprises, and I'm very tired. I'll eat in my office, Paroi. Send me Paneb when he arrives and tell Kenofer I'll want to get onto my couch as soon as possible."

Paroi nodded. "Shall I send for Royal Physician Seneb?"

"No. Have hot water ready for me in the bathhouse after Paneb and I have glanced at the letters." The steward bowed and left and Huy made his way slowly to his office. The room was blessedly cool and smelled faintly of new papyrus and the scent of lilies. Huy saw Amunhotep's seal on the top of a large pile of scrolls on the desk and unwillingly unrolled the papyrus. "To my dear Uncle and revered mer kat, greetings on your return," he read. "I look forward to hearing all your news, but first I eagerly anticipate a disclosure of the contents of the Seeing you performed for Prince Amunhotep. I expect to receive you the day after you have read this. Thus I give you time to recover from your journey. Dictated to Chief Royal Scribe Mahu and signed by myself."

Huy did not bother with the King's long list of titles. Pushing the scroll aside, he sat back in his chair, folding his arms and staring at the wall opposite with its niches full of scrolls. He could hear the arrival of the men with whom he had travelled and the servants who were handling his boxes. Laughter and commands blended with thumps and thuds. *They're happy to be home*, Huy thought, then dismissed the cheerful bustle from his mind. *I must go to the palace early tomorrow morning*, he mused while he felt his heart turn over in trepidation. *I don't want to face a drunken Amunhotep.*

Paroi knocked and entered with a tray. Absently Huy pushed the correspondence aside. Paroi set the food on the desk, bowed, and withdrew. The sight of roasted gazelle meat, steaming lentil stew, and dried fruit turned Huy's stomach, but he forced himself to eat and to drink the barley beer. *I won't send word that I'm back*, he decided, stirring the lentils round and round, not really aware of what he was doing. *I particularly don't want the Empress warned. If Atum wills it, she'll be sitting in the reception hall dealing with the business of the day and then hearing petitions. I must convince Amunhotep of the seriousness of the matter before Tiye appears, even if he reacts with incredulity. Atum help me! Tiye will want me torn limb from limb.*

Another knock heralded Paneb's arrival. He bowed, settled himself cross-legged on the floor, arranged his utensils, and Huy quickly began to sift through the messages looking for seals from the most important ministries, pushing his apprehension away with great effort. He had eaten the stew and half the dried fruit, but he could not face the gazelle's cold flesh.

By the time he and Paneb had dealt with the scrolls and Paneb had taken them away to be delivered to Chief Herald Ba-en-Ra, Huy was exhausted, more from the thought of what awaited him the following day than from the task he had completed. Leaving the office, he went along the passage outside to the bathhouse, where Kenofer was keeping the water hot. Later, washed and oiled, he took the stairs to his bedchamber, Kenofer behind him. Walking in, Huy went straight to the invitation of fresh white linen on his couch, shedding the sheet Kenofer had draped around him. The window covering had been lowered and hazy sunlight lay across the floor in bands of muted light between the thin shadows of the reed slats. Huy sat, swung his legs up onto the couch, and was about to lie down when he caught movement in the corner beside his shrine to Khenti-kheti. He froze.

A hyena was sitting on its haunches and staring at him, and even as he realized what he was seeing, its musty, pungent odour filled his nostrils. Opening its mouth, it yawned then licked its lips with a black tongue, but this was not the hyena Huy had seen drowsing against Imhotep in the Beautiful West. That creature had regarded him with mild golden eyes; this beast's eyes were black, like its tongue. But that made no sense either, Huy knew, because hyenas inhabiting the desert and seeking offal in the fields and villages had pink tongues.

"Master, what's wrong?" Kenofer said, but Huy hardly heard him. The hyena took two steps forward into one of the strips of sunlight and with horror Huy saw that it had no markings—its hide was as black at its eyes. Pausing, it settled onto its haunches again and went on considering him. After the first shock of seeing it, Huy realized that he was not overly surprised by its presence. He had been free of it for weeks, but now he was back in Weset and the gods were watching.

"Kenofer, do you see anything out of place here? Smell anything?" he asked without much hope.

The man examined the room with a practised eye, took several deep breaths, then shook his head. The beast did not stir. "No, Master, all is as it should be," Kenofer answered. "Do you see something amiss?"

Huy's mouth had gone dry. "It doesn't matter," he managed. "Go and sleep. I'll call if I need you." Once alone, Huy regarded the hyena more calmly. He read no menace in its stance or in the sooty eyes fixed so steadily on him. It came no nearer. After a while Huy lay down on his side, facing it. It still did not stir. "I don't know what you want," he whispered. "Has Ma'at sent you from the depths of the Judgment Hall to lead me to an ultimate destruction, or do you come from the Beautiful West with a message for me that I am unable to understand? I have the oddest feeling that I know you."

There was no response, just that steady regard, and after a while Huy began to relax. He closed his eyes, opening them again to see if the hyena had come any closer, but it had remained where it was, although the light no longer limned it. With a moment of astonishment at his ability to do so, Huy went to sleep.

16

HE SLEPT FITFULLY THAT NIGHT, waking often to peer into the shrouded room until he could see the outline of the hyena, a blacker shape amongst the thick shadows. He spent the hour before dawn lying on his back, alert for any animal sound, drawing that fetid odour into his lungs and willing himself to remain calm. As soon as he could see the details of the scene painted on his ceiling, he forced himself to leave the couch and raise the window hanging. The pink of an early sunrise washed over and past him and he turned into the newly lit space, praying that it might be empty. The hyena's head had followed his movements and Huy found himself staring straight into eyes so glossy that he believed he was able to see himself reflected in them. He stood still for some time, senses straining to detect any hint of malice coming from the beast, but its gaze remained politely neutral. Only when he dared to walk right up to it did it move, rising clumsily on all fours so that its ugly hindquarters appeared, and opening its black mouth to snarl at him. The snarl became a growl as he stubbornly bent to touch it. Black lips lifted away from black, moist teeth, and then it laughed at him, a series of highly pitched warning barks. Its hackles rose. Repulsed and wary, Huy stepped away.

Outside the door, Kenofer was snoring on his pallet and the guard at the end of the passage gave Huy a short nod. Obviously neither of them had heard any sound. Gently, Huy pressed Kenofer's shoulder and the body servant was fully alert at once. "I must go to the palace," Huy said. "If Amunmose hasn't ordered hot water for the bathhouse yet, you'll have to see to it yourself. Also, I want to wear a blue kilt and shirt today. Do I have these?"

Kenofer was on his feet and listening carefully. "Master, you want to wear mourning clothes?" he responded doubtfully. "Has there been a death in the palace?"

"No. I won't be wearing any jewellery, and my usual sandals will be fine. Bring me my dose of poppy before you do anything else." Kenofer had already wrapped yesterday's kilt around himself and was slipping into his reed sandals. Huy returned to his couch, sitting on its edge and meeting the hyena's stare. "I will not let you unnerve me," he said. "Anubis refuses to tell me why you have begun to haunt me, or even who sent you. I cannot let you pre-occupy my mind today. I must open my shrine. Move back." He did not expect a reaction, but the hyena got up and shambled to the far corner, settling down where a shadow still hung. *I can learn to ignore you,* Huy went on silently as he opened Khenti-kheti's shrine and bowed to the totem of his birth sepat. *I can learn to stop asking questions about you. I can make you as anonymous and disregarded as the tiles under my feet.* He knelt and prostrated himself before the god, reminding Khenti-kheti of the devotion he had shown in the design and ongoing construction of the new temple at Hut-herib and begging him for his help when he faced the King. He prayed to Amun also, speaking of the blasphemy he had seen in his vision. He tried to maintain a proper attitude of worship, but his thoughts kept slipping out of his control to circle the moment when he must open his mouth and probably destroy himself.

As he got up from the floor and stepped forward to close the doors of the shrine, Kenofer entered with the poppy. "One of the kitchen staff is tending the fire for the water," he said as Huy drained the vial. "I'm sorry that you must wait, but it's still very early." He took the empty vial, set it on the table beside the couch, and began to empty one of Huy's chests in search of the blue linen.

Huy glanced into the corner. Two black eyes glittered back at him. Deliberately, he turned his back on them.

Within the hour he was bathed, kohled, and dressed, and Kenofer had woven his hair into one long braid that hung along his spine and bumped lightly against the small of his back. The man had brought food—bread, goat's cheese, and milk and water—and although Huy drank, his stomach revolted against anything solid. In one lunatic moment he tore off a piece of the flatbread intending to toss it at the hyena, but common sense reasserted itself and, half ashamed, he returned the portion to the tray.

Going downstairs to the reception hall, he was about to summon Perti and his soldiers as an escort when he decided against any show of force. *There must be no suggestion of violence, no reason for the King to even imagine a threat.* Sending for his scribe, he waited just inside the cedar doors that gave out onto his vast arouras. He felt numb inside and out thanks to the poppy. His thoughts had slowed and calmed so that by the time Paneb came gliding up to him, palette under his arm, and together they went out into the early sunlight, he had begun to plan what he would say. Paneb had glanced swiftly at his attire and then away, keeping the obvious question to himself as a good servant should, and Huy did not enlighten him. Paneb had recorded the Seeing in the baby Prince's nursery and had made two copies of it, one for the King and the other for Huy's archives. He knew its details as well as Huy did.

They were carried in separate litters through the dusty poppy fields, along the bank of the sunken river, and into the palace compound. Huy needed to be alone and undistracted. He missed the comfort of Perti's presence and felt naked without a barrier of soldiers between himself and Weset's citizens, but he knew that he had made the right decision in leaving them behind in spite of Perti's vehement insistence to the contrary.

At the southern gate of the outer wall, his bearers were stopped. Huy pushed the litter's curtain aside to see Commander-in-Chief Wesersatet coming towards him. At the sight of Huy's face the man broke into a smile. He bowed. "Mer kat, your message from Mennofer took us all by surprise! You were not expected back so soon! I trust your business there was concluded successfully?"

Huy nodded, returning the smile. "It was. I'm happy to see you, Wesersatet, but I'm in a hurry to speak to the King. Is His Majesty still in his private quarters?" He asked without much hope of an answer. It was not necessary for a commander to be in the royal presence unless summoned. To Huy's surprise, Wesersatet replied immediately.

"The King has already left his couch in favour of a chair, but when I left him he was in no hurry to be bathed. He seldom rises so early, but I had requested a private audience with him before I began my duties for the day. I'm retiring, Huy."

"What? No, you can't!" Huy protested. "You'll thoroughly demoralize every division in the army! There'll be soldiers weeping in the streets! Who will replace you?" He was joking, but it was true that the men of Egypt's army loved him. *Another link with my past is being severed,* Huy thought sadly beneath the forced humour. *Wesersatet deserves to leave the court on a tide of gifts and adulation, but I dread the time when every face in the palace is strange to me.*

Wesersatet laughed. "You give me too much credit. I'll miss the hours we spent together here in your office, devising the military strategies that have played their part in the creation of Egypt's empire. We did well, didn't we? I've recommended to His Majety that Navy Commander Nebenkempt take my place as Chief Commander, or rather, I recommended him to the Queen, who sits in audience every morning. I think you know him well, as your older nephew's father-in-law."

"A good choice. But I'll miss you very much. Enjoy a long and peaceful retirement, Commander."

He was about to signal the bearers to go through the now open gate, but Wesersatet put his mouth to Huy's ear. "The King is suffering from a hangover and will want to spend the rest of the morning lying on his couch in order to recover from that and the annoyance of having to personally grant me permission to go home instead of being able to leave the matter to Tiye. I just thought I'd warn you." Withdrawing, he bowed and strode away, and Huy and Paneb entered the palace precincts.

Leaving the litter-bearers under the shade of the many trees dotting the area between the outer wall and the sprawling buildings, they sought admittance through a side door, where Huy sent one of the palace heralds to ask if the King would see him. The man returned quickly. "His Majesty is very eager to receive you, mer kat. His Majesty is in his bedchamber. Shall I call a house servant to escort you?"

"Thank you, but I know the way. Is the Empress with him?"

"Not yet. She is hearing the petitions at present."

I hope she'll go from there to the administrative offices, Huy prayed as he and Paneb moved into the labyrinth of intersecting passages. *That's what we used to do.* As he walked through the palace, the noise and laughter of the groups of courtiers already congregating at every intersection died away at his approach. Heads were bowed and arms outstretched in reverence. A few of them made sure that their fingers brushed him. *As if by merely touching me they might be healed or given a glimpse of their future*, Huy thought as he passed them. Thothmes' comments regarding Huy's titular godhead came to mind and were quickly dismissed. The wide, statue-lined corridor leading to Amunhotep's imposing double doors was directly ahead, and the King's personal bodyguard stood with Chief Steward Nubti, watching Huy and Paneb approach. Nubti rose with his usual misshapen grace. Reverencing Huy with a smile, he opened the door behind him, and Huy and Paneb waited, listening to his deep voice announce them. He waved them in.

At once they knelt and performed a full prostration. Huy, with his nose to the floor, could smell a faint trace of Tiye's perfume, her odd blend of cardamom and myrrh. *Has she spent the night here*, he wondered, *or was she here a short time ago? If so, she may not return and my luck will continue to hold.* Amunhotep's happy voice bade them stand and approach and they did so, bowing again as they came up to him. He was relaxing in the wide chair beside his couch, swathed to his ankles in crumpled linen, a white cap on his head and his face unpainted. He was beaming at Huy, and for a moment Huy was returned to his office at Hut-herib, where his precious royal charge sat behind his desk with the plans for constructing a ship under his hands, his brown face lifted to Huy's with a question. Free of cosmetics he was simply an older version of that impatient child, all innocence and anticipation, and Huy's heart filled with love for him as Amunhotep left his seat and threw his arms around Huy.

"Uncle, this is a great and welcome surprise!" he said as he released Huy and returned to his chair. "I was grumbling at Wesersatet for making me leave my couch so early, but now I'm overjoyed! Your presence has cured the pain in my head! Why didn't you send me word that you had come home? Sit. Sit!"

"I needed to rest before approaching you," Huy replied, "and if

Your Majesty doesn't mind, I'd rather stand for now." He repressed an urge to reach down and stroke the King's soft cheek. "It's good to see you also, Amunhotep."

Some of the cheerfulness went out of the younger man's brown eyes. "You want to be serious. True to your word, you bring me the vision of my little Prince's future now that matters in Mennofer have been concluded. I'm anxious to hear it, particularly since for once the gods did not predict an early death for him, but you come to me unadorned and wearing blue. Not all the events in the Seeing are good, are they? I think that the Empress must hear it too." He beckoned Nubti. Huy noted that Amunhotep had not asked for the results of his visit to Ptah's temple. Hastily he put out a hand.

"Please, Majesty, not yet," he said. "What I have to say is for you alone at present."

Amunhotep sobered. "I have no secrets from Tiye. You are my right hand, Uncle, and she is my left. I insist on her presence. Nubti, bring me wine."

The chief steward came forward quickly. "But Your Majesty, you have eaten no food yet this morning. Wine on an empty stomach will simply give you another headache, and you had planned to hunt later today."

Amunhotep flicked his fingers, a gesture of irritable dismissal. "You do not exist in order to mother me! Do as I order you. Stop trying to catch my uncle's eye, and don't frown. It makes you look like a cat about to vomit." Nubti bowed and went out.

The time when Huy might have corrected the King's rudeness was long gone. He waited in silence, Paneb behind him. The King began to drum his fingers on the gilded arm of his chair. A line of sweat had broken out across his forehead, darkening the band of his cap and sending a whiff of sour rosemary oil into the air. "If the Seeing had been full of promise, you would have told us all of it before you left Weset," he ventured after a while. "You assured us that my second son will not die in his youth, therefore Anubis showed you some other form of anguish, something terrible."

"Yes."

"Then I shall drink before I allow you to speak, mer kat, and Tiye must definitely hear what Atum showed you."

"But Amunhotep—"

"No buts, Uncle. The boy was spawned from her body. Already she adores him and spends every afternoon in his nursery. He is completely healthy and suckles well. Amulets of protection surround him—"

Huy cut in, leaning towards him. "Majesty, he needs no protection against any Khatyu. No god wishes to unleash a force of demons against him—not yet."

"Not yet? What does that mean? Senu!" he shouted. "Are you outside my door?"

At once the Chief Palace Herald appeared and sketched a bow. "Majesty?"

"Find the Empress, somewhere in the administrative quarter. She's to come here at once. Escort her."

Senu kept his expression bland, but Huy saw astonishment flit swiftly across his features. *Amunhotep doesn't often issue orders to Tiye,* Huy reflected, *and I wager she will be annoyed at both the summons and the interruption.* Senu bobbed a reverence and went away, closing the door behind him, but it was reopened by a young man Huy did not know, a silver tray bearing a large flagon, a golden cup, and a dish of sweetmeats held ceremoniously before him.

"I don't need a tedious repetition of the vintage, Tiawi," Amunhotep said irritably, "and you can take the almond cakes away. I'm not hungry. Just pour and leave."

Unperturbed, the man did as he was bidden, his movements fraught with solemnity, then turned to bow to Huy. "I am Royal Cup Bearer of Wine Si-Renenut, mer kat, recently appointed to the service of His Majesty. His Majesty and the members of my family call me Tiawi. May I fetch a cup for you also?"

"It would do the Seer no good unless it was laced with lotus flowers, Tiawi," the King interposed.

Tiawi bowed again. "Unfortunately, the shipment of grape wine that arrived yesterday has not yet been opened," he explained. "Therefore I have not tasted it nor set aside the required amount for the inclusion of the lotus. However, there are plenty of juices stored beside the kitchens."

Huy would have liked a cup of pomegranate juice. His mother and the family's one servant, Hapzefa, used to make it after every harvest and the taste would have brought back to him the security and peace of his earliest years at Hut-herib. But Amunhotep waved Tiawi away. "Thank you, Tiawi," he snapped. "You may go."

Tiawi managed to include Huy in his bow. Then, tray in hand, he backed away, bowed once more, and went out.

"I have four wine and beer bearers now," Amunhotep said. "Tiye complains that I'm getting fatter because of the amount I drink, but as long as I'm able to hunt and satisfy my women, why should I care? Egypt is in more capable hands than mine anyway. You and she took over the government years ago." He raised the cup and took a mouthful of wine.

"Your mother and I raised you to govern, not Tiye," Huy reminded him sharply. "As for me, I would like nothing better than to pass the reins of Egypt's control back to you and spend my time with Thothmes and Nasha, or overseeing the progress of the tomb you have graciously allowed me to place between those of your mighty forebears the Osiris-ones Thothmes the First and the Second of that name, or choosing the final decorations for my totem's new temple. Why are you suddenly so peevish, Majesty?"

Amunhotep smiled faintly over the rim of his cup. Huy could see that he was doing his best to regain his good humour. "I don't know, Uncle," he admitted ruefully. "I want to be bathed and dressed and then visit my stables. I ought to be more than eager to learn the details of the Seeing now that I've waited for months, but if something appalling waits to overtake the Prince years from now, why do I need to concern myself with it today?"

Huy was saved from answering. The doors were flung back and Tiye swept into the room followed by her body servant Heria, carrying her spare sandals, whisk, and cosmetic box, Chief Palace Herald Senu, Tiye's steward, the King's steward Nubti, and a couple of palace guards. The room was suddenly full of bowed heads.

"Senu, you should have told me that the Seer was here," Tiye said as she passed Huy without acknowledging his obeisance and settled herself into the vacant chair next to her husband. "Nubti, bring me a footrest and another cup—I might as well refresh myself. Chief Treasurer Sobekhmose and I have been talking together ever since I left the audience chamber and my throat is dry." Coolly her eyes met Huy's. She was wearing a sheath of pale green that emphasized the red lights in her loose hair. Her jewellery, from the circlet on her brow to the anklets on her half-hidden feet, was made of gold unrelieved by any embellishment. Even the rings on each of her fingers were bereft of any stone, the patterns on them etched into the metal. Huy thought that she looked magnificent and powerful, the impression of self-assurance evident in her heavily lidded eyes and the cruel downward turn of her hennaed mouth. Still in her mid-twenties, she exuded the authority of complete competence.

We worked so well together, you and I, in the days when we argued ourselves and the various ministers into policies from which grew the empire Egypt now controls, he said to her mutely. *I wish that we had remained friends.*

Nubti was approaching with a small footrest, which he set on the floor in front of her, and another cup. Half filling it with wine, he bowed and retreated.

Tiye swung her feet onto the footrest, took a mouthful of wine, and set the cup down loudly on the table between herself and Amunhotep. "Well?" she said sharply to Huy. "The gods know I've waited quite long enough for this revelation. What did Anubis show to you in the matter of the Prince's future?"

She glanced at Paneb as though uninterested in him, but a brief twist of what Huy could only interpret as jealousy marred her face. *The lowly scribe Paneb already knows what you do not*, Huy thought.

Amunhotep raised his voice. "Leave us, all of you. Wait in the passage. Nubti, Seer Huy will come for you when we have finished." Obediently they all bowed themselves out. The double doors closed behind them and Amunhotep's attention returned to Huy. He reached across the small table to grasp Tiye's hand. "You look pale, Uncle," he said kindly to Huy. "Perhaps you should sit after all."

A sudden weakness was beginning to make Huy's knees tremble. Dragging a stool from Amunhotep's cosmetics table, he placed it before them and sank onto it gratefully.

"Now, Uncle, tell us everything. You wear blue in order to warn us, don't you?" Huy saw him tighten his hold on Tiye, whose gaze was already fixed coldly on Huy's face.

At Huy's signal Paneb went to the floor and prepared to record the proceedings. He had not been ordered to leave with the other servants. *I want an accurate account of everything said today, and so does Amunhotep,* Huy decided. *He's not as obtuse as he would like his courtiers to think.* Clearing his throat, trying not to clench his fists, Huy began.

He spoke of the strange city in which he had found himself, the malformed body of the King who stood with several women and girls above the crowd, the awarding of the Gold of Favours, the distressing answers to Huy's questions given by Anubis in the guise of the anonymous man beside him. He spoke of temples left empty, priests turned out to wander begging from village to village, the gods' storehouses cleared of gold and grain that went into the silos of the Aten and its worshippers at Akhet-Aten while the rest of Egypt starved. Paneb's brush remained poised over the papyrus on his palette as Huy repeated the details of the vision already copied and filed away. As Huy went on, Amunhotep sat frozen, oblivious to the wine cup resting on his thigh or Tiye's fingers curled tightly around his own. Tiye's eyes stayed fixed on Huy. He was able to read nothing in them. At his first words a dull red had flushed her cheeks, fading almost at once to a patchy sallowness, and her features had gone blank, but he could see the gradual tensing of the rest of her body.

Today I am atoning for the loss of courage I displayed before the Osiris-one Amunhotep the Second, he thought as his bleak words filled the room. *I am discharging my debt to you, Ma'at, and to you, mighty Atum. If the hyena is haunting me because of that perfidy, dismiss it, I beg you, and let me live out the remainder of my days in peace!*

When there was nothing left to say, no detail overlooked, he closed his mouth. A deep silence descended. Neither the King nor Tiye moved, and Huy, free at last from an oppressive burden, felt a tide of giddy elation spread out from his dry throat and surge along his limbs, leaving them limp with relief. Out of the corner of his eye he saw Paneb dip his brush into the ink and hold it ready, but still the pair were motionless. A low murmur of conversation from the group of servants waiting outside the door came drifting faintly through the wood. The odour of Tiye's perfume mingled with the King's sweat. The blend seemed to intensify, hanging both acrid and unpleasantly magnetic in the still air. Finally Huy left the stool, and at his movement Amunhotep let go his grip on his wife's fingers, unsteadily set the cup he had been holding on the table, and bent forward. When he spoke, his voice was reedy.

"Let me be sure I understand," he said. "You are telling me that my son will grow up to be physically deformed, inherit the Horus Throne, blaspheme against every one of Egypt's deities but the Visible Disc, and desert Amun's home for a new city? This is the future Anubis showed you?"

"Yes, Majesty."

"I will have no more legitimate sons besides Prince Thothmes, who is already destined to die, and my princely namesake, who will deliberately destroy everything precious in this country and leave us at the mercy of famine and disease?"

"Yes, Majesty. Since the day when Anubis showed me these things, when I took the baby's hand in my own, I have been overwhelmed by what I saw and heard."

"He will render Amun powerless?" The King looked increasingly puzzled, as though confused by Huy's words and yet impelled to contradict their clarity.

Huy was about to reply when Tiye loudly slapped one hennaed palm on the surface of the table and sprang to her feet. "It's a lie! All a lie!" she said through gritted teeth. "You gave this ... this peasant more power to rule than anyone else in the realm, ignoring the years of faithful service my older brother Ay devoted to you, and my parents to your father before that! Anen, my younger brother, still wears the simple robes of a priest although he should be here at court where his talents would not be wasted. As for myself ..." She faced her husband, placing both hands on the table and inclining stiff-armed towards him. "As for myself, my competence to govern Egypt is only required when the Son of Hapu is away on some errand of his own. This so-called vision is nothing but a ploy to make sure that every fully royal son dies. Then you will be forced to name one of the male bastards born to any one of your harem women as the Horus-in-the-Nest and grant him legitimization by marrying him to one of our daughters. And you may be sure that the boy will be chosen by Huy himself!"

Huy knelt, holding his arms out palms up in the universal gesture of submission. "Not only will he render Amun powerless, he will send masons throughout Egypt to obliterate the names of every god but the Aten," he said clearly and deliberately to Amunhotep, forcing the King to hold his gaze. "In removing the name of Amun, he not only commits the gravest blasphemy against Egypt's saviour, he annihilates you also. You are the Incarnation of Amun. Your name contains the name of the god, but if it is excised, your ka will be lost."

"This is not to be believed." Amunhotep shook his head and slumped back in his chair. "What have I done to deserve such a fate? What evil has Egypt done, that Ma'at should desert her? No, Uncle. Your vision must be false, and if not false, then you have misinterpreted what you saw."

"What a kind assumption you make, my husband!" Tiye broke in sarcastically. She folded her arms and, brushing past Huy, began to pace. He was no longer able to read her expression. "How generous you are! 'Misinterpreted'? What proof have we that our trusty mer kat was granted any vision at all? Only his word and the word of his scribe, who will of course swear on behalf of his master."

Amunhotep ignored her. "I have known you all my life, Huy," he said quietly, "and indeed when I was still a baby in my mother's arms with no claim to the Horus Throne you saw me bathed in royal gold. Through the years you have served and protected me, and worked tirelessly to give me an empire. You've grieved with me at the deaths of my children, deaths predicted by your visions. It was very hard for you to tell me that my beloved Prince Thothmes would not outlive me. Now you confess a future for me and my country more terrible than I could ever have imagined." His voice faltered. Lifting his cup from the table, he drank deeply, wiping his mouth on the sleeve of his shift. "Without the history of many accurate Seeings behind you, I might agree with the Empress," he continued. "As it is, we must discover how this future might be averted. Get up! And you, Tiye, such outbursts do no good. You hate Huy for matters beyond his control."

On the contrary, you hate me for everything within my control, Huy thought as he regained the stool and watched her return to perch rigidly on the edge of her chair.

"There are many feast days for Osiris this month," Amunhotep went on. "We will beg him for his wisdom, and you and I, Tiye, will process to Ipet-isut at every sunrise, and while the Holiest of Holiest is open so that the High Priest may minister to Amun, we will prostrate ourselves and ask what it is that we have done wrong."

"But we've done nothing wrong!" Tiye protested hotly. "If the Son of Hapu speaks the truth, which I still doubt, the seeds of disaster are in our son, not in ourselves!" She reached across the little table and gripped his forearm with both hands. "We must watch over him at all times, choose his tutors with the utmost care, make sure he learns to sincerely venerate the gods, teach him the correct position the Visible Disc holds! Then he will have no inclination to drift into heresy."

As Huy listened to their interchange, an agitation grew in him that he dared not show. *Your father and grandfather openly preferred to worship the sun in all his aspects, and Ra's priests encouraged the enmity that ensued between them and the servants of Amun. Amun is superior, the essence of godhead. The Aten is merely one of Ra's energies, his rays of light, the Visible Disc striking the earth and becoming lions. Unfortunately, it's a far more exciting concept for a boy to imagine than Amun the Great Cackler with his double plumes. Lions are the representations of the rays of both Amun and Ra. The Aten is the rays themselves. Aten worship has been a court religion for hentis. It's always been too sophisticated, too complex, to appeal to the ordinary citizen. This second royal son will make it his obsession.* "Majesty, Anubis did not so much as hint at a way out—none at all!" Huy addressed Tiye directly. "Everything I saw in that gleaming new city seemed distorted, every face in the crowd marked with a despair that only I could see. The Prince is already cursed. His affliction will spread."

Amunhotep shook himself free of his wife's grasp and, picking up his cup, stared into the dregs. The cup trembled in his grasp.

Tiye went very still. "Then what does Anubis want His Majesty to do with our poor little cursed Prince?" she whispered venomously, eyes half shut. "Surely he does not expect Amunhotep to violate a law of Ma'at and thus become a feast for Ammut beneath Ma'at's scales in the Judgment Hall when his heart inevitably weighs more heavily than her feather? Oh, but I forgot." She made a parody of recollection. "The King does not undergo the test of the Judgment Hall. He ascends to ride in the sacred barque with his royal ancestors. He is thus exempt from any punishment for his abuses—but Egypt is not. Egypt suffers in his place. So I ask you again, mer kat, Great Seer, what does Anubis expect my husband to do with his son? That is, if your vision spoke true at all."

"Enough!" Amunhotep's voice was unsteady. "Leave us alone now, Uncle. Go home and stay there until you're summoned. Paneb, give me my copy of the Seeing. Send Nubti and Tiawi in at once. You're both dismissed."

Huy rose carefully. *It was too much to expect that the King would simply take my word for this Seeing,* he thought in a brief burst of panic that had every one of his muscles suddenly tensed for flight. *When he reads the full account, it will seem so preposterous to him, so blasphemous, that any hope I had of belief on his part will be gone. As for Tiye, she will demand my punishment and use every argument she can muster against me.* "Paneb, give me both scrolls," he said quietly. Paneb left the floor with ease, reaching into his pouch and handing them over. Huy stood looking down at them, two neat curls of papyrus, while the rich possessions he had worked to amass over his lifetime grew flimsy, shredded, and blew away, leaving him as naked and vulnerable as a child.

"Majesty, I have not told you everything," he said huskily, holding the scrolls out to him with shaking hands. "Many years ago, before you married Amunhotep, I Scryed for you, Tiye. Anubis showed me the King's coronation day with you beside him, resplendent in the formal garb of a Queen, but that was only the first part of the vision. I kept the second part to myself because I wanted the marriage to take place, and the will of Atum was not clear. However, I did dictate all of it." He swallowed. "The whole vision of the baby Prince Amunhotep's future that I received is on this other scroll. Anubis showed me more than I have dared to say. I am too afraid to put it into words. You will understand when you read it, and I beg you, both of you, to remember as you do so that I have served Egypt and the Horus Throne with complete loyalty."

Tiye's arm went out, but Amunhotep snatched the scrolls first and held them securely in his lap. "Does anyone else know the full extent of what these contain?" he demanded sharply.

Huy hesitated before deciding that the time for deceit, even kindly deceit to spare another's pain, was long past. "I discussed the contents of the older vision with your royal Mother in her capacity as Regent," he acknowledged, and did not go on to say that Mutemwia had also thought it best to keep silent regarding any description in its entirety. Tiye had gone white. Both hennaed lips were clamped tightly closed. The King merely looked pensive.

"Dismissed, both of you," he repeated. Huy and Paneb bowed themselves to the door. Tiye's hostile eyes stayed on Huy, but Amunhotep's gaze had returned to the scrolls he continued to hold firmly against his linen-draped thighs.

As soon as Huy stepped out into the passage, he knew the hyena was there. Its odour assailed his nostrils, a foul miasma far stronger than the tang that had invaded his bedchamber and more pungent than that of any wild animal. Resisting the urge to cover his mouth and nose, drained and on edge, he spoke quickly to Nubti and Tiawi, then started along the statue-lined way to the palace entrance, Paneb behind him. He could not think. He hardly saw the deferential comings and goings around him or heard any greeting. His ears were full of the soft, sinister footfalls only he could hear, and the slow panting of hot breath over a wet black tongue. Grimly, he prayed that in the sunlight flooding the vast stone concourse before the pillars of the reception hall the apparition would dissolve away or at least become invisible.

At first it seemed as though his prayer had been answered. The bearers saw him and came hurrying with the litters. He and Paneb got in, were lifted, and began the ride home, but one glance beyond the open curtains showed Huy the beast padding in the shadow abreast of his litter. When the bearers changed direction and the shadow moved, the hyena moved also, staying within its reach. Huy drew the curtains, closing himself in, and his head sank onto his raised knees. *I am being haunted by a demon,* he thought dully. *Anubis has unleashed a member of his Khatyu against me—but for what reason? I have solved the riddle of the Book of Thoth. In spite of knowing that Tiye will do her best to ruin me or even have me killed, I have finally released the details of both Seeings. Atum is allowing me to age at last, I feel it; therefore he has no more use for me. Unless I'm required to go further, sacrifice myself, fill my heart so full of the heavy stones of evil that the scales will not balance and Ma'at will condemn me to annihilation.* Huy groaned aloud. *Murder a child and save Egypt, but destroy myself. Let him live and destroy Egypt, but in disobeying Anubis's direct command to undo the damage my arrogance has already caused, condemn myself anyway. There is no choice at all—I am damned whatever I do. I used to hate you, Atum, for treating me as though, with the gift of Seeing you bestowed on me and the permission to read the Book of Thoth you granted me, you purchased my soul to do with as you pleased. As I grew, I came to understand and accept the uniqueness with which you compensated me. But now I will return to hating you. You and your mouthpiece Anubis are more cruel than any of us mortals.* Huy knew that the clarity and venom of the words passing through his mind were largely a reaction against the tension of the morning, interspersed as they were with images of Tiye's furious face and the King's puzzlement. But the naked facts of Huy's dilemma were undeniable. The presence of the hyena dogging his steps was also undeniable. Nauseated and oddly cold, Huy hugged his knees and gave himself up to despair.

Amunmose and Kenofer were waiting for him as he entered his house. Paneb left him to file away the record of the meeting with the King and Tiye, and his steward and body servant approached him, but suddenly Huy could not move. A paralysis of mind and body had seized him so that the faces of his servants and the details of his surroundings were all at once unfamiliar. Only the hyena had substance. It squatted beside him, so close to his naked calf that he could feel the heat of its body. A need to look down at it grew in him, a conviction that reality would quickly warp out of all recognition unless he did so. With a flicker of rebellion and fear, he compelled his head to turn, his gaze to drop. The creature was peering up at him, and as their eyes met, the room and the people in it regained perspective.

Both men were watching him cautiously. "Rakhaka is keeping the noon meal hot for you, Master," Amunmose said. "Will you eat?"

"No." With an effort of the will Huy thrust the instant of distortion away. "Kenofer, bring me poppy, and you, Amunmose, find Perti. I want to see both of you immediately." *Amunhotep would never harm me*, Huy thought as he walked through the hall towards the stairs, *but Tiye would not hesitate to have me assassinated if she believed that my death would somehow change her son's destiny. In spite of her bluster, she knows that my visions do not lie.* Reaching his bedchamber, he shook off his sandals and exchanged the blue shirt and kilt for a white shift. Lifting the lid of one of his cedar tiring chests, he felt past the neatly folded clothes to the boxes beneath. Most of them held jewellery and treasured mementoes from the past. Huy drew out one of them, slightly longer and less ornate than the others, and untying the cord that kept it closed, he took out a dagger. He had not held it for many years. Thothmes had given it to him on a Naming Day long gone, partly as a joke but mainly so that he might carry a weapon at his waist during one of his official journeys away from Egypt. The blade was of plain iron, but the haft was of gold inlaid with buttons of red carnelian, crafted so that a hand might grasp it smoothly. Huy hefted it briefly, aware that the hyena was watching him from a corner of the room, then replaced it in its box and carried it to the chair beside his couch.

Kenofer knocked and entered. Huy had just passed the empty opium vial back to him when Perti swung through the doorway, followed by Amunmose. Perti bowed briskly, bringing with him an odour of worn leather and dust that momentarily overlaid the hyena's stench. Huy regarded him carefully. Pharaoh's Commander-in-Chief Wesersatet had occasionally approached Huy with a request for Perti's service in the army and the promise to Perti himself of a division to administer, but Perti had always refused. "With you I travel the empire, Master," he had explained to Huy. "I learn of new weapons and tactics, I have the opportunity to observe the great of many lands, and best of all you give me full authority to organize the defence of your household and the activities of your spies. I answer to no one but you. Where else would I enjoy such freedom and responsibility?" Now he stood waiting, his eyes on Huy, Amunmose beside him.

"Kenofer, close the door," Huy said. "Perti, how many soldiers are in my employ?"

"Fifty at present," Perti replied promptly. "Wesersatet approved an increase from the usual twenty when your partner Prince Amunnefer needed your guards to assist his in the protection of the poppy fields. The arouras are completely open, as you know. Ten men are away in Punt with the myrrh caravan. Thirty stand watch in the house and grounds and accompany you when you go to the palace or into the city. Master, why do you ask?"

Perti had earned the right to question him. So had Kenofer and Amunmose, although Kenofer seldom did so. Huy cast about for a way to tell them that his life might be in danger without having to provide clarification, but before he could do so, Amunmose spoke up.

"You're afraid, aren't you, Huy? We've known each other for hentis and I can interpret your moods almost as well as Anhur could. In the few days since you returned from Iunu you've been distraught, not sleeping or eating, and standing in the hall a while ago after your visit to the palace I saw you completely lost. If an angry ghost was seeking revenge on you, you would be sending for an exorcist, not for us." He made a wide gesture that included the other two. "We're not asking why, only what we must do."

"Thank you, Amunmose. All I may say is this: I have made Their Majesties very distressed, so much so that one or both of them might try to kill me. Amunmose, let no food into the kitchens that you haven't procured yourself from the market or the garden, and warn Rakhaka to stop sampling the meals as he cooks." Perti's black eyebrows rose. He opened his mouth to protest, but Huy forestalled him. "No one is to risk death on my behalf. Perti, delegate a soldier to be with Amunmose at all times and have guards appointed to keep watch in the kitchens. Kenofer, the only water I'll drink will be carried from the river by you and there'll be another soldier to help you. No wine or beer to come from open containers. Perti, have this knife sharpened for me and bring it back. Impress on your men that no one is to be allowed onto the estate or into the house, and if there are messages for me, they must be left at the gate. Perti, I want you outside my door day and night. Kenofer can bring a pallet and bedding for you." He handed Perti the dagger.

"Master, do you really believe that our Horus or the Goddess would deliberately break a law of Ma'at because you have distressed them?" The voice was Kenofer's. "The balance of Ma'at is not disturbed by the condemnation of a criminal justly tried before the judges, but a secret murder by the One who stands in the Holiest of Holiest on our behalf will be seen by the gods as a transgression committed by all of us—every Egyptian."

Only until the One enters into the transforming ritual of the heb sed, Huy thought, moved by the innocent perplexity suffusing his body servant's face. *Then he truly becomes a god in the flesh, no longer accountable for anything he has done. Few down the ages have really believed this. In fact, only a tiny handful of those who have followed the Book of Thoth to its end have been aware that it is more than an account of creation or a series of manuals explaining how to acquire the skills of magic or read the stars.* "I have grieved them greatly, particularly the Empress," Huy told him. "I expect to be summoned back to the palace, but in the meantime I need you all to keep me safe." *I no longer trust Anubis to do that,* Huy's bitter thoughts ran on. He glanced to the corner beyond the shrine to Khenti-kheti. The hyena was staring back at him. With an effort, he pulled himself out of the chair. "You're dismissed. Kenofer, I'll take my afternoon sleep now. Please take the mourning clothes away."

It did no good to appear in blue today, he told himself as the servants filed out and the door was closed. *Neither Amunhotep nor Tiye recognized or shared the grief for Egypt herself that imbued my vision with such horror and sadness.* "Stay or go, I don't care," Huy said to the creature crouching in the dimness. Crawling onto his couch, he pulled the sheet up over himself and determinedly closed his eyes.

He began to dream of frogs, dozens of them, crawling over each other at his feet. They were all black. A strong light shone from somewhere behind him and he was casting an elongated shadow so deep that it was difficult to see one creature divided from another, but he could feel their cold sliminess against his skin. He half turned in order to see them more clearly, kicking at them as he did so. The light moved with him, settling at his back again. Plunging both hands into the seething mass of tiny bodies,

Huy began to fling them away, but the more feverishly he dug into the repulsive pile, the faster their number increased. Waking with a cry, he fought himself free of his sweat-soaked sheet and hastily left the couch, expecting to see it and the floor around him alive with frogs; but there was nothing, only the hyena engaged in delicately licking its paws. For once it was not staring at him. All its attention appeared to be fixed on cleaning itself. *I wish you were still alive, Henenu,* Huy whispered to himself, standing watching it. *From the time you came to Hut-herib to exorcise me and found no demon, you became my protector from the evil forces wanting to ruin me and the gift of Seeing. I grew to love you, to trust your judgment. If you were here, you could tell me why that bau haunts me, why it takes the form of an offal eater, why it is blacker than any moonless night, who sent it to torment me. There's no one left alive to confide in—only Thothmes, who would listen but could offer no help. I dare not approach any priest with this, not even the archivist at Mennofer, particularly now, when my position as mer kat is threatened, let alone my life, and I must betray no weakness. More than anything, I wish that I might stare into my copper mirror and be given a vision of my own future!* The animal had finished washing itself and had resumed its steady but oddly indifferent gaze at him, and Huy shouted for Kenofer, wanting to sluice away not only his own rank smell but the repugnant feel of the frogs' cold scum lingering on his feet.

Over Perti's objections, Huy had an awning erected on the grass by the garden, where he dictated a letter to Thothmes and Nasha and then lay on his back, hands behind his head, and tried to think of nothing at all. The estate was quiet, the heat slowly intensifying. A letter had come from the steward of Huy's holdings in the north. Henenu had left her estate in the oasis to him. The soil around the lake of Ta-she was particularly fertile, and the abundant crops grown there added to Huy's wealth year by year. He was careful to take the steward's advice regarding what to plant, but now the scroll lay unread, rustling in the breeze where Paneb had left it, inches from the hyena sitting motionless beside Huy. Perti and several of his soldiers were standing guard within earshot. The quiet conversation of two passing servants seemed to embody the timelessness of the season. But Huy, outwardly relaxed, knew that unless he kept his eyes closed and his mind distracted, he would leap up screaming and run to the gate, through the opium fields, into the muddy depths of the dwindling river, and embrace at last a welcome oblivion where his ghostly shadow could not follow.

Many times in the days when he and Ishat had lived together in the slums of Hut-herib and he was driving himself to exhaustion in Atum's service, they had answered an urgent request for a Seeing only to enter some poverty-stricken hut and find a child already drowned. Huy, kneeling helplessly beside the pallid grey flesh and colourless eyes of the little corpse, would feel the desperation of the parents and, even worse, their frantic hope. Lay your hands on my baby and bring her back to life. You have the power. The gods gave it to you when they made you live again and granted you the gift of Seeing and healing. Were your parents more deserving than us? Were you? Why you and not my baby? Why will you not help us? The accusation would hang unspoken in the air. He had heard it before. He had tried to explain something that even he did not understand, and in the end he had given up. Now he clung to the memories of those times, allowing them to blend with a desire for his own death so that the noisy street on which they had lived, the food they had eaten, even the vibrant personality of Ishat herself, became part of a losing struggle against the relentless omnipresence of the flood itself.

All the rest of the afternoon, he managed to keep himself in the gloom of a Hut-herib of distorted invention so that by the time Amunmose came to summon him to the evening meal he had almost forgotten the curse that now followed him everywhere. By the time he unwillingly entered his bedchamber for the night, there had still been no message from the palace.

17

THAT NIGHT HE DREAMED OF FROGS again, but this time he was struggling for breath in the deep waters of the lake fronting the wide forecourt to Ra's temple while the ugly creatures swarmed over and around him, trying to hold him down. He and Thothmes had been walking past the entrance to Ra's outer court on their way to the practice ground, Thothmes gauntleted in preparation for a lesson with the chariot master and Huy with his bow slung over one shoulder. *I've been attacked,* Huy thought, lungs bursting, arms and legs flailing as he struggled to free himself from the smothering mass of bodies. *Sennefer knocked me into the lake with his throwing stick. Where have all these frogs come from? Why are they trying to drown me? Thothmes, help me! Help me! Where are you?* He felt his consciousness begin to fade. Unable to hold his breath any longer, he exhaled. Panic overtook him as his mouth filled with water and something more, something worse. Frogs were sitting on his tongue, grazing the back of his throat. He retched, and then the panic turned to madness. Thothmes' hand gripped his shoulder, but it was too late—he was dead.

"Master, you must wake up! Wake up! The Queen is here!"

Huy opened his eyes onto darkness. In a moment of confusion he expected to find himself in the Judgment Hall facing Ma'at and her scales, but instead he was on his couch, entangled in his sheet, and Perti was bending over him. He struggled to sit up. His head was thick and aching and his throat was sore.

"Perti," he croaked. "I was a student again, twelve years old and dying in Ra's lake. What's happening?"

Perti stepped away to make room for Kenofer, who was carrying a bowl of water that he set on the bedside table. Swiftly he pulled Huy's twisted sheet away and, tossing it on the floor, urged Huy to his feet. "The Queen is in your office, Huy. She walked here from the palace with only Wesersatet to guard her. She must see you at once." Perti had gone out into the passage while he was speaking and returned with a lamp.

Huy's wits had come back. He glanced sharply at his captain's drawn features. "She's in my office alone? You left her alone?"

"No. Two of your soldiers are with her. I've woken Paneb."

Whatever she has to say won't be recorded, Huy thought, shivering briefly as Kenofer's wet cloth moved over him. *Otherwise she'd have summoned me to the palace. This matter is entirely secret.*

"I'm sorry that the water is cold," Kenofer said. "I was unable to—"

"It doesn't matter. Get me a clean kilt. Wake Paroi and have him bring date wine and something to eat to the office. And Kenofer, make sure the wine is unopened and the food's been under the guard's eye since it was sent back to the kitchens after the evening meal. Tell Paroi not to offer any of it before I arrive. Perti, come with me, but I want you to stand outside the office where Wesersatet will be."

Kenofer had finished his cursory wash and had gone to one of Huy's chests, extracting a kilt and coming to wrap it around Huy's waist before hurrying away. *I won't wear sandals*, Huy thought as he followed Kenofer into the passage, Perti behind him. *I can run better in bare feet.* Then he laughed aloud, an abrupt bark without humour. *If Tiye has already conceived of a way to put an end to me and this is her first move, then no escape as crude as physical flight will succeed,* he acknowledged to himself, *not even if I take the long journey into a self-imposed exile somewhere on the edge of the empire.*

Paneb and the customary household guard at the foot of the stairs both looked up as he and Perti descended. Apart from slightly swollen eyelids and an unpainted face, Paneb gave no indication that he had been roused from a deep sleep. He was fully dressed and shod. A droplet of gold hung from one lobe and the red carnelian sweret bead inscribed with Thoth's hieroglyph and Paneb's name hung as usual on his chest. He bowed to Huy, his palette tucked comfortably under his arm, and for the hundredth time Huy blessed the day when the scribe had entered his employ. "Be as unobtrusive as you can," he told Paneb as together they turned away from the front of the house and started along the gloomy corridor lined with closed doors leading to the rear gardens. Huy could see the vague shape of Pharaoh's Commander-in-Chief standing outside the office. Perti moved deftly ahead, his hand going to the hilt of his sword. As they came up to Wesersatet, he bowed.

"I am here only to accompany Her Majesty," he said. "She understands your increased security, Great Seer, and knows that in any case she is perfectly safe beneath your roof." Huy nodded, Perti took up his position beside the Commander, and Huy opened the door. He did not knock.

His soldiers were stationed to each side of the figure sitting behind the desk, a respectful but watchful distance away from her. A dun-coloured cloak had been flung over the back of a second chair in front. The desk itself held a small pile of scrolls. Two alabaster lamps burned steadily beside them, casting a peaceful glow into the room that encompassed not only the surface of the desk but the woman who perched with knees to her chin under the voluminous white linen gown that covered her from neck to ankles. Her arms were folded across her knees. A pair of tiny leather sandals had been tossed under the desk. She did not stir as Huy came forward and halted, astonished. He and Paneb prostrated themselves. As he knelt, Huy saw a dark, ungainly shape melt into the shadows lurking in one of the far corners. The hyena. He closed his eyes and pressed his nose against the tiles. There was a long period of silence. Slowly the mixed perfume of lotus, narcissus, and henna in satke oil began to tickle Huy's nostrils. One of the lamps sputtered. Then she sighed.

"Dismiss your guards, Huy," she said. She had not given him permission to rise. Craning his head to one side, he gave the order. The two men reverenced her and strode past Huy and Paneb, both still embarrassingly supine, and the door closed quietly behind them.

There was another silence, this one pregnant with uneasy expectancy. Huy heard a creak and rustle as she left the chair, and when she spoke again he realized that she was directly above him. "Get up, both of you," she ordered. "Paneb, you may make notes, but afterwards the scroll is mine." Huy regained his feet and at once she raised her face to him. "You agreed to come to me first when you returned from Mennofer. You did not do so. The King is thoroughly drunk and Tiye has shut herself up in the nursery with her little Prince and screams death to anyone who tries to reason with her. Apparently you have turned all the nursery staff into assassins. I have been obliged to take her place during the morning audiences and make the rounds of the administrative offices. I am not pleased. If you had related the vision to me, we might have avoided these consequences."

With a rush of affection, Huy scrutinized the delicate features. Scoured of paint, the fans of lines at her temples and running from her nostrils to either side of her mouth were clearly visible. The long cap of gleaming black hair was slivered through with streaks of grey. But the small, graceful hands and lithe movements of her body belied her age.

"Majesty, I could not in good conscience keep my word to you," Huy answered. "The things I saw belonged directly to the King and the Empress."

"And not to Egypt? The deformed King and his heresy will do more harm to this beloved country than any transgression of yours."

"You've read the scroll."

"Of course. Both of them." She gathered up the folds of her gown and, pacing back to the desk, settled herself on the chair behind it. At once her heels sought the edge of the chair. Tugging the capacious linen down over her shins, she rested both outstretched arms on her hidden knees, and at the gesture Huy found himself back in the office of his home at Hut-herib with her little son asleep upstairs in the care of Royal Nurse Heqarneheh and he and she deep in an intimate conversation that might continue for hours as the night waxed and then gradually waned towards the dawn. Neither she nor Egypt's Horus-in-the-Nest liked to take to their couches early, he remembered. Prince Amunhotep required story after story, and Huy had often met his mother wandering through the house or in the garden when everyone else in the household was asleep. He and she had developed a close bond. Huy had never overstepped the gulf of blood and station between them, but they had come to trust and respect one another. Mutemwia's approach to chairs in the privacy of Huy's home had been decidedly informal, and with a pang of homesickness for the past and genuine love for this royal woman Huy watched her succumb to an old habit. She waved him down into the opposite chair.

"Amunhotep and I have always been close, and the link between us became even stronger during my years as his Regent," she continued. "He confides everything in me eventually. He confides in Tiye also, but if he needs advice he can trust he comes to me. He doesn't need to seek advice from you, Huy. He made you mer kat. He knows that you make excellent decisions and carry them out and thus Egypt prospers without the necessity for him to do anything more than stand between the gods and the people. Yes, he's lazy and I'm sorry for it, but it does make him easy to control." She grimaced. "At least, that was true until you neglected your duties and left for Mennofer." Huy began to protest, but she held up a warning hand. "Tiye took over your responsibilities. You knew she would, didn't you? The scrolls sent north to you merely let you know what decisions she had taken. Not one refutation came back from you. Our administrators were compelled to do her bidding whether they agreed with her policies or not."

"Majesty, you know why I had to leave Weset," Huy protested, "and while I was away I read every letter. There was nothing to refute. Tiye and I used to work together regularly in the ministries. Her judgments were sound."

"That's not the point. You must take control of Egypt again, before Tiye has completely won the loyalties of the governors and administrators. A Queen in charge of the country sets a dangerous precedent. We need you, Huy, Amunhotep and I, not only to take up Egypt's reins again but also to make a barrier between Tiye and the power she craves." She indicated the scrolls on the desk. "This morning, after a long conversation with the King, I had the correspondence of the day brought to me. There it is. I've read it. Chief Architect Kha needs your advice on the west bank, at the site of the new palace. Hori and Suti need you to settle an argument between them regarding their work at

Ipet-isut. They're extremely talented, but foolishly they divided their responsibilities into the west side and the east side of Amun's temple. Promotions are long overdue within the Semenu family. I think it would be wise to make Sobekhmose's son Sobekhotep Overseer of the Treasury now that Sobekhmose is Overseer of the Works of Upper and Lower Egypt. You gave Sobekhmose the position yourself, Huy. Do you remember? Sobekhotep is eager to oversee the Treasury, having learned from his father, but first he asks that you allow him to travel to Rethennu and assess the potential of the turquoise mines we own there. I suggest that your nephew Amunhotep-Huy be given the task of planning and overseeing a new mortuary for the sacred Apis bulls. His competence in directing the repairs and additions to Ptah's temple in Mennofer was exemplary. Give the Viziership to Aper-el. Oh, and you should give some thought to the building of more granaries—the crops continue to be more abundant than we have seen in several seasons. Shall I go on?"

"No, Majesty, and you're right, I have been negligent in my duties and allowed personal concerns to come before my larger responsibilities." The words were correct, but behind them was a flood of desperation. Mutemwia was eyeing him steadily, her chin resting on the forearms still folded loosely across her linen-swathed knees.

"The Empress must not become mer kat," she said. "The weaknesses in my son's character are becoming distressingly obvious. He cannot resist the requests of his women. Jewellery and other fripperies don't matter—the careless granting of sincecures does. He and Tiye love each other, but Tiye is already becoming adept at manipulating his defects. Perhaps we should have abandoned plans for the marriage after the first vision, in which you saw her with the malformed King whom Anubis has now identified for us as her son."

Huy's shoulders hunched. "At the time, we spoke of the possibility of altering the future, changing fate. Atum had appeared to choose Tiye for Amunhotep." He glanced at Paneb, but the scribe was writing calmly, head down over the papyrus.

"Had he?" Mutemwia uncurled. One by one her legs straightened, and she sat back, shook out the drape of her gown, tucked both bare feet under the chair, and crossed her arms. "What if Anubis was showing you what would happen if we designated Tiye as Queen, not what her future would be if we did not?"

"I forced the union," Huy said slowly. "I elected to ignore the portion of the vision I didn't like because I was full of the arrogance of my new power. I was eager to test it. A foreign commoner as Queen? Atum had sanctioned the bond, unlikely though it was. You were dismayed, but out of reverence for the god and trust in me you agreed to it." His fingers met and clenched. "The result will be a disaster for Egypt's future. With the birth of Prince Amunhotep the seed of that disaster was sown. It's up to me to put everything right. Isfet must not be allowed to spread and enfeeble Ma'at because of me."

Mutemwia pursed her lips. "A terrible word, Isfet. Whatever you do, you're damned, aren't you, my Huy? Your dilemma is perfectly clear to me. But of course you will not murder my grandson. Such ruthlessness is beyond your nature, no matter how fully the deed occupies your mind. Do you really think that the fate of the entire country will result from your conceit? That belief is unmitigated conceit itself."

The hyena was staring at him. Huy could feel its unwavering regard as an unclean caress between his naked shoulder blades. "Majesty, I will tell you how I know that I am not tormented by conceit but accountability," he said hoarsely, rising from the chair in one stiff movement and walking around it, his hands reaching for the support of its back. "I am being haunted. For some time I saw the animal only occasionally, but now it is with me night and day ..." Recklessly, no longer caring how he sounded, he spoke of the three hyenas, one fleshly, one belonging in the Beautiful West, and now the third plaguing him, the words tumbling into the room. It was both a relief and an agony to rid himself of the burden he had carried for so long, *and will continue to carry*, he thought bleakly under the torrent of his voice. His gaze swept from door to desk to the dusky height of the painted ceiling and back again. He noted subconsciously that she had unfolded her arms and placed them along the polished arms of her chair. Lost in the painful vortex, he saw Paneb as if from a great distance, a man he did not recognize sitting on the black and white tiled floor and performing some inexplicable task. *The frogs are a part of it too*, his rational self said from the bottom of some inner well where sense and control had taken shelter. *I must tell it all.* He went on without volition, wanting to stop but unable to do so until he had purged himself and there was nothing left to say. His mouth seemed to close of its own accord. He stumbled, caught himself as Paneb reached across and pressed a palm against his outer thigh to balance him, and awkwardly sat down. His heart was pounding. The muscles of his legs were quaking.

At that moment there was a knock on the door. Huy tried and failed to call out, and it was Mutemwia who sharply replied. Paroi and a kitchen servant entered, and seeing the Queen, Paroi bowed as respectfully as he could with the loaded tray he was carrying. "There is hot garlic and chickpea soup and bread from this morning," he said as he unloaded the contents of the tray onto the desk. "There are also slices of ox liver in dilled cabbage, dried figs, and as you can see, Master, the wine jar is unopened. Kenofer fetched the water in the jug himself. That's why I have taken so long." He cast a keen glance at Huy as he removed the wax plug from the neck of the wine jar and picked up the empty tray. The kitchen servant was placing a large bowl of water and a stack of folded linen cloths beside the dishes. Huy took one, dipped it in the water, and wiped his face and neck.

"Thank you, Paroi," he said, trying to catch his breath. "Please make sure that the Commander is fed." He dismissed Paroi before the under steward could ask the obvious question hovering on his tongue. The two servants backed down the room and the door closed behind them. Mutemwia slid upright and stood, folded back her sleeves, and, pouring a cup of wine, came around the desk and wrapped Huy's hands around it, lifting it to his mouth. The gentle service was a singular honour. Her touch was warm and the wine refreshing. While he sipped, Mutemwia returned to her chair and, perching on its edge, began to spoon up the soup.

"It's a long walk to your house from the palace," she said. "I'm hungry, and I expect Wesersatet is also." Huy waited, the thudding in his chest and the tremors in his legs gradually decreasing. Presently she looked across at him. "The bau of Anubis can be messengers or demons. You assume that the thing afflicting you is one of the Khatyu, but what if the hyena is Habyu instead, bringing you a message you need to understand? As for the frogs, to see them in a nightmare is very puzzling. They delight us because they represent resurrection, and we venerate them because they belong to the First Time, before Atum created the world. This is excellent soup." Putting down her spoon, she dabbed her mouth with a piece of linen and surveyed the dish of liver and cabbage. "You know all this, Huy," she went on. "You have been with Imhotep in the Beautiful West. You speak with Anubis every time you perform a Seeing. Ever since you were twelve years old, you have lived in two worlds, the present and the future, where time does not yet exist. You have forgotten your power and uniqueness, and fear and confusion rule you."

Selecting another spoon, she scooped up a quantity of liver and cabbage and ate it, chewing thoughtfully. "Why was Imhotep sitting reading under the blessed Ished Tree with a hyena tamed and docile beside him?" she wondered. "I can't help you, my dear old friend, not in matters of the gods that are beyond my comprehension, and I suspect beyond the comprehension of any High Priest or even a Master of Mysteries. All I can do is support and encourage you in your temporal duties as mer kat. Are you feeling better? Good. Then finish your wine and let me eat this meal."

Cradling his cup, Huy watched her delicate movements. Neither the spoon nor her mouth were ever too full. She allowed no sound, not even the clink of silver utensil against golden platter. She did not lean over the food. She used each linen napkin only once, and when she had finished, she dabbled her fingers in the bowl of water, glanced about for a moment and remembered that there was no servant to dry them, picked up the last spotless linen, dried them herself, and rose. "I must leave before Ra is born. I would prefer that neither Tiye nor Amunhotep learns of this visit. Amunhotep intends to summon you early. I have already told him that you will be sitting in audience instead of Tiye from now on. Incidentally, one of those scrolls contains a list of courtiers requiring a Seeing from you. Find your courage again, Great Seer. Let the contents of the Book of Thoth go back to gathering dust."

It was the first time she had referred to the successful culmination of his lifelong search for the Book's ultimate meaning. He understood that it was far less important to her than the continued stability and prosperity of her son and thus Egypt herself, and he wondered how she might regard the true purpose of the heb sed ceremonies. *One day I'll tell her*, he promised. Catching up the dun-coloured cloak, he laid it across her arm. "I will make no attempt to harm Prince Amunhotep, Majesty," he said reluctantly, "but you're wrong if you believe me incapable of smothering him in his cot. He carries within him a disease that will one day render Ma'at and Egypt's greatest divinities impotent. I will face the Judgment Hall leaving my greatest reparation undone. Therefore I beg you to beseech forgiveness for me from both Amun and Atum himself."

A peculiar expression Huy could not decipher flitted across her exquisite little face. "The gods will not desert you, and you have nothing to fear from the Empress." Rising on the tips of her toes, she put her hands to either side of his neck and kissed him directly on the mouth, enveloping him in a cloud of her perfume. Shock drove him to step back, and a full, generous smile lit up her face. "I am always available to assist you in your duties, mer kat," she finished, walking to the door and rapping on it. "Come and tell me when you've solved the riddle of the hyena." Her words seemed to shrink the enigma to the status of a minor conundrum, and she had closed the door behind her before he was able to complete his bow.

Kenofer was waiting for him as he walked into his bedchamber. The oil in his bedside lamp had been replenished, the debris of his hurried exit removed, and wordlessly Kenofer held out a vial of poppy. Huy drank it at once. Crawling onto his couch, he ordered Kenofer to raise the reed covering on the small window. There was no hint of dawn in the pressing darkness, but a puff of wind stirred the sheet Huy was holding and the flame inside the thin curves of the alabaster lamp fluttered briefly. The hyena was settling itself in the dense shadows beyond the range of light. Huy distinctly heard the scrabble of its claws against the tiling as it lowered its scrawny hindquarters onto the floor and immediately turned its black gaze to him. "Are you Khatyu or Habyu?" he murmured, feeling the opium enclose and ease the familiar nagging ache in his stomach and begin to soften his emotions.

"Kenofer, I'll be summoned to the palace early tomorrow. Or this morning," he said drowsily. "You might as well set out one of my kilts of the twelfth grade and whatever jewellery will be appropriate before you go back to your pallet." He did not hear Kenofer's reply. He was already wandering beside the river, watching one frog after another emerge miraculously from the murky water and hop up onto the bank beside him. Under the influence of the drug there would be no nightmares.

It was not Kenofer who woke him but a dishevelled Amunmose, shaking him unceremoniously until he opened his eyes and batted the man's arm away. "Chief Royal Herald Senu is here, Huy," Amunmose said. "He was ordered to deliver an official summons to you at dawn. There's a confirmation. The scroll is signed by the King himself."

"I was expecting it." Struggling to clear his mind, Huy left the couch. "How long have I slept?"

"Not long. Kenofer's gone to heat your water in the bathhouse. I'll send Senu away, get Rakhaka up to prepare you some food, then I'll wash myself. Do you remember how difficult it used to be to persuade young Amunhotep to get off his couch in time for the noon meal? Not any more, apparently. I'm too old for any of this." He paused at the door and turned. "There's no trouble from the Empress already, is there, Huy? Is that why Her Majesty the Queen came to see you in the night? Should I be packing up the household for a flight into Rethennu or Zahi?"

"No, I don't think so. I'll take an escort, though. Please tell Perti."

"He's on his pallet outside the door. He's awake."

Mutemwia said that I have nothing to fear from Tiye, Huy's thoughts ran on as the last vestiges of sleep blew away under Kenofer's scrubbing. *She's very eager to see Tiye returned to an inferior place in Egypt's day-to-day governmental affairs, and I under-*

stand why, but would she minimize the danger to me in her keenness to have me take up my duties as mer kat again? I'd have done so soon in any case. According to her, Tiye has shut herself up with her son and is screaming at everyone, but it's only a matter of time before she calms down and appears in the audience hall again. Mutemwia wants me to return to the palace before the Empress's rage is spent and she regains control of herself. Mutemwia adores her son. Does she fear that one day Tiye will have him assassinated and so wield the total authority of a Regent on behalf of the one Prince who is destined to survive? If so, it means that in spite of her sneers she believes my vision. Goddess as Regent, not as wife? Mutemwia knows what it's like to be a Regent, the stresses and temptations of the position. She and I have been friends since the King was a baby. She is an extremely astute woman who sees the crevices in Amunhotep through which an ambitious wife might creep. But Tiye loves Amunhotep. Of that I have no doubt.

"Electrum or the purple gold, Master?" Kenofer asked, and Huy sighed and came to himself. The sun had risen fully by now but still hung low in the east, its first rays sending thin morning shadows snaking across Huy's fields, and he knew that he must hurry. Dressed in a kilt woven of gold-wrapped linen threads, his face meticulously painted, his waist-length hair braided and entwined with thick gold bands each portraying the feather of Ma'at, and shod in leather sandals studded with golden ankhs, he was frowning at the display of jewellery laid out on his couch.

"I really don't care," he snapped, "but I suppose that, seeing I may be going straight to the audiences once the King has finished with me, it had better be the purple gold." He held out his arms for the wide bracelets shot through with traces of purple and bent his head so that Kenofer could hang the linked double plumes of Amun on his chest. Purple gold was too expensive for any but the wealthiest Egyptians to own. The native craftsmen, brilliant though they were, had never been able to reproduce whatever composed the reddish tinge in the jewellery. Kenofer was handling it with reverence, but Huy's eyes rested on the two rings he had not removed since Henenu the Rekhet, controller of demons, had made them for his protection. *Perhaps they are what's keeping the hyena at a distance—the Soul Protector and the Frog of Resurrection. Now why didn't I remember that I wear the Frog on my finger, and wonder why it allowed the nightmares? Because the hyena is indeed Habyu, not Khatyu?* Kenofer had finished setting the cascade of tiny scarabs into Huy's earlobe and was holding up the copper mirror. Huy waved it away and left the room.

He and Paneb were carried to the palace in separate litters as before, Paneb with the scrolls the Queen had left tucked into his battered leather pouch. Perti and twenty of Huy's soldiers surrounded them both, and Huy's Chief Herald Ba-en-Ra strode in front to keep the way clear. There were not many people about to hear the herald's warning. Huy kept his curtain closed against the early sun, his mind as much as possible on what Mutemwia had told him so that he might remain unruffled by any thought of the coming interview. If the King ordered his arrest, there would be nothing Perti and his men could do. Of course Perti knew it, but the sound of his cheerful voice as he chatted with one of his officers gave Huy a fragile sense of security.

At the entrance to the palace, Wesersatet and a contingent of royal guards were waiting. Wesersatet bowed as Huy left his litter. "Greetings, mer kat. You are expected. Please order your escort to wait. Refreshment will be provided for them." His words and features were politely impersonal. Nothing in his manner betrayed the escapade of the night before. He strode towards the forest of pillars fronting the reception hall and at once the guards surrounded Huy and Paneb as they followed him. Huy did not need to be shown the way to the King's apartments. Usually a guide would be summoned for a newcomer and the Commander-in-Chief would disappear to attend to other duties. It had been a long time since Huy had become lost in the maze of the palace, but today Wesersatet did not even slow his pace and the soldiers gave no sign of dispersing. The small groups of courtiers already drifting along the corridors quickly gave way as Wesersatet swept past them. A few recognized Huy between the sturdy bodies around him and bowed hesitantly. Huy knew what was in their minds, and in his also. *Am I a prisoner or not?*

At the wide double doors to the royal quarters, Nubti left his stool. He smiled and reverenced Huy, and Wesersatet and his men moved to either side of the passage, but they did not disband. Huy glanced at Paneb. The scribe's demeanour was as imperturbable as ever. Nubti opened one of the doors, called Huy's name, and waved the pair of them inside. The door closed behind them with an echo.

Amunhotep was still in his nightshirt, sitting slumped in a chair, his head covered with the white cap of strict custom. Both hands were resting in large bowls of water, one to either side of him on small tables. A servant was busily massaging one bare foot. The other, still bearing traces of henna, was stretched out on a stool. The King's face was slightly swollen. Kohl was smeared across one temple, but his other eye was clean although bloodshot. To Huy he looked as though one of his eyes was missing. A man Huy had not seen before stood patiently off to one side, a large jug in his grasp. The air in the huge room was heavy with the scent of rosemary and a haze of myrrh smoke. Huy and Paneb went to the floor in a full prostration, and immediately Amunhotep grunted that they should get up. "Paneb, go over there and be quiet," he said. "Uncle, you're late. Come closer so that I don't have to shout. My head is threatening to burst and every part of my body aches. I should not have left my couch, but before the festivities last night my Mother the Queen requested that I speak to you before the hour of audience this morning."

Huy stepped up to him. "I'm sorry you're ill, Majesty," he offered.

Amunhotep grunted again. "I'm more hungover than ill," he acknowledged surprisingly. "Nubti, get rid of everyone except Huy and Paneb, and send Nebmerut in. He should be hovering outside in the passage. And you, Neferronpet," he snapped at the man Huy did not recognize, "what kind of a butler are you? The last thing I need is sweet date wine. Bring me sermet." He turned back to Huy. "Nothing really helps but cold water on my wrists and myrrh smoke," he said as the room promptly emptied. "Often sermet takes the headache away, but I don't particularly like beer. Sometimes a massage to my feet makes magic. But not today." He lifted his hands from the bowls of water. Huy picked up a linen towel and, wrapping the King's hands, carefully dried each finger. Amunhotep watched him. "You've always loved me, haven't you?" he said quietly after a while. "Ever since I spent the flood months with you and Anhur when I was a young boy. I love you too, and I trust you. In fact, I think that you and my Mother the Queen are the only two people I trust completely."

There was a knock on the door that reverberated throughout the vast space and Nubti entered followed by a man Huy identified as Seal Bearer and Chief Royal Scribe Nebmerut. Without being told to do so, Nebmerut joined Paneb on the floor, greeted him, and set his palette across his thighs.

Amunhotep ignored the small disturbance. "I have no doubts at all that your gift is from Atum himself and your visions speak true," he went on. "The things you saw in my little son's future filled me with fear and despair. How does any Incarnation dare to repudiate the god who is his father, and moreover send masons to every temple and monument and stela in Egypt, and even beyond, to hack out his name and thus make it as though he never existed? I had a terrible fight with Tiye. She accused you of wanting the Horus Throne for yourself and your nephews. She called you a charlatan and vowed to have you arrested and imprisoned to starve until you were dead. Then she ran into the nursery."

Another knock on the door boomed. Amunhotep winced in pain. Butler Neferronpet advanced with a clay jug and a silver cup. Pouring a draft and bowing, he passed it to Amunhotep, who drank thirstily. Huy took the jug, set it on one of the tables, and curtly dismissed Neferronpet. After a swift glance at the King, the man went away. Huy dropped the linen he had been absently holding into the water and sat back on the stool.

"I went to talk to my Mother the Queen and then I drank all night," the King continued. "I wanted oblivion, Huy. I cannot kill my little son, but neither can I pretend that I did not hear the prediction. To imagine Tiye actually marrying our Prince goes far beyond the borders of sanity, let alone the edicts of Ma'at, but your voice followed me into one jug of wine after another. I couldn't escape it. If Ma'at is wounded, Egypt will be unprotected from drought and famine and disease and—who knows?—maybe even from invasion and military defeat." He pressed the tip of a finger against his right eye, where he was obviously in pain. "Therefore I have given the one command open to me," he said miserably. "Prince Amunhotep is now confined to the harem. He may not leave its precinct for any reason at all. Ever. Chief Harem Steward Userhet and his successors will answer with their lives if he goes free. My royal seal is on the injunction and the grounds for it. I have also ordered that Tiye be removed from the harem and only allowed to visit the Prince with my permission. It has all been so hard and so horrible, Uncle. Have I done the right thing?"

Huy longed to take him in his arms, to cuddle and rock him as he used to do when Amunhotep was young. Instead, he gathered the King's hands into his own once more. "You did the right thing, the only thing possible without breaking a law of Ma'at," he said quietly. "You were wise. Tiye will eventually accept your decision. I'll return to my duties as your mer kat at once if you are agreeable. And Amunhotep, never doubt that you may trust me with your life." Huy felt his fingers squeezed and then released. Amunhotep nodded.

"The ministers and ambassadors and boon-seekers in the audience hall will be restless," he said. "Get on with it, Uncle, and tell Nubti on your way out that I'm hungry now. You can bring anything that needs my seal to my quarters this evening."

"Were you able to hear everything, Paneb?" Huy asked once the heavy doors were closed behind them and they were hurrying along the corridor.

Paneb nodded. "Every word, Master," he replied. "May I suggest that you obtain the royal seal on the papyrus?"

You are no fool, my dear scribe. This time I definitely need insurance against whatever vagaries might be in my own future. He swept into the audience hall and took the empty seat on the dais, looking down at the sea of bowed heads. "Mahu, who should be dealt with first?" he said.

The Mitanni ambassador presented a long letter full of wordy praise from his King to Amunhotep, but as always, Huy thought as he listened to the seemingly endless phrases extolling Amunhotep's virtues, Mitanni wanted gold and plenty of it. Surprisingly, this time the King of Mitanni was offering a few horses and chariots in exchange. Huy cut the recitation short and referred the matter to the Overseer of Foreign Affairs. Merimose, Viceroy of Kush and Wawat and also the Overseer of the Gold Lands of Amun, sent his humble greetings to Amunhotep and a request for more soldiers to protect the gold routes. That letter required an investigation by the Chancellor together with Wesersatet as Commander-in-Chief. Huy would be required to approve any decision.

Once the hall had emptied, Huy and Mahu began their tour of the administrators. Mahu remained silent. Only Nebmerut, Royal Scribe and Seal Bearer, was his superior. Huy had always enjoyed working with Mahu. Like Paneb, he knew how to keep his thoughts to himself unless his opinion was required, in which case his replies were succinct and to the point. His load was heavy, noting down the details of each day's discussions and decisions and making copies of every encounter for the palace archives, but he did not complain. Today Huy was reflecting on his meeting with the King as he and Mahu approached the large office shared by Hori and Suti, Architect Kha's undoubtedly accomplished twin sons. Huy did not expect them to be present; architects and stonemasons did much of their outdoor work in the cool early hours of the morning. But one of their assistants and probably a couple of scribes would be busy inside, and Huy simply wanted to make sure that the two young men would be there to speak with him the following day.

Amunhotep has made it plain that he doesn't doubt my visions, Huy mused as he and Mahu paced easily along the paved path fronting the row of administrative cells to their left. On their right a well-watered lawn ended in a section of the towering wall that encircled the palace precincts. The sun had not yet reached its zenith. Huy's shadow, though truncated, lay on the grass beside him. Deliberately he refused to glance at it, knowing that the hyena was there in its shade, keeping pace with him. Grimly he forced his mind away from it. *Mutemwia often used to tell Amunhotep the story of what I Saw the first time I inadvertently touched him, when no route to the Horus Throne seemed possible. He surely knows it all by heart. But I have no such history with Tiye. I Saw for her first when she was already a girl on the verge of womanhood, and I lied by omission when I recounted it to her. Now she's read all of it. I've given her good reason to mistrust me, and like any mother her instinct is to shield her son from harm no matter what. Coupled with an excuse to label me a sham, she will want me as far away from the Prince as possible. Given the power she wields as Empress, and her undoubted fury at her husband but most especially at me, she will look for a way to see me dead and Amunhotep's edict rescinded. No matter what Mutemwia said, I'll make sure that my estate and all of us in it are protected. Will Atum help me, even though I've fulfilled my agreement to decipher the meaning of the Book and my only use to him now is as a Seer? Will Anubis?* He could hear the hyena panting, and in a spasm of disgust he swung round and aimed a kick at it, aware even as his foot shot out that the action was futile.

"Master?" Mahu said.

Huy exhaled noisily. "It's nothing. I thought I saw a scorpion," he replied. "Let's finish our business quickly. I'm hungry."

They had arrived at the open cell door. Huy could hear a casual conversation going on inside. The interior was pleasantly dim. Two men were bending over a scroll that had been unrolled and spread out across the surface of a wide table. As Mahu stood aside to let Huy enter first, they bowed courteously.

"Let us call light First—but it is known only through darkness," one of the men said, and all at once Huy could not see his face. The room was much more murky than it had appeared to be. He turned, but there was no door behind him, no sun-drenched grass, no sliver of intensely blue sky.

"Mahu?" he called, and at the sound of his voice utter blackness suddenly descended. It was so thick that Huy experienced it as a suffocating weight, and for one panic-stricken moment he could not breathe.

"The ponderous inevitability of consequence," another voice intoned. In spite of his disorientation Huy heard something in its quality that he recognized. It woke faint echoes in him from long ago. A High Priest? Of Ra or Thoth's temple? What had it meant? He couldn't remember.

"Anubis, are you here?" he whispered, his words muffled by the impenetrable gloom that seemed to have bulk as well as depth. "Have you come to lead me into the Judgment Hall?"

There was no reply. Instead the first voice shouted, "Only through darkness, darkness, darkness! The Light cast a shadow, grim and terrible, like restless water with spume like smoke! Peril in the water and menace in the smoke!" It began to wail.

Huy broke out in a cold sweat. The sound was unearthly, a series of chilling howls without a hint of human breath, but he remembered where he had seen those words. He had gone to Thoth's temple at Iunu to read the second part of the Book of Thoth. Anhur and a young Amunmose had gone with him. Amunmose had used the time to visit his family. Huy, intimidated by everything and everyone at Thoth's home, continuously aware of the god's strong magic, had clung to Anhur and forged a bond with the soldier that had only been broken by Anhur's death. The portion of the Book he had been expected to untangle had made no sense to him at all, not until he and Thoth's High Priest had begun to talk of frogs. He began to repeat the mysterious stanza aloud. The whole of the Book was there, lodged faultlessly in his mind. "I am One that transforms into Two. I am Two that transforms into Four. I am Four that transforms into Eight. After this I am One."

Immediately the moaning stopped and Huy's recitation was taken up and repeated by a chorus that slowly grew from several guttural voices to the deafening clamour of a multitude. Huy covered his ears. Still he could see nothing. Then his right hand was pulled roughly away from his head, forced to grip what felt like a portion of a metal rod, and he found himself towed backward. He struggled to keep his balance. His other hand slid along a wall, caught against the edge of a door jamb, and without warning he was outside. The cacophony ceased. The silence made his head ring. He realized that he was clutching a tall golden Staff of Office halfway down its length. It was topped with the face of a jackal, and Anubis was holding it just under the talisman. Hastily Huy let it go and looked about.

He was standing on the grass opposite Hori and Suti's cell, but the door was closed. So was every other door along the block of administrative offices. Nothing stirred. No insect moved in the grey lawn. No wind lifted the hem of Huy's kilt. No bird troubled the leaden grey sky. The lack of sound was absolute, and everything Huy's eyes rested upon was the colour of death except his own shadow. Pitch-black, it snaked across the lawn, crawled up the side of the grey wall, and continued to climb into the sky until Huy had to crane his neck to see the enormous, misshapen head. He did not look at it for long. Not far from his feet the hyena squatted, inky dark within the blurred outline of the shadow. It was not staring at him. Its attention was fixed on Anubis.

"What did Mighty Atum do when he saw his shadow, Great Seer?" Anubis said harshly. "I am ashamed to be here, asking this question, and you should be ashamed to be standing in the place of No-Time without an answer." His lips lifted in scorn. "How often have I warned you to look to your house? How many words of caution have I wasted on such a pathetically weak ka as yours?" Stepping close to Huy, he snarled, his wet white teeth bared. His skin gleamed. The golden ankh resting on his black chest glittered. The pleats of his golden kilt swung shimmering against the perfect musculature of his legs as he moved. He was the only vibrant, living thing in all that tomblike drabness, and Huy, glancing down at himself, saw his own dusty greyness. "Tell me," Anubis growled, "what does a triad represent?"

"It represents eternal and unchanging truths."

"And what of a doubling?" Huy watched the long furred nose, the pink tongue, those lethal jaws, form the words. The god's breath was warm and smelled of the sacred kyphi perfume reserved for temple rites.

"A doubling is all fleeting, earthly wisdom."

"Tell me, then, what is the heb sed?"

Huy stared at him. Anubis waited, black eyes half closed, majestic ears stiffly raised. "I have discovered, Most Dread God of the Judgment Hall, that the heb sed takes the King and transcends his doubling. He becomes eternal, infinite. He enters the mathematical certainty of the triad. His nature is changed. Thus the heb sed is the mathematics of eternity."

"You have discovered this, and yet you do not remember what Mighty Atum did when he became Light and saw his shadow? Frogs, Son of Hapu. Frogs. Look!"

He stretched out his Staff over Huy's distorted shadow and to Huy's horror the hyena crouching within it began to grow. It swelled, lengthened, began to fill the contours of the shadow, until the shape of the head high against the slate-grey sky was not Huy's anymore but a huge, grotesque thing of tuft and snout. Within the darkness flowing across the grass from Huy's feet there was movement, seething on the wall, churning into the sky, and with it came a stench Huy recalled. It was not the whiff of a wild animal. It was putrefaction, rotting flesh, *but that was only half the odour emanating from the Ished Tree in Ra's temple*, Huy thought with a jolt of recognition. *Honey and garlic and orchard blossoms as well* ... The creatures trapped inside his shadow were struggling towards him. Frogs. With a shriek he stumbled backward, but his shadow went with him, attached to him, part of him, and so did the frogs.

"Stop it, Anubis! Please stop it!" he begged.

The god shrugged his broad shoulders. "Stop it? How can I? You and your shadow are one, foolish Seer, even as Atum's shadow belonged to him."

"But Atum saw the chaos within his shadow and calmed it! He commanded the harmony of pairs, two, four, eight, male and female, frogs, Anubis, oh yes, of course! Frogs! I remember all of it now! Water, endless space, darkness, and what is hidden, and so the cosmos was conceived, before creation could take place. But I'm not a god! I can't command concord inside my shadow!"

"So you recollect the meaning of the second scroll at last." Anubis's grating tone was caustic. "All these years Atum has waited, Thoth has waited, I have waited, for you to understand. No human being is able to bring order into his darkness. He may try. He may succeed for a little while. But his shadow will always shelter a hyena." With a flick of one beringed finger, the frogs vanished and Huy's shadow returned to an ordinary size. The hyena had also disappeared. "It's still there," Anubis said. "It has been there all your life. You were no more than thirteen when you read the substance of the second Book and you and Thoth's High Priest unravelled its meaning together. Why did you forget it so soon?"

Huy shook his head. Excuses flashed through his mind—*I was very young, I was uneasy in Thoth's temple, I didn't concentrate on the task because I was aware all the time of Sennefer's presence in the temple's school*—but they would be unacceptable to the jackal god who had taunted and goaded him for years. It came to him that perhaps Anubis had been instructed purposely to provoke him, to force a return to obedience when the path of rebellion beckoned.

Anubis sighed, an exaggerated gush of scented breath. "Fear, proud Huy," he said, his animal throat making the word an inadvertent growl. "Fear that the future you saw in your visions was flawed. Fear that the wounds and diseases you treated under my instructions would eventually be transferred elsewhere. And you saw it happen, didn't you? Not often, but often enough to trouble your sleep. Were you forced to think of yourself as infallible so that blame could be placed somewhere else? I am infallible, human, but you are not. The answer was deep within your ka, but you refused to face it for fear that you would have to admit your shortcoming to those who sought your help." Rapidly he passed his tongue over the soft fur of his lips. "The insurmountable disorder in your shadow, the insurmountable disorder in the shadows of those for whom you Scryed, warped the truths that Atum gave you through me. Not always, and usually insignificantly, but often enough to cause you, and them, distress." To Huy's alarm, Anubis leaned forward and, putting an arm around Huy's neck, licked his cheek. The god's nose was damp and cool. "You carry needless guilt, dear human," he purred. "Only the merest fraction of responsibility for Egypt's destiny lies with you. The King has behaved correctly, and Ma'at is pleased. She sees into your heart also. Get about your business, mer kat. Govern this blessed country and Scry for its people."

He stood away and, taking his Staff in both black hands, spoke in a language Huy did not know. At once the heavy rings on his fingers sparkled in new sunlight, the grass flushed green, and a flock of birds piped as they flew by. Beyond the open cell door two men looked up, saw him, and bowed. Beside him Mahu waited politely. Huy glanced about. Anubis had gone, but a faint trace of kyphi perfume lingered in the warm air. Huy nodded at Mahu, smiled, drew a deep breath, and stepped past him into the office.

EPILOGUE

AMUNHOTEP SON OF HAPU lived well into his eight-
ies. He had declared that he would reach the age of
110, a purely symbolic number, although given his
longevity he may well have meant the figure literally. During his
life he was responsible for a staggering amount of work throughout Egypt on behalf of the gods and his King. He oversaw the
construction of Amunhotep the Third's funerary temple on the
west bank of the Nile, an edifice estimated to have covered over
4,200,000 square feet. With floors of silver, doors of electrum,
and gold throughout, it was larger than the temple of Ipet-isut
(Karnak) itself. It was erected so that only the inmost shrine
remained dry during the annual flood. Unfortunately, due to
earthquakes, later plundering, and the weak foundations of the
pylons and columns, nothing remains of it but the two huge
statues known as the Colossi of Memnon. Standing seventy-five
feet tall, they are of a seated Amunhotep the Third accompanied by a much smaller effigy of Tiye on the southern statue and
with his mother Mutemwia beside him on the northern one. On
the base of one of the colossi Huy records, "I have established
the statue in this great temple that it might endure as long as the
heavens. You are my witnesses, you who shall come later." One
of the statues was reputed to have "sung" at dawn. This phenom-
enon drew a steady stream of ancient tourists, including the

Roman emperor Hadrian. The music ceased when an attempt was made to repair the image. It's assumed that when a crack in the sandstone was struck by the rising sun, the rock expanded and produced a sound.

Under Huy and their father Kha, the twins Hori and Suti laboured to complete their major work at Ipet-isut, Amun's home, and in the twenty-ninth year of Amunhotep's reign it was finished and the temple was dedicated. Men, the stonemason and sculptor, obeyed the commission to construct two quartzite likenesses of the King to be set up at Ipet-isut. They towered seventy feet into the air above one of the pylons on the south side of the temple. Only a pair of feet remain. A series of statues of the King as Osiris, each twenty-five feet high, were ranked on either side of the Nile along the east and west banks. Amunhotep's beautiful temple to celebrate his own divine birth at Luxor (the southern Apt) was not finished until after Huy's death.

In Year 26 of the King, a temple to Horus was begun at Hebenu, close to Thoth's great home at Khmun. A temple to Mut, Amun's consort, had been started the year before in the southwest area of Ipet-isut. It was surrounded on three sides by a horseshoe-shaped sacred lake, linked to Amun's temple by an avenue of sphinxes, and more than six hundred black basalt statues of the goddess Sekhmet stood around it. These are just a few examples of the steady building and beautifying that took place throughout Amunhotep the Third's reign.

In Year 17, Huy was granted permission to begin his own funerary temple just behind that of Amunhotep and in the company of other great Kings below the cliffs that conceal the famous Valley of Kings. It was a singular honour. Amunhotep himself richly endowed it in perpetuity. Huy added his own curse on anyone in the future who might allow the endowment to fall into decay or steal any of the male and female slaves cultivating its fields. The temple was completed in Year 31.

In the King's twentieth year on the throne, Huy began the research and planning that would culminate with Amunhotep's first heb sed festival in May (Epophi) of his thirtieth year. The most complete record of this major event dates back to the Twelfth Dynasty. Not only did the rites themselves have to be perfect, but there were shrines to be built and statues of the King to be set up throughout Egypt. The ceremonies took place at the ancient capital of Mennofer. Amunhotep bestowed the honorary, and temporary, titles of "festival leader" and "hereditary Prince in the offices of the sed festival" upon Huy. In painted fragments from Huy's temple, he is depicted wearing a decorated headband commemorating the occasion. In that same Year 30, Egypt enjoyed an enormous agricultural harvest from Kush in the south to Naharin in the east. A delighted King showered rewards on all his Treasury officials. At this time he renamed the Palace of the Dazzling Aten; it became the House of Rejoicing. However, the worship of the Aten, once a cult adhered to almost exclusively by a handful of Egypt's aristocrats and those of Amunhotep's foreign wives who revered the sun, began to be even more firmly established, thus paving the way for Akhenaten's disastrous reign. Amunhotep held three more heb seds in the following three years.

Amunhotep the Third has rightly been called "The Magnificent." Under him, Egypt became an empire. Gold poured into the country from Kush, far to the south, and trade with conquered and satellite nations was brisk. Egypt basked in over thirty years of increasing wealth and power. More statues were erected throughout that time than at any other period in Egypt's history. The art of embalming reached its highest degree of skill. Indeed, the mummy of Yuya, Tiye's father, who died in Amunhotep's twentieth year on the throne, is regarded as the most expertly preserved. Thuyu, Tiye's mother, died soon after her husband. Her mummy is also proof of the embalmers' skill. Yet representations of the King in later life show him as overweight beneath the drape of the loose female linens he began to prefer. There is an air of listlessness about him, a jaded boredom, as though being the most significant ruler in the world and able to have everything he desired had left him empty. He died in Year 38 of his reign at an age somewhere in his early fifties.

His son Thothmes had predeceased him by almost ten years, leaving no Hawk-in-the-Nest but his much younger brother Amunhotep. This Prince eventually inherited his father's glorious legacy, an Egypt bursting with vigour, prosperity, and influence. In a scant seventeen years he became a fanatical heretic, changed his name to Akhenaten in honour of his god, closed all temples but those of the Aten, lost most of the empire, plunged the country into poverty, and brought Egypt to the brink of invasion. (I have told his story in my novel *The Twelfth Transforming*.)

Queen Mutemwia was in her sixties when she died in her son's thirty-second year on the throne. He had loaded her with titles, and tells us that "Everything she commanded was done."

As for Huy, he died rich and highly respected in the King's Year 34. The previous year, the King had ordered two statues of Huy to be placed along the processional route through Ipet-isut, near the ninth pylon, thus inviting Amun himself to regard Huy as a god. On the statues, Huy made Amun's worshippers aware that they could bring their prayers and libations to him and he would take their petitions directly to Amun. He had been named by the King to do so. Amunhotep must have grieved deeply for the loss of the friend he had loved and trusted. Over the following centuries Huy gradually attained true godhead by healing the sick, and particularly the blind, who came to pray to him. He may have lost his own sight before he died.

Tiye's younger brother Anen died in the same year. Anen's great friend Ramose, Huy's younger nephew, finished Anen's tomb at his own expense. Ramose became Mayor of Weset at this time. Huy's other nephew, the harsh Amunhotep-Huy, did not long survive his uncle. He was in his fifties when he died in the year following Huy's death. The Empress Tiye lived on well into the reign of her second son.

ACKNOWLEDGMENT

MANY THANKS to my researcher Bernard Ramanauskas, whose diligence and insight into what remains of both the Book of Thoth and the heb sed festival have been invaluable in the creating of this trilogy.